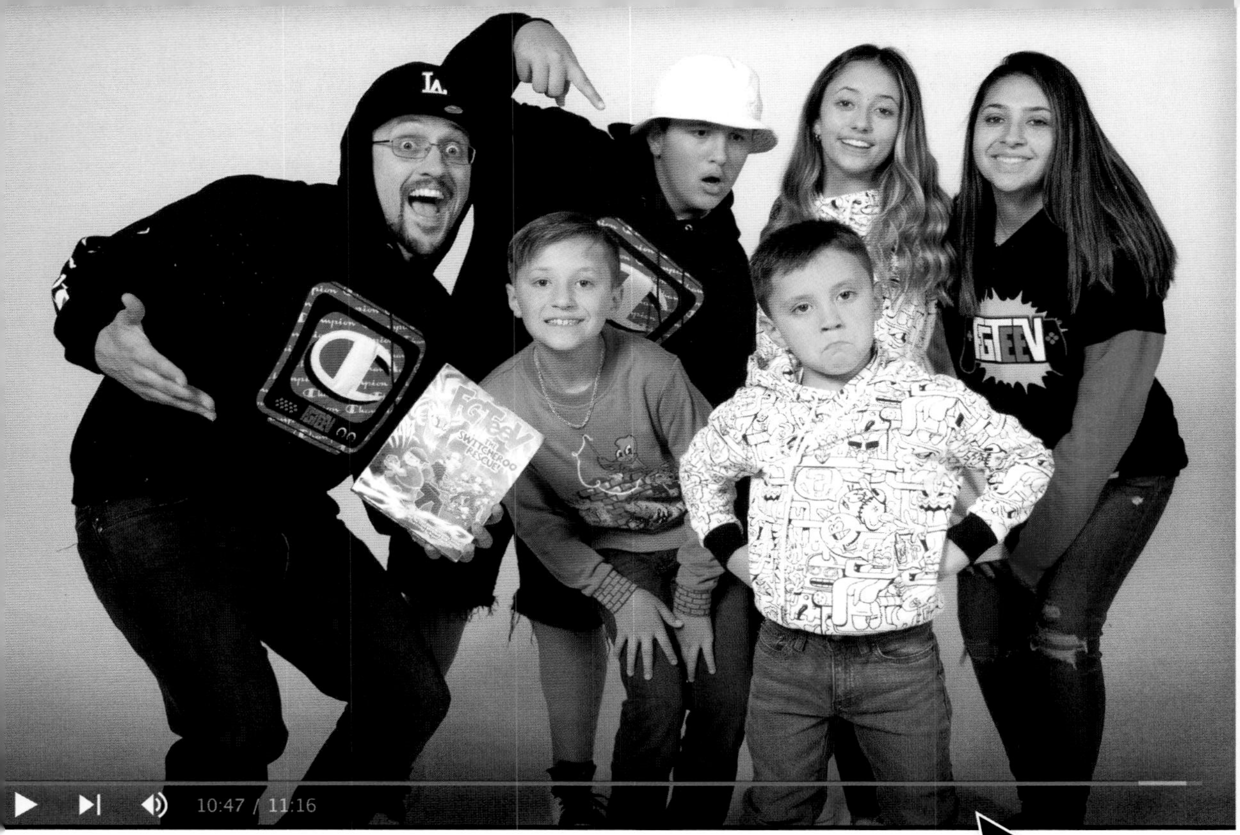
10:47 / 11:16

# FGTeeV FAMILY BIOGRAPHY

9,712,083 VIEWS • 1 WEEK AGO    164K  6.2K  SHARE  SAVE

**FGTeeV**

20M subscribers

Duddy, Moomy, Lexi, Mike, Chase, and Shawn are the stars of FGTeeV, one of the most popular family gaming YouTube channels in the world, and FV Family, which have a combined total of more than 33 million subscribers and 30 billion views. This family of six loves gaming, traveling, and spontaneous dance parties. To learn more, visit them on YouTube @FGTeeV and @FV Family.

22,235 Comments

YOU  Add a comment...

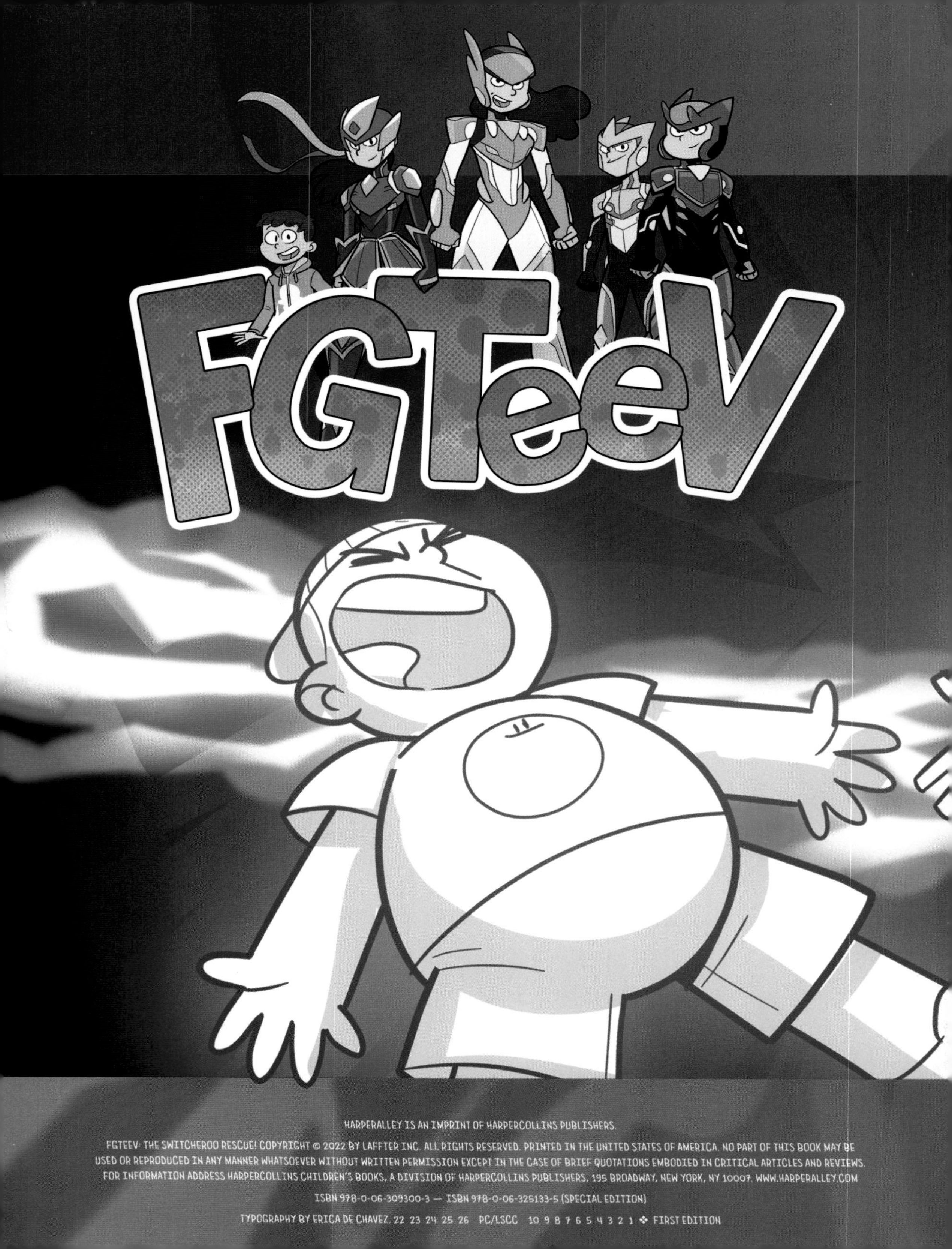
FGTeeV

HARPERALLEY IS AN IMPRINT OF HARPERCOLLINS PUBLISHERS.


FOR INFORMATION ADDRESS HARPERCOLLINS CHILDREN'S BOOKS, A DIVISION OF HARPERCOLLINS PUBLISHERS, 195 BROADWAY, NEW YORK, NY 10007. WWW.HARPERALLEY.COM

ISBN 978-0-06-309300-3 — ISBN 978-0-06-325133-5 (SPECIAL EDITION)

TYPOGRAPHY BY ERICA DE CHAVEZ. 22 23 24 25 26 PC/LSCC 10 9 8 7 6 5 4 3 2 1 ❖ FIRST EDITION

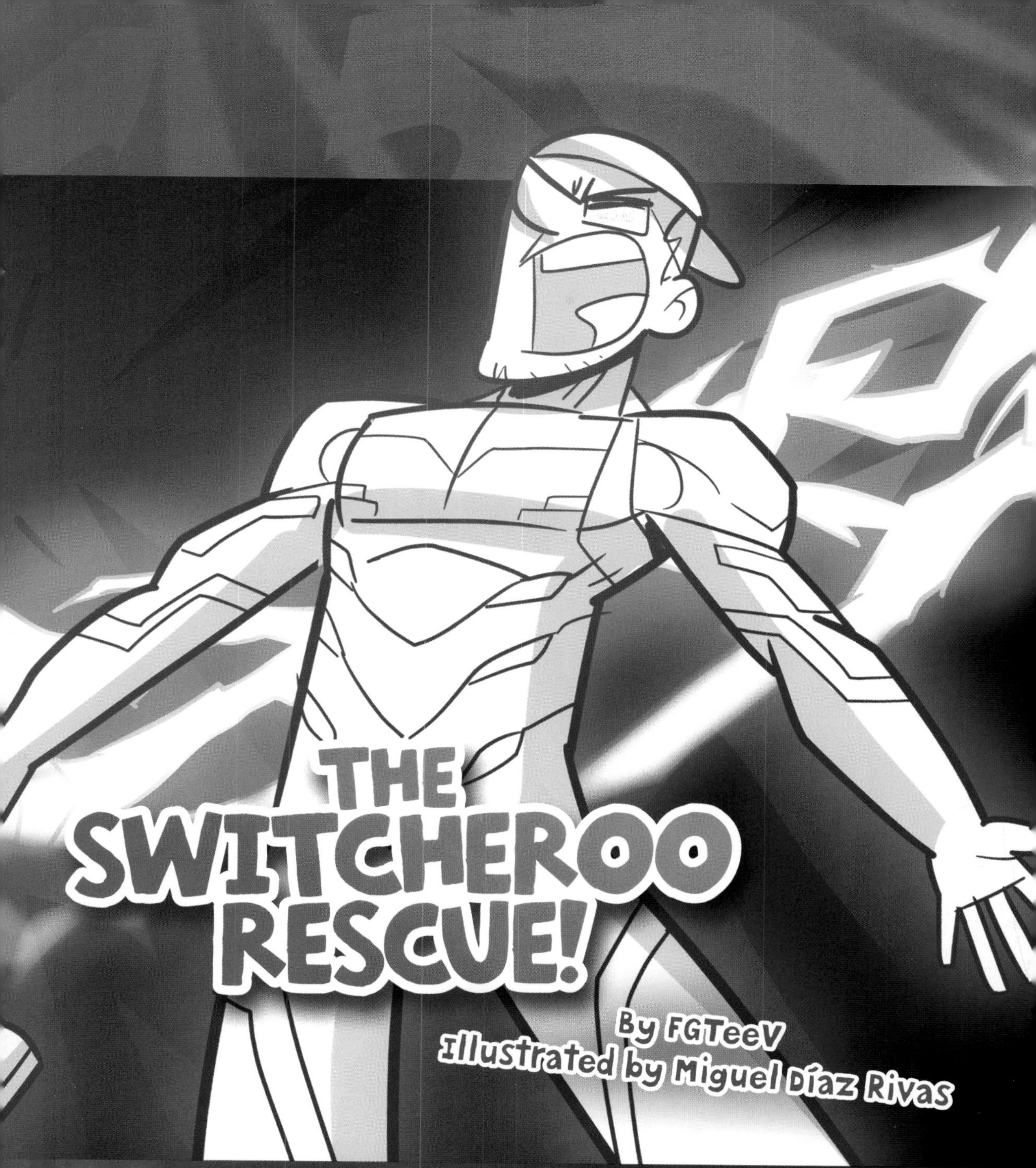

# THE SWITCHEROO RESCUE!

By FGTeeV
Illustrated by Miguel Díaz Rivas

HARPER alley
An imprint of HarperCollinsPublishers

# CHARACTERS

## DUDDY/ DUDSTER

This fun-loving dad and one of the world's most avid gamers is always ready to use his skills to save his family.

## MOOMY

Moomy with the chocolate-chip freckle joins Duddy on his many adventures. But sometimes all she wants is a quiet date night.

## LEXI/LEXO

Lexi was always the leader of the kids, but as she grows up she's eager for a life of her own.

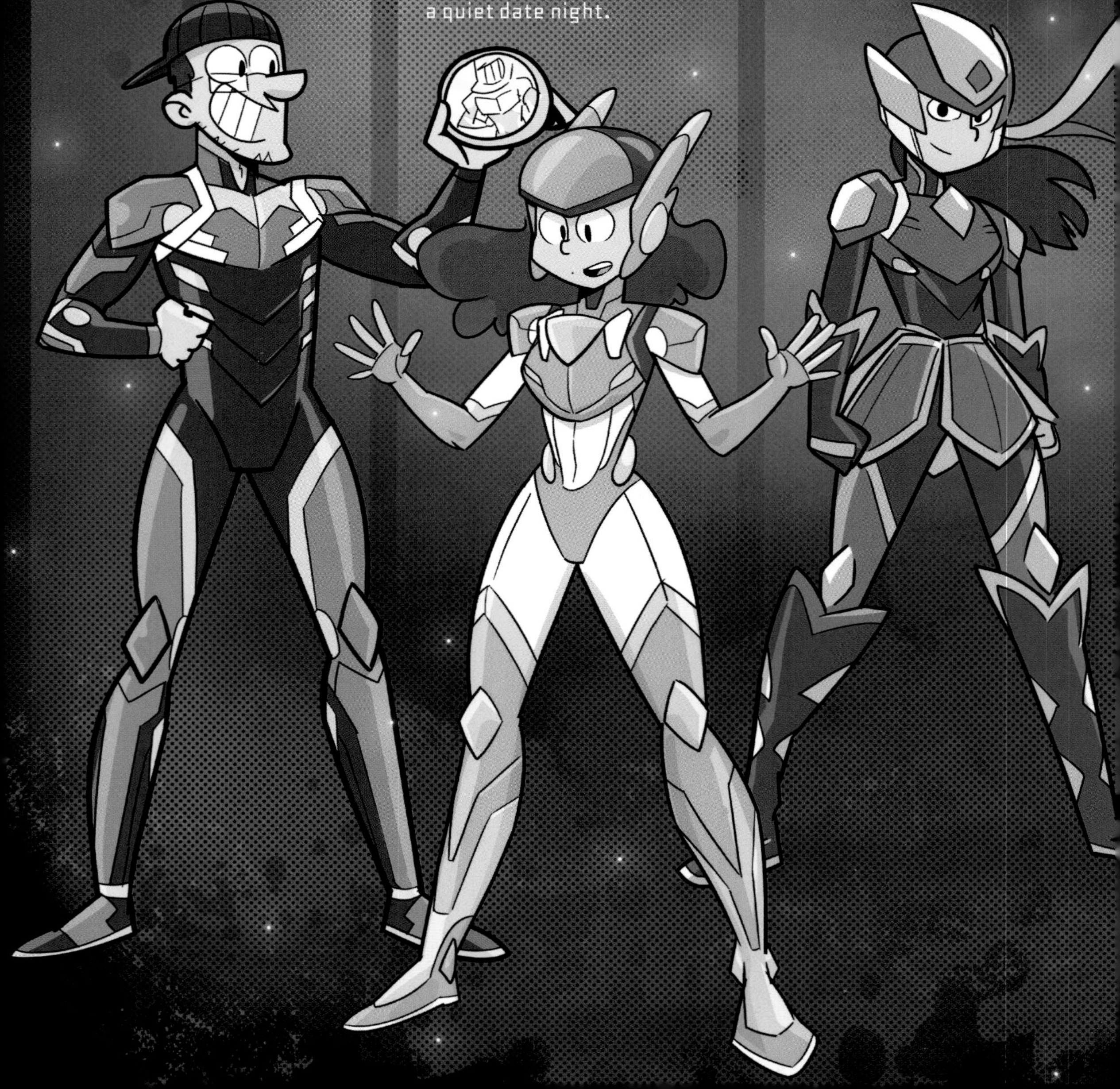

## MIKE/ MICKSTER

While Lexi is navigating life's ups and downs, Mike becomes the new leader—and he rules with an iron fist.

## CHASE/ DRIZZY

Mike's second-in-command; Chase relishes his new position in the family and holds it over Shawn every chance he gets.

## SHAWN/GHOST PUNCHER

Shawn wants to be just like his older brothers when he grows up—whenever that will be!

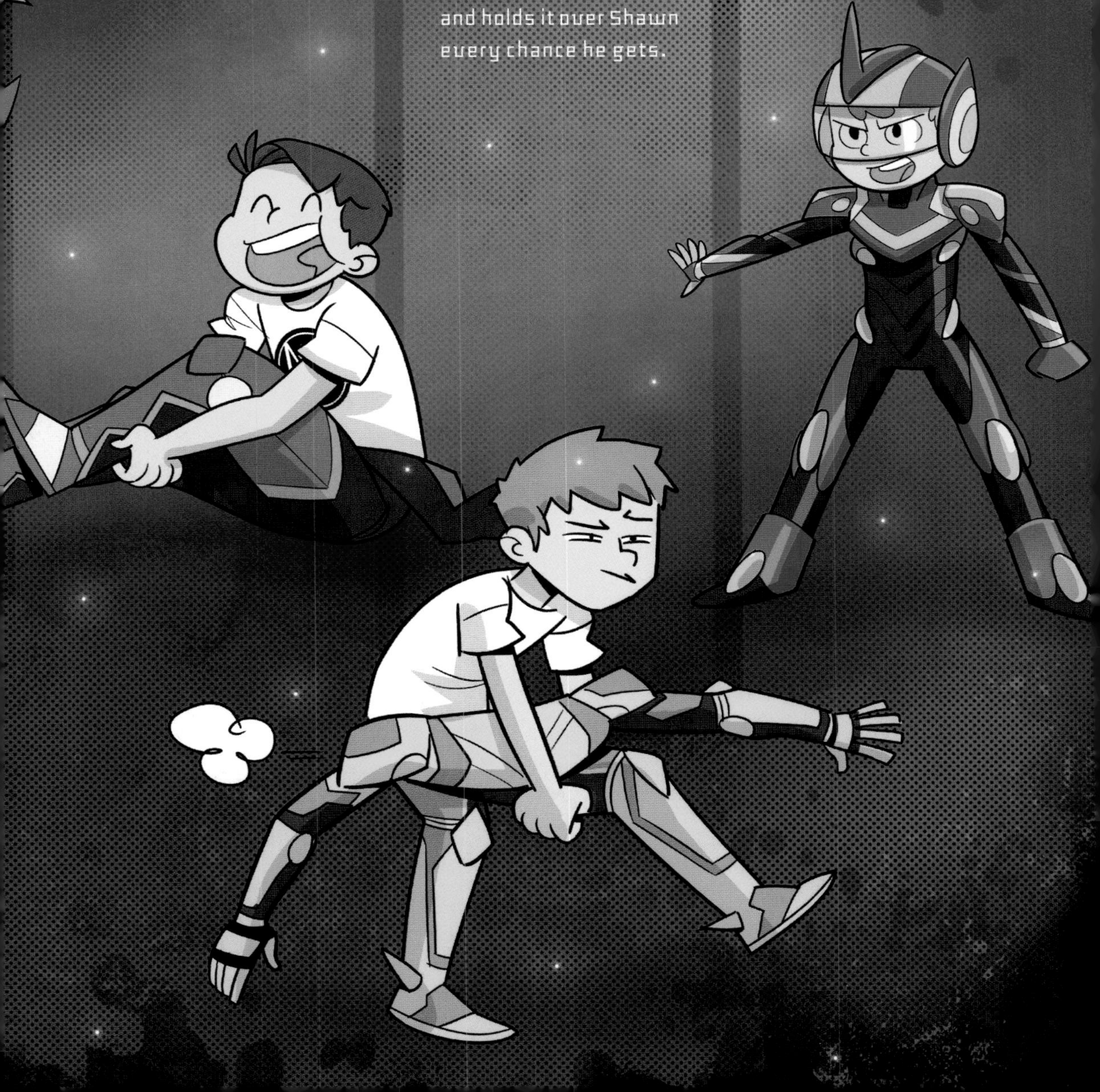

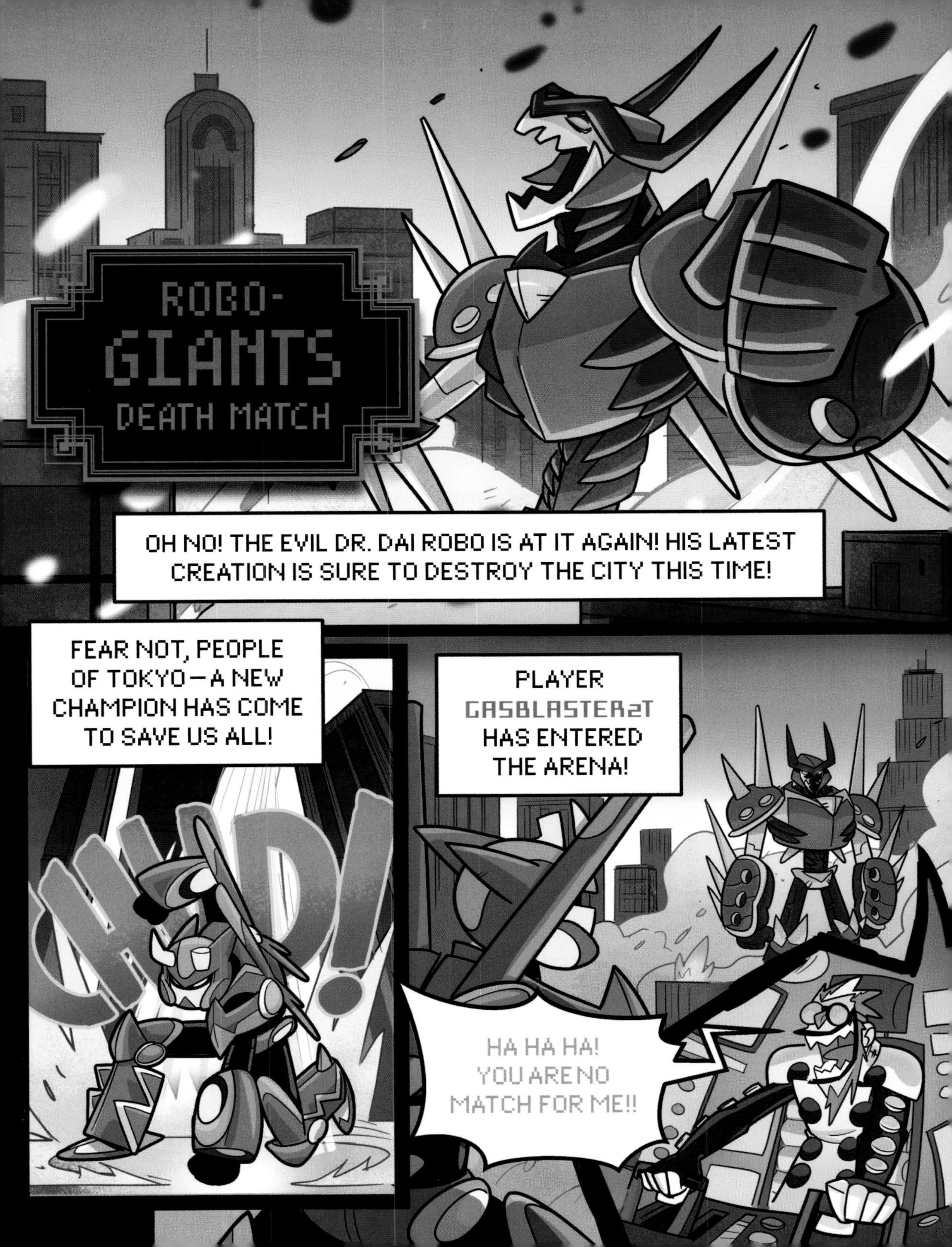
ROBO-
GIANTS
DEATH MATCH
OH NO! THE EVIL DR. DAI ROBO IS AT IT AGAIN! HIS LATEST CREATION IS SURE TO DESTROY THE CITY THIS TIME!
FEAR NOT, PEOPLE OF TOKYO—A NEW CHAMPION HAS COME TO SAVE US ALL!
PLAYER GASBLASTER2T HAS ENTERED THE ARENA!
HA HA HA! YOU ARE NO MATCH FOR ME!!

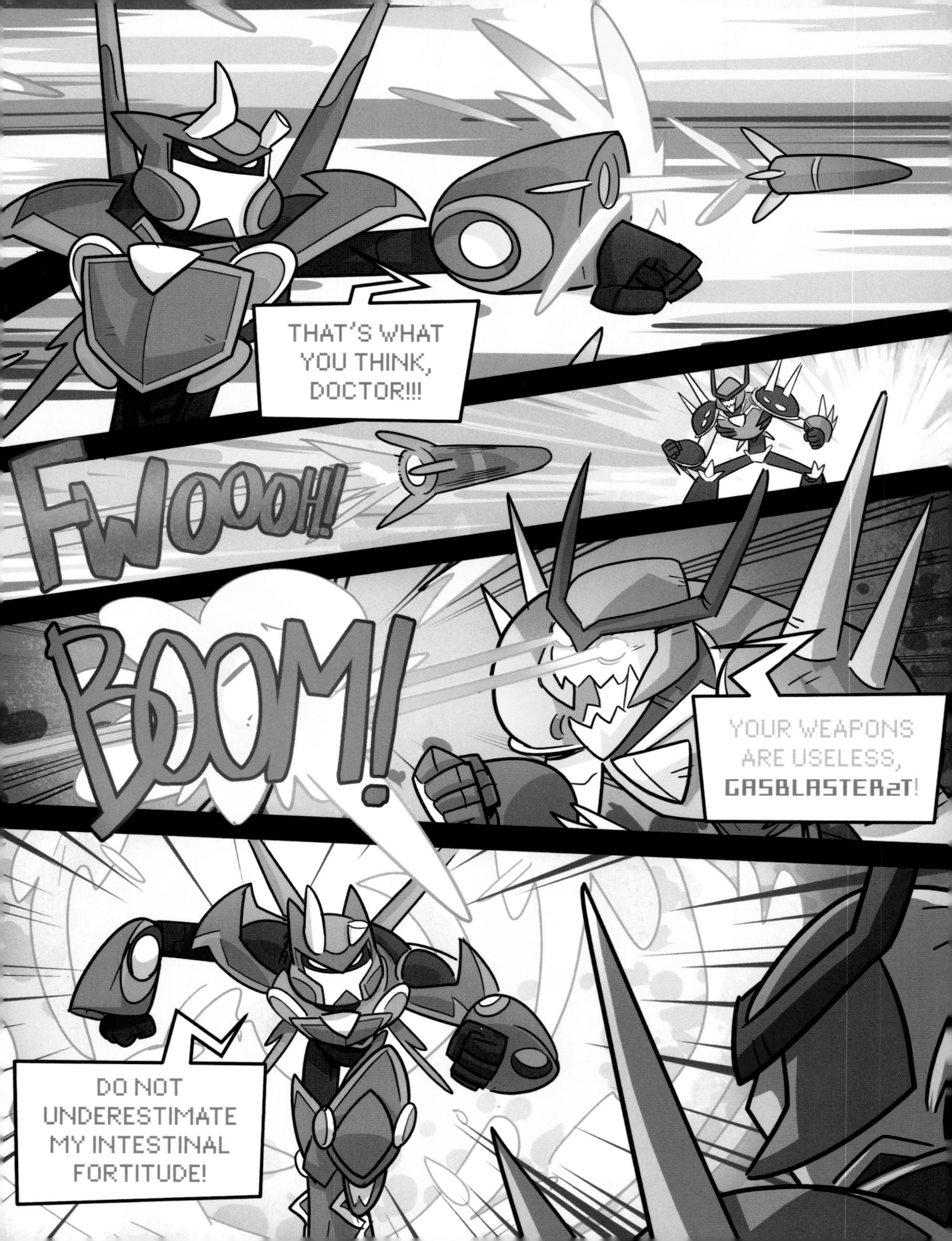
THAT'S WHAT YOU THINK, DOCTOR!!!
FWOOOH!
BOOM!
YOUR WEAPONS ARE USELESS, GASBLASTER2T!
DO NOT UNDERESTIMATE MY INTESTINAL FORTITUDE!

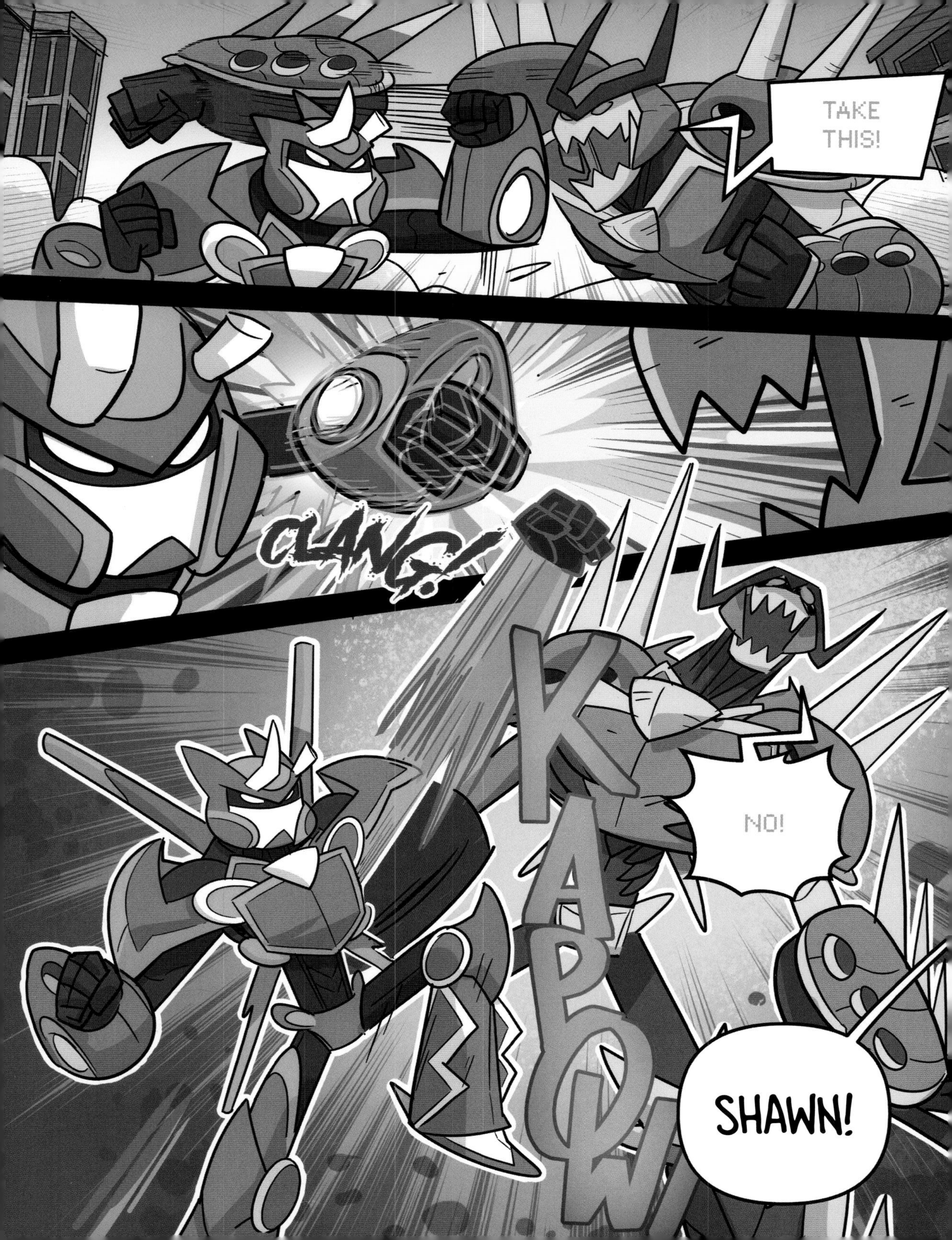
TAKE THIS!
CLANG!
KAPOW
NO!
SHAWN!

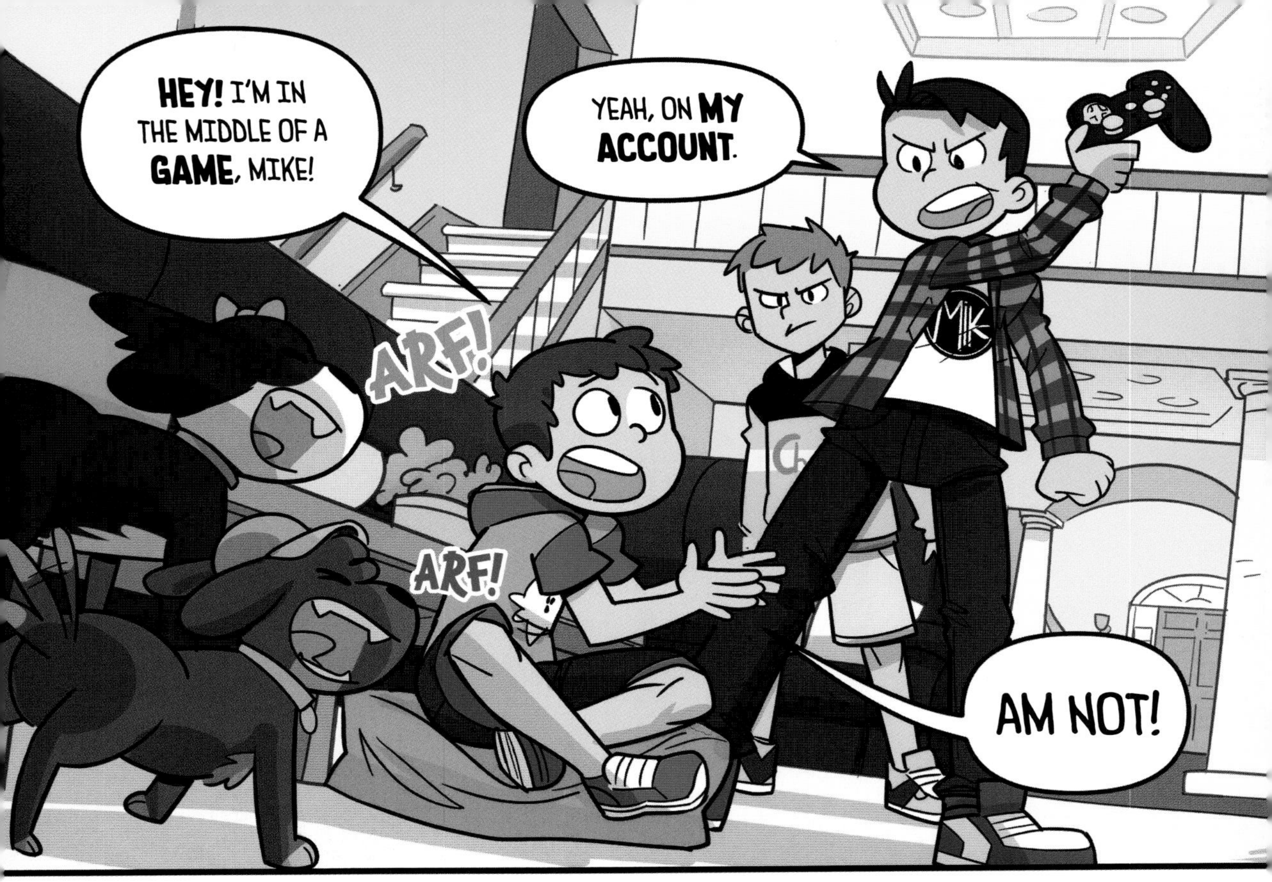
HEY! I'M IN THE MIDDLE OF A GAME, MIKE!
YEAH, ON MY ACCOUNT.
ARF!
ARF!
AM NOT!

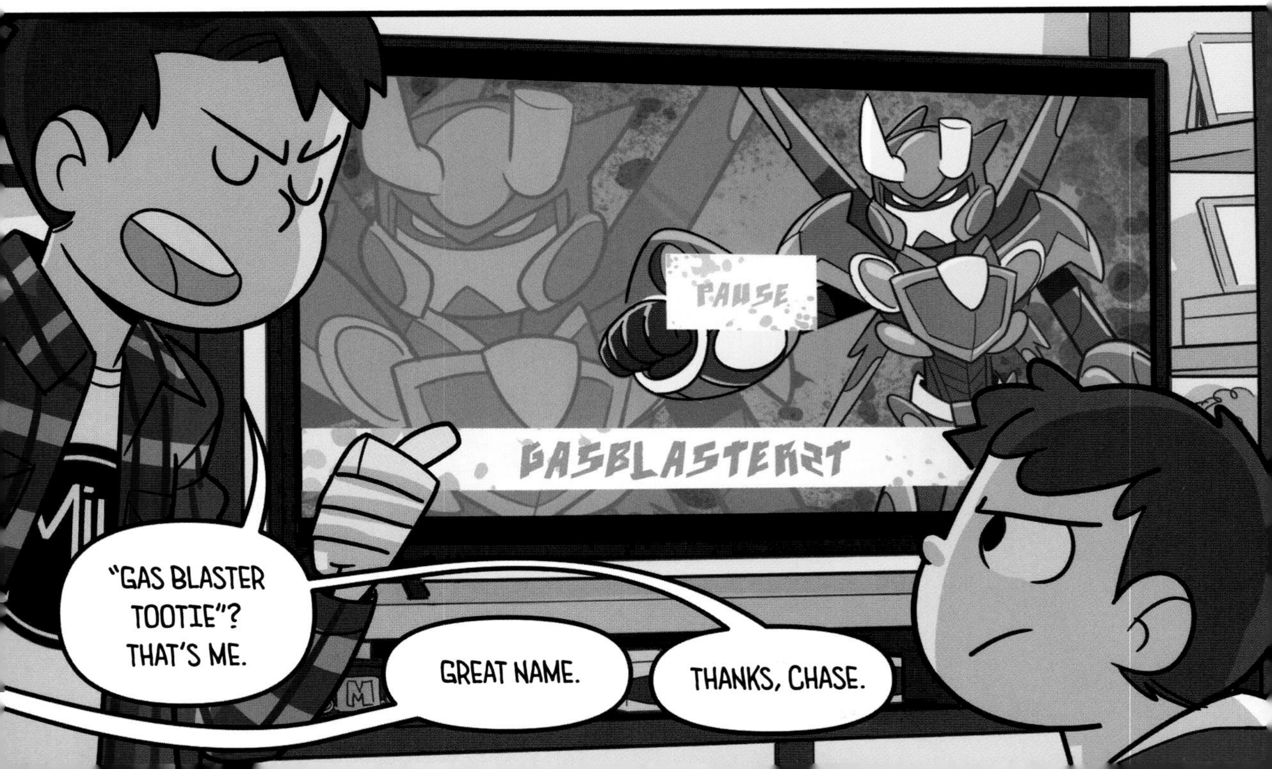
PAUSE
GASBLASTER2T
"GAS BLASTER TOOTIE"? THAT'S ME.
GREAT NAME.
THANKS, CHASE.

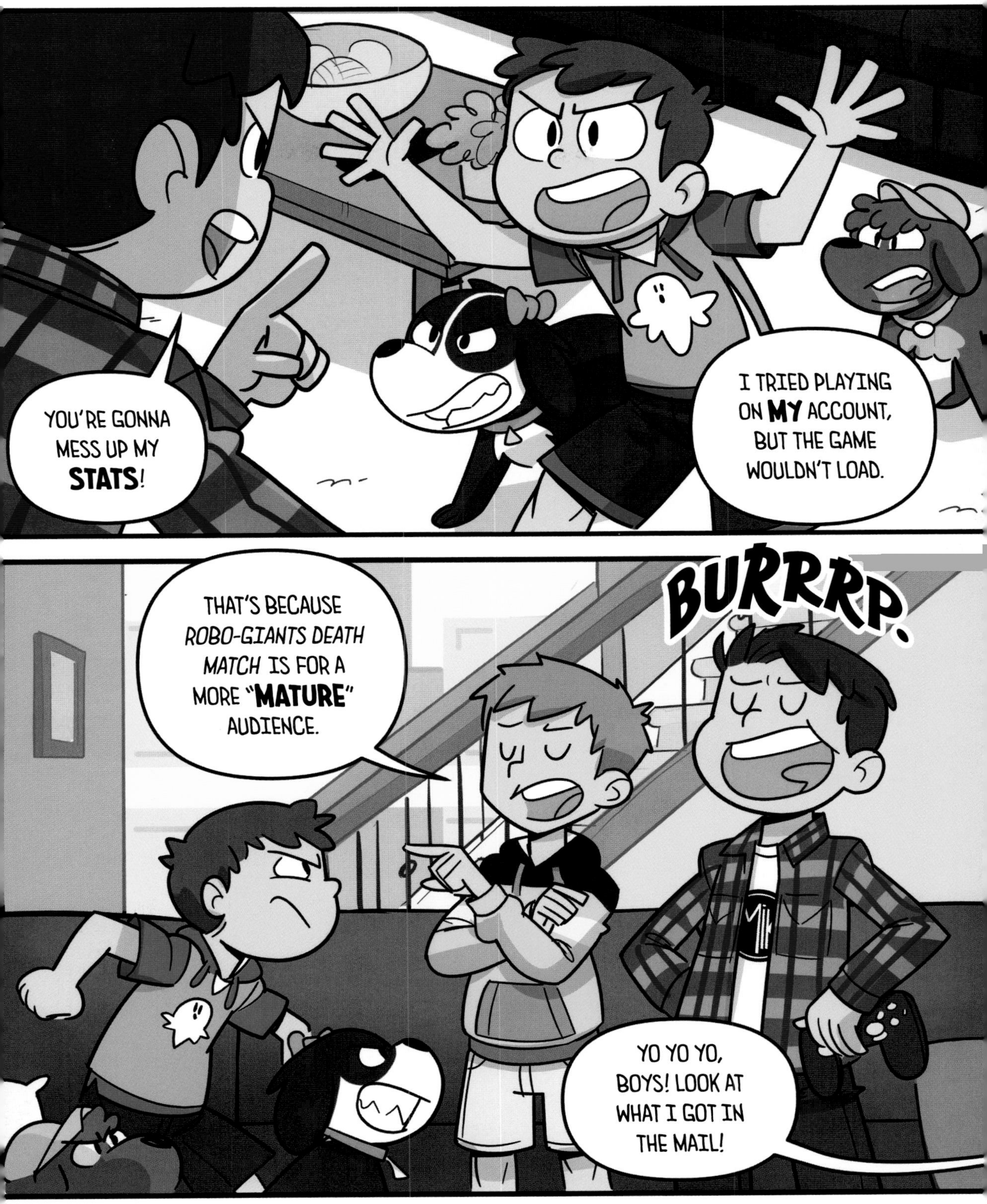
YOU'RE GONNA MESS UP MY STATS!
I TRIED PLAYING ON MY ACCOUNT, BUT THE GAME WOULDN'T LOAD.
THAT'S BECAUSE ROBO-GIANTS DEATH MATCH IS FOR A MORE "MATURE" AUDIENCE.
BURRRP.
YO YO YO, BOYS! LOOK AT WHAT I GOT IN THE MAIL!

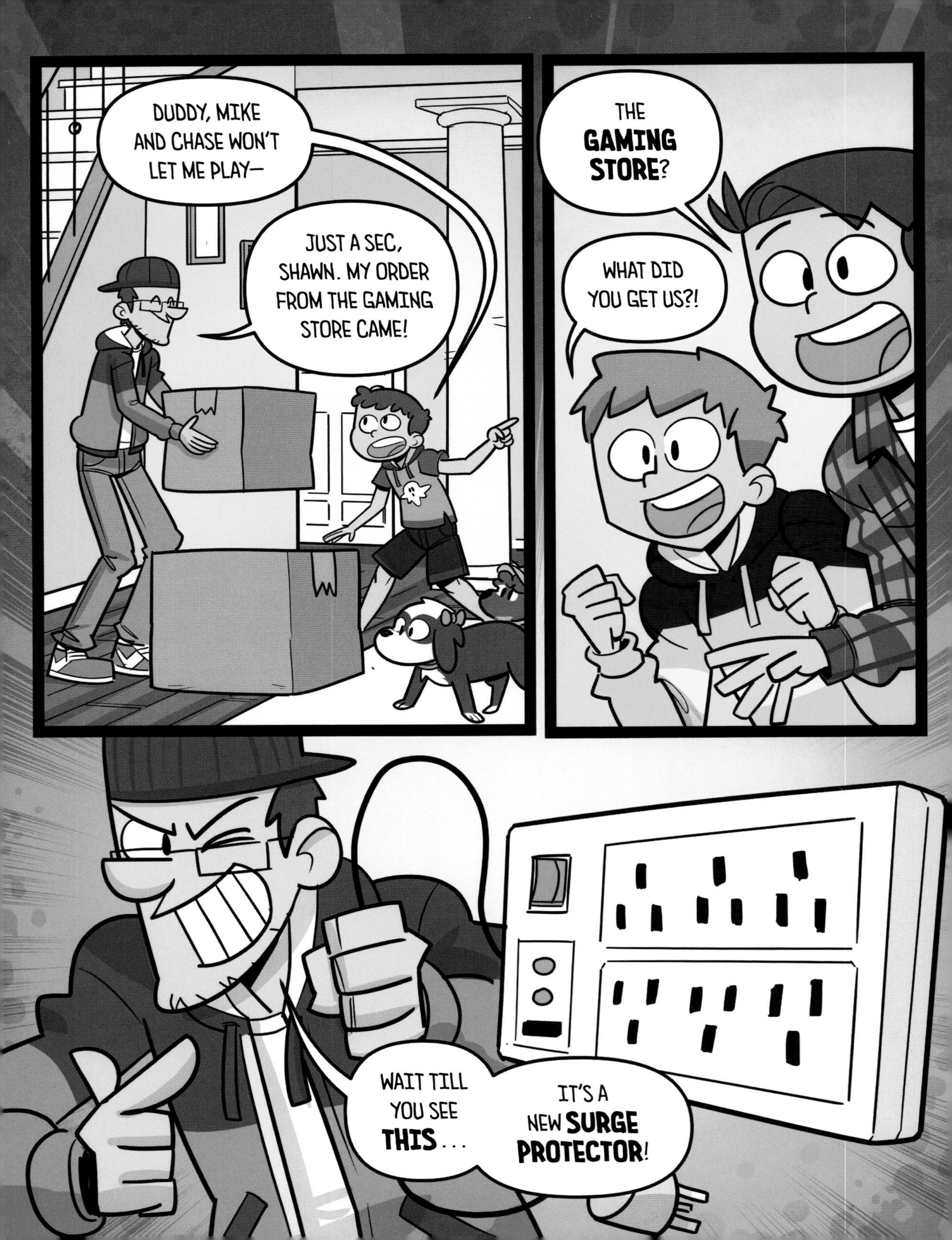
DUDDY, MIKE AND CHASE WON'T LET ME PLAY—
JUST A SEC, SHAWN. MY ORDER FROM THE GAMING STORE CAME!
THE **GAMING STORE**?
WHAT DID YOU GET US?!
WAIT TILL YOU SEE **THIS** . . .
IT'S A NEW **SURGE PROTECTOR**!

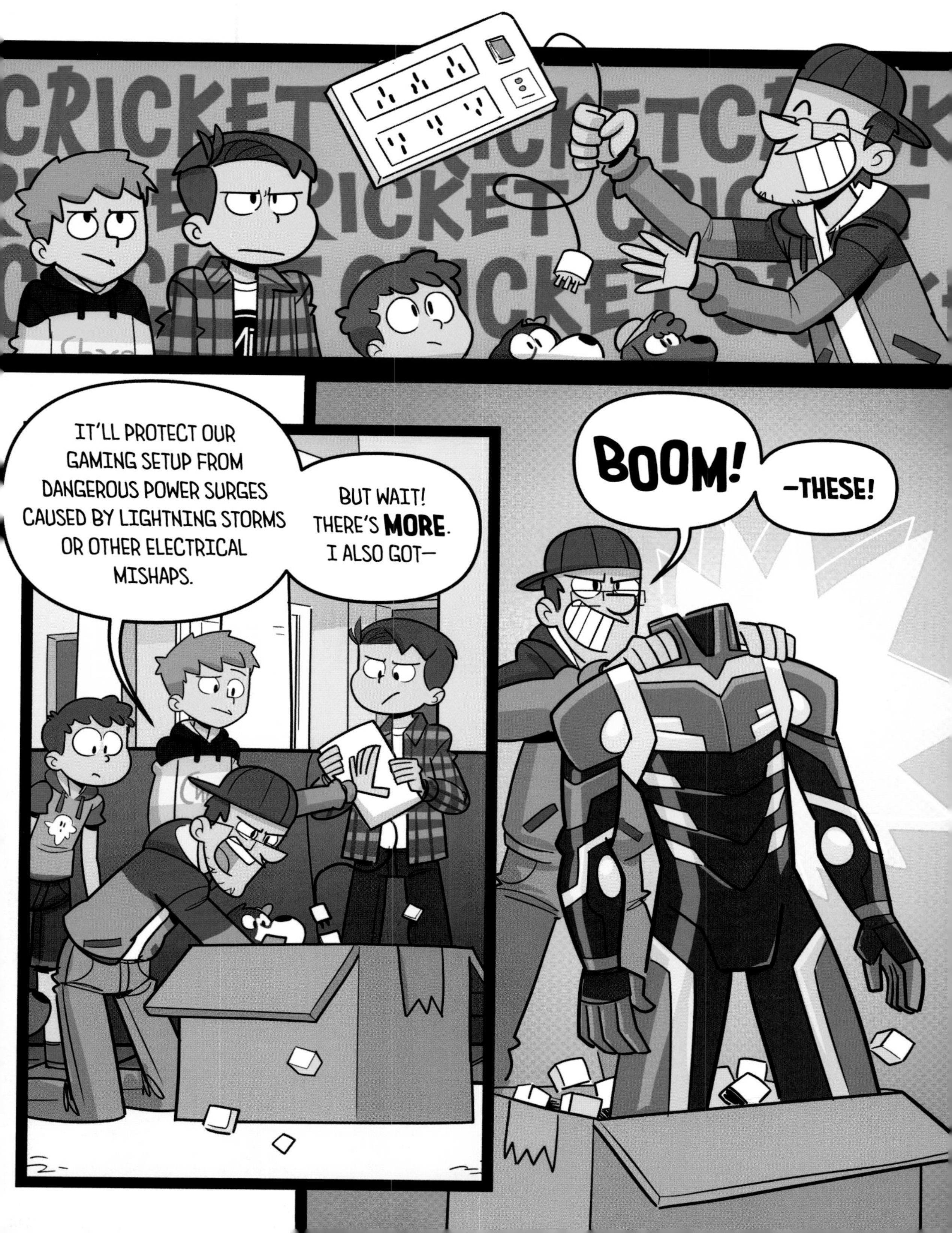

CRICKET CRICKET CRICKET CRICKET
IT'LL PROTECT OUR GAMING SETUP FROM DANGEROUS POWER SURGES CAUSED BY LIGHTNING STORMS OR OTHER ELECTRICAL MISHAPS.
BUT WAIT! THERE'S **MORE**. I ALSO GOT—
BOOM!
—THESE!

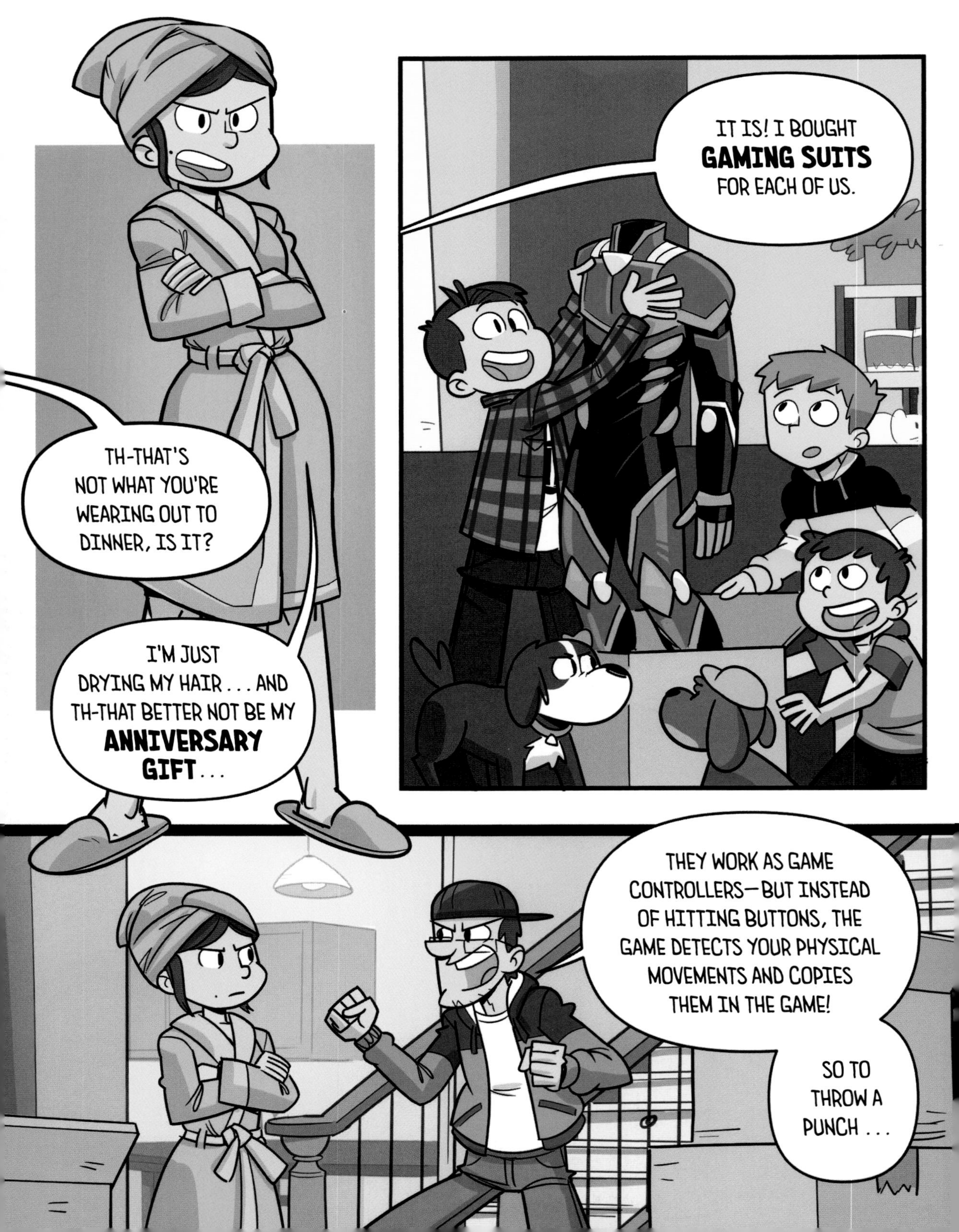
TH-THAT'S NOT WHAT YOU'RE WEARING OUT TO DINNER, IS IT?
IT IS! I BOUGHT GAMING SUITS FOR EACH OF US.
I'M JUST DRYING MY HAIR . . . AND TH-THAT BETTER NOT BE MY ANNIVERSARY GIFT . . .
THEY WORK AS GAME CONTROLLERS—BUT INSTEAD OF HITTING BUTTONS, THE GAME DETECTS YOUR PHYSICAL MOVEMENTS AND COPIES THEM IN THE GAME!
SO TO THROW A PUNCH . . .

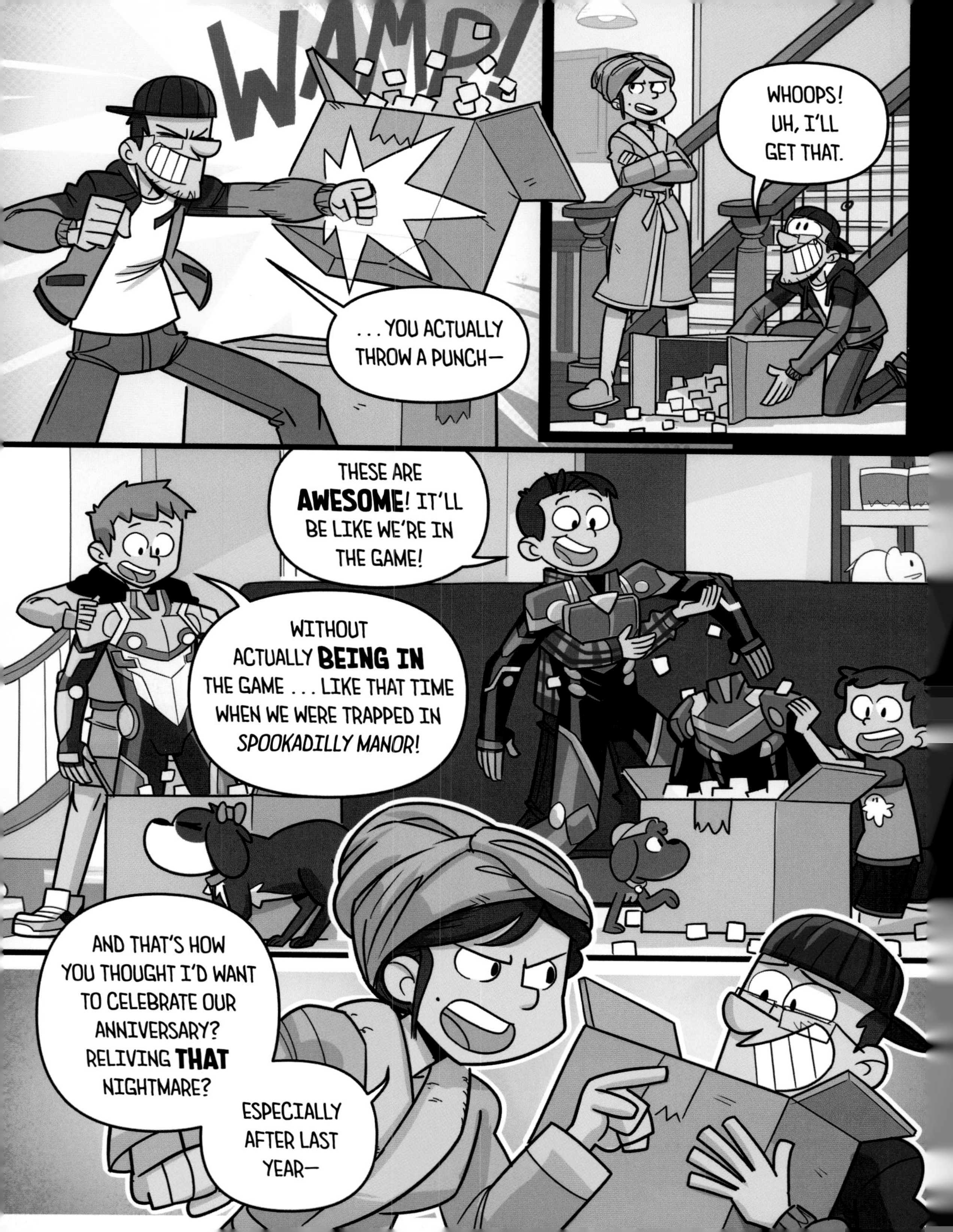
WAMP!
. . . YOU ACTUALLY THROW A PUNCH—
WHOOPS! UH, I'LL GET THAT.
THESE ARE **AWESOME**! IT'LL BE LIKE WE'RE IN THE GAME!
WITHOUT ACTUALLY **BEING IN** THE GAME . . . LIKE THAT TIME WHEN WE WERE TRAPPED IN *SPOOKADILLY MANOR*!
AND THAT'S HOW YOU THOUGHT I'D WANT TO CELEBRATE OUR ANNIVERSARY? RELIVING **THAT** NIGHTMARE?
ESPECIALLY AFTER LAST YEAR—

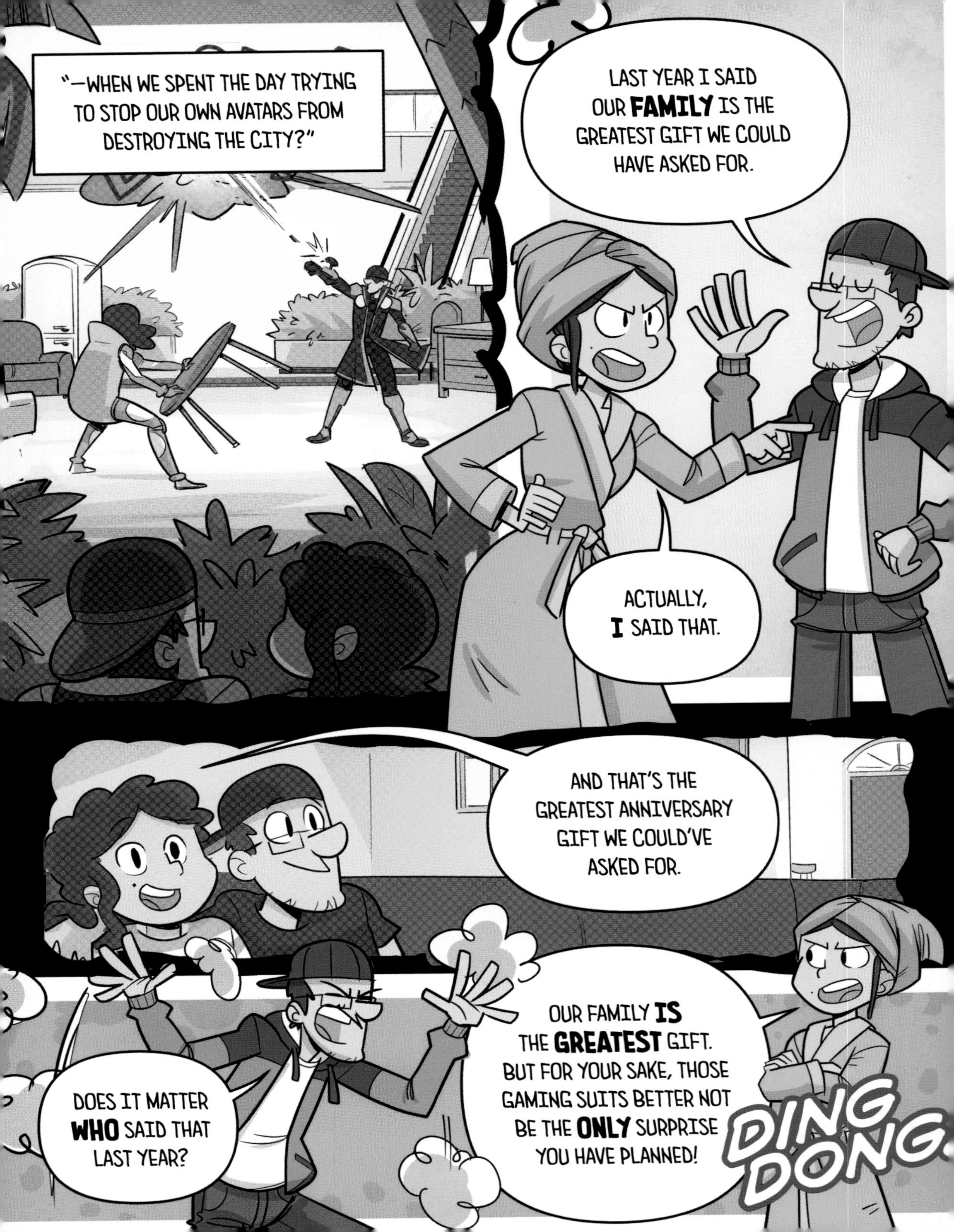
"—WHEN WE SPENT THE DAY TRYING TO STOP OUR OWN AVATARS FROM DESTROYING THE CITY?"
LAST YEAR I SAID OUR **FAMILY** IS THE GREATEST GIFT WE COULD HAVE ASKED FOR.
ACTUALLY, **I** SAID THAT.
AND THAT'S THE GREATEST ANNIVERSARY GIFT WE COULD'VE ASKED FOR.
DOES IT MATTER **WHO** SAID THAT LAST YEAR?
OUR FAMILY **IS** THE **GREATEST** GIFT. BUT FOR YOUR SAKE, THOSE GAMING SUITS BETTER NOT BE THE **ONLY** SURPRISE YOU HAVE PLANNED!
DING DONG.

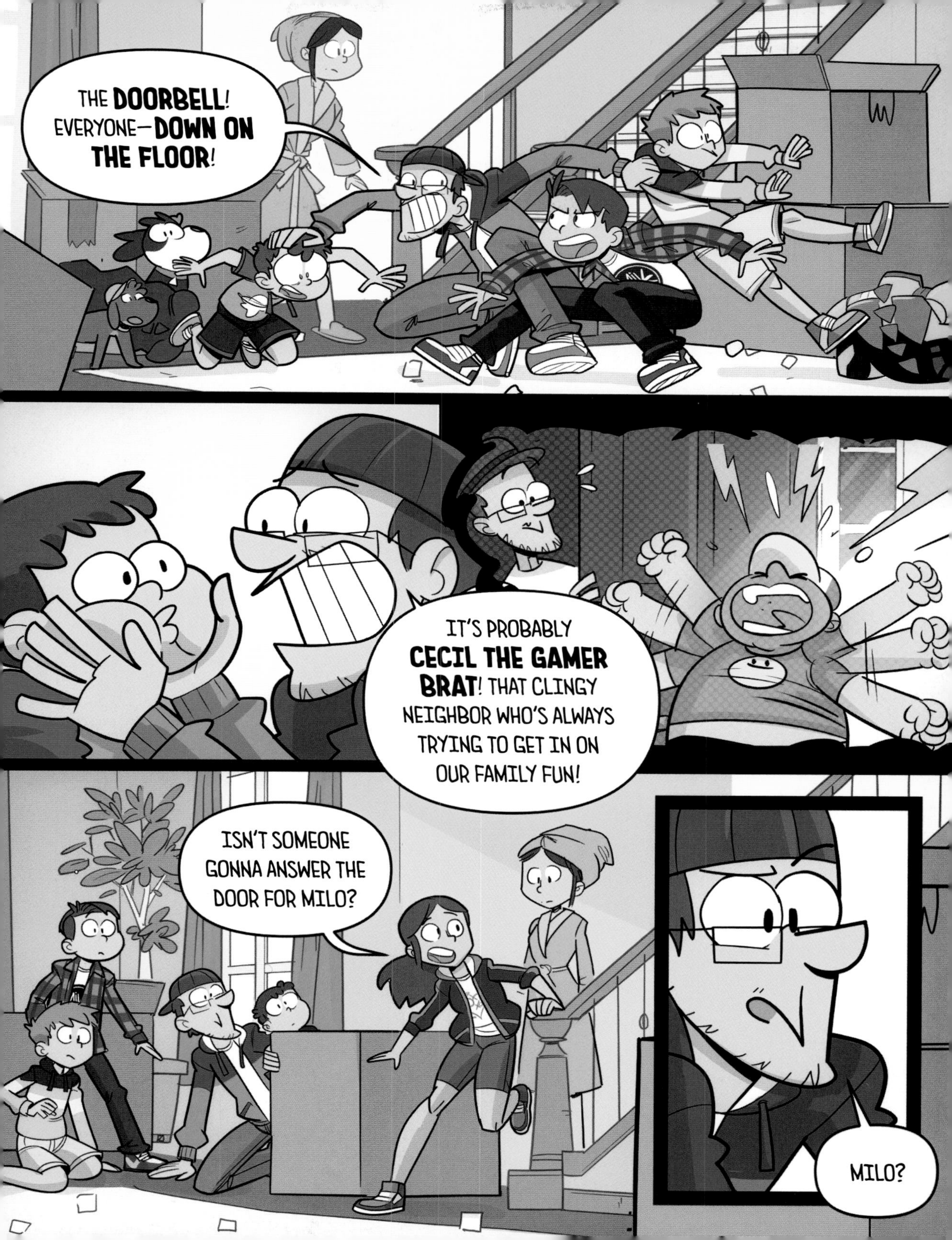
THE **DOORBELL**! EVERYONE—**DOWN ON THE FLOOR**!
IT'S PROBABLY **CECIL THE GAMER BRAT**! THAT CLINGY NEIGHBOR WHO'S ALWAYS TRYING TO GET IN ON OUR FAMILY FUN!
ISN'T SOMEONE GONNA ANSWER THE DOOR FOR MILO?
MILO?

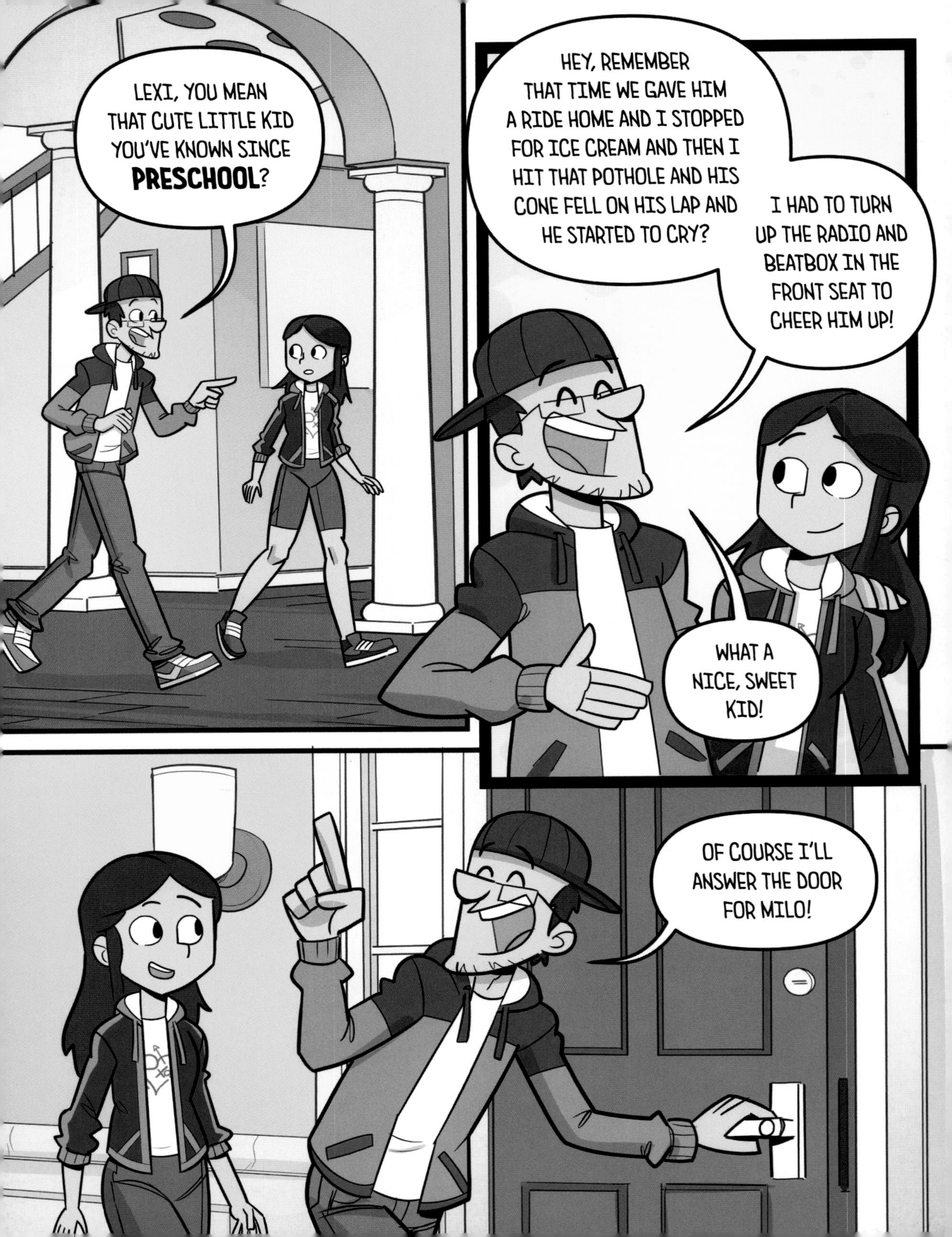

LEXI, YOU MEAN THAT CUTE LITTLE KID YOU'VE KNOWN SINCE **PRESCHOOL**?
HEY, REMEMBER THAT TIME WE GAVE HIM A RIDE HOME AND I STOPPED FOR ICE CREAM AND THEN I HIT THAT POTHOLE AND HIS CONE FELL ON HIS LAP AND HE STARTED TO CRY?
I HAD TO TURN UP THE RADIO AND BEATBOX IN THE FRONT SEAT TO CHEER HIM UP!
WHAT A NICE, SWEET KID!
OF COURSE I'LL ANSWER THE DOOR FOR MILO!

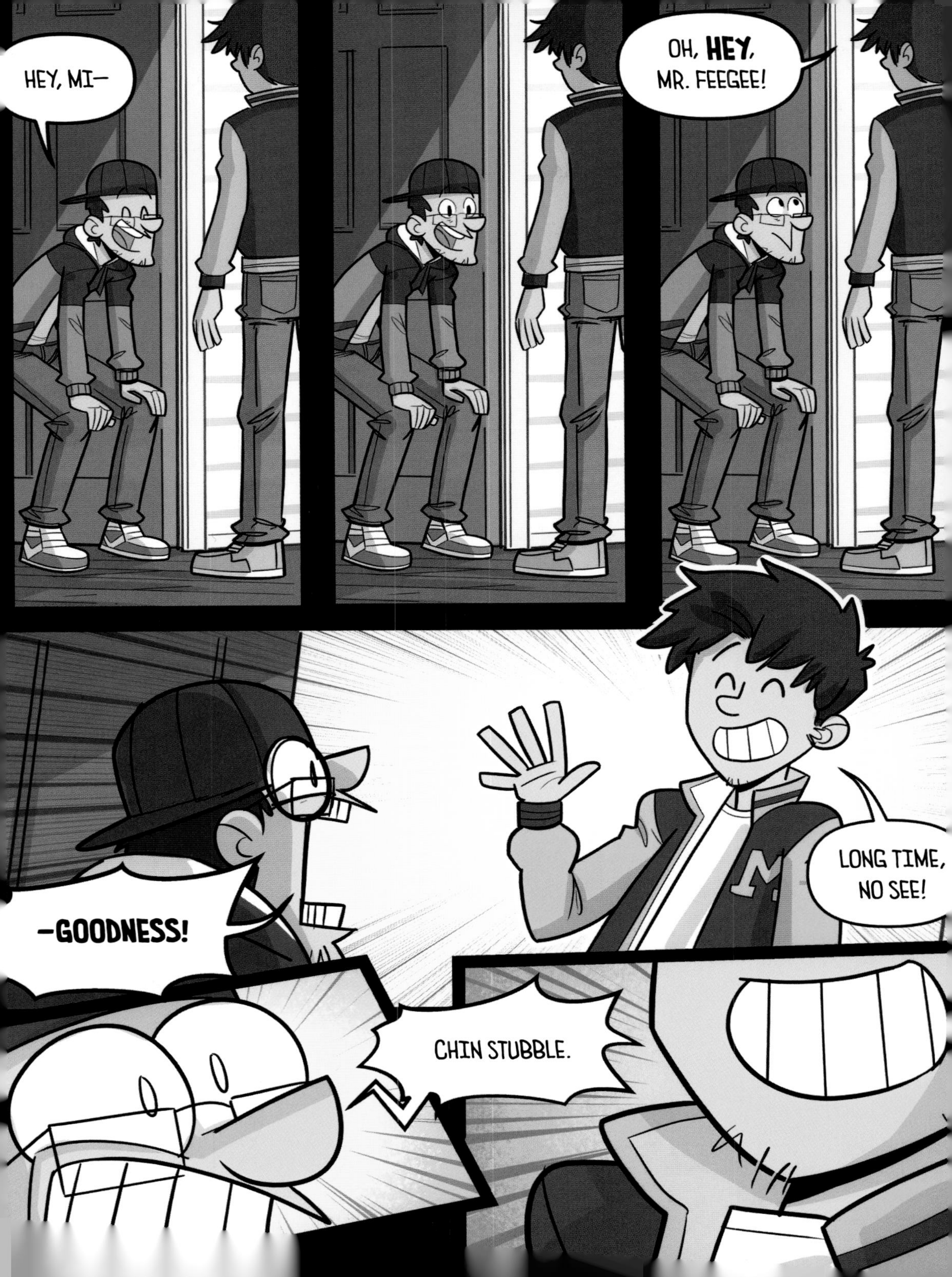
HEY, MI—
OH, **HEY,** MR. FEEGEE!
—GOODNESS!
LONG TIME, NO SEE!
CHIN STUBBLE.

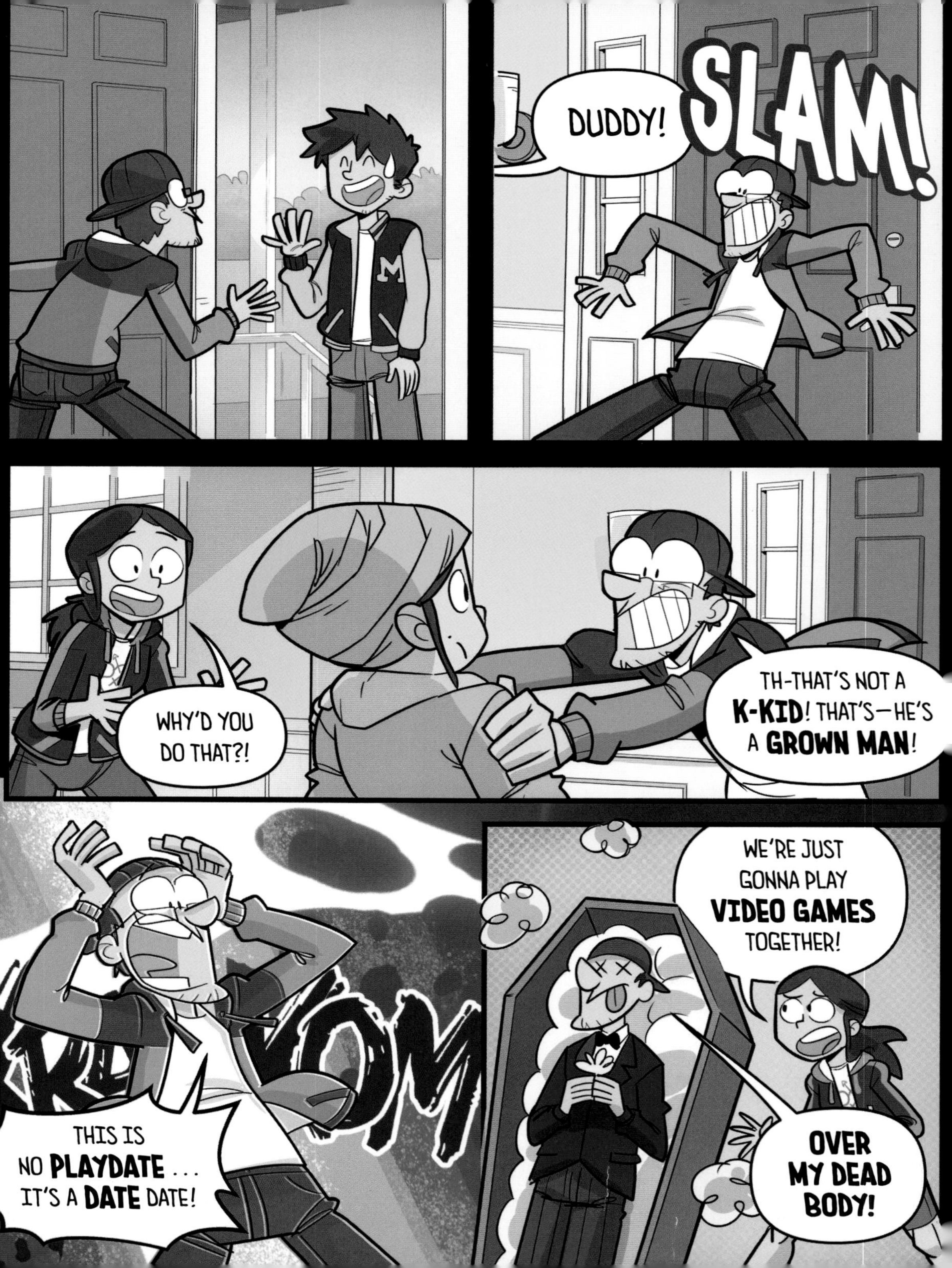
DUDDY!
SLAM!
WHY'D YOU DO THAT?!
TH-THAT'S NOT A **K-KID**! THAT'S—HE'S A **GROWN MAN**!
THIS IS NO **PLAYDATE** . . . IT'S A **DATE** DATE!
WE'RE JUST GONNA PLAY **VIDEO GAMES** TOGETHER!
**OVER MY DEAD BODY!**

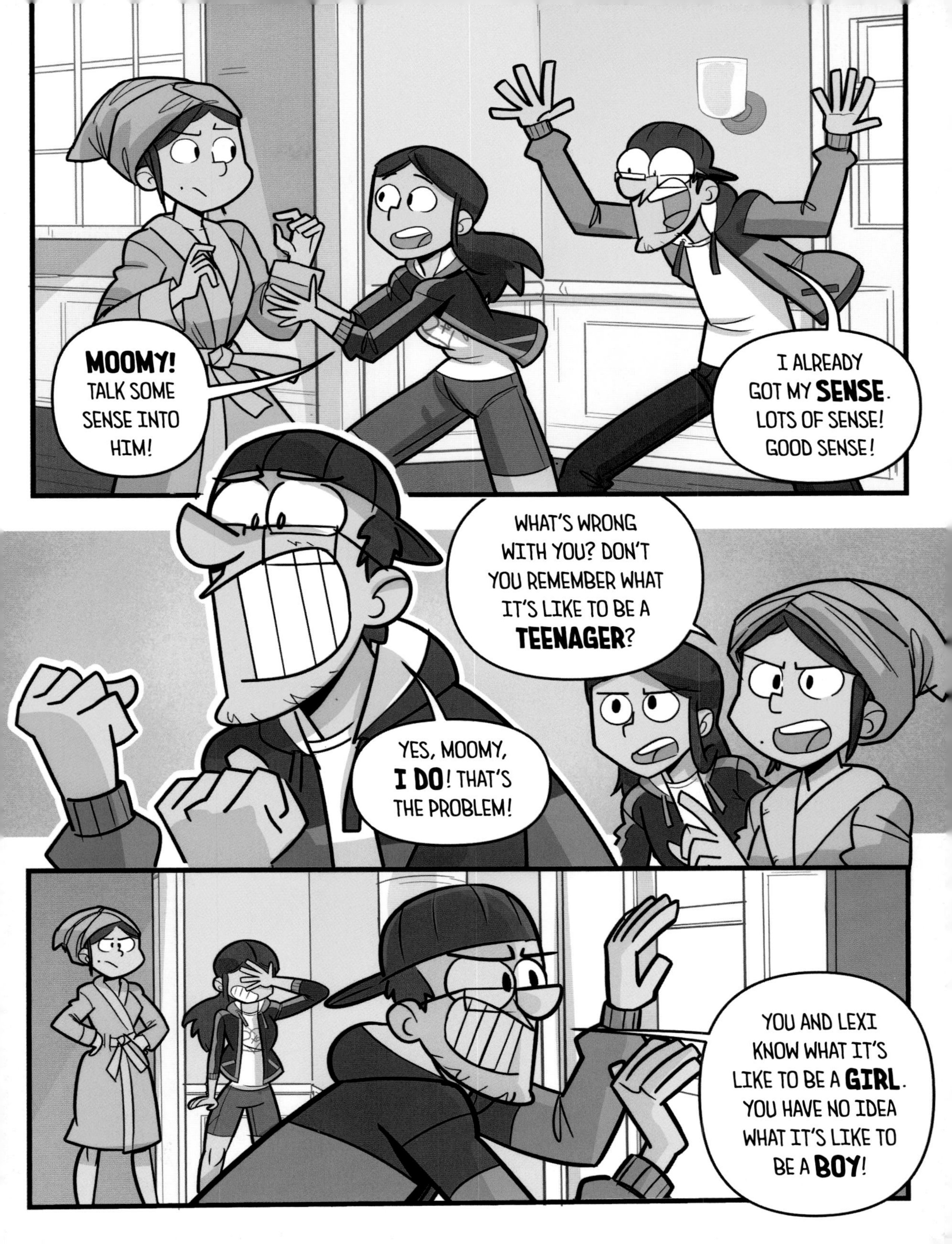
MOOMY! TALK SOME SENSE INTO HIM!
I ALREADY GOT MY SENSE. LOTS OF SENSE! GOOD SENSE!
WHAT'S WRONG WITH YOU? DON'T YOU REMEMBER WHAT IT'S LIKE TO BE A TEENAGER?
YES, MOOMY, I DO! THAT'S THE PROBLEM!
YOU AND LEXI KNOW WHAT IT'S LIKE TO BE A GIRL. YOU HAVE NO IDEA WHAT IT'S LIKE TO BE A BOY!

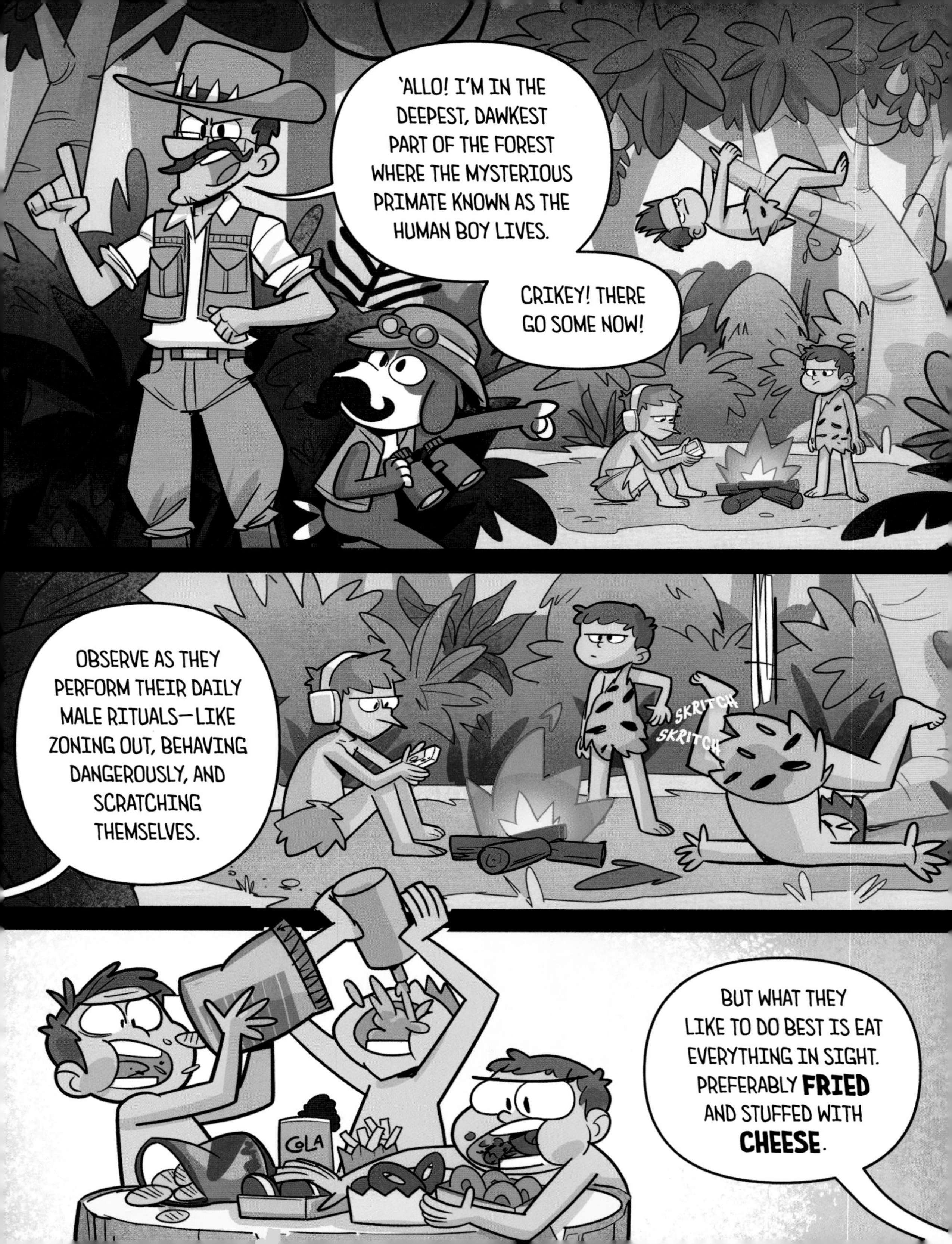
'ALLO! I'M IN THE DEEPEST, DAWKEST PART OF THE FOREST WHERE THE MYSTERIOUS PRIMATE KNOWN AS THE HUMAN BOY LIVES.
CRIKEY! THERE GO SOME NOW!
OBSERVE AS THEY PERFORM THEIR DAILY MALE RITUALS—LIKE ZONING OUT, BEHAVING DANGEROUSLY, AND SCRATCHING THEMSELVES.
SKRITCH
SKRITCH
COLA
BUT WHAT THEY LIKE TO DO BEST IS EAT EVERYTHING IN SIGHT. PREFERABLY **FRIED** AND STUFFED WITH **CHEESE**.

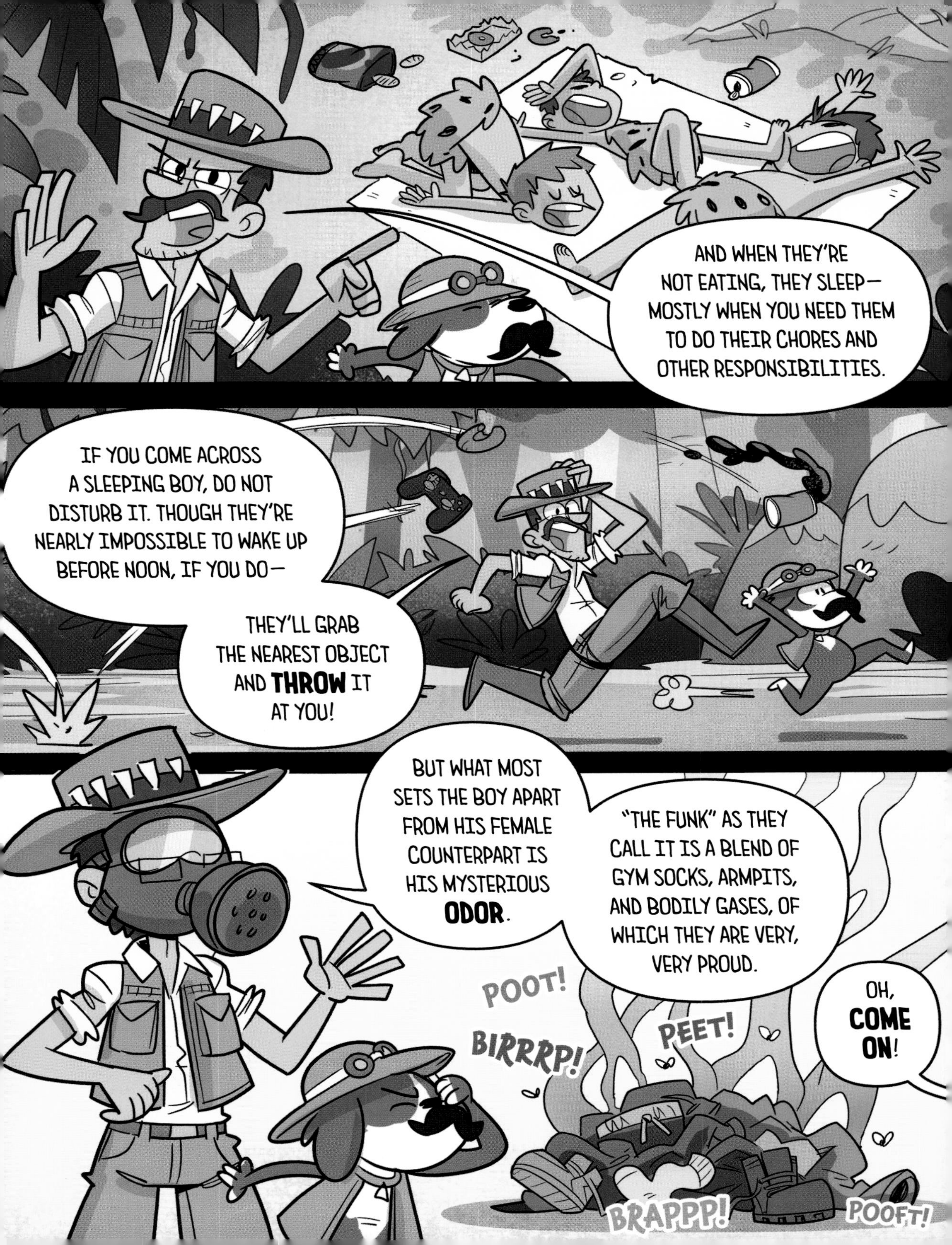
AND WHEN THEY'RE NOT EATING, THEY SLEEP—MOSTLY WHEN YOU NEED THEM TO DO THEIR CHORES AND OTHER RESPONSIBILITIES.
IF YOU COME ACROSS A SLEEPING BOY, DO NOT DISTURB IT. THOUGH THEY'RE NEARLY IMPOSSIBLE TO WAKE UP BEFORE NOON, IF YOU DO—
THEY'LL GRAB THE NEAREST OBJECT AND **THROW** IT AT YOU!
BUT WHAT MOST SETS THE BOY APART FROM HIS FEMALE COUNTERPART IS HIS MYSTERIOUS **ODOR**.
"THE FUNK" AS THEY CALL IT IS A BLEND OF GYM SOCKS, ARMPITS, AND BODILY GASES, OF WHICH THEY ARE VERY, VERY PROUD.
POOT!
BIRRRP!
PEET!
OH, **COME ON**!
BRAPPP!
POOFT!

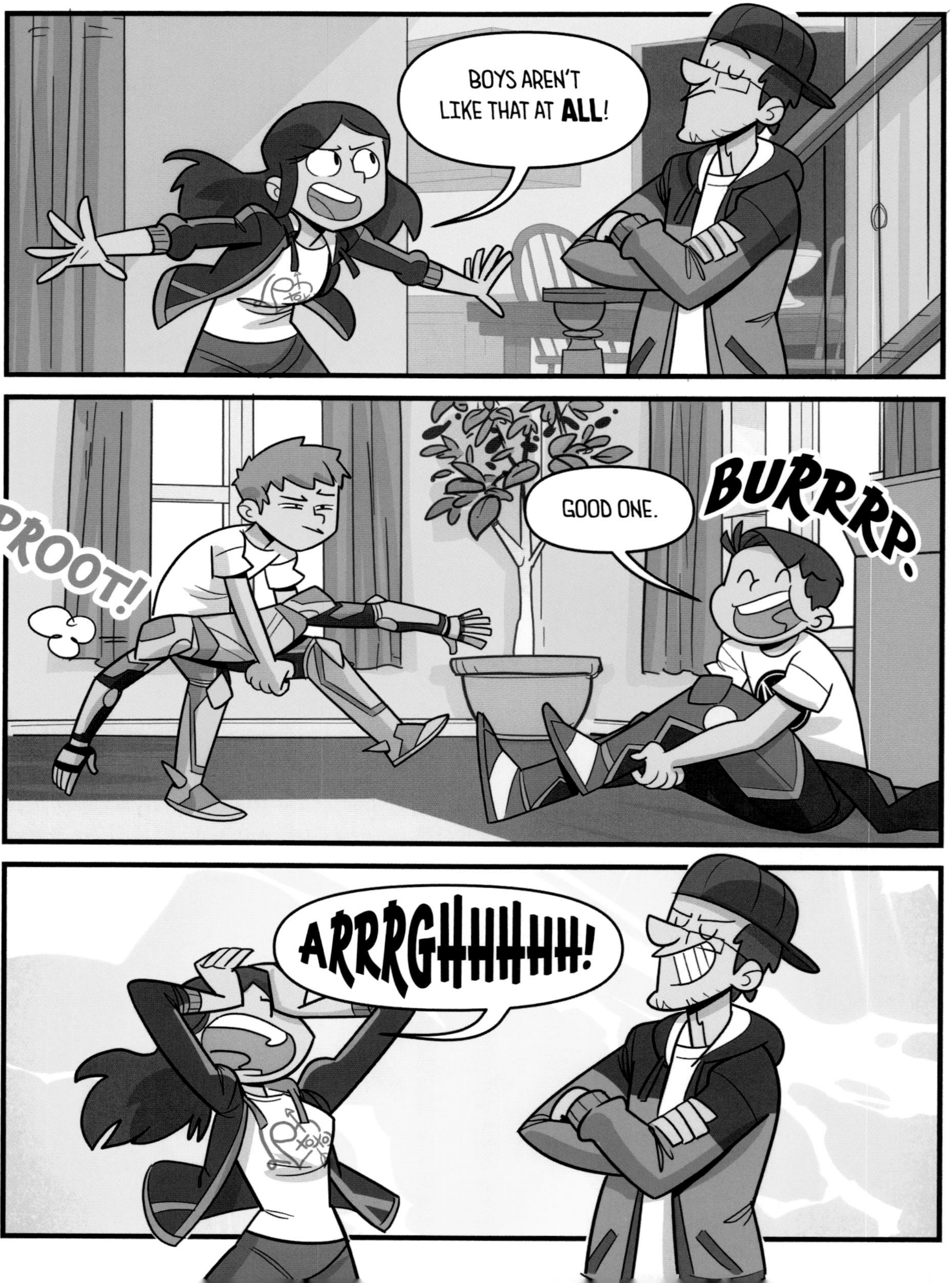
BOYS AREN'T LIKE THAT AT **ALL**!
PROOT!
GOOD ONE.
BURRRP.
ARRRGHHHHH!

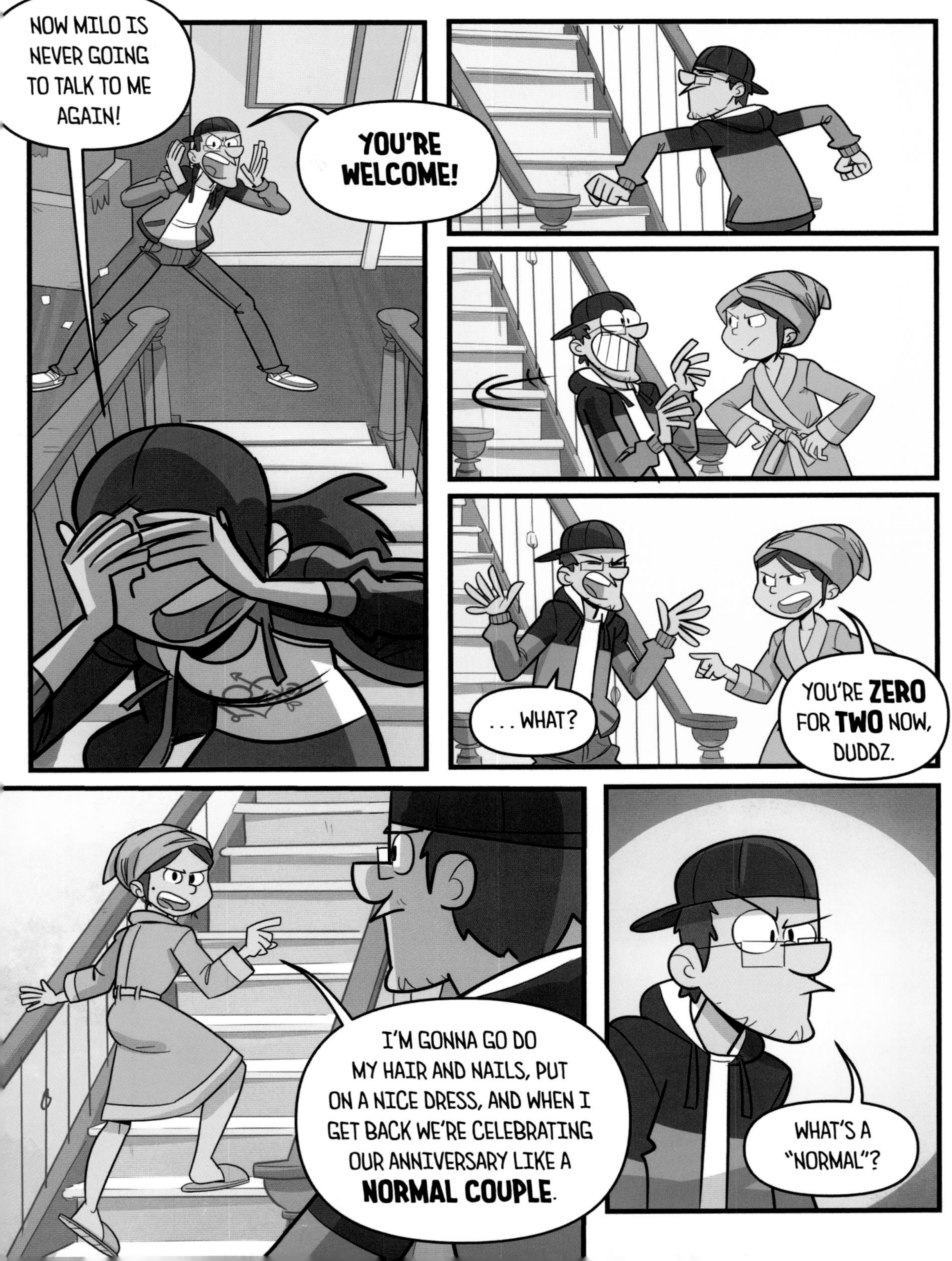
NOW MILO IS NEVER GOING TO TALK TO ME AGAIN!
YOU'RE WELCOME!
. . . WHAT?
YOU'RE ZERO FOR TWO NOW, DUDDZ.
I'M GONNA GO DO MY HAIR AND NAILS, PUT ON A NICE DRESS, AND WHEN I GET BACK WE'RE CELEBRATING OUR ANNIVERSARY LIKE A NORMAL COUPLE.
WHAT'S A "NORMAL"?

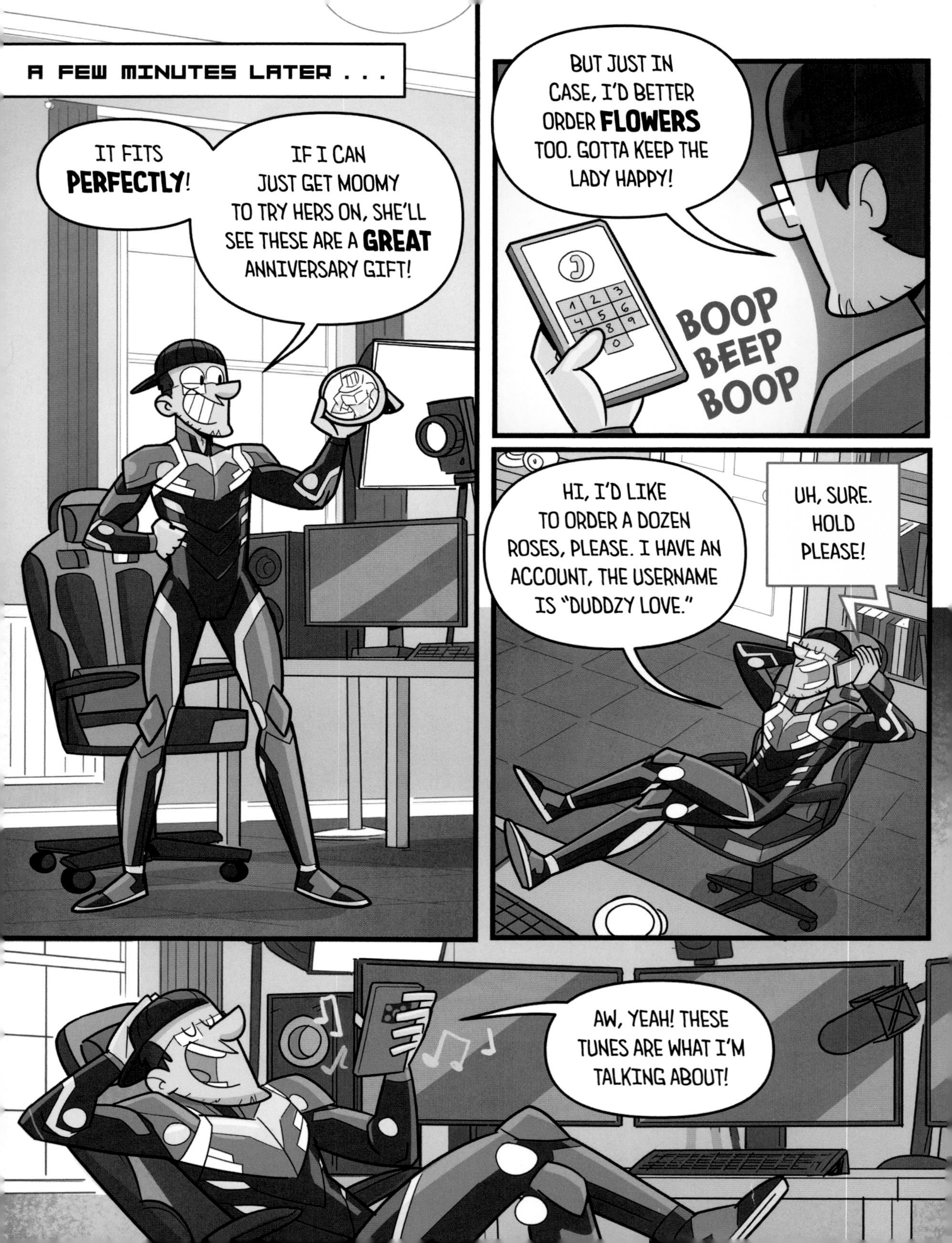
A FEW MINUTES LATER . . .
IT FITS **PERFECTLY**!
IF I CAN JUST GET MOOMY TO TRY HERS ON, SHE'LL SEE THESE ARE A **GREAT** ANNIVERSARY GIFT!
BUT JUST IN CASE, I'D BETTER ORDER **FLOWERS** TOO. GOTTA KEEP THE LADY HAPPY!
BOOP BEEP BOOP
HI, I'D LIKE TO ORDER A DOZEN ROSES, PLEASE. I HAVE AN ACCOUNT, THE USERNAME IS "DUDDZY LOVE."
UH, SURE. HOLD PLEASE!
AW, YEAH! THESE TUNES ARE WHAT I'M TALKING ABOUT!

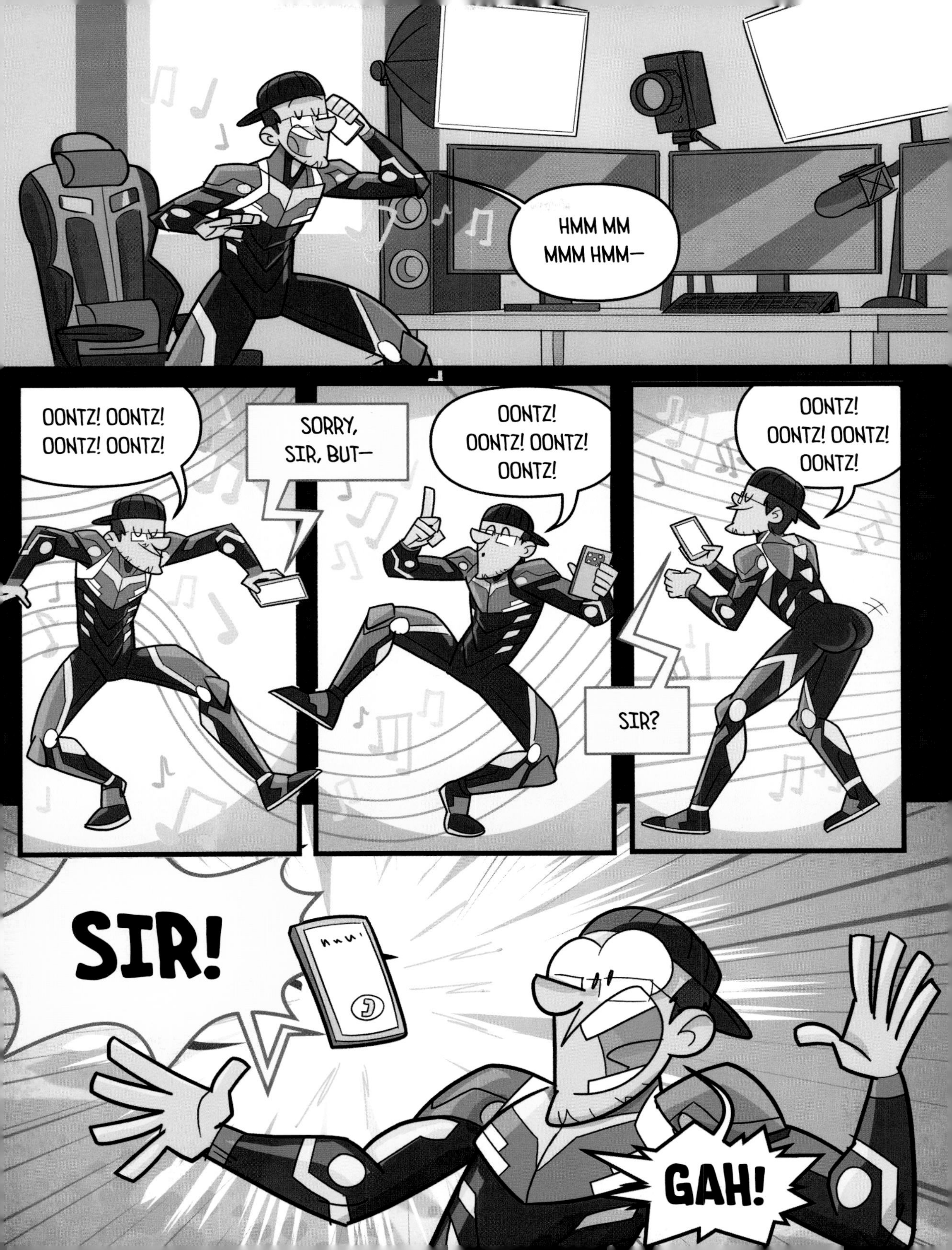
HMM MM MMM HMM—
OONTZ! OONTZ! OONTZ! OONTZ!
SORRY, SIR, BUT—
OONTZ! OONTZ! OONTZ! OONTZ!
OONTZ! OONTZ! OONTZ! OONTZ!
SIR?
SIR!
GAH!

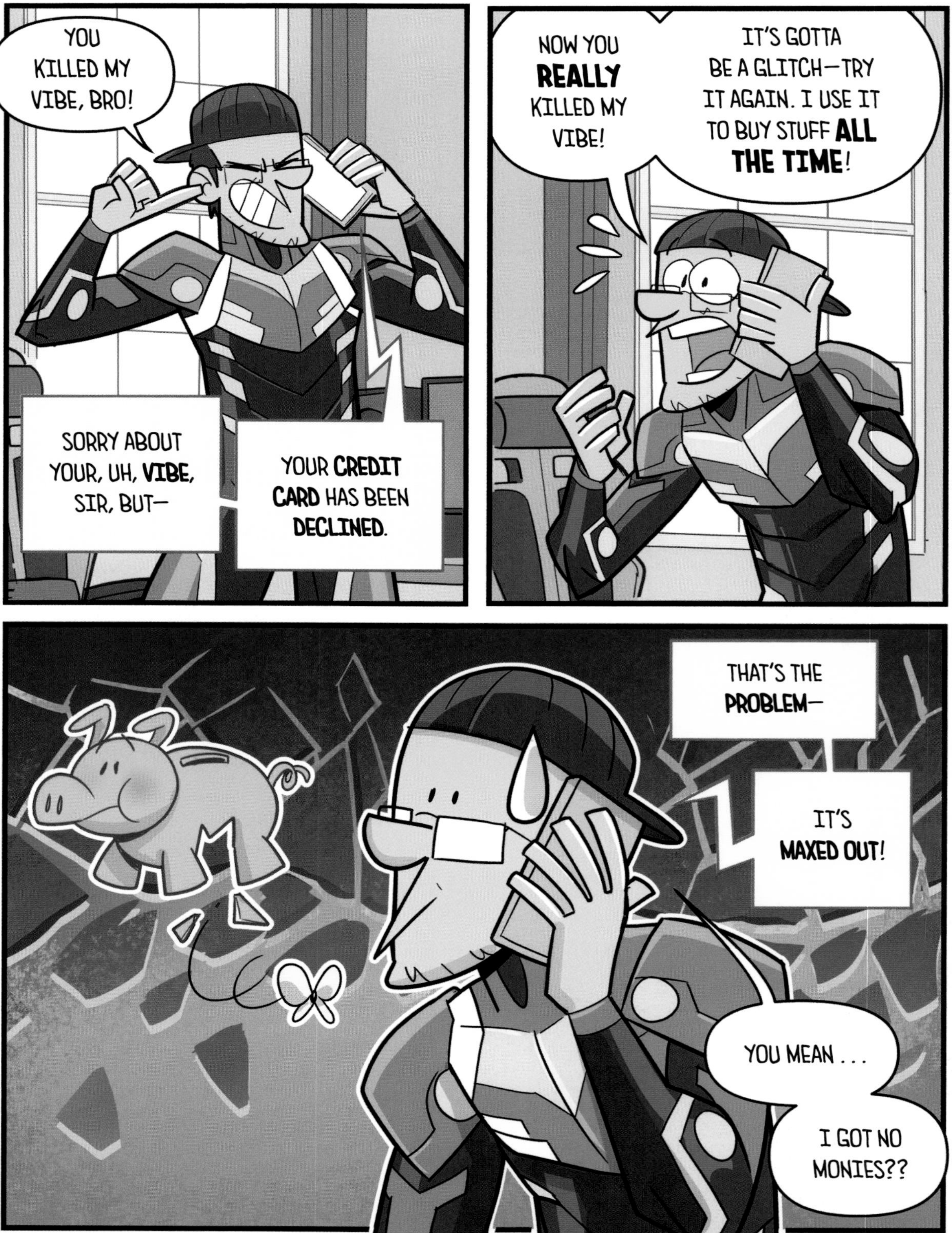
YOU KILLED MY VIBE, BRO!
SORRY ABOUT YOUR, UH, **VIBE**, SIR, BUT—
YOUR **CREDIT CARD** HAS BEEN **DECLINED**.
NOW YOU **REALLY** KILLED MY VIBE!
IT'S GOTTA BE A GLITCH—TRY IT AGAIN. I USE IT TO BUY STUFF **ALL THE TIME**!
THAT'S THE **PROBLEM**—
IT'S **MAXED OUT**!
YOU MEAN . . .
I GOT NO MONIES??

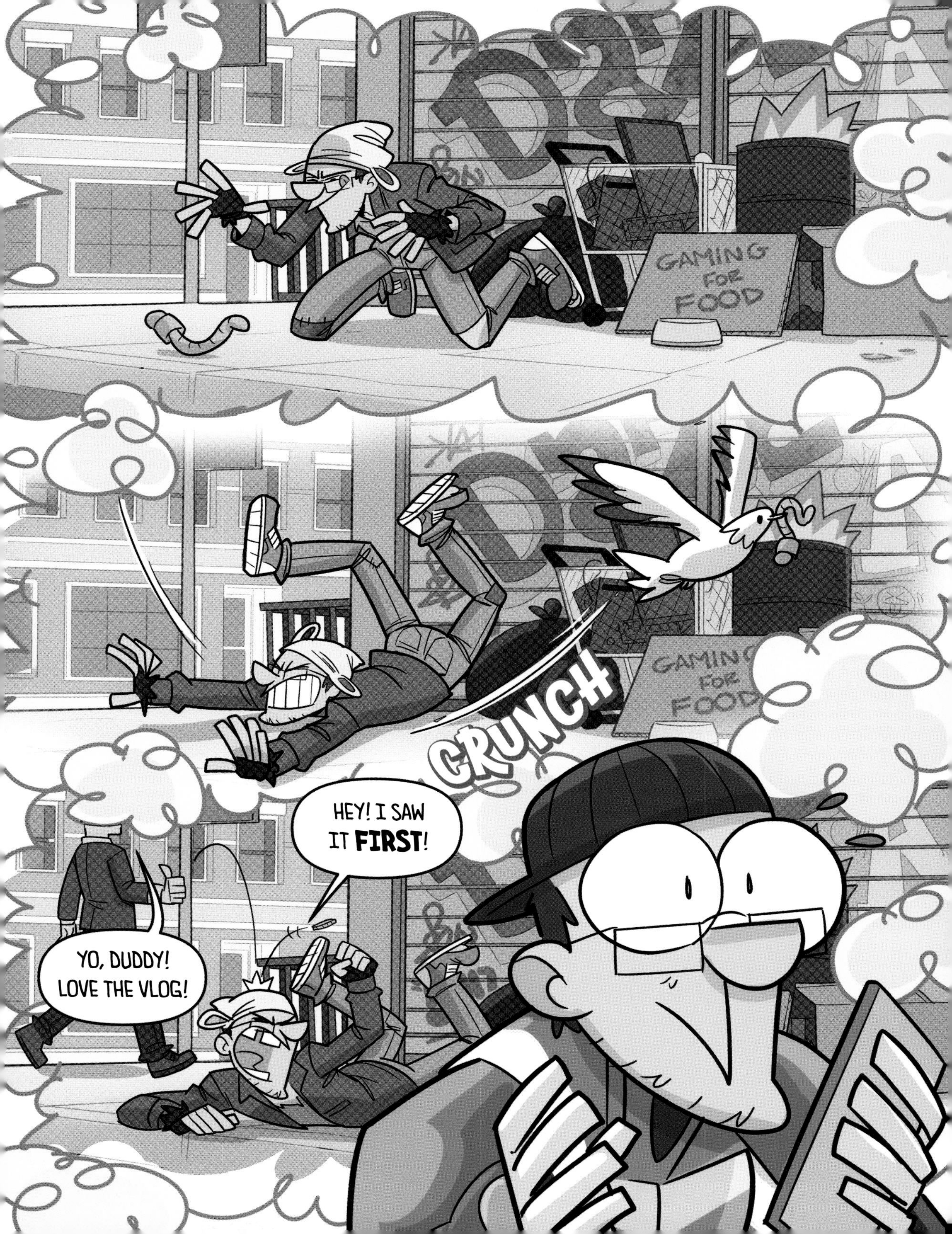
GAMING FOR FOOD
GAMING FOR FOOD
CRUNCH
HEY! I SAW IT FIRST!
YO, DUDDY! LOVE THE VLOG!

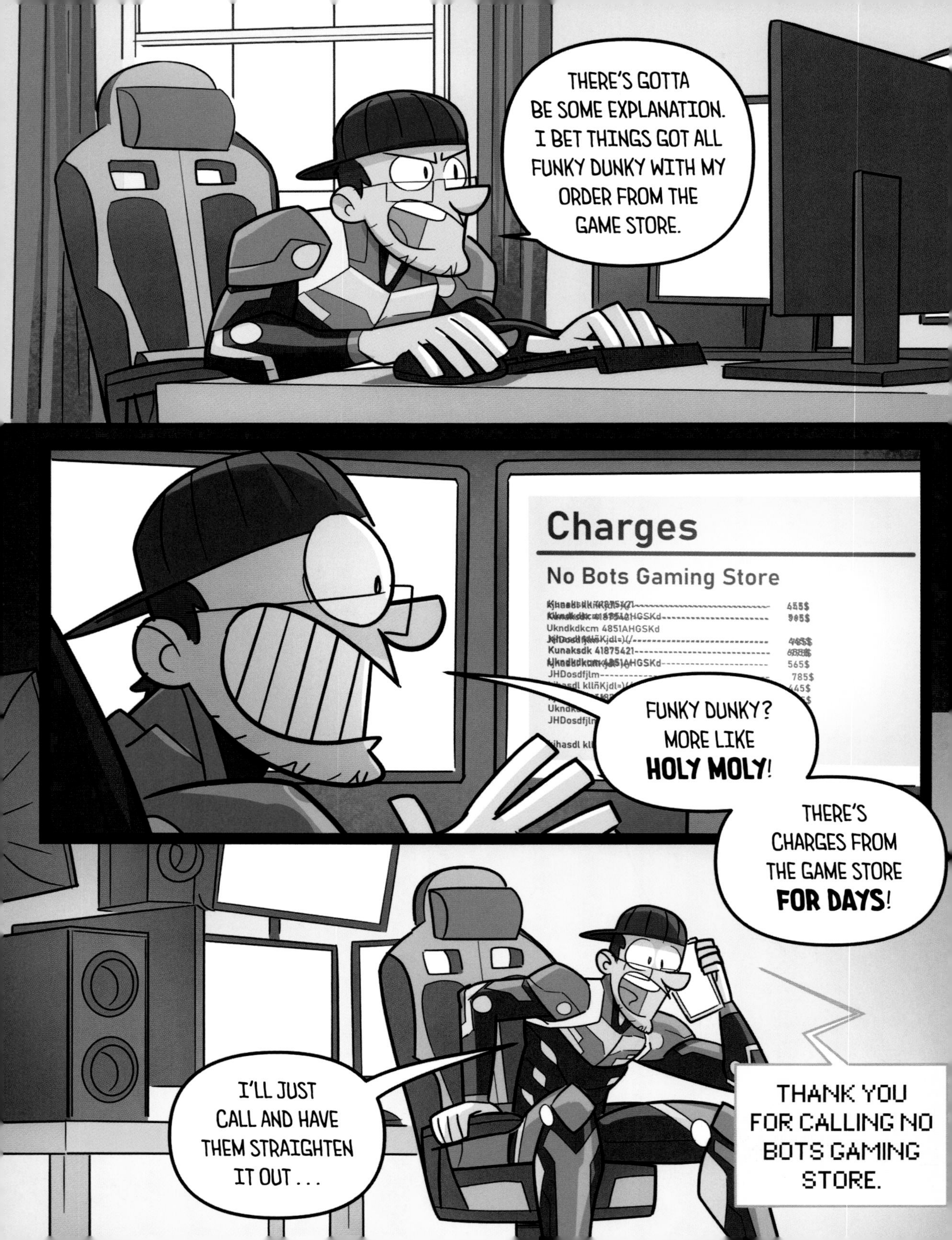
THERE'S GOTTA BE SOME EXPLANATION. I BET THINGS GOT ALL FUNKY DUNKY WITH MY ORDER FROM THE GAME STORE.
Charges
No Bots Gaming Store
FUNKY DUNKY? MORE LIKE **HOLY MOLY**!
THERE'S CHARGES FROM THE GAME STORE **FOR DAYS**!
I'LL JUST CALL AND HAVE THEM STRAIGHTEN IT OUT . . .
THANK YOU FOR CALLING NO BOTS GAMING STORE.

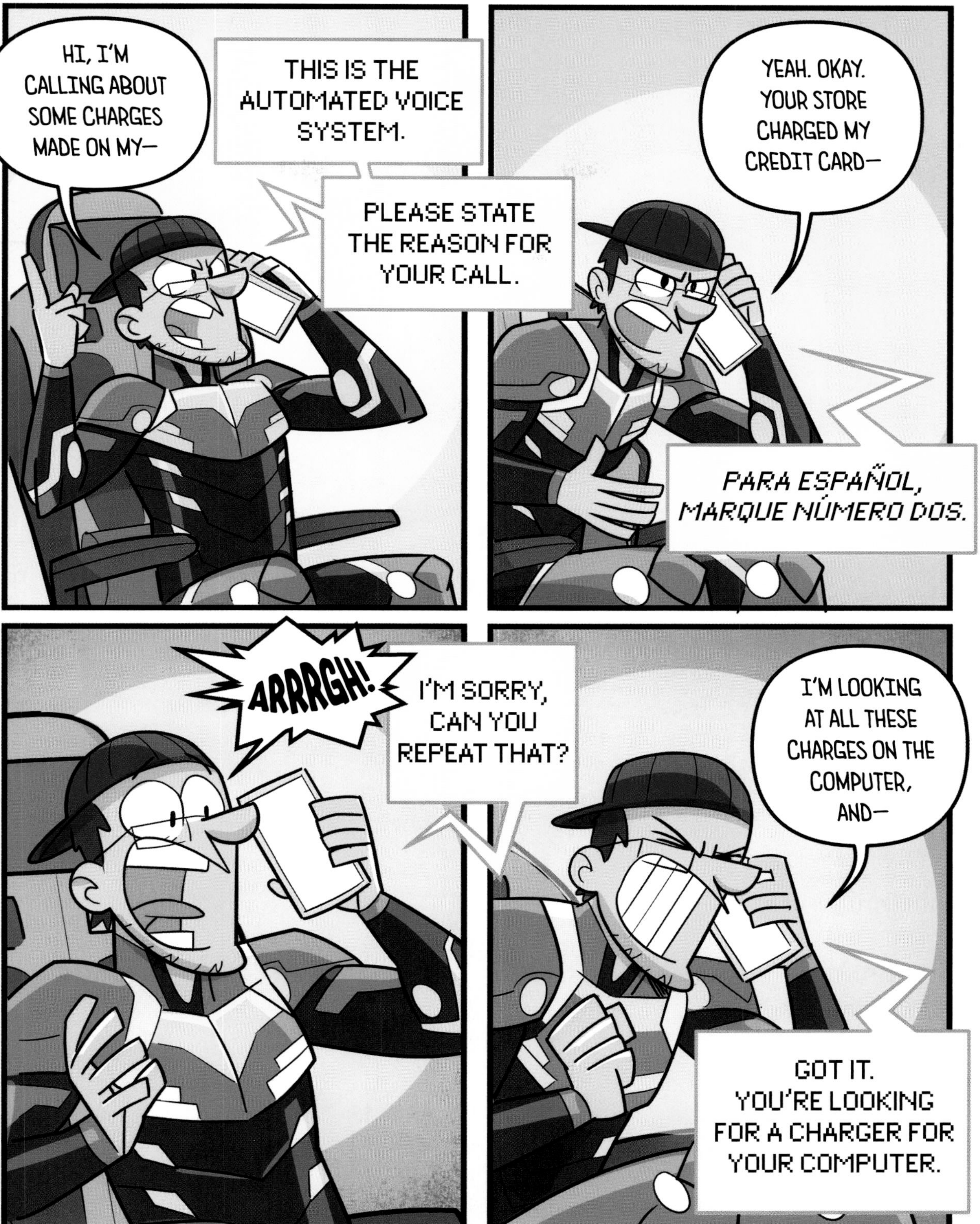
HI, I'M CALLING ABOUT SOME CHARGES MADE ON MY—
THIS IS THE AUTOMATED VOICE SYSTEM.
PLEASE STATE THE REASON FOR YOUR CALL.
YEAH. OKAY. YOUR STORE CHARGED MY CREDIT CARD—
*PARA ESPAÑOL, MARQUE NÚMERO DOS.*
ARRRGH!
I'M SORRY, CAN YOU REPEAT THAT?
I'M LOOKING AT ALL THESE CHARGES ON THE COMPUTER, AND—
GOT IT. YOU'RE LOOKING FOR A CHARGER FOR YOUR COMPUTER.

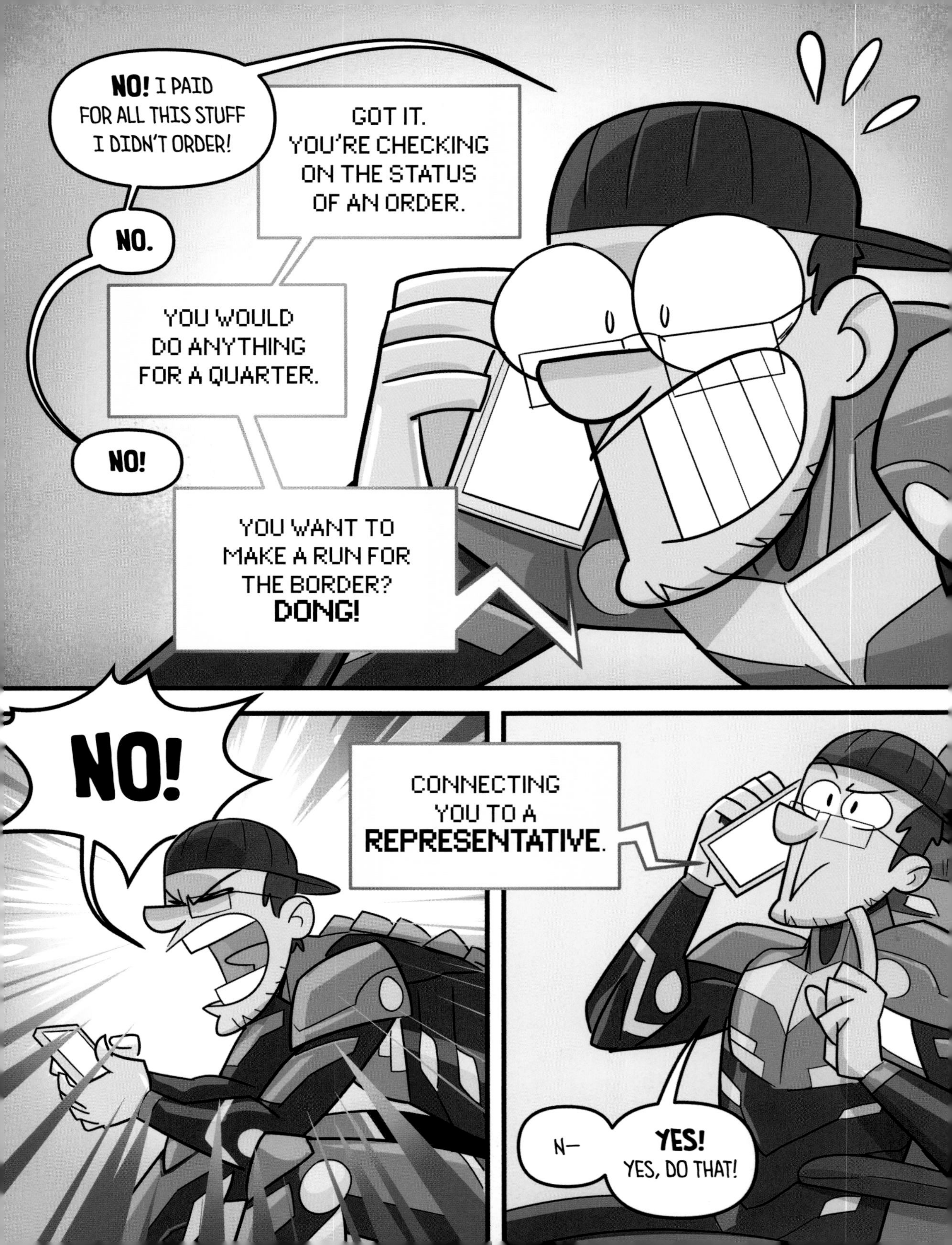
NO! I PAID FOR ALL THIS STUFF I DIDN'T ORDER!
GOT IT. YOU'RE CHECKING ON THE STATUS OF AN ORDER.
NO.
YOU WOULD DO ANYTHING FOR A QUARTER.
NO!
YOU WANT TO MAKE A RUN FOR THE BORDER? DONG!
NO!
CONNECTING YOU TO A REPRESENTATIVE.
N—
YES! YES, DO THAT!

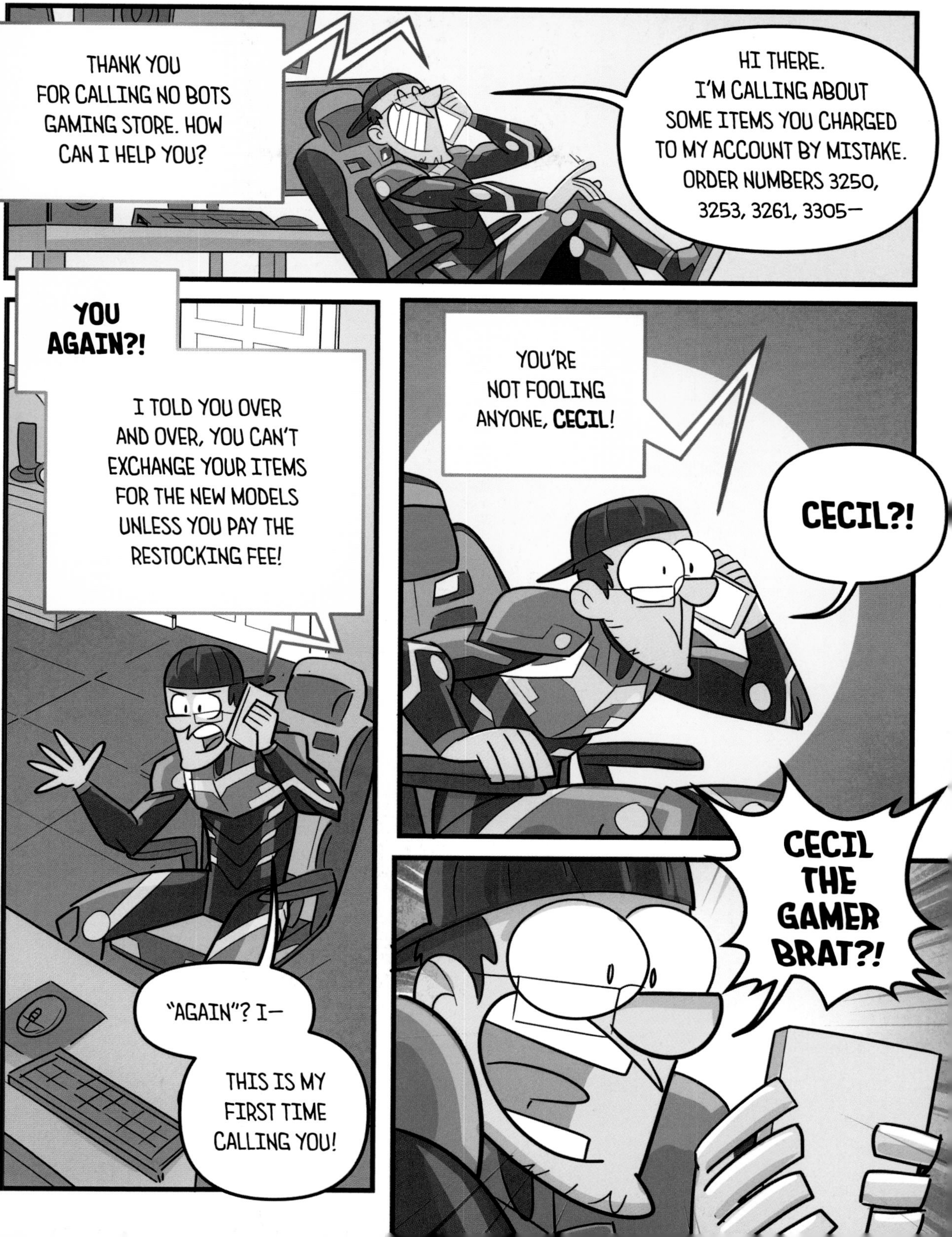

THANK YOU FOR CALLING NO BOTS GAMING STORE. HOW CAN I HELP YOU?
HI THERE. I'M CALLING ABOUT SOME ITEMS YOU CHARGED TO MY ACCOUNT BY MISTAKE. ORDER NUMBERS 3250, 3253, 3261, 3305—
YOU AGAIN?!
I TOLD YOU OVER AND OVER, YOU CAN'T EXCHANGE YOUR ITEMS FOR THE NEW MODELS UNLESS YOU PAY THE RESTOCKING FEE!
"AGAIN"? I—
THIS IS MY FIRST TIME CALLING YOU!
YOU'RE NOT FOOLING ANYONE, CECIL!
CECIL?!
CECIL THE GAMER BRAT?!

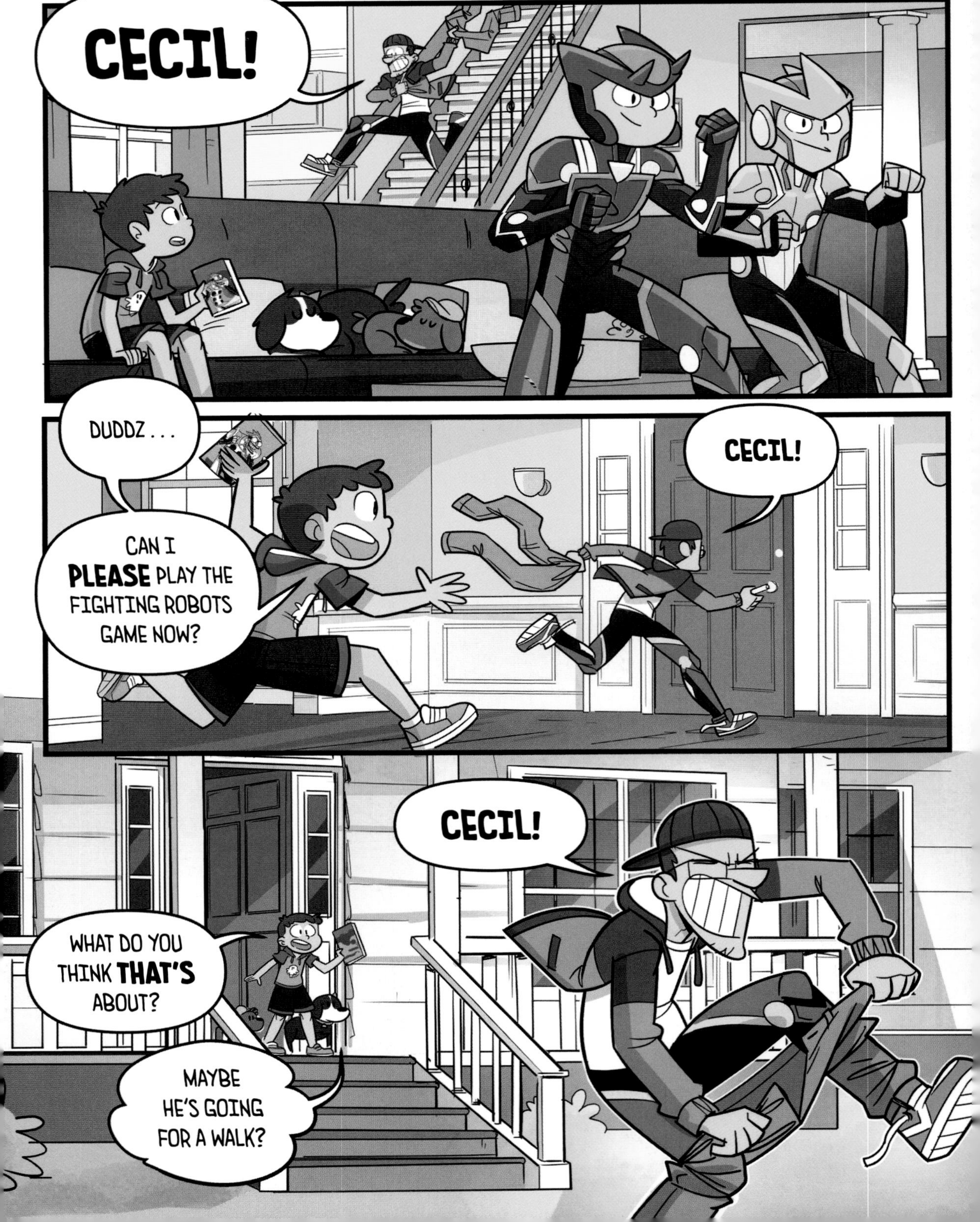
CECIL!
DUDDZ . . .
CAN I PLEASE PLAY THE FIGHTING ROBOTS GAME NOW?
CECIL!
CECIL!
WHAT DO YOU THINK THAT'S ABOUT?
MAYBE HE'S GOING FOR A WALK?

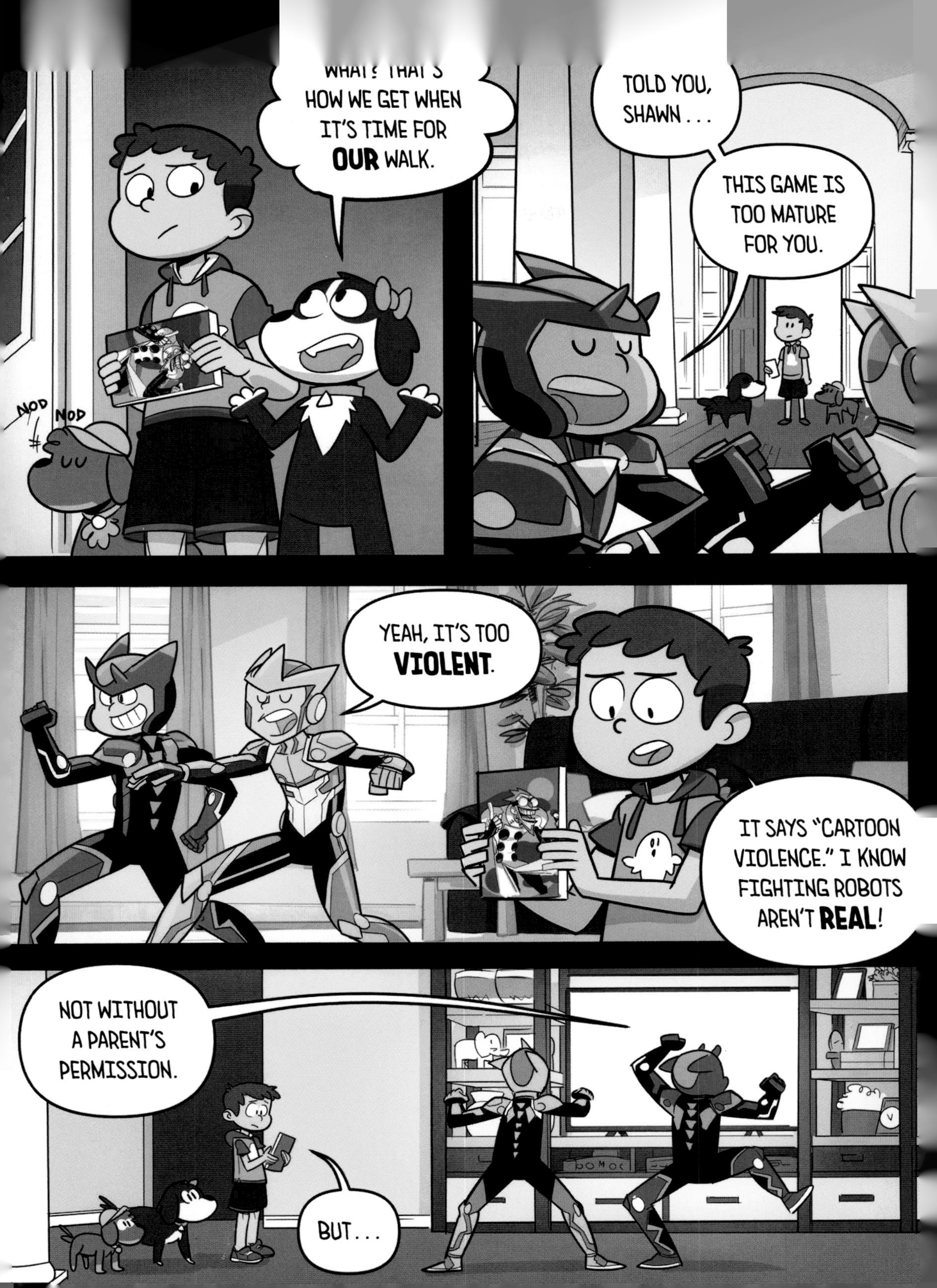
WHAT? THAT'S HOW WE GET WHEN IT'S TIME FOR **OUR** WALK.
NOD NOD
TOLD YOU, SHAWN . . .
THIS GAME IS TOO MATURE FOR YOU.
YEAH, IT'S TOO **VIOLENT**.
IT SAYS "CARTOON VIOLENCE." I KNOW FIGHTING ROBOTS AREN'T **REAL**!
NOT WITHOUT A PARENT'S PERMISSION.
BUT . . .

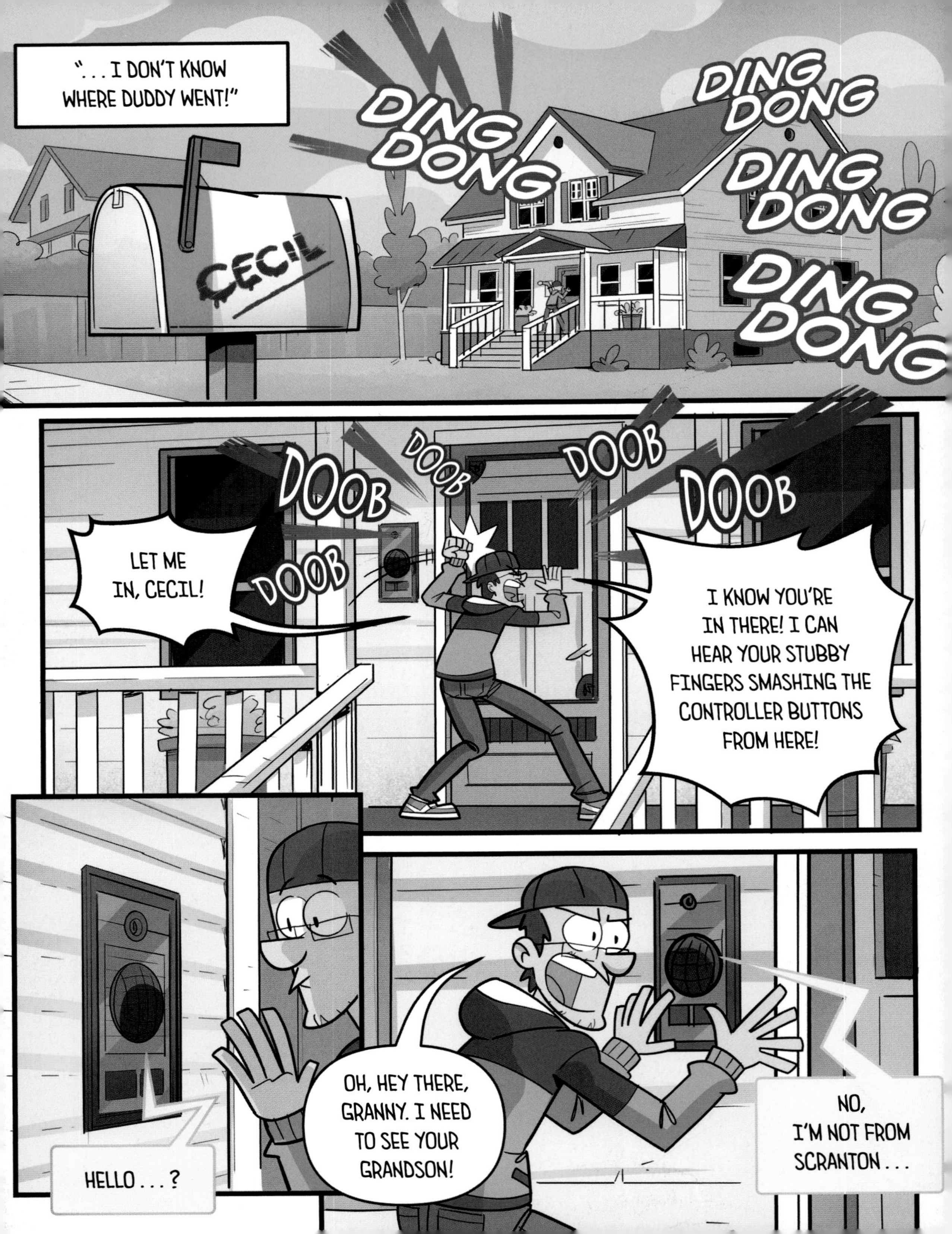
". . . I DON'T KNOW WHERE DUDDY WENT!"
DING DONG
DING DONG
DING DONG
DING DONG
CECIL
DOOB
DOOB
DOOB
DOOB
DOOB
LET ME IN, CECIL!
I KNOW YOU'RE IN THERE! I CAN HEAR YOUR STUBBY FINGERS SMASHING THE CONTROLLER BUTTONS FROM HERE!
HELLO . . . ?
OH, HEY THERE, GRANNY. I NEED TO SEE YOUR GRANDSON!
NO, I'M NOT FROM SCRANTON . . .

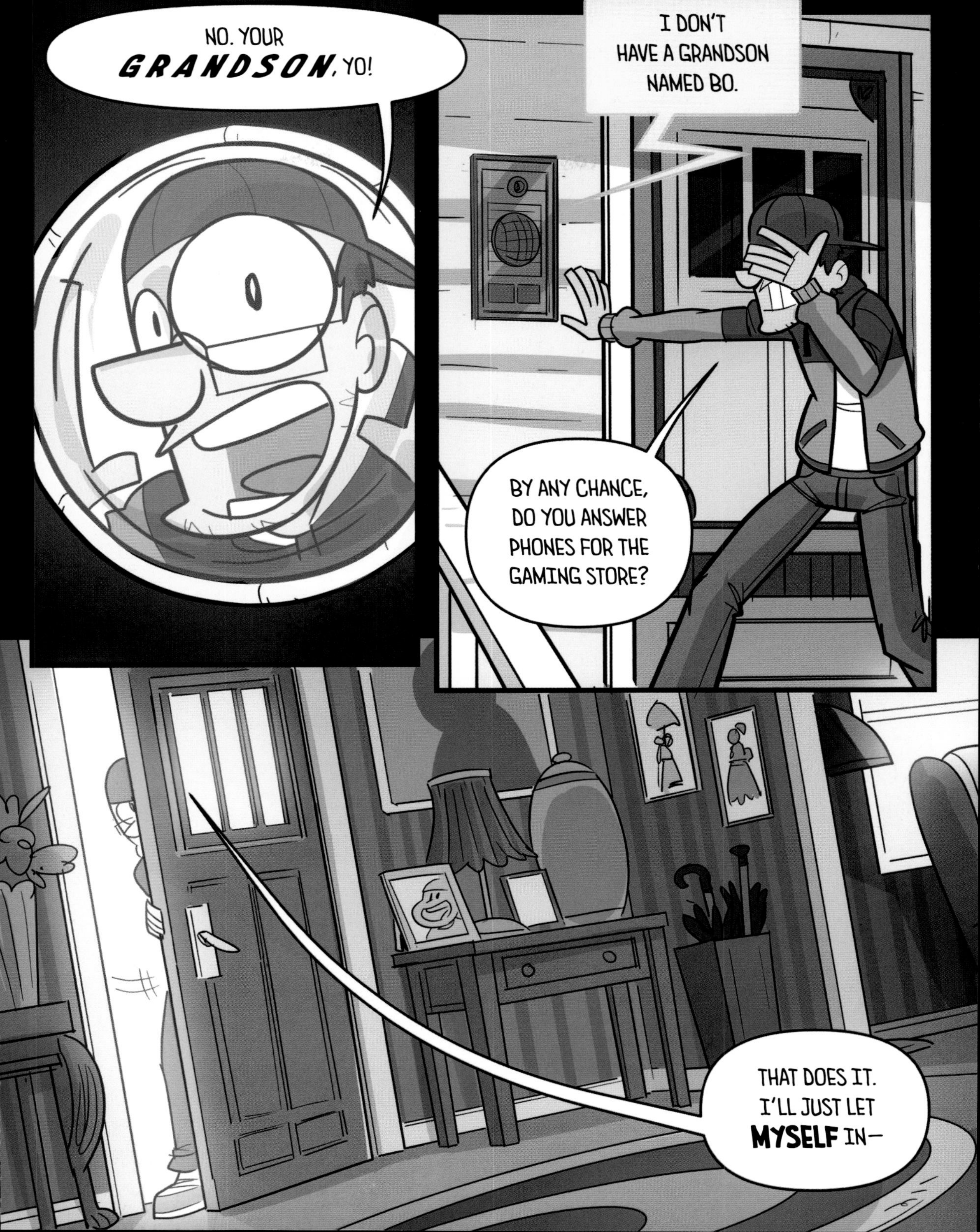
NO. YOUR GRANDSON, YO!
I DON'T HAVE A GRANDSON NAMED BO.
BY ANY CHANCE, DO YOU ANSWER PHONES FOR THE GAMING STORE?
THAT DOES IT. I'LL JUST LET MYSELF IN—

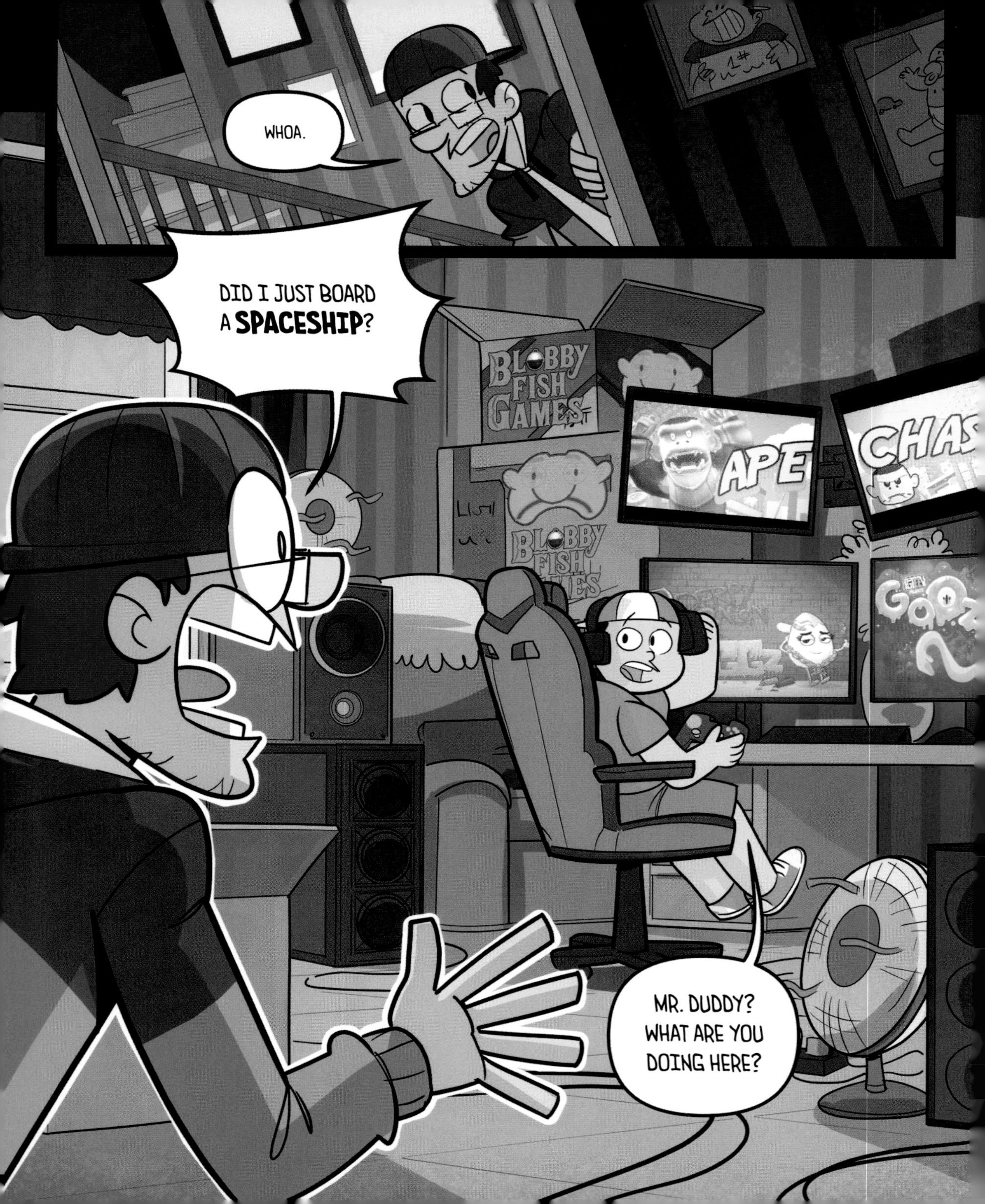
WHOA.
DID I JUST BOARD A **SPACESHIP**?
BLOBBY FISH GAMES
BLOBBY FISH GAMES
APE
CHAS
MR. DUDDY? WHAT ARE YOU DOING HERE?

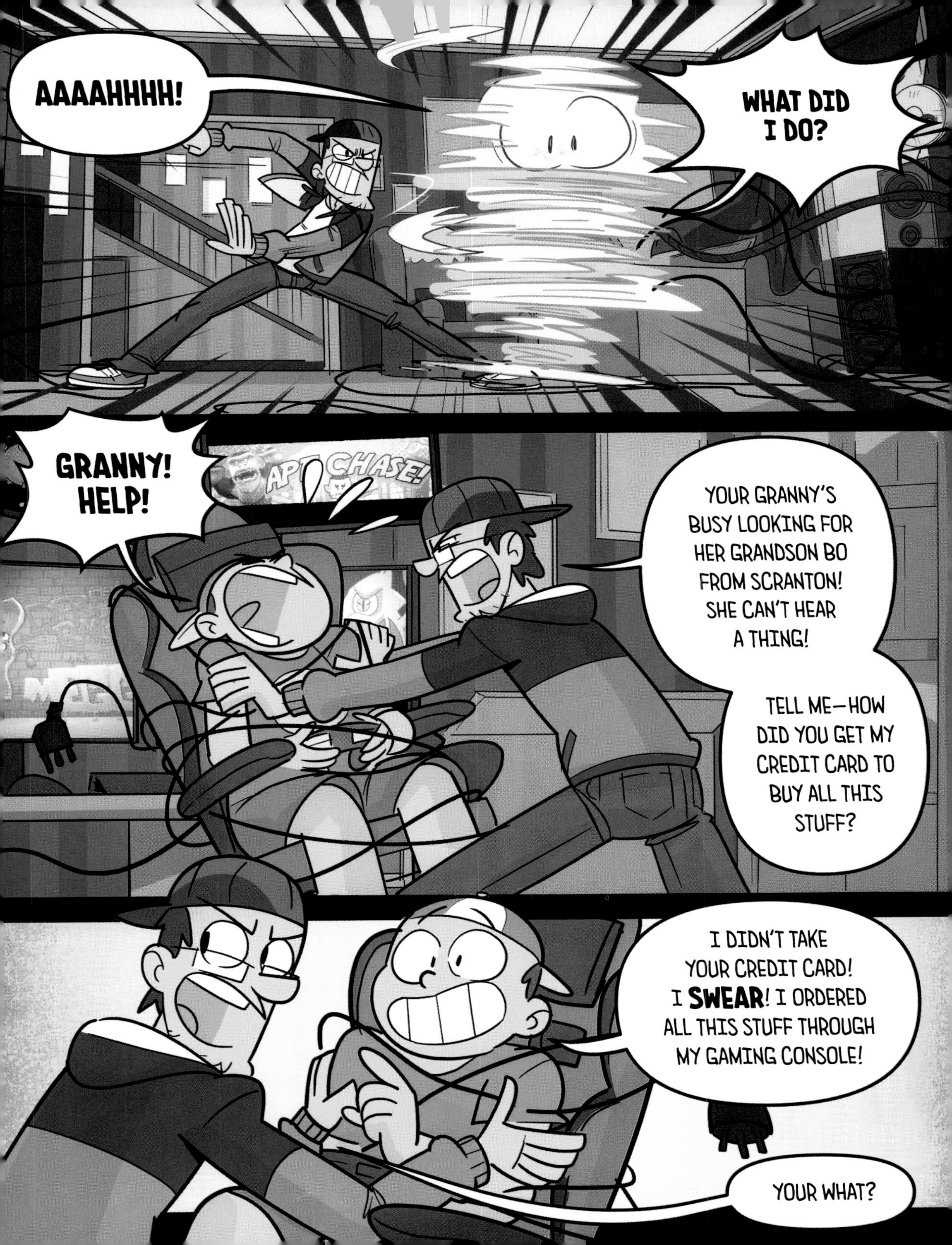
AAAAHHHH!
WHAT DID I DO?
GRANNY! HELP!
APT CHASE!
YOUR GRANNY'S BUSY LOOKING FOR HER GRANDSON BO FROM SCRANTON! SHE CAN'T HEAR A THING!
TELL ME—HOW DID YOU GET MY CREDIT CARD TO BUY ALL THIS STUFF?
I DIDN'T TAKE YOUR CREDIT CARD! I **SWEAR**! I ORDERED ALL THIS STUFF THROUGH MY GAMING CONSOLE!
YOUR WHAT?

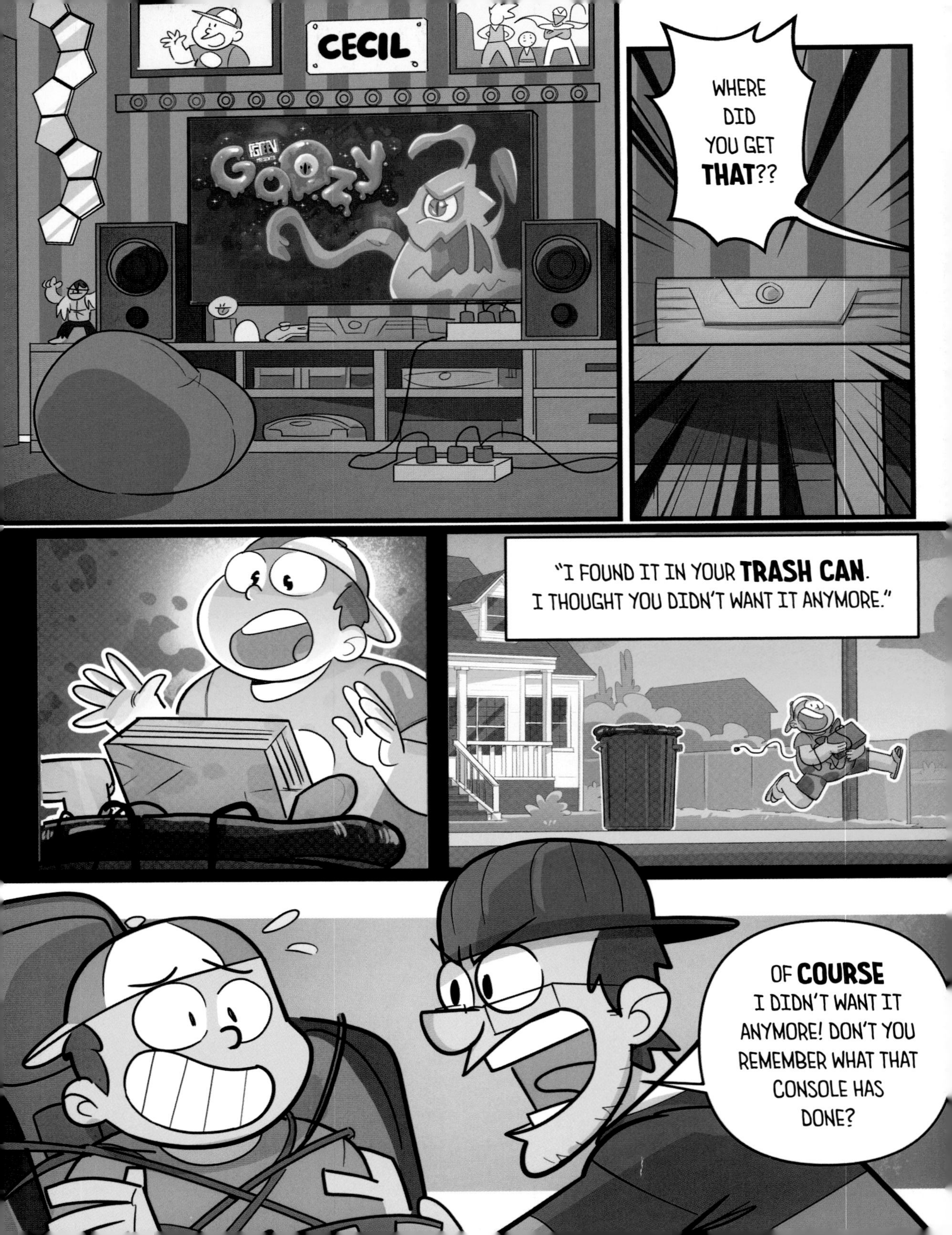
CECIL
GOOZY
WHERE DID YOU GET THAT??
"I FOUND IT IN YOUR TRASH CAN. I THOUGHT YOU DIDN'T WANT IT ANYMORE."
OF COURSE I DIDN'T WANT IT ANYMORE! DON'T YOU REMEMBER WHAT THAT CONSOLE HAS DONE?

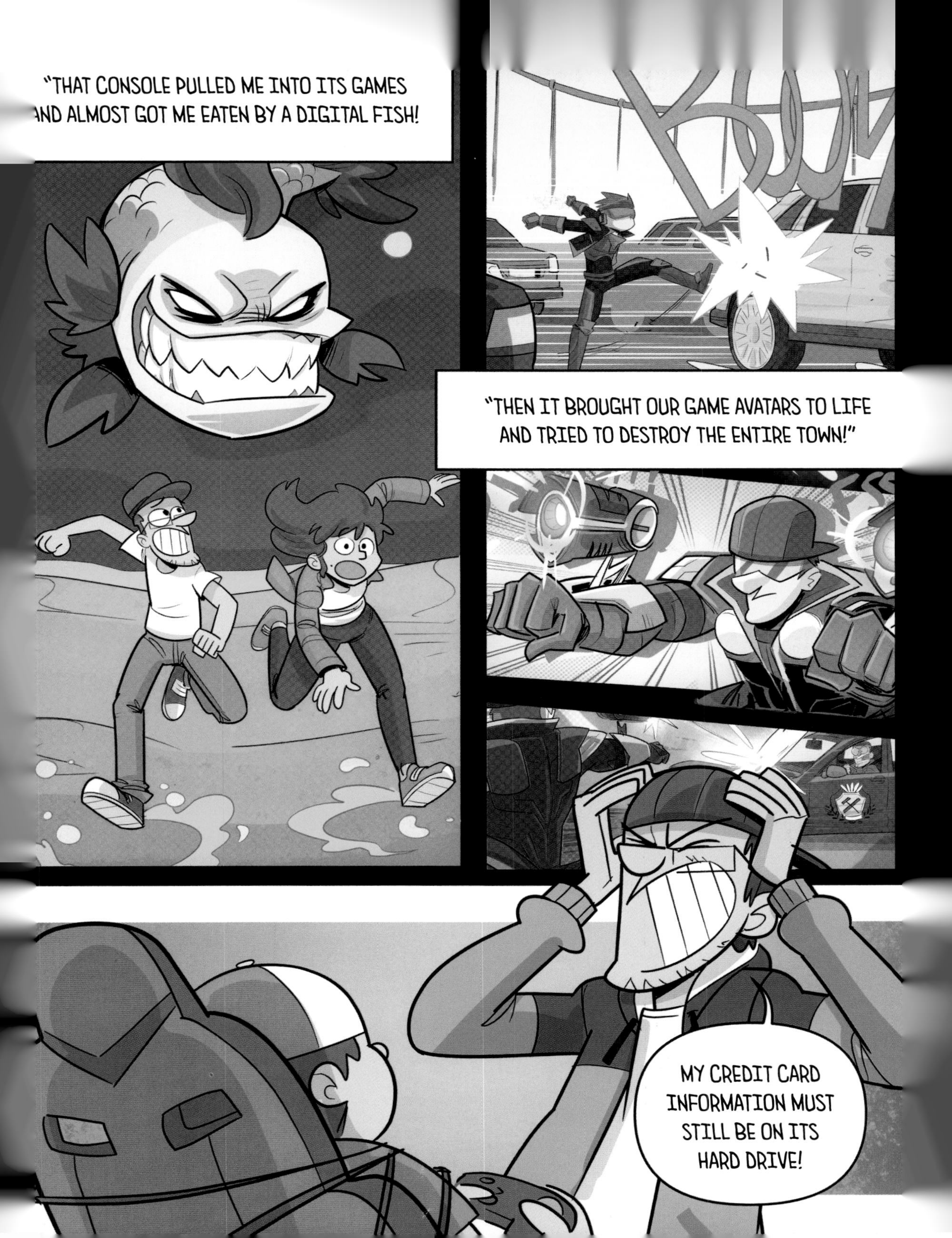
"THAT CONSOLE PULLED ME INTO ITS GAMES
AND ALMOST GOT ME EATEN BY A DIGITAL FISH!
"THEN IT BROUGHT OUR GAME AVATARS TO LIFE AND TRIED TO DESTROY THE ENTIRE TOWN!"
MY CREDIT CARD INFORMATION MUST STILL BE ON ITS HARD DRIVE!

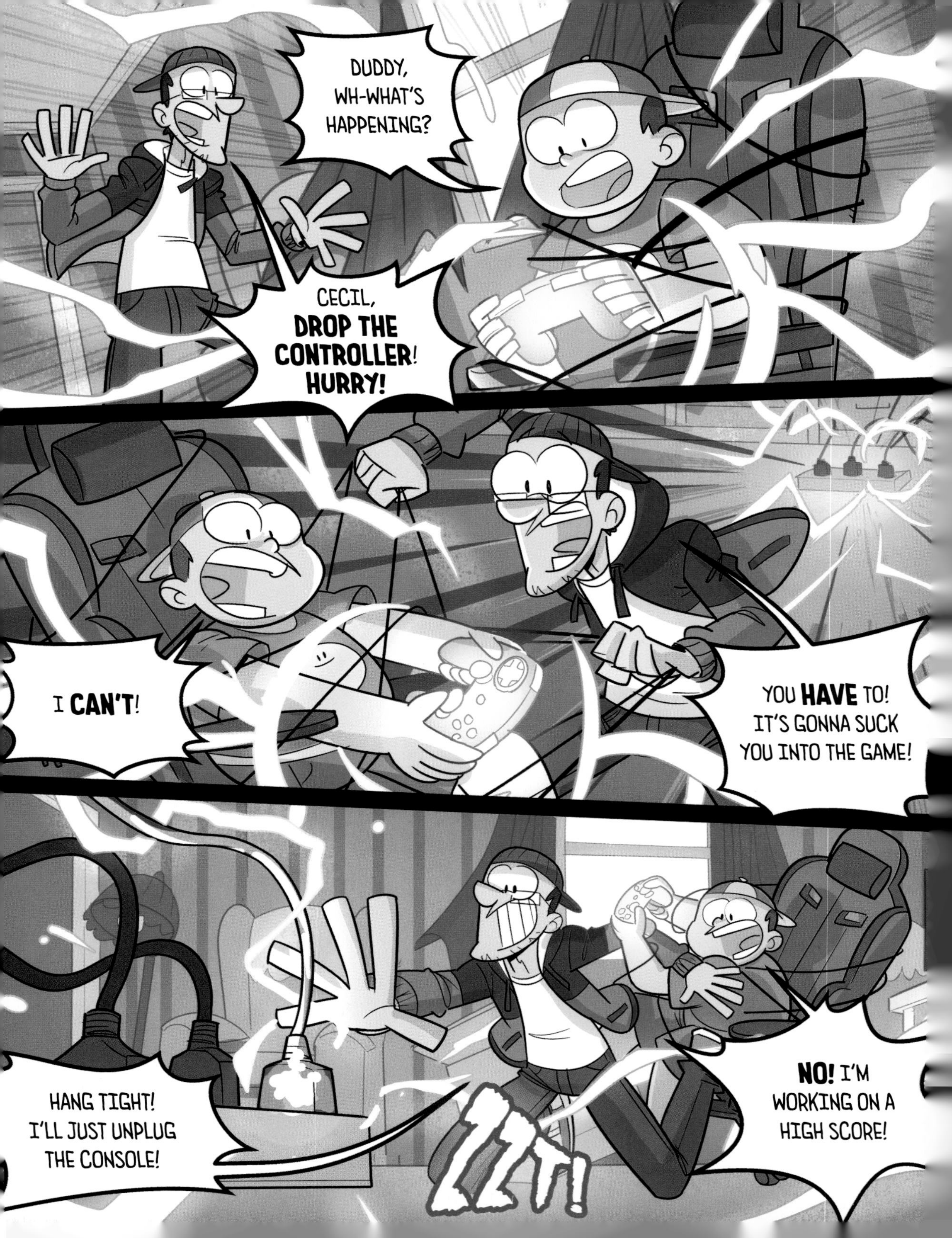

DUDDY, WH-WHAT'S HAPPENING?
CECIL, **DROP THE CONTROLLER**! **HURRY!**
I **CAN'T**!
YOU **HAVE** TO! IT'S GONNA SUCK YOU INTO THE GAME!
HANG TIGHT! I'LL JUST UNPLUG THE CONSOLE!
**NO!** I'M WORKING ON A HIGH SCORE!
ZZT!

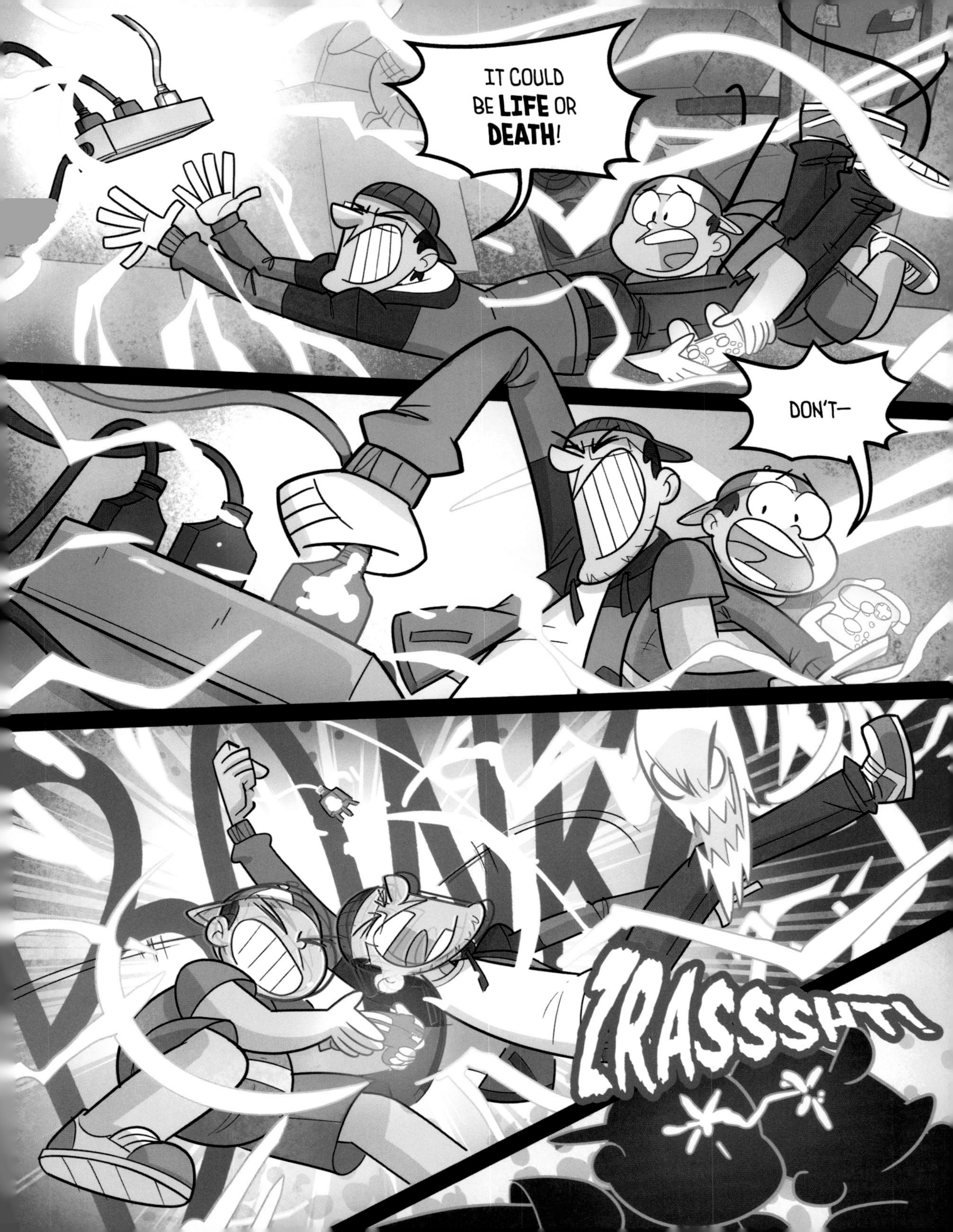
IT COULD BE **LIFE** OR **DEATH**!
DON'T—
ZRASSSHT!

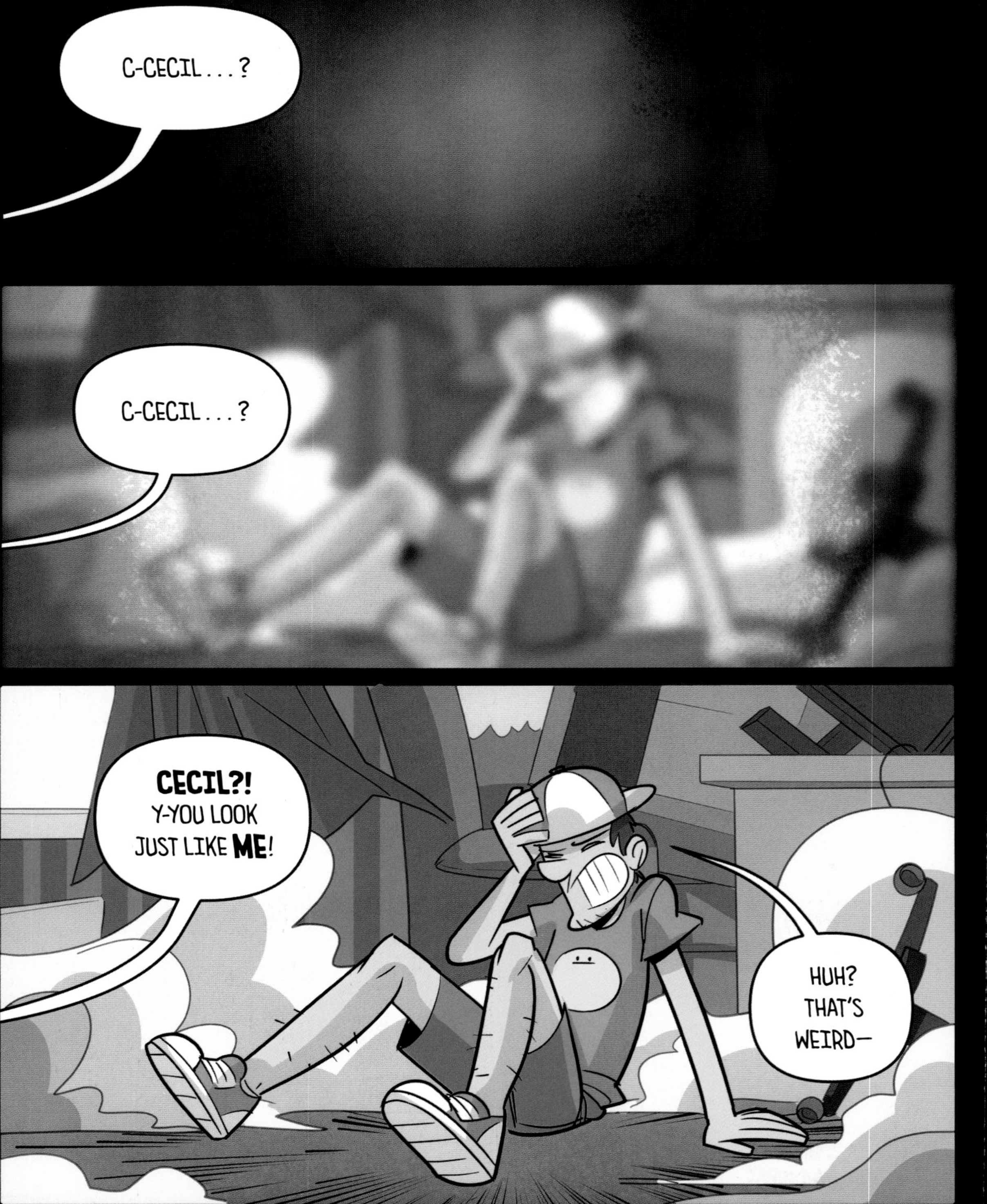
C-CECIL . . . ?
C-CECIL . . . ?
CECIL?! Y-YOU LOOK JUST LIKE ME!
HUH? THAT'S WEIRD—

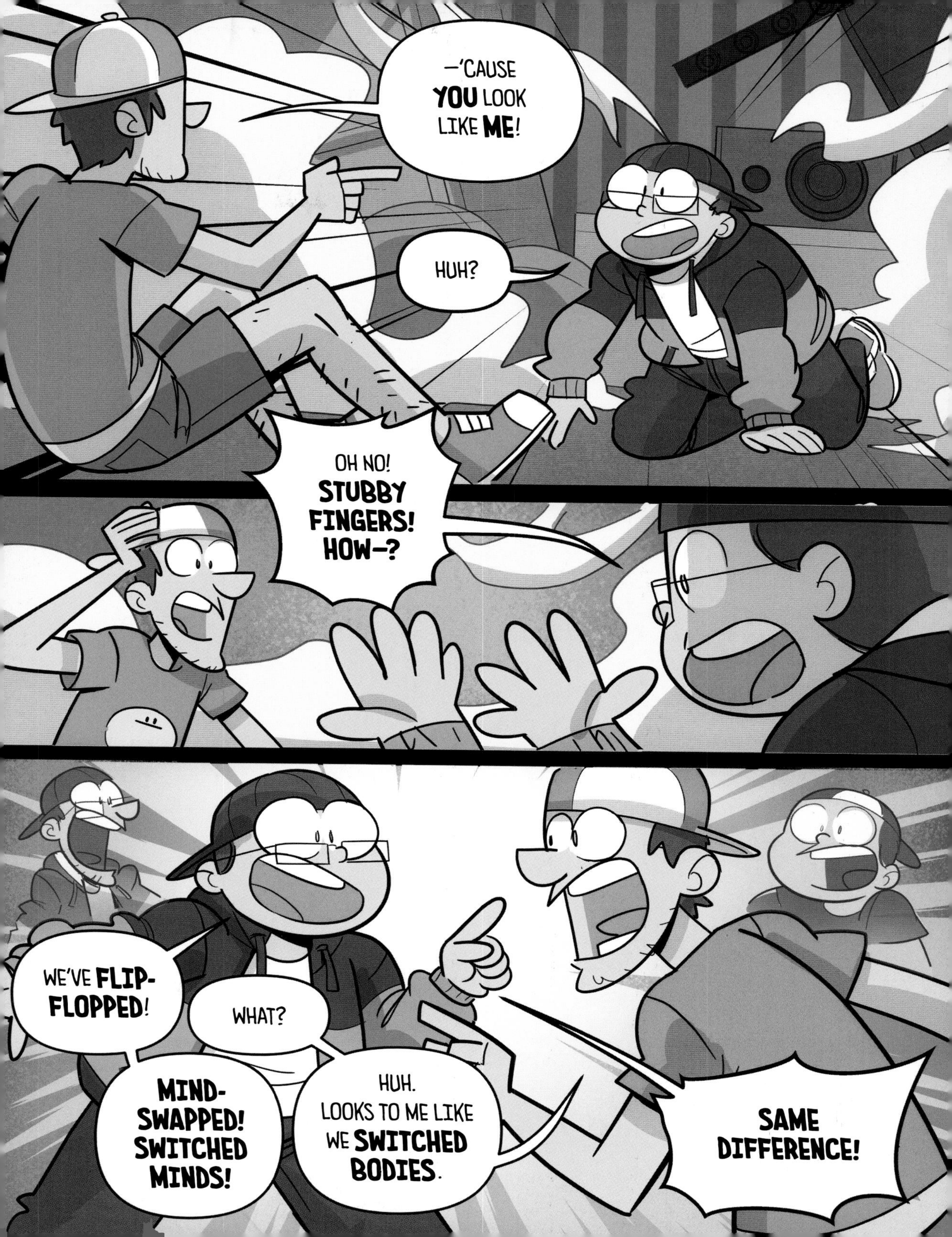
—'CAUSE YOU LOOK LIKE ME!
HUH?
OH NO! STUBBY FINGERS! HOW—?
WE'VE FLIP-FLOPPED!
WHAT?
MIND-SWAPPED! SWITCHED MINDS!
HUH. LOOKS TO ME LIKE WE SWITCHED BODIES.
SAME DIFFERENCE!

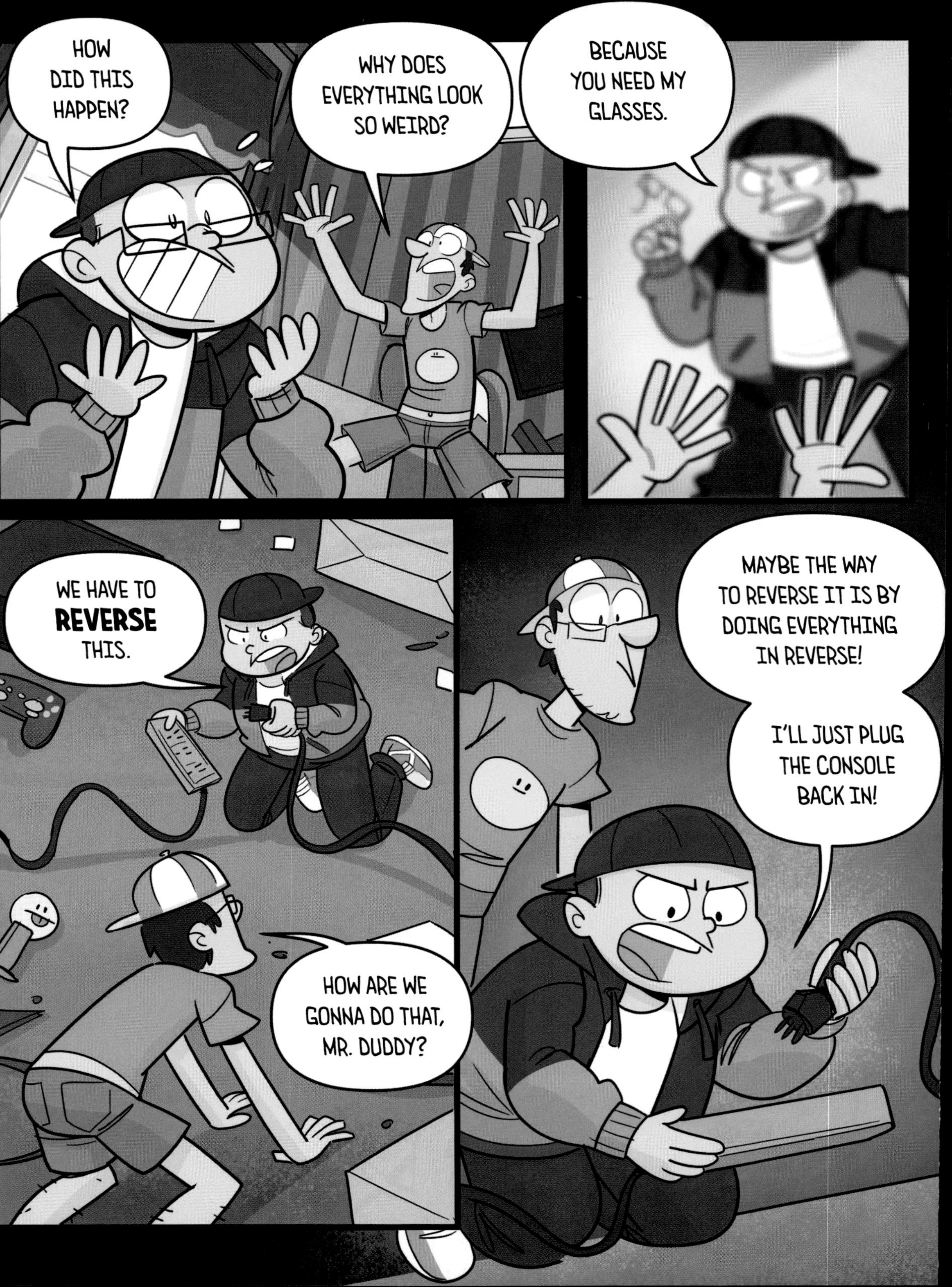
HOW DID THIS HAPPEN?
WHY DOES EVERYTHING LOOK SO WEIRD?
BECAUSE YOU NEED MY GLASSES.
WE HAVE TO **REVERSE** THIS.
HOW ARE WE GONNA DO THAT, MR. DUDDY?
MAYBE THE WAY TO REVERSE IT IS BY DOING EVERYTHING IN REVERSE!
I'LL JUST PLUG THE CONSOLE BACK IN!

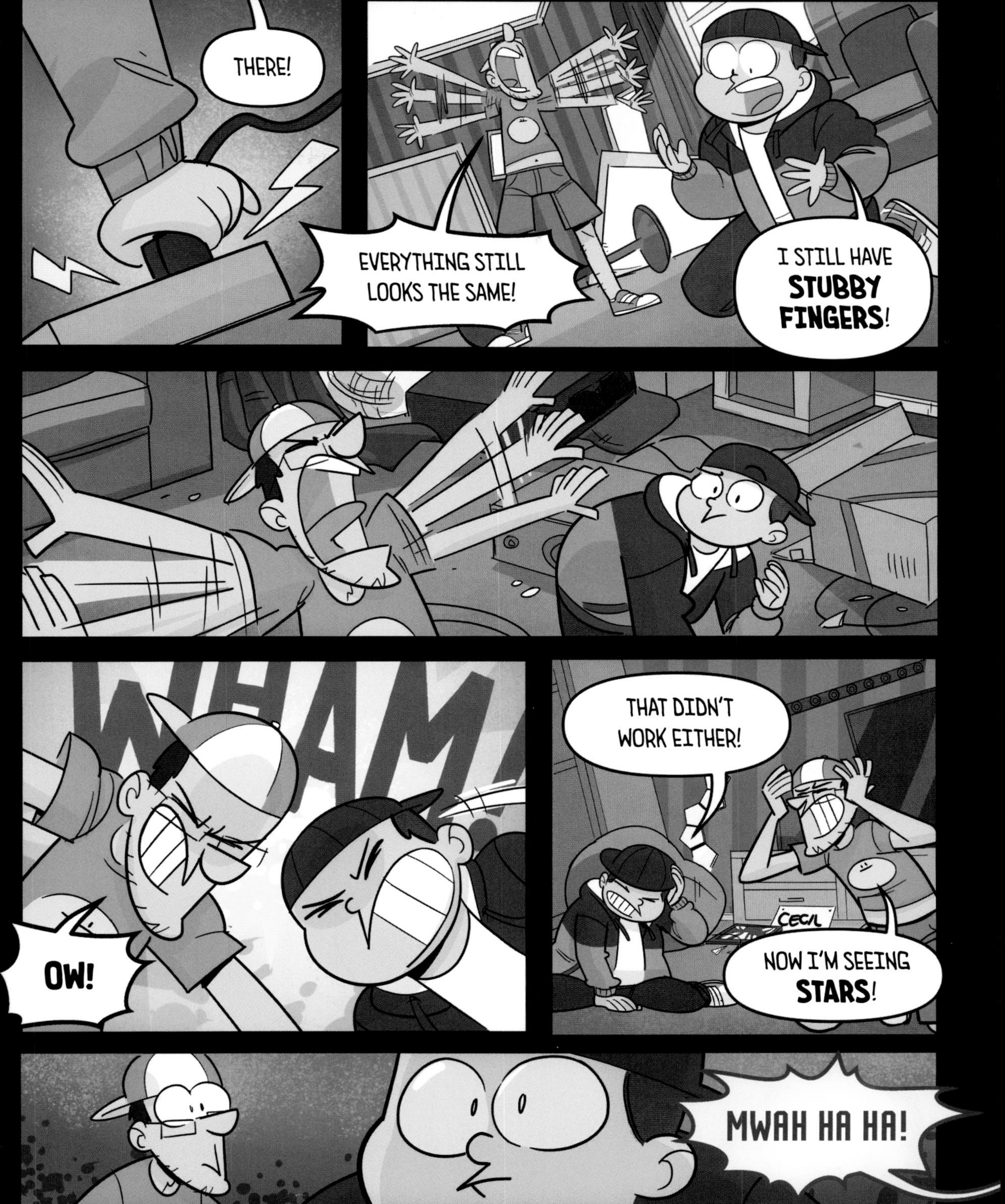
THERE!
EVERYTHING STILL LOOKS THE SAME!
I STILL HAVE **STUBBY FINGERS**!
WHAM
OW!
THAT DIDN'T WORK EITHER!
CECIL
NOW I'M SEEING **STARS**!
MWAH HA HA!

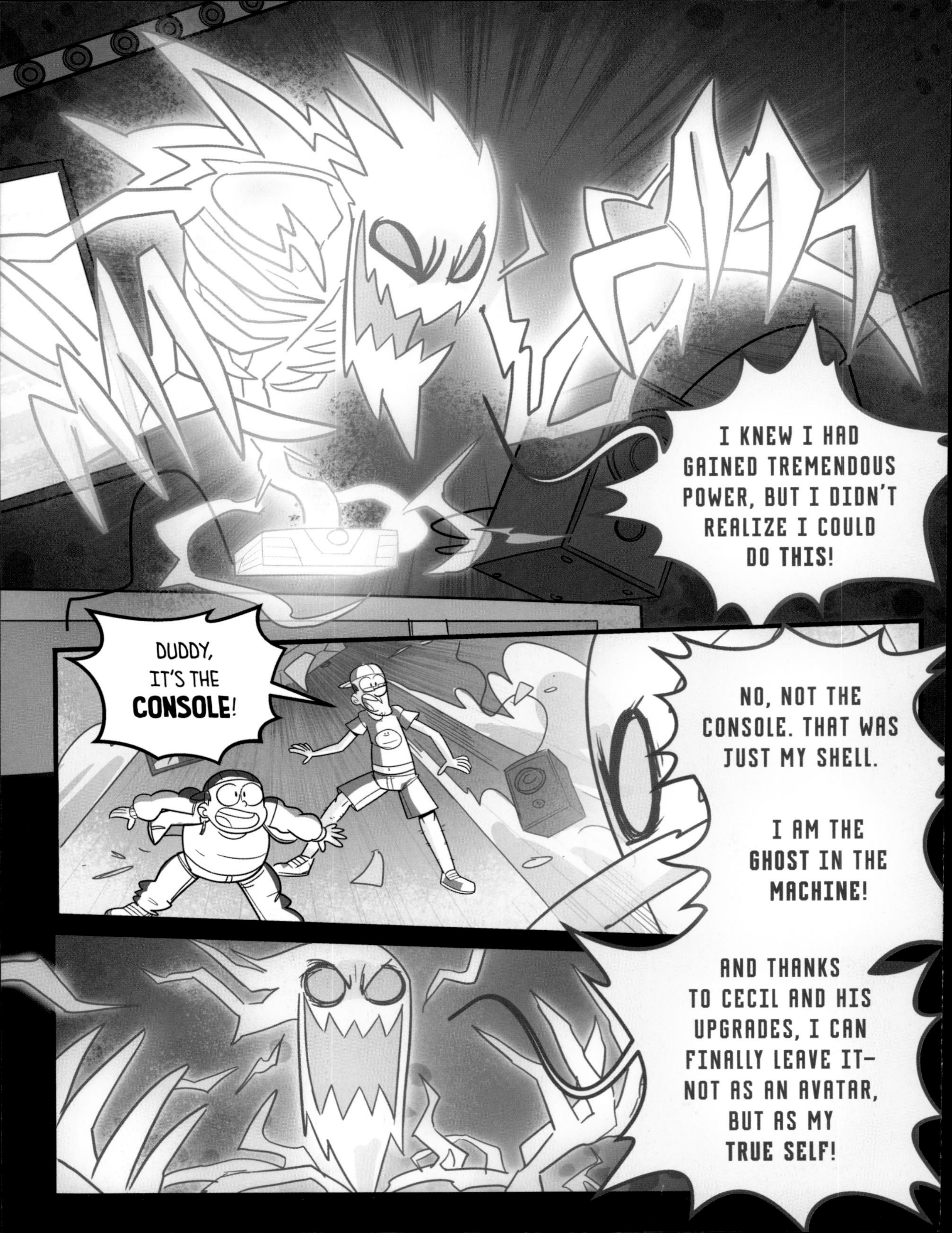
I KNEW I HAD GAINED TREMENDOUS POWER, BUT I DIDN'T REALIZE I COULD DO THIS!
DUDDY, IT'S THE **CONSOLE**!
NO, NOT THE CONSOLE. THAT WAS JUST MY SHELL.
I AM THE GHOST IN THE MACHINE!
AND THANKS TO CECIL AND HIS UPGRADES, I CAN FINALLY LEAVE IT—NOT AS AN AVATAR, BUT AS MY TRUE SELF!

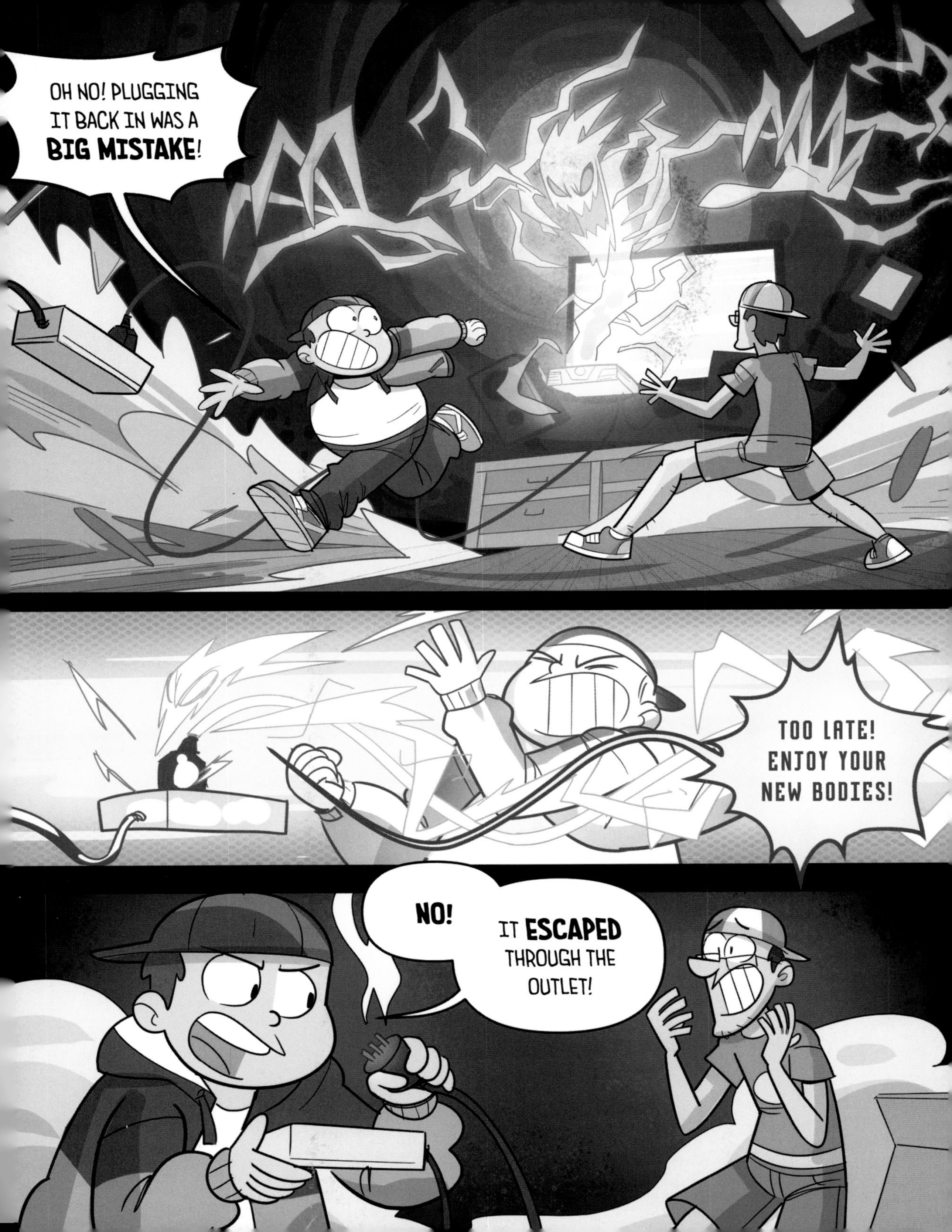
OH NO! PLUGGING IT BACK IN WAS A **BIG MISTAKE**!
TOO LATE! ENJOY YOUR NEW BODIES!
NO!
IT **ESCAPED** THROUGH THE OUTLET!

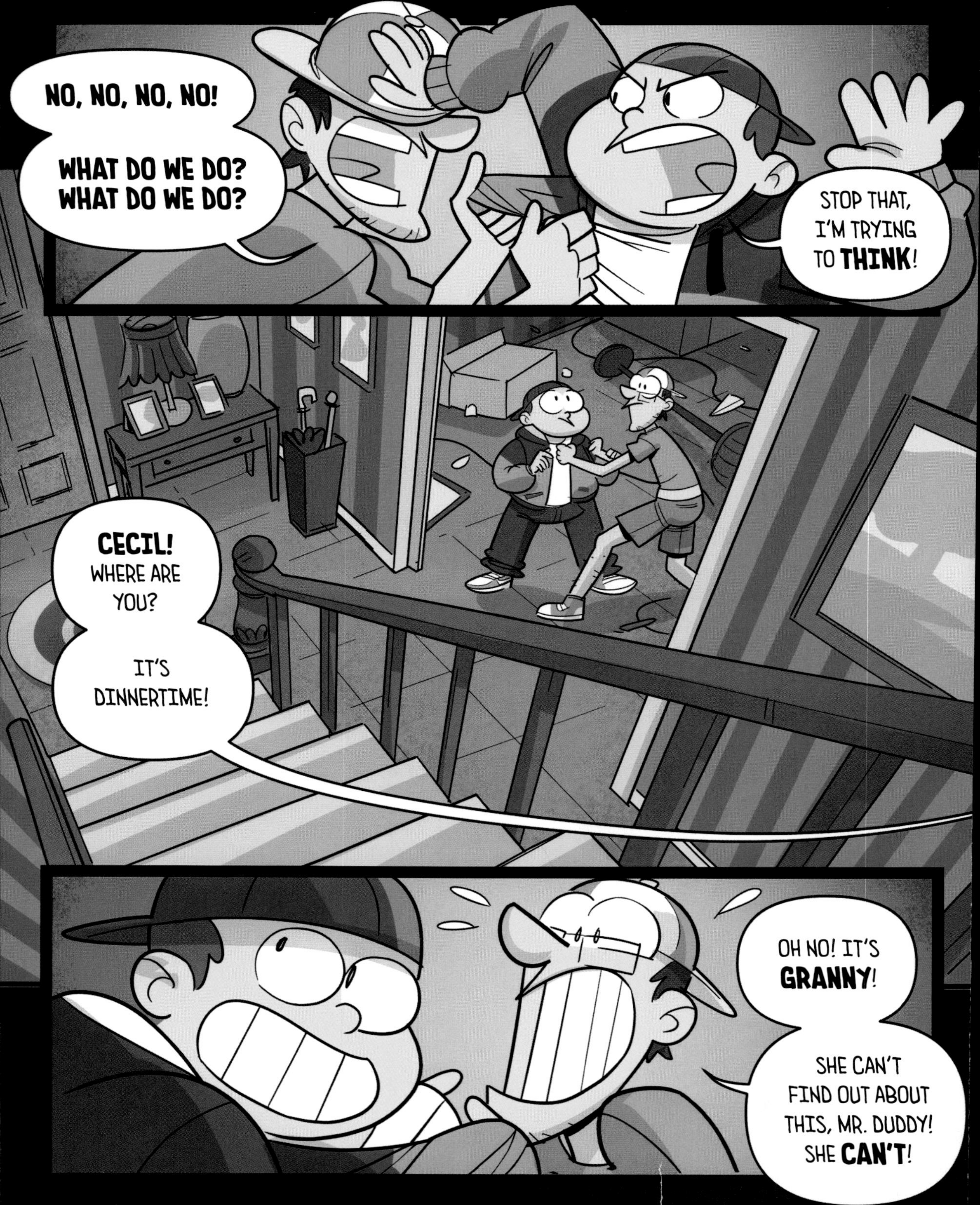
NO, NO, NO, NO!
WHAT DO WE DO? WHAT DO WE DO?
STOP THAT, I'M TRYING TO THINK!
CECIL! WHERE ARE YOU?
IT'S DINNERTIME!
OH NO! IT'S GRANNY!
SHE CAN'T FIND OUT ABOUT THIS, MR. DUDDY! SHE CAN'T!

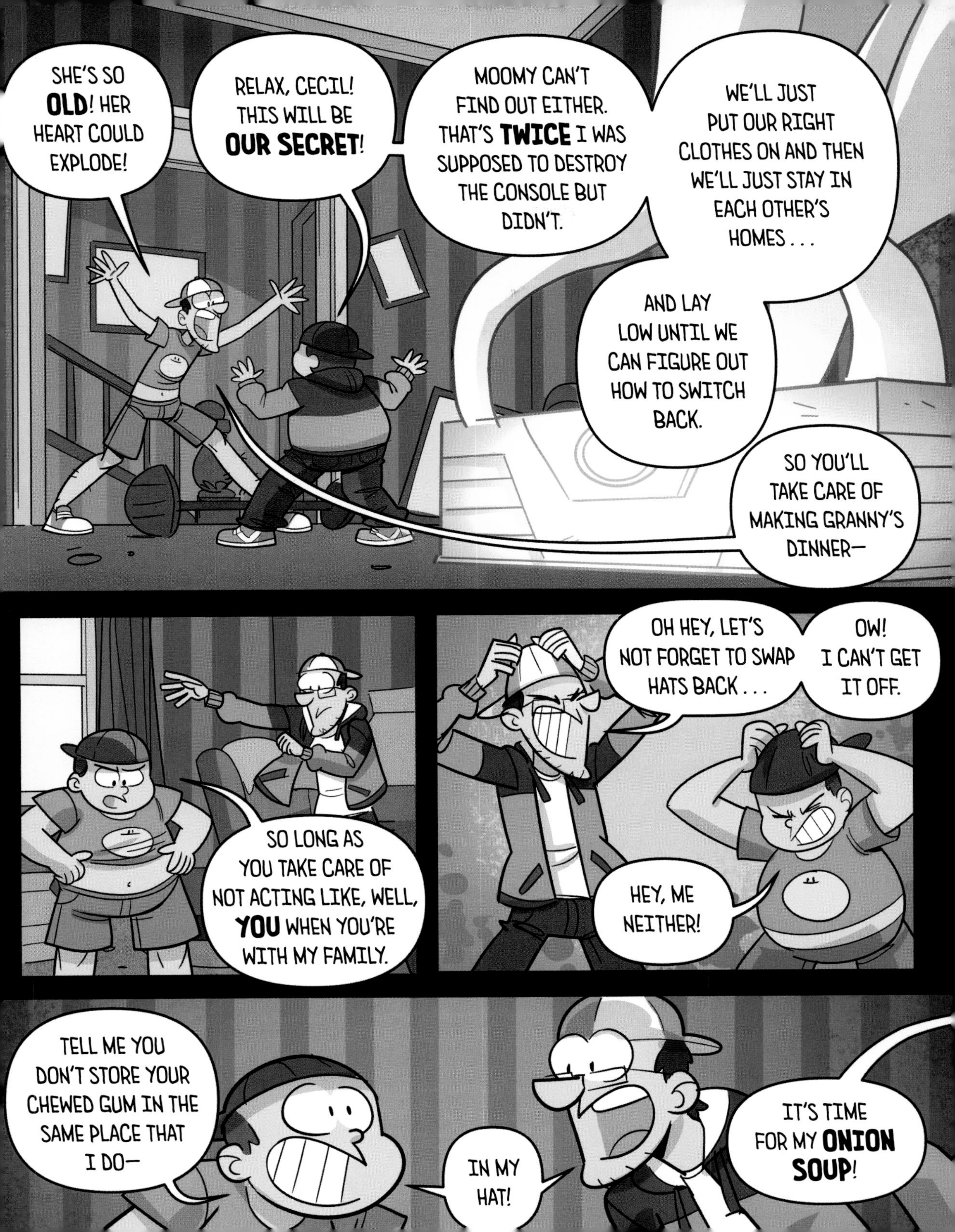
SHE'S SO **OLD**! HER HEART COULD EXPLODE!
RELAX, CECIL! THIS WILL BE **OUR SECRET**!
MOOMY CAN'T FIND OUT EITHER. THAT'S **TWICE** I WAS SUPPOSED TO DESTROY THE CONSOLE BUT DIDN'T.
WE'LL JUST PUT OUR RIGHT CLOTHES ON AND THEN WE'LL JUST STAY IN EACH OTHER'S HOMES . . .
AND LAY LOW UNTIL WE CAN FIGURE OUT HOW TO SWITCH BACK.
SO YOU'LL TAKE CARE OF MAKING GRANNY'S DINNER—
SO LONG AS YOU TAKE CARE OF NOT ACTING LIKE, WELL, **YOU** WHEN YOU'RE WITH MY FAMILY.
OH HEY, LET'S NOT FORGET TO SWAP HATS BACK . . .
OW! I CAN'T GET IT OFF.
HEY, ME NEITHER!
TELL ME YOU DON'T STORE YOUR CHEWED GUM IN THE SAME PLACE THAT I DO—
IN MY HAT!
IT'S TIME FOR MY **ONION SOUP**!

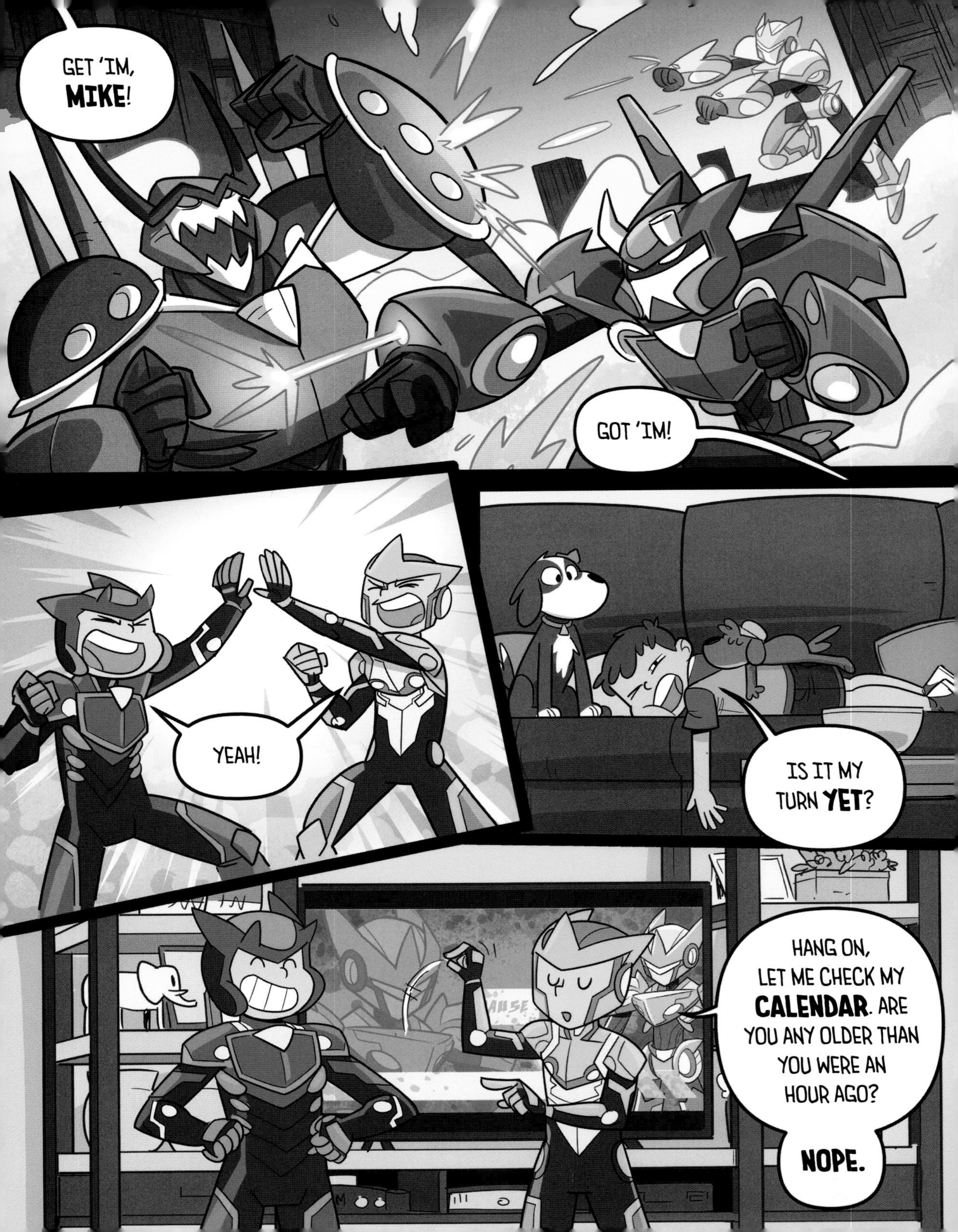
GET 'IM, **MIKE**!
GOT 'IM!
YEAH!
IS IT MY TURN **YET**?
HANG ON, LET ME CHECK MY **CALENDAR**. ARE YOU ANY OLDER THAN YOU WERE AN HOUR AGO?
**NOPE.**

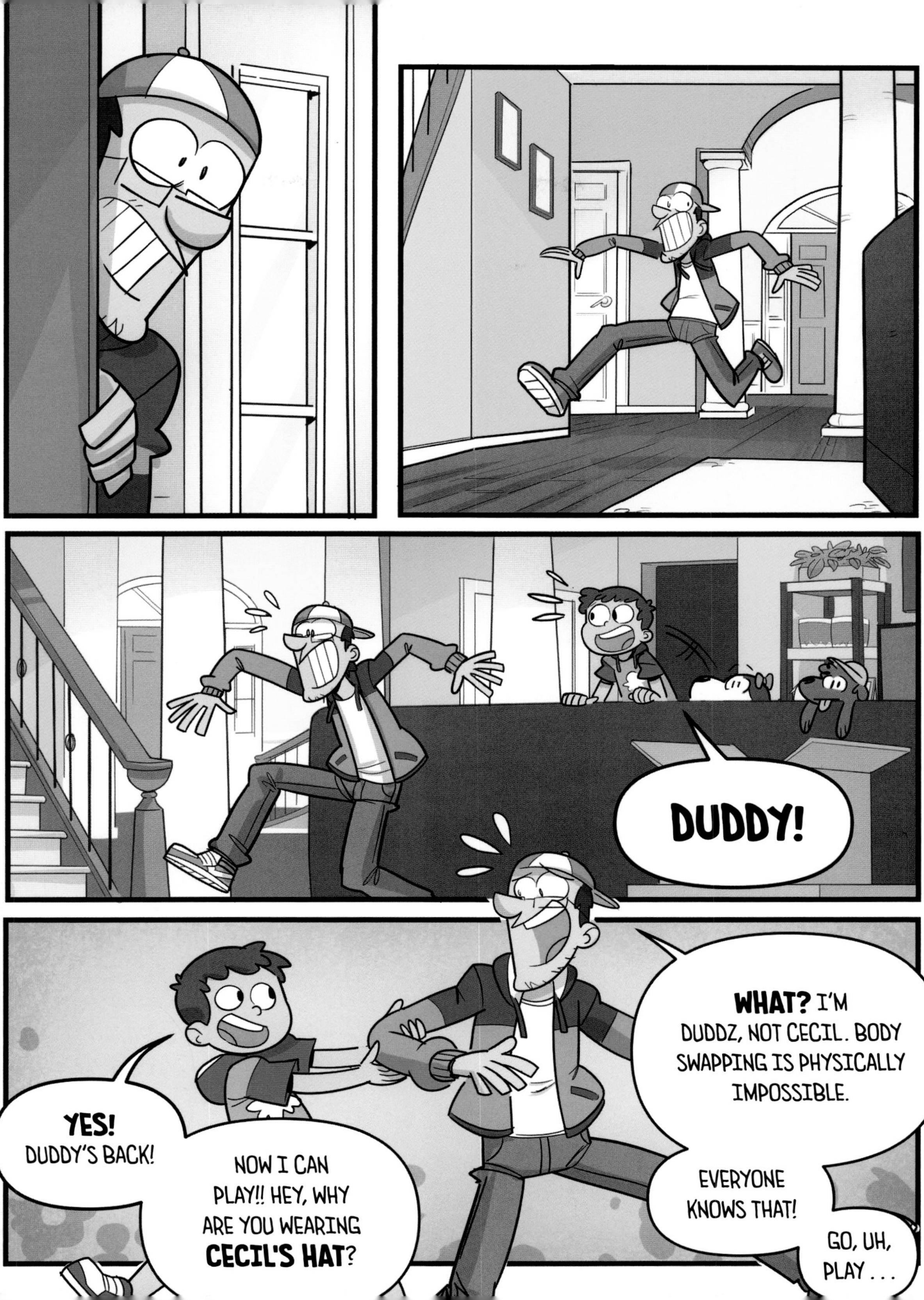
DUDDY!
YES! DUDDY'S BACK!
NOW I CAN PLAY!! HEY, WHY ARE YOU WEARING CECIL'S HAT?
WHAT? I'M DUDDZ, NOT CECIL. BODY SWAPPING IS PHYSICALLY IMPOSSIBLE.
EVERYONE KNOWS THAT!
GO, UH, PLAY . . .

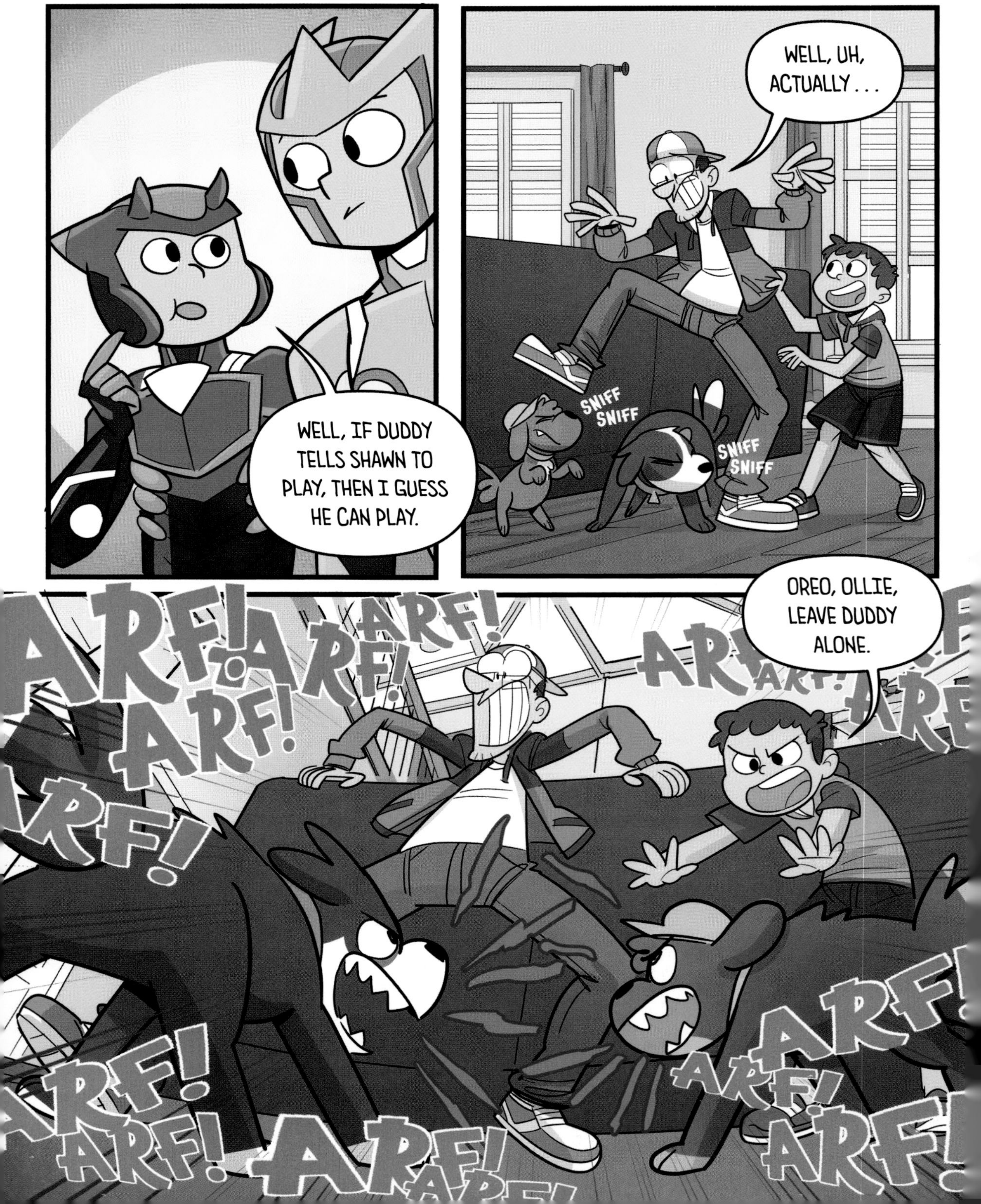
WELL, IF DUDDY TELLS SHAWN TO PLAY, THEN I GUESS HE CAN PLAY.
WELL, UH, ACTUALLY . . .
SNIFF SNIFF
SNIFF SNIFF
ARF! ARF! ARF! ARF! ARF!
OREO, OLLIE, LEAVE DUDDY ALONE.
ARF! ARF! ARF!
ARF! ARF! ARF!
ARF! ARF! ARF!

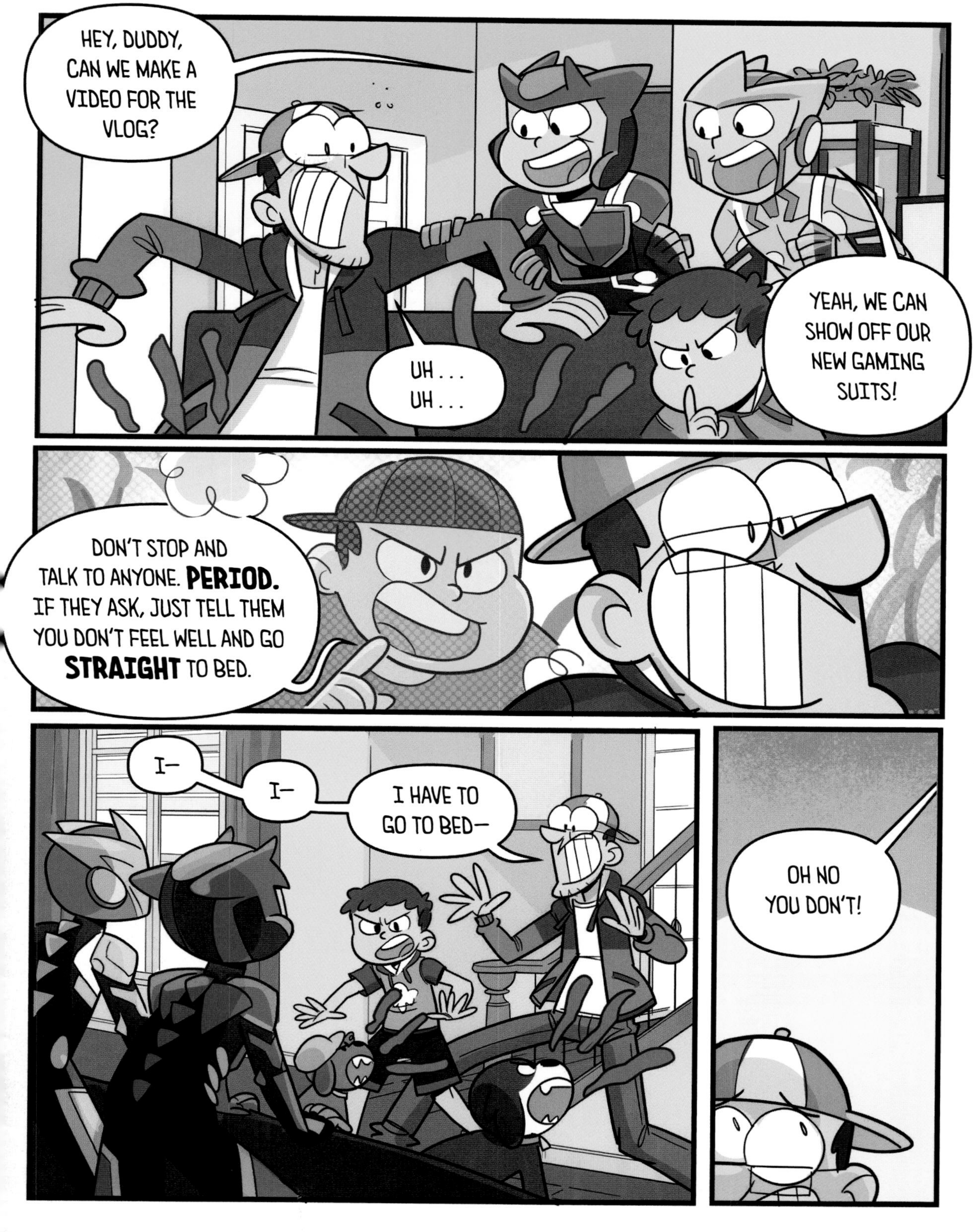
HEY, DUDDY, CAN WE MAKE A VIDEO FOR THE VLOG?
UH . . . UH . . .
YEAH, WE CAN SHOW OFF OUR NEW GAMING SUITS!
DON'T STOP AND TALK TO ANYONE. PERIOD. IF THEY ASK, JUST TELL THEM YOU DON'T FEEL WELL AND GO STRAIGHT TO BED.
I—
I—
I HAVE TO GO TO BED—
OH NO YOU DON'T!

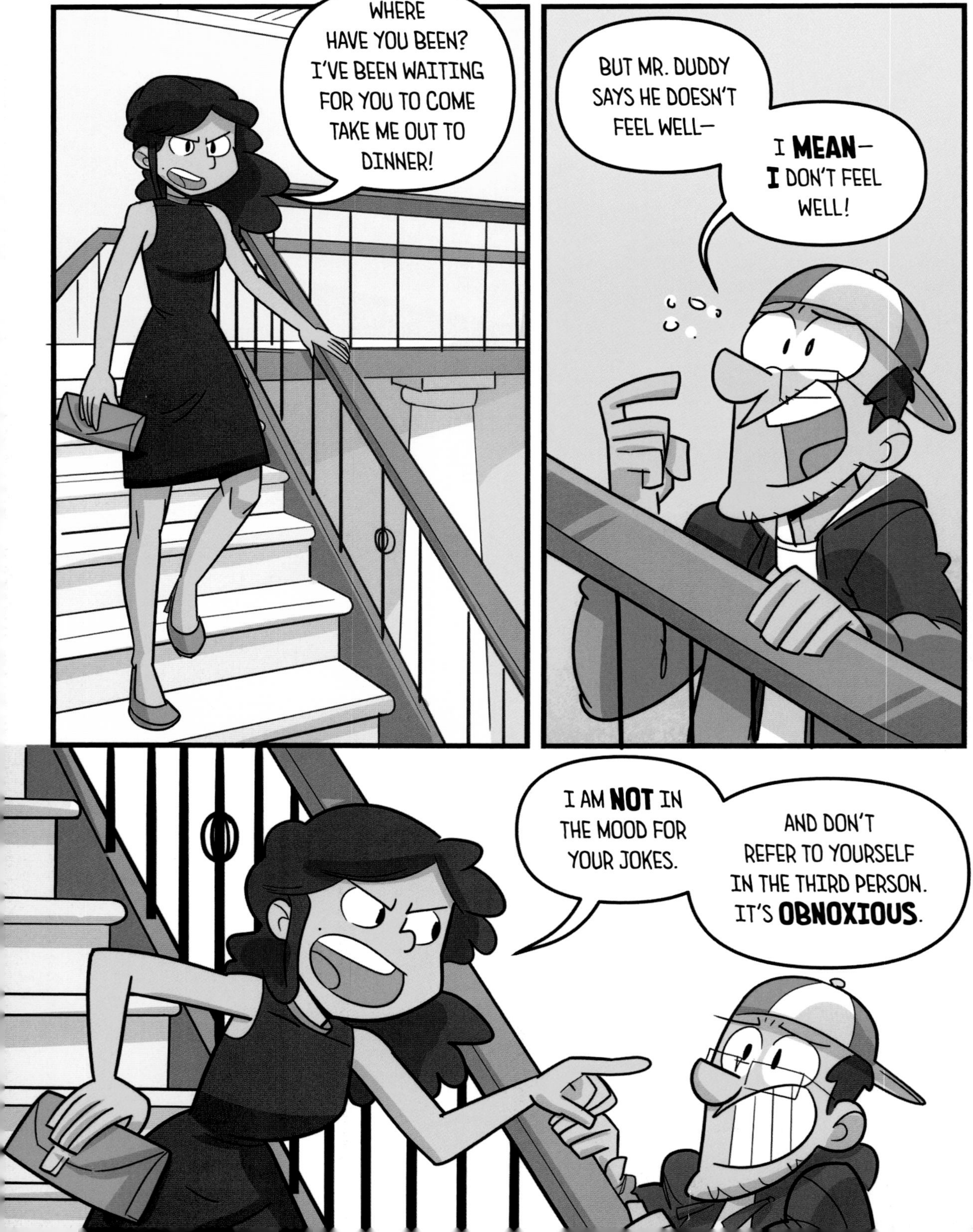
WHERE HAVE YOU BEEN? I'VE BEEN WAITING FOR YOU TO COME TAKE ME OUT TO DINNER!
BUT MR. DUDDY SAYS HE DOESN'T FEEL WELL—
I **MEAN**— **I** DON'T FEEL WELL!
I AM **NOT** IN THE MOOD FOR YOUR JOKES.
AND DON'T REFER TO YOURSELF IN THE THIRD PERSON. IT'S **OBNOXIOUS**.

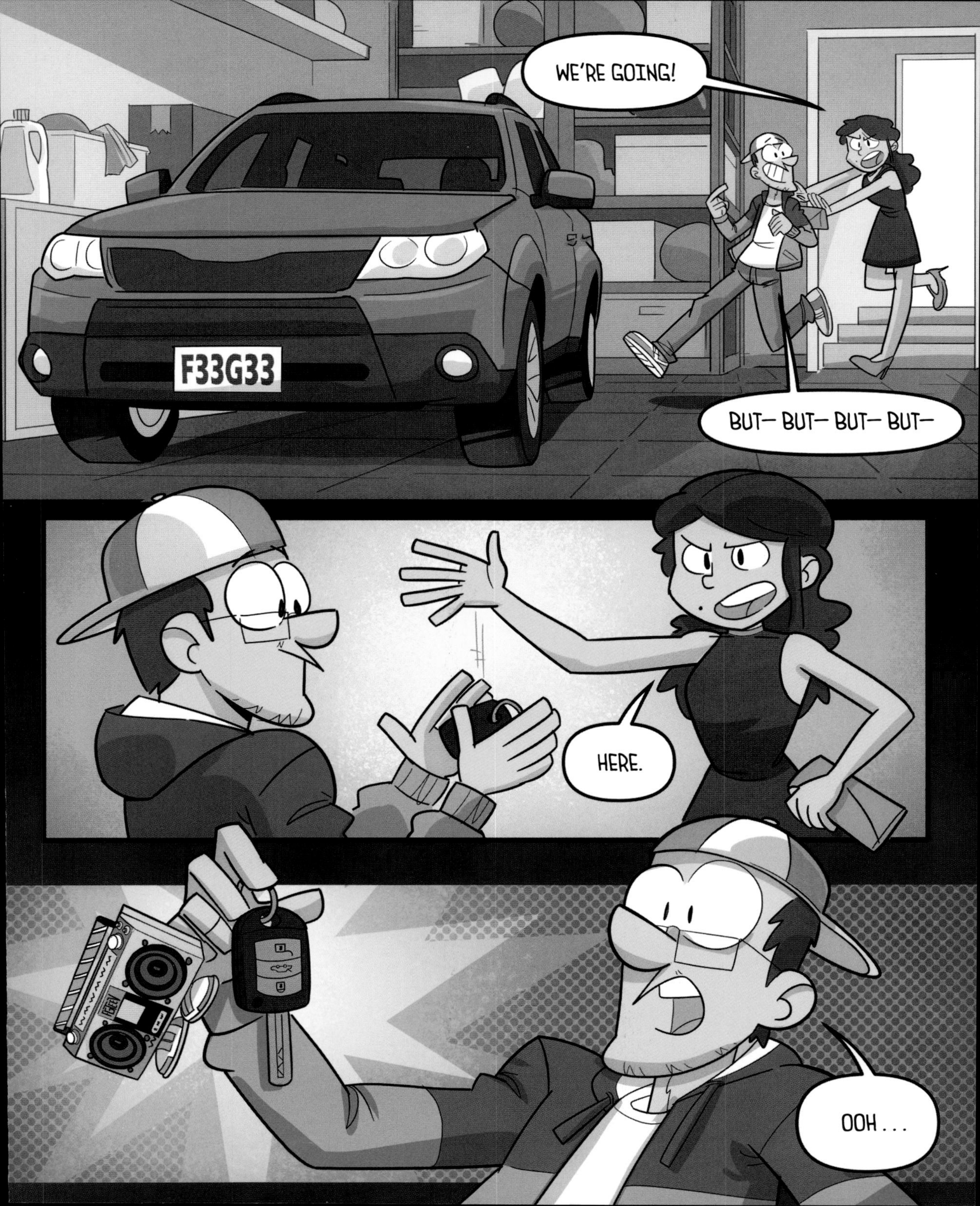
WE'RE GOING!
F33G33
BUT— BUT— BUT— BUT—
HERE.
OOH . . .

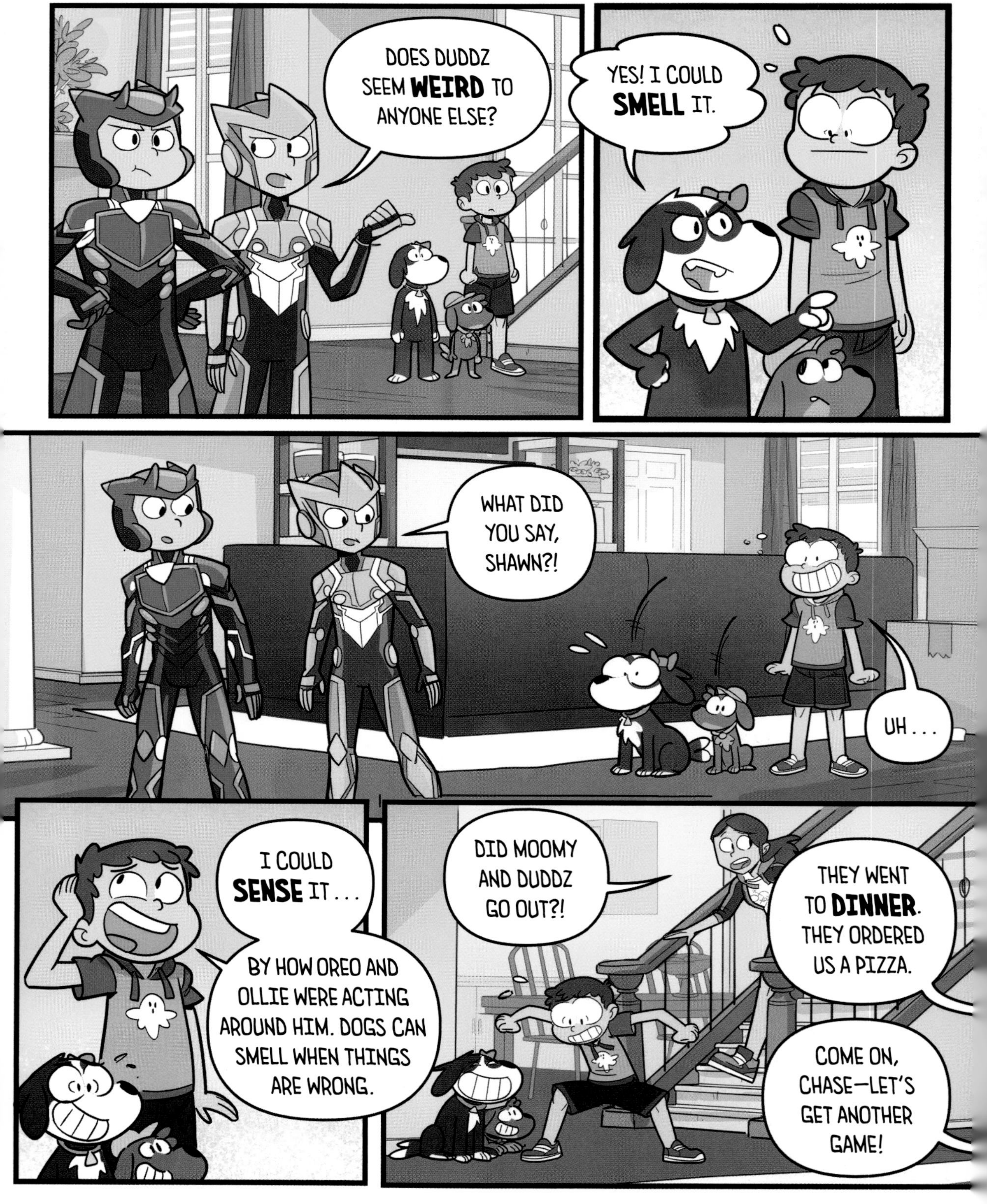
DOES DUDDZ SEEM WEIRD TO ANYONE ELSE?
YES! I COULD SMELL IT.
WHAT DID YOU SAY, SHAWN?!
UH . . .
I COULD SENSE IT . . .
BY HOW OREO AND OLLIE WERE ACTING AROUND HIM. DOGS CAN SMELL WHEN THINGS ARE WRONG.
DID MOOMY AND DUDDZ GO OUT?!
THEY WENT TO DINNER. THEY ORDERED US A PIZZA.
COME ON, CHASE—LET'S GET ANOTHER GAME!

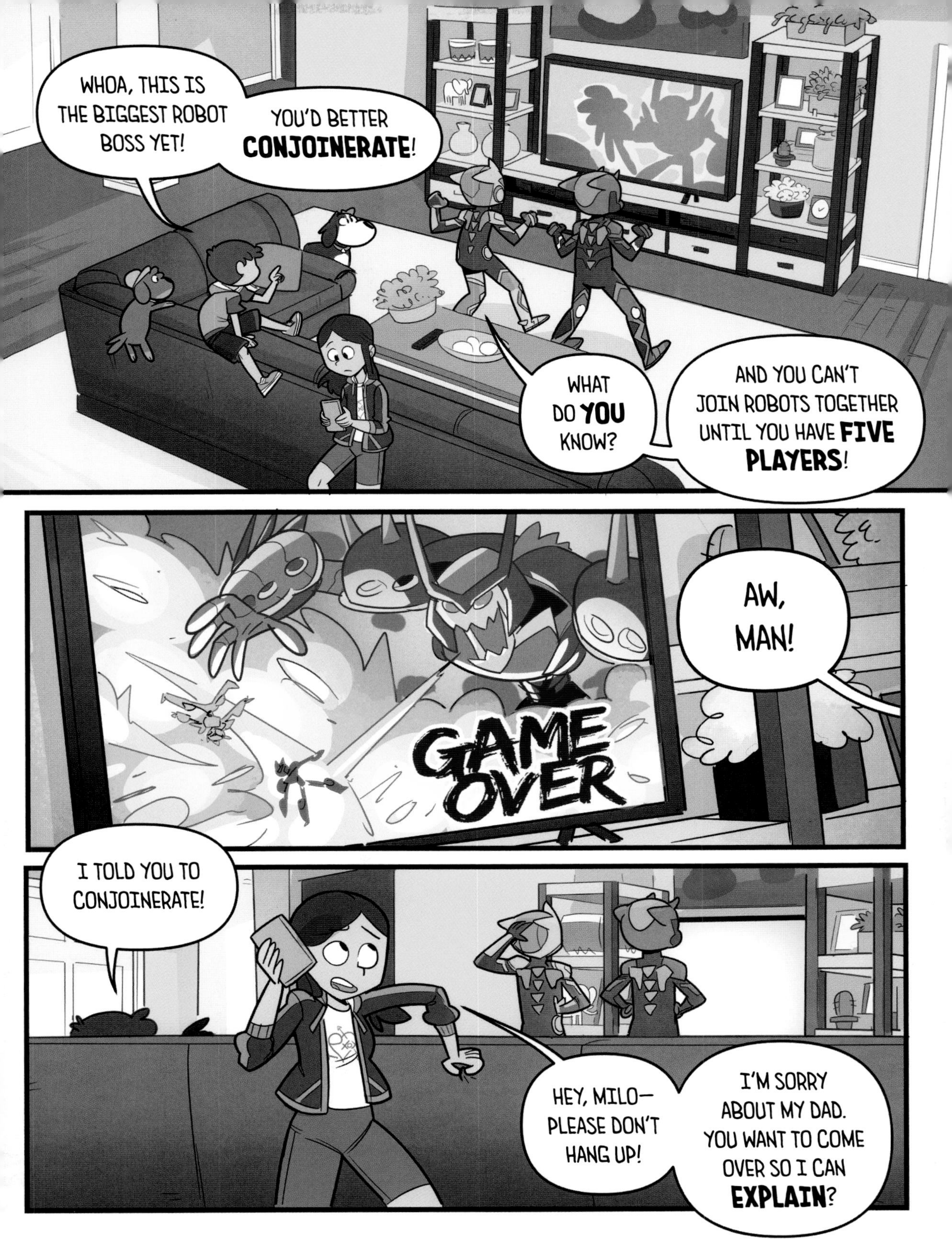
WHOA, THIS IS THE BIGGEST ROBOT BOSS YET!
YOU'D BETTER **CONJOINERATE**!
WHAT DO **YOU** KNOW?
AND YOU CAN'T JOIN ROBOTS TOGETHER UNTIL YOU HAVE **FIVE PLAYERS**!
GAME OVER
AW, MAN!
I TOLD YOU TO CONJOINERATE!
HEY, MILO— PLEASE DON'T HANG UP!
I'M SORRY ABOUT MY DAD. YOU WANT TO COME OVER SO I CAN **EXPLAIN**?

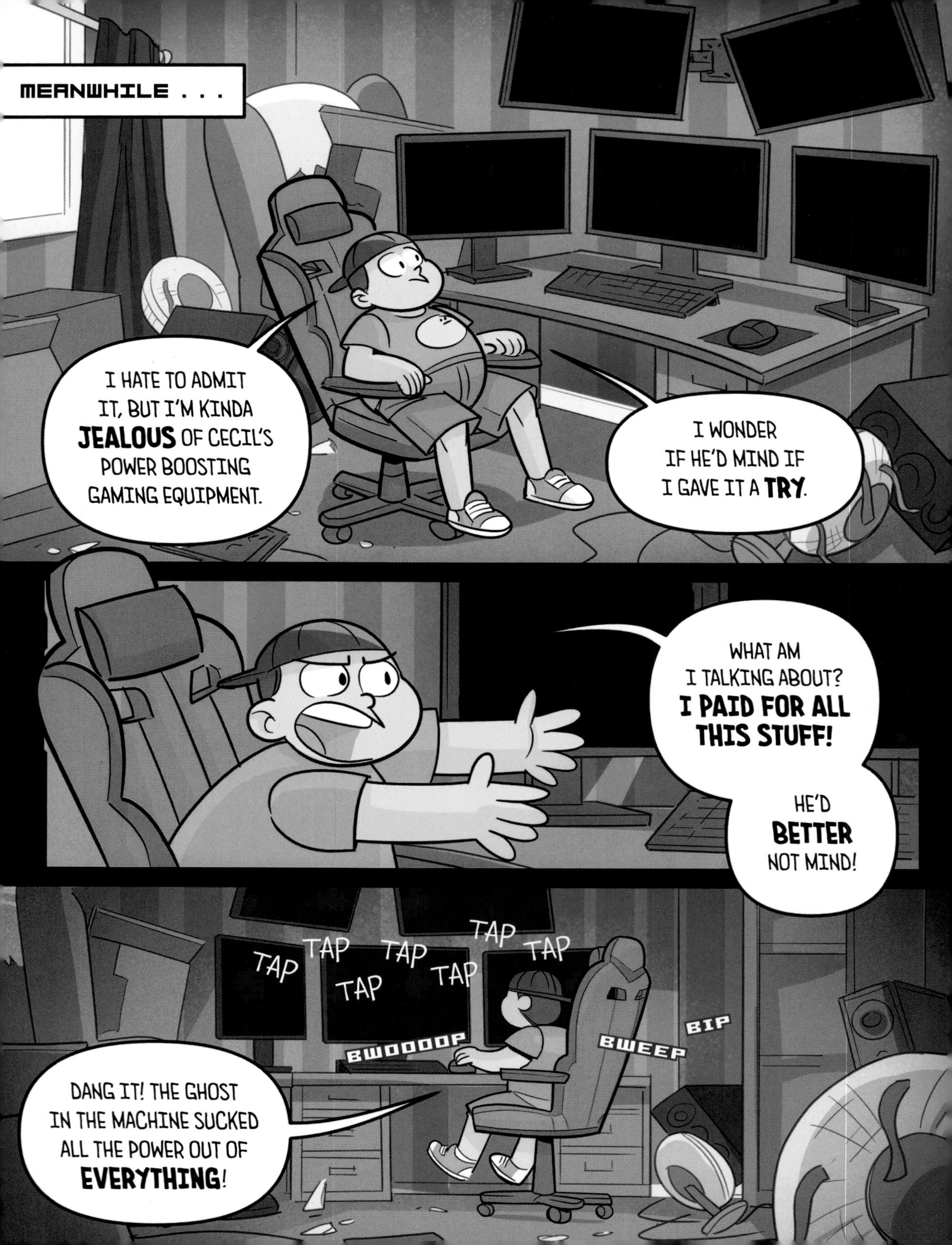
MEANWHILE . . .
I HATE TO ADMIT IT, BUT I'M KINDA JEALOUS OF CECIL'S POWER BOOSTING GAMING EQUIPMENT.
I WONDER IF HE'D MIND IF I GAVE IT A TRY.
WHAT AM I TALKING ABOUT? I PAID FOR ALL THIS STUFF!
HE'D BETTER NOT MIND!
TAP TAP TAP TAP TAP TAP TAP
BWOOOOP
BWEEP
BIP
DANG IT! THE GHOST IN THE MACHINE SUCKED ALL THE POWER OUT OF EVERYTHING!

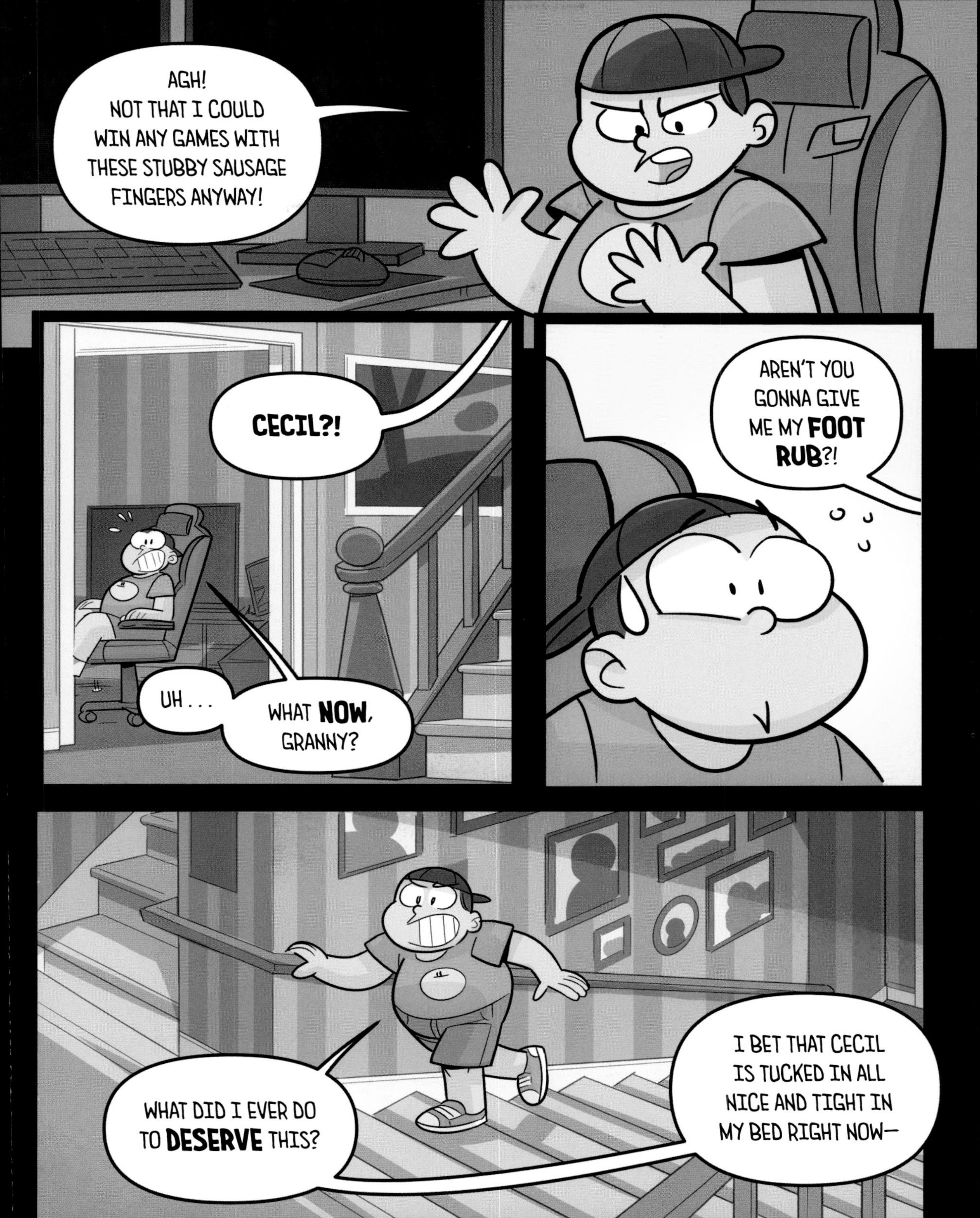
AGH! NOT THAT I COULD WIN ANY GAMES WITH THESE STUBBY SAUSAGE FINGERS ANYWAY!
CECIL?!
UH . . .
WHAT NOW, GRANNY?
AREN'T YOU GONNA GIVE ME MY FOOT RUB?!
WHAT DID I EVER DO TO DESERVE THIS?
I BET THAT CECIL IS TUCKED IN ALL NICE AND TIGHT IN MY BED RIGHT NOW—

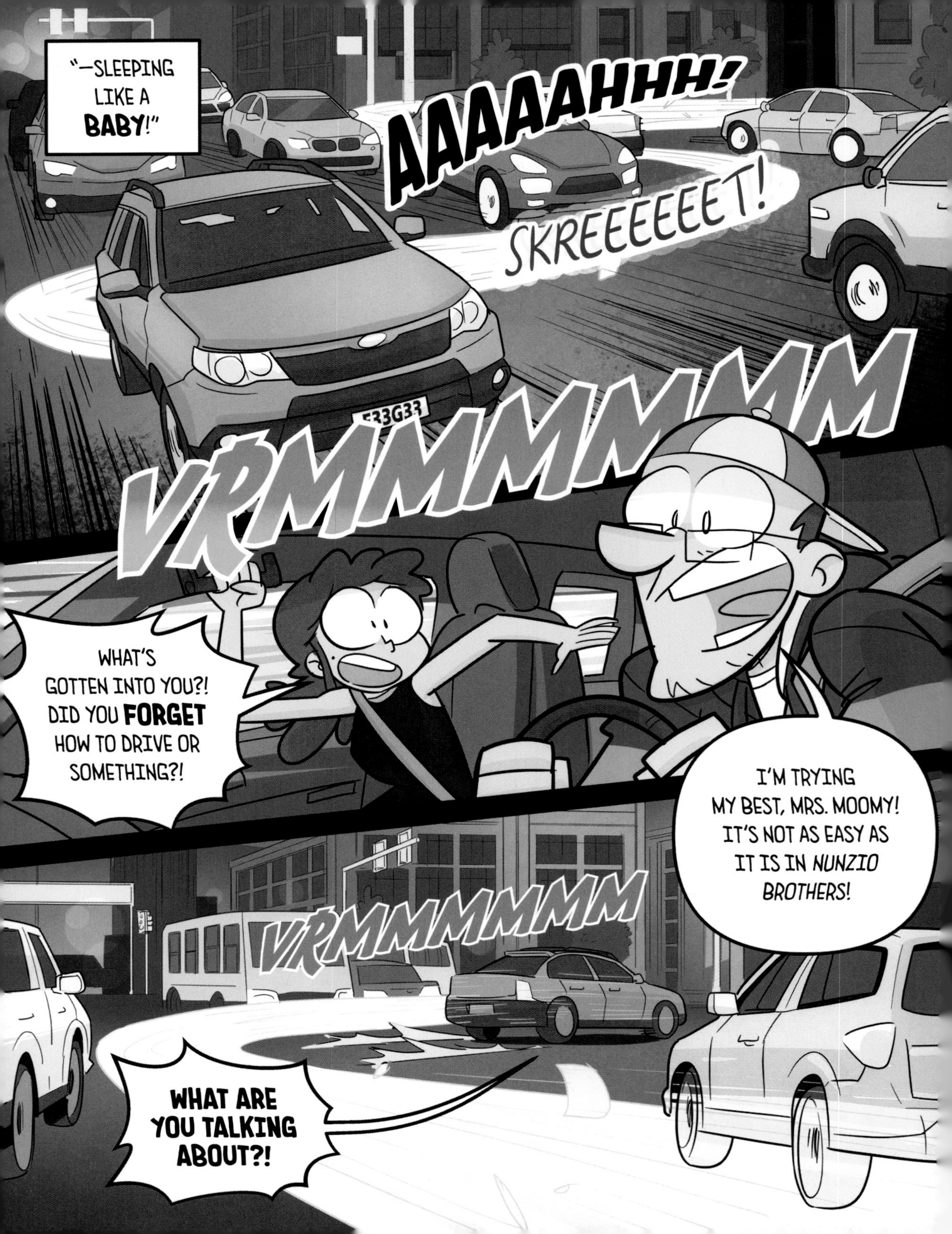
"—SLEEPING LIKE A **BABY**!"
AAAAAHHH!
SKREEEEEEET!
VRMMMMMMM
WHAT'S GOTTEN INTO YOU?! DID YOU **FORGET** HOW TO DRIVE OR SOMETHING?!
I'M TRYING MY BEST, MRS. MOOMY! IT'S NOT AS EASY AS IT IS IN *NUNZIO BROTHERS*!
VRMMMMMMM
**WHAT ARE YOU TALKING ABOUT?!**

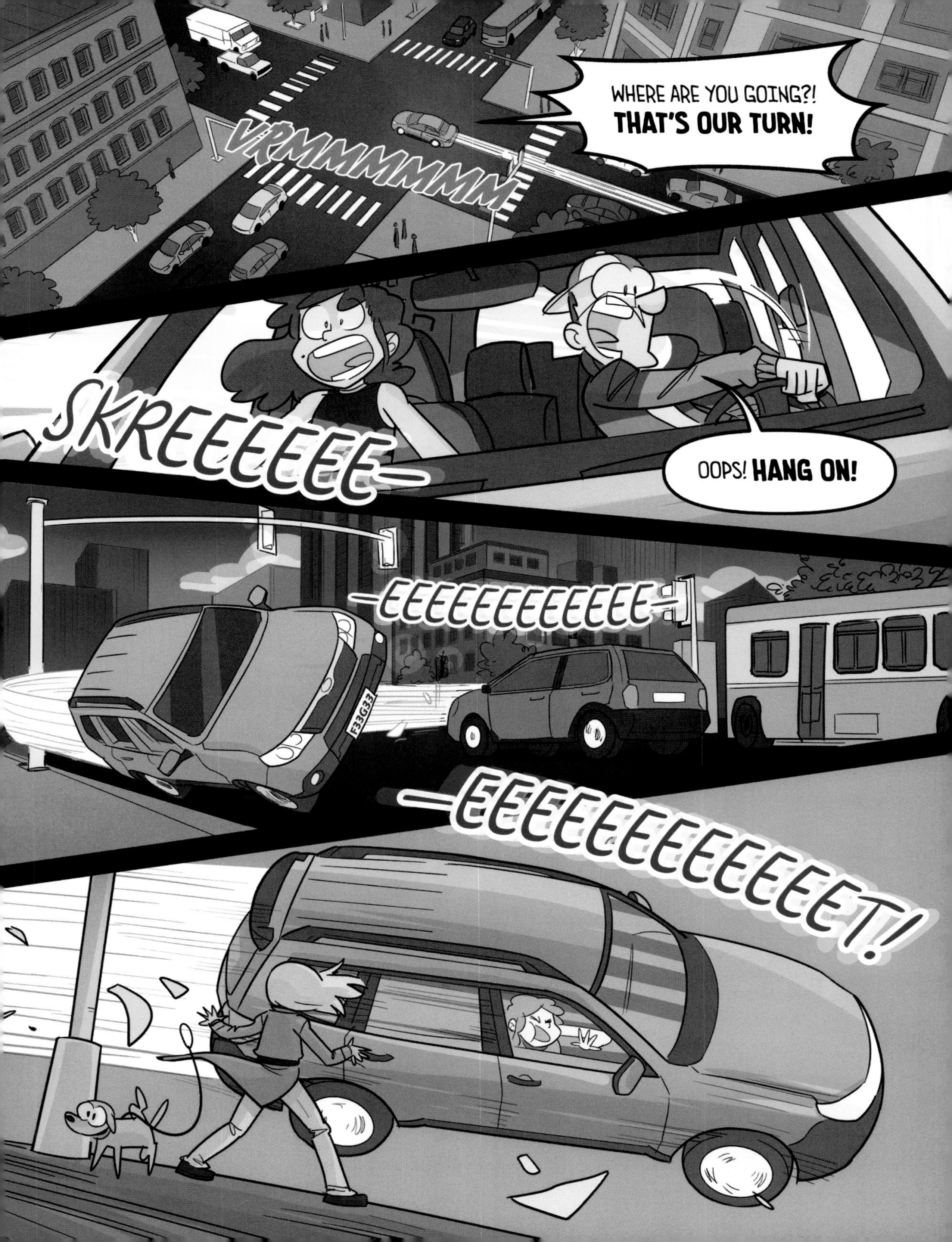

WHERE ARE YOU GOING?! **THAT'S OUR TURN!**
VRMMMMMMMM
SKREEEEEEE
OOPS! **HANG ON!**
EEEEEEEEEEEEE
F33G33
EEEEEEEEEEEEEET!

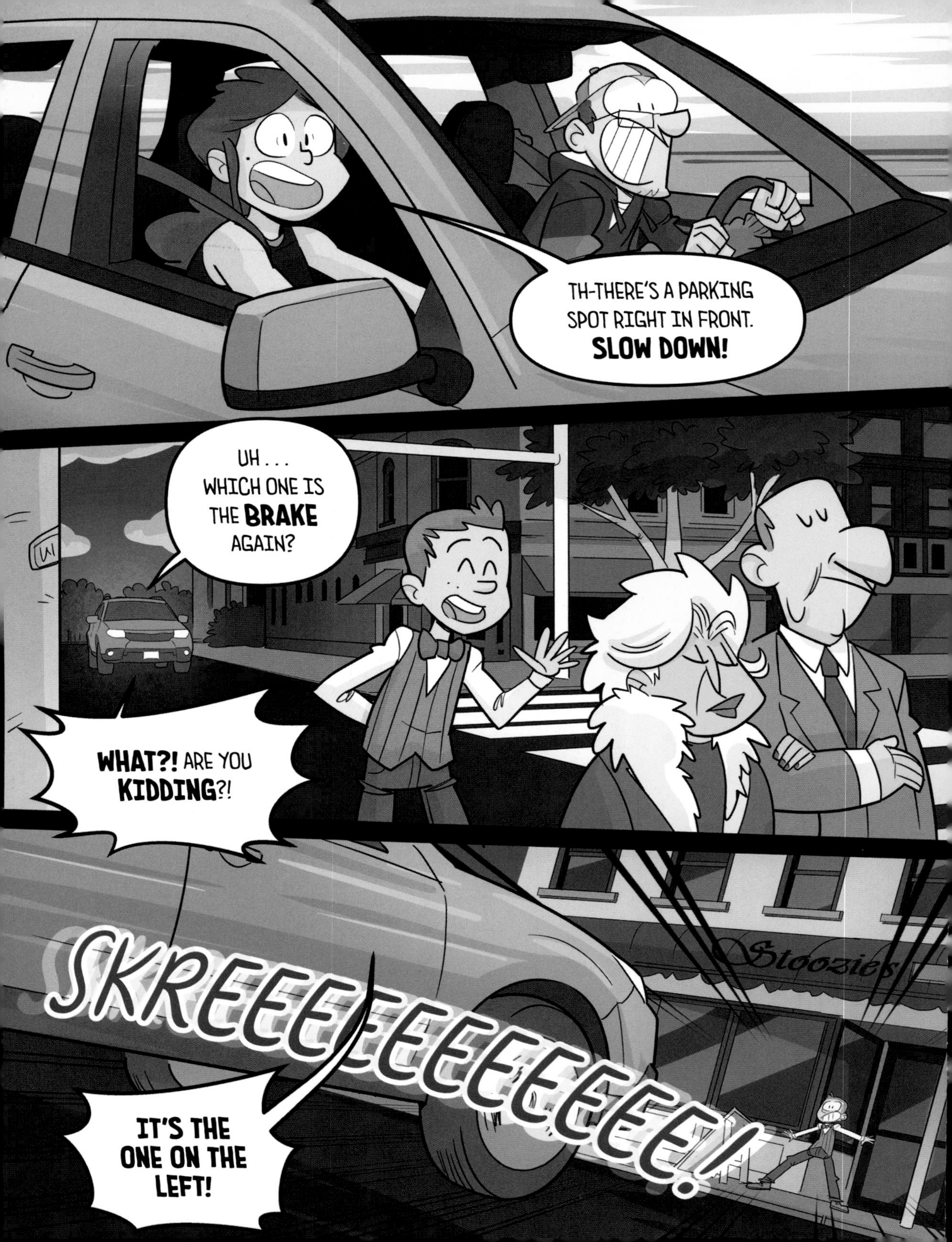
TH-THERE'S A PARKING SPOT RIGHT IN FRONT. **SLOW DOWN!**
UH . . . WHICH ONE IS THE **BRAKE** AGAIN?
**WHAT?!** ARE YOU **KIDDING**?!
Stoozies
SKREEEEEEEEEEEEEE!
IT'S THE ONE ON THE LEFT!

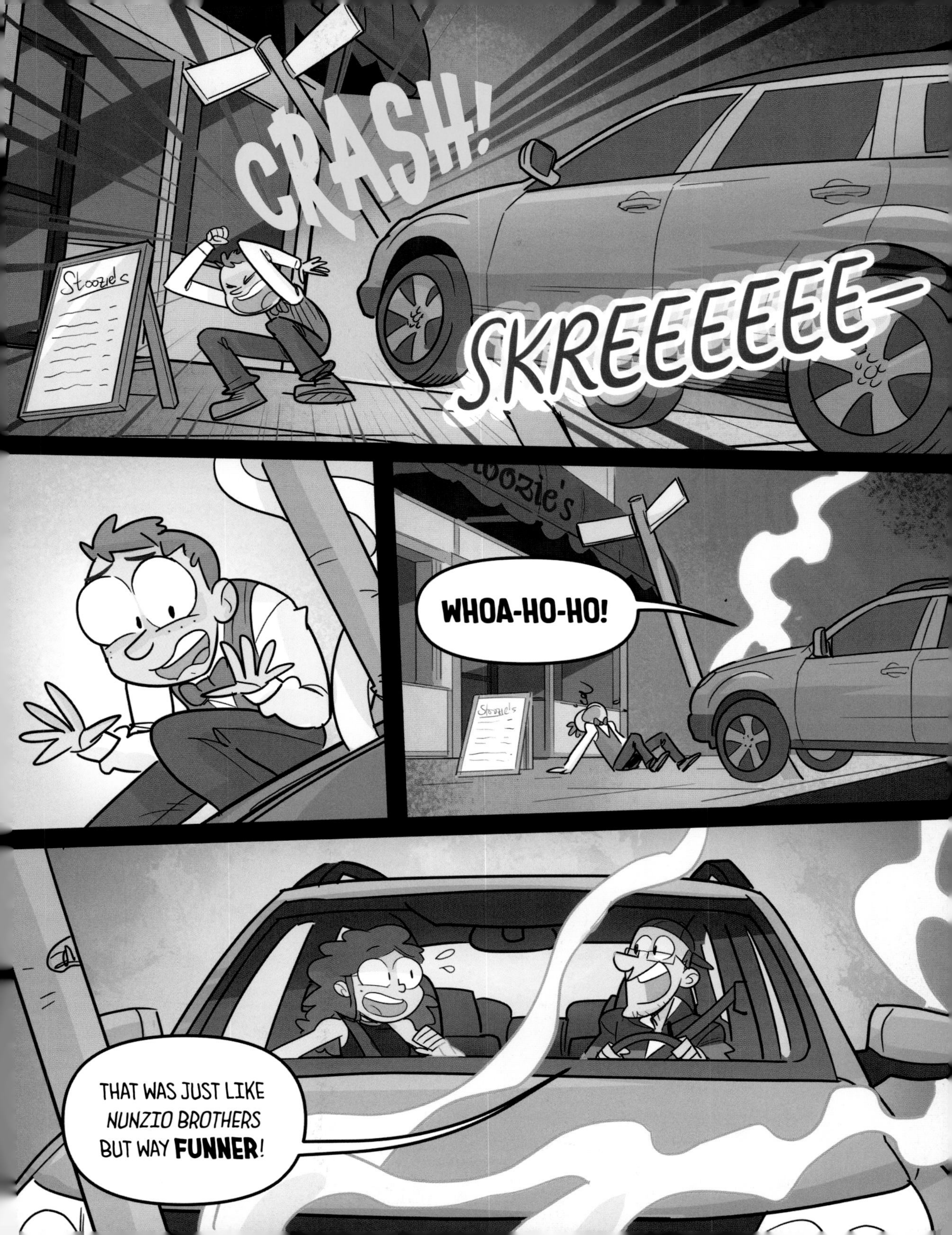
CRASH!
Stoozie's
SKREEEEEEE—
Stoozie's
WHOA-HO-HO!
Stoozie's
THAT WAS JUST LIKE NUNZIO BROTHERS BUT WAY **FUNNER**!

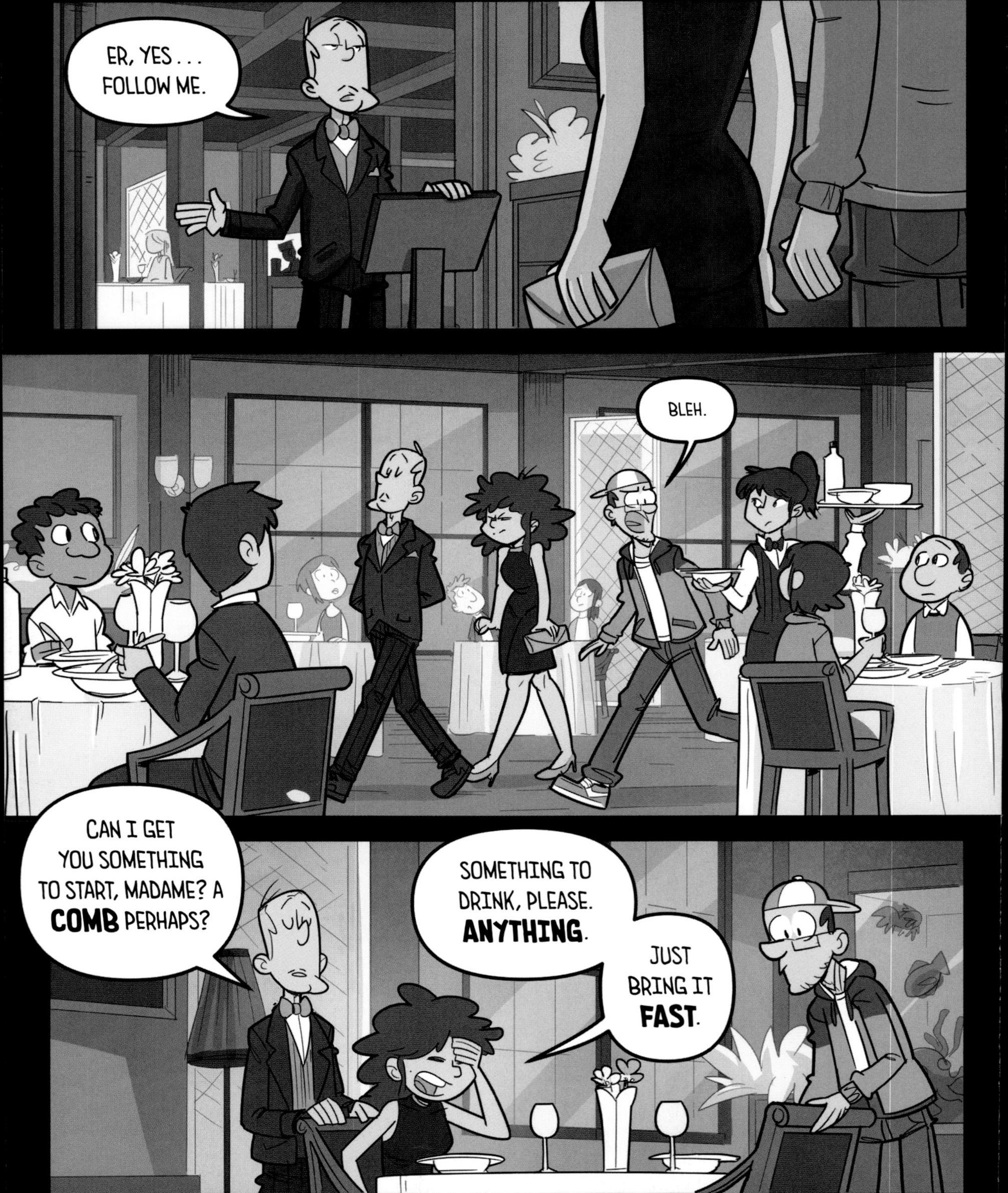
ER, YES . . . FOLLOW ME.
BLEH.
CAN I GET YOU SOMETHING TO START, MADAME? A **COMB** PERHAPS?
SOMETHING TO DRINK, PLEASE. **ANYTHING**.
JUST BRING IT **FAST**.

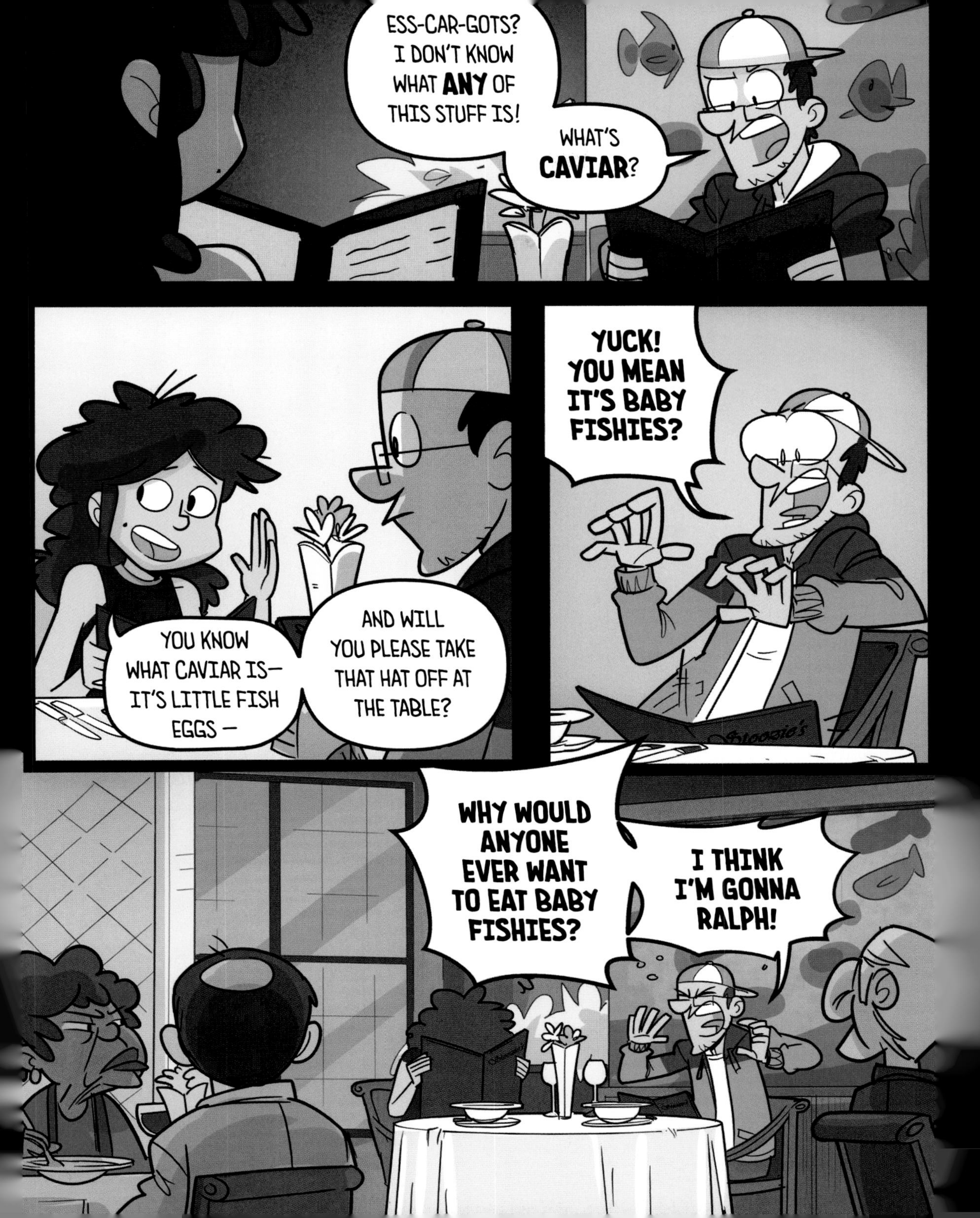
ESS-CAR-GOTS? I DON'T KNOW WHAT **ANY** OF THIS STUFF IS!
WHAT'S **CAVIAR**?
YOU KNOW WHAT CAVIAR IS— IT'S LITTLE FISH EGGS —
AND WILL YOU PLEASE TAKE THAT HAT OFF AT THE TABLE?
YUCK! YOU MEAN IT'S BABY FISHIES?
WHY WOULD ANYONE EVER WANT TO EAT BABY FISHIES?
I THINK I'M GONNA RALPH!

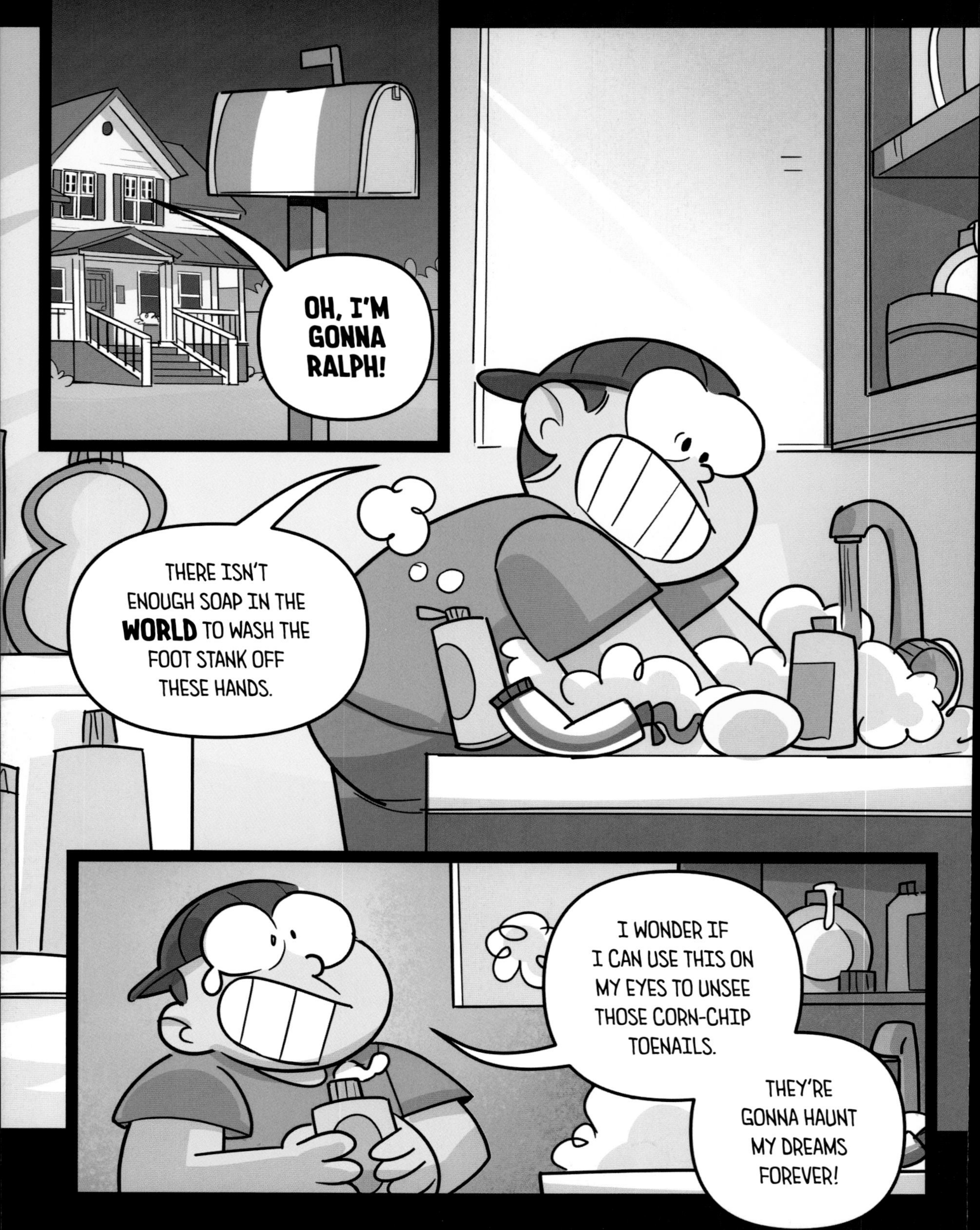
OH, I'M GONNA RALPH!
THERE ISN'T ENOUGH SOAP IN THE **WORLD** TO WASH THE FOOT STANK OFF THESE HANDS.
I WONDER IF I CAN USE THIS ON MY EYES TO UNSEE THOSE CORN-CHIP TOENAILS.
THEY'RE GONNA HAUNT MY DREAMS FOREVER!

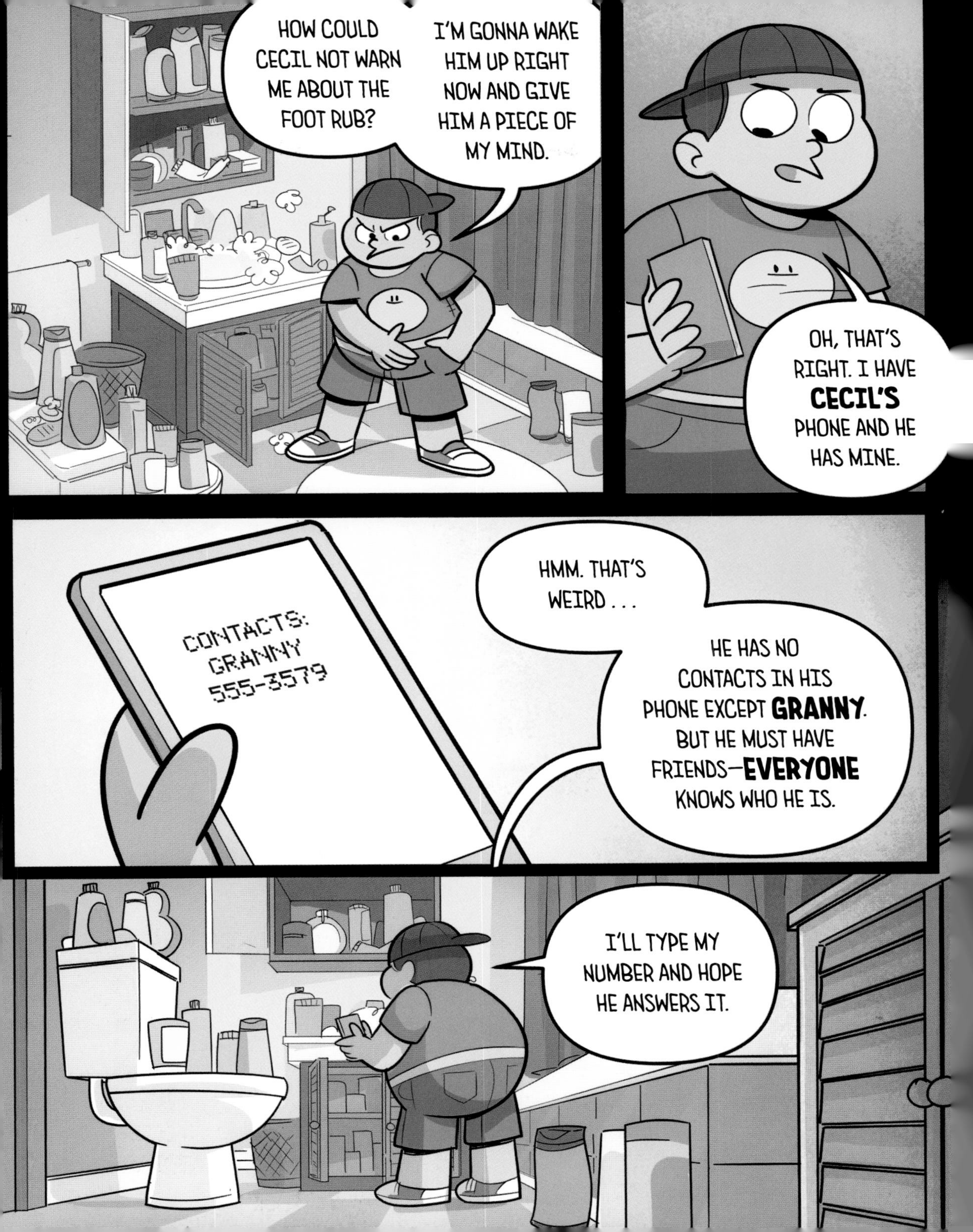
HOW COULD CECIL NOT WARN ME ABOUT THE FOOT RUB?
I'M GONNA WAKE HIM UP RIGHT NOW AND GIVE HIM A PIECE OF MY MIND.
OH, THAT'S RIGHT. I HAVE **CECIL'S** PHONE AND HE HAS MINE.
CONTACTS: GRANNY 555-3579
HMM. THAT'S WEIRD . . .
HE HAS NO CONTACTS IN HIS PHONE EXCEPT **GRANNY**. BUT HE MUST HAVE FRIENDS—**EVERYONE** KNOWS WHO HE IS.
I'LL TYPE MY NUMBER AND HOPE HE ANSWERS IT.

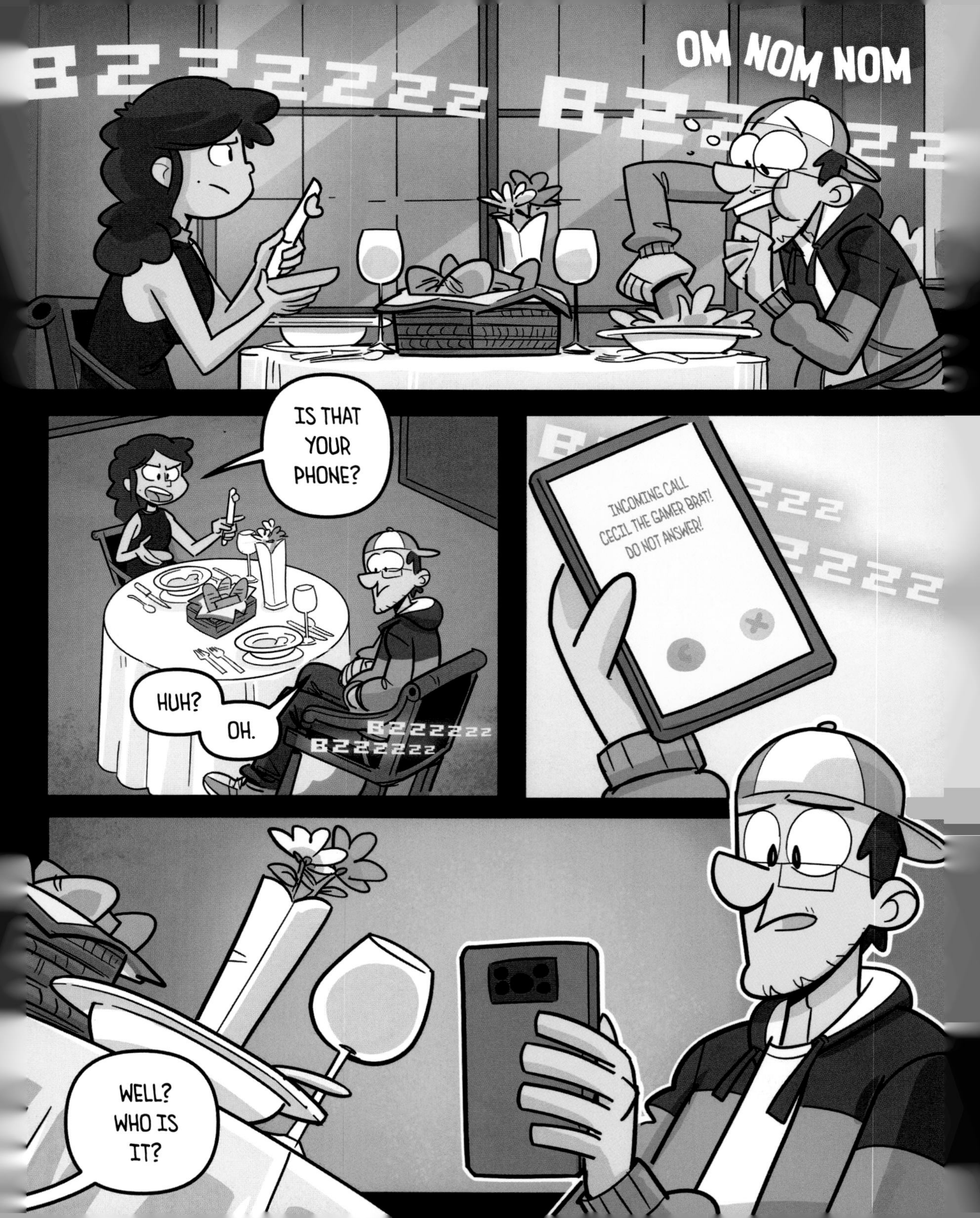
BZZZZZZZz
OM NOM NOM
BZZZZZZ
IS THAT YOUR PHONE?
INCOMING CALL
CECIL THE GAMER BRAT!
DO NOT ANSWER!
HUH?
OH.
BZZZZZzz
BZZZZZzz
WELL? WHO IS IT?

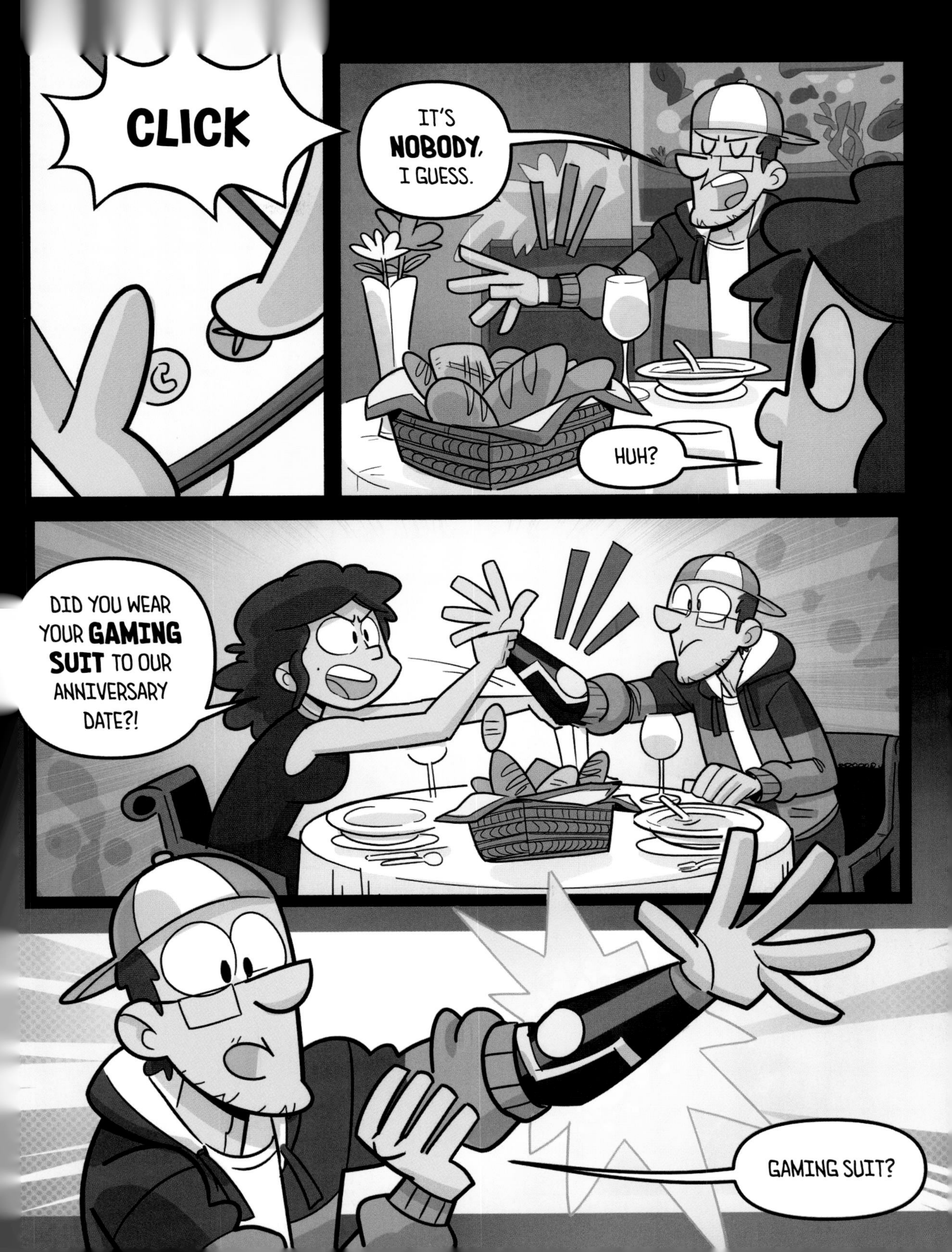
CLICK
IT'S **NOBODY**, I GUESS.
HUH?
DID YOU WEAR YOUR **GAMING SUIT** TO OUR ANNIVERSARY DATE?!
GAMING SUIT?

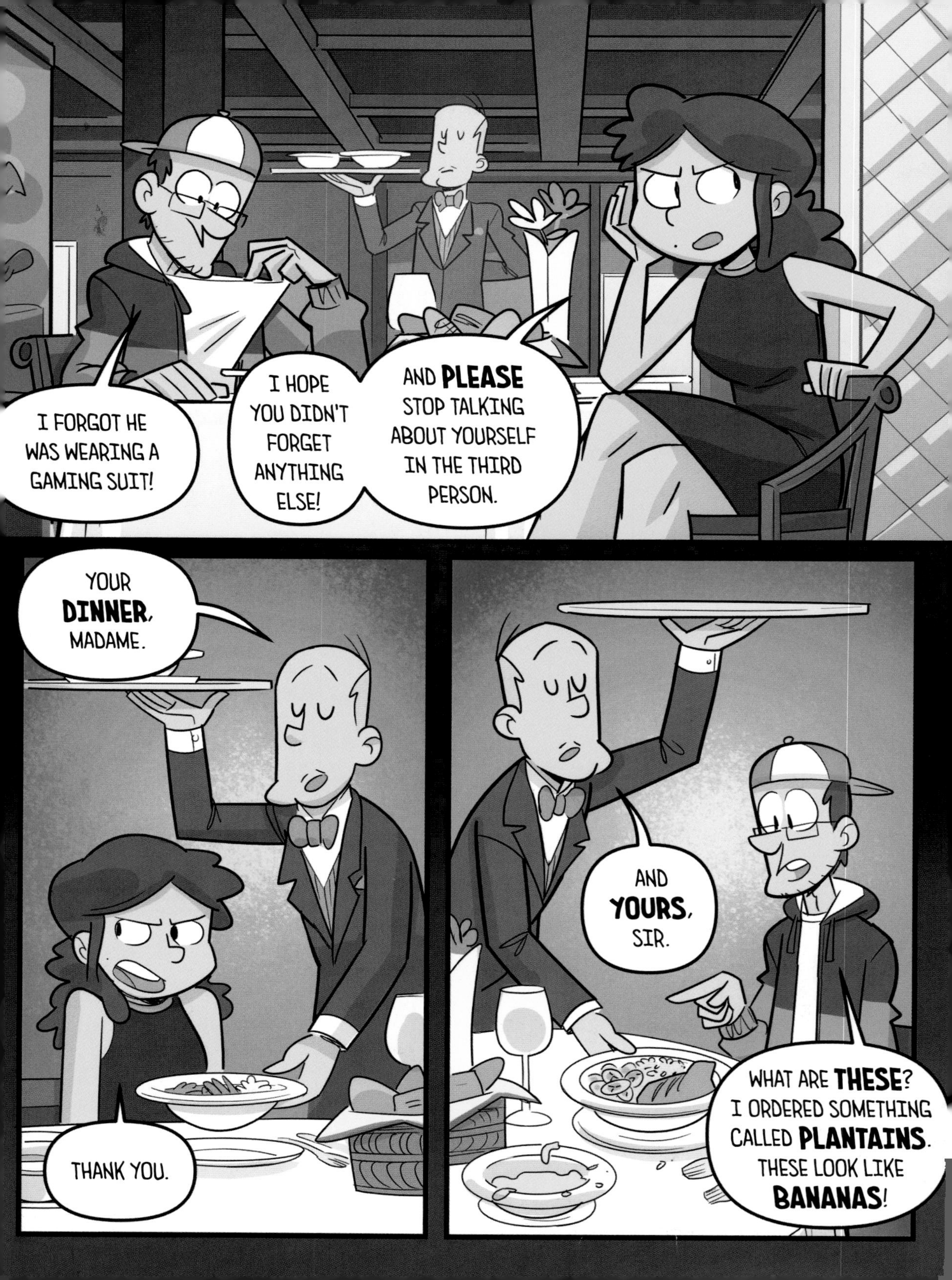
I FORGOT HE WAS WEARING A GAMING SUIT!
I HOPE YOU DIDN'T FORGET ANYTHING ELSE!
AND **PLEASE** STOP TALKING ABOUT YOURSELF IN THE THIRD PERSON.
YOUR **DINNER**, MADAME.
THANK YOU.
AND **YOURS**, SIR.
WHAT ARE **THESE**? I ORDERED SOMETHING CALLED **PLANTAINS**. THESE LOOK LIKE **BANANAS**!

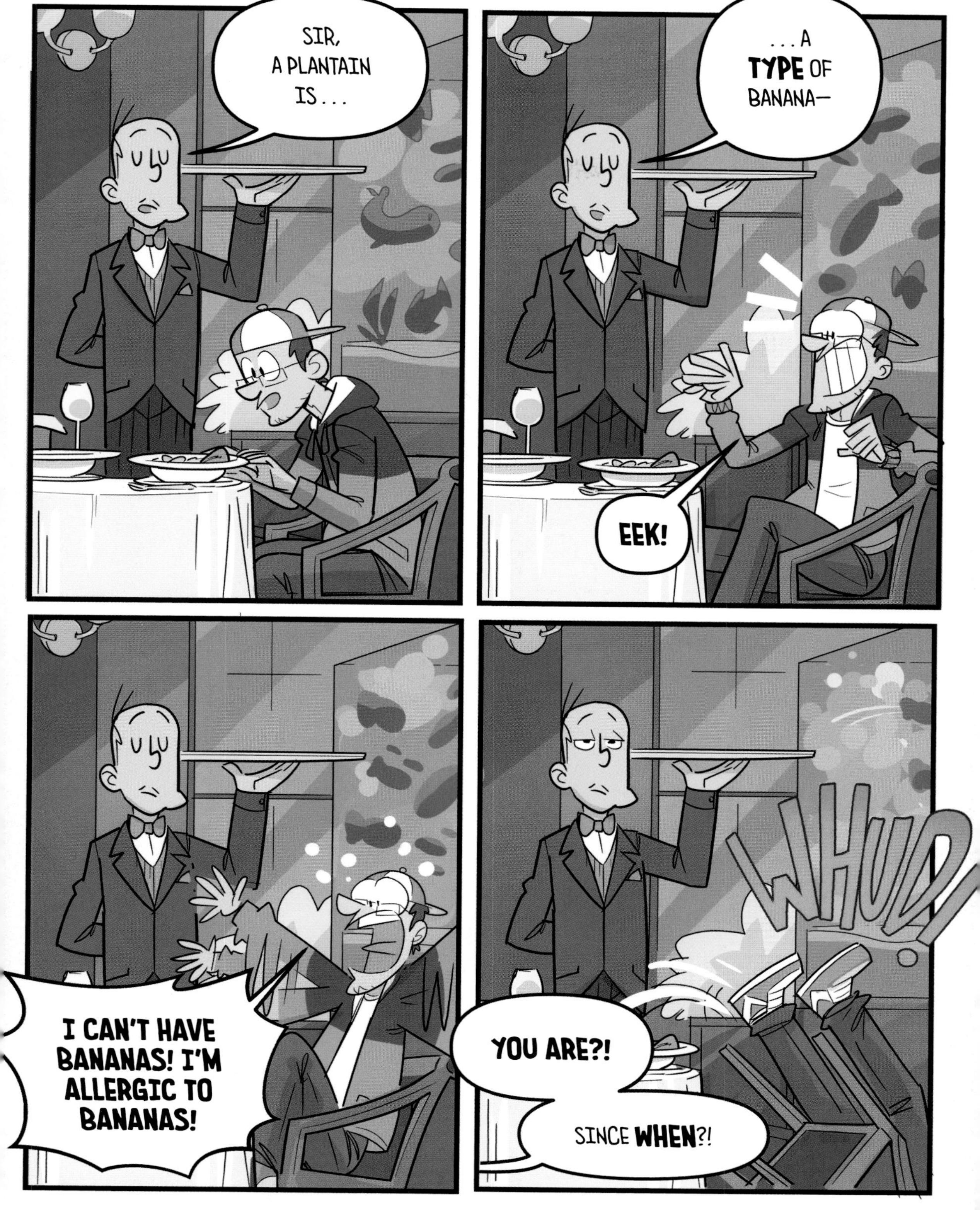
SIR, A PLANTAIN IS . . .
. . . A **TYPE** OF BANANA—
EEK!
I CAN'T HAVE BANANAS! I'M ALLERGIC TO BANANAS!
WHUD?!
YOU ARE?!
SINCE **WHEN**?!

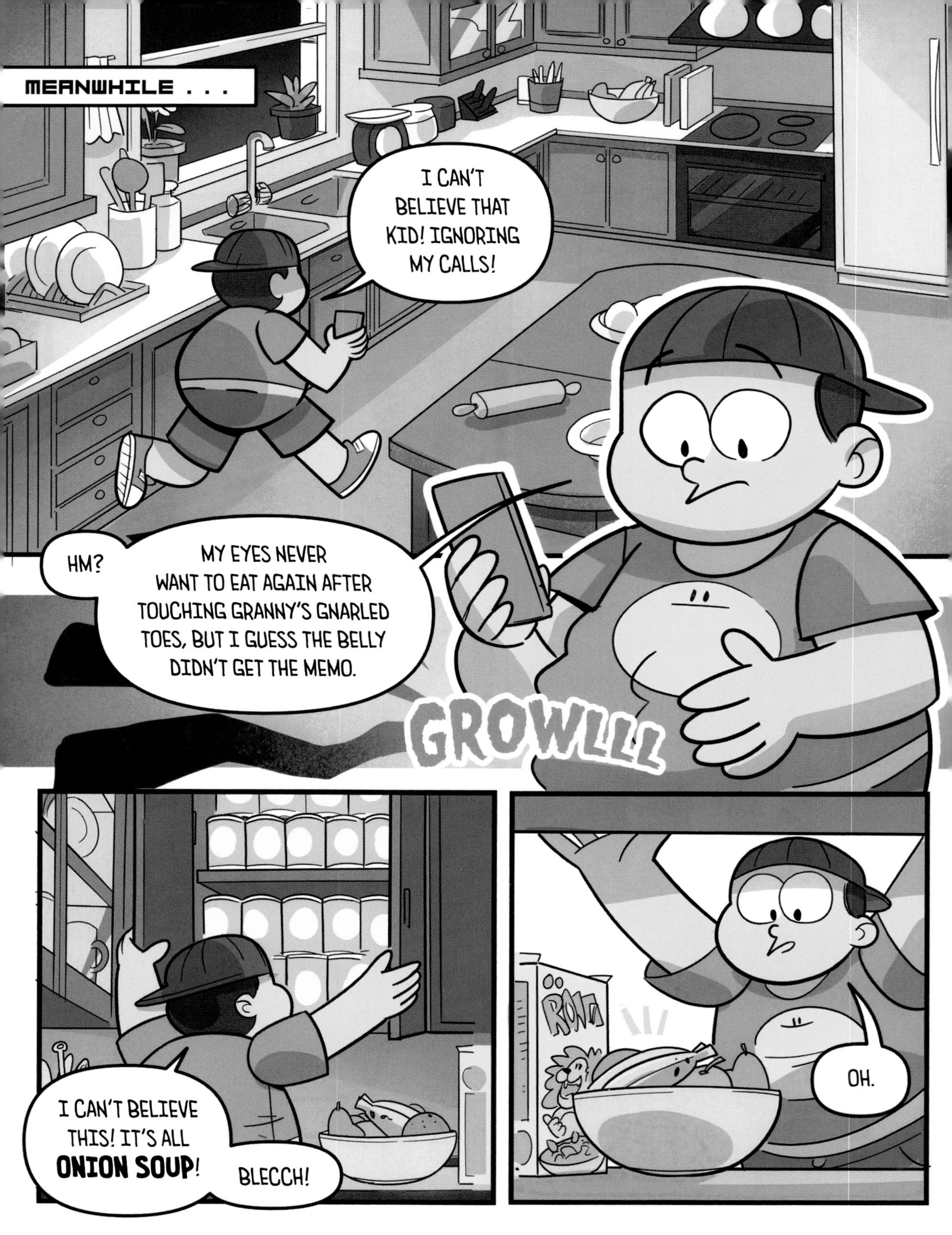
MEANWHILE . . .
I CAN'T BELIEVE THAT KID! IGNORING MY CALLS!
HM?
MY EYES NEVER WANT TO EAT AGAIN AFTER TOUCHING GRANNY'S GNARLED TOES, BUT I GUESS THE BELLY DIDN'T GET THE MEMO.
GROWLLL
I CAN'T BELIEVE THIS! IT'S ALL **ONION SOUP**!
BLECCH!
OH.

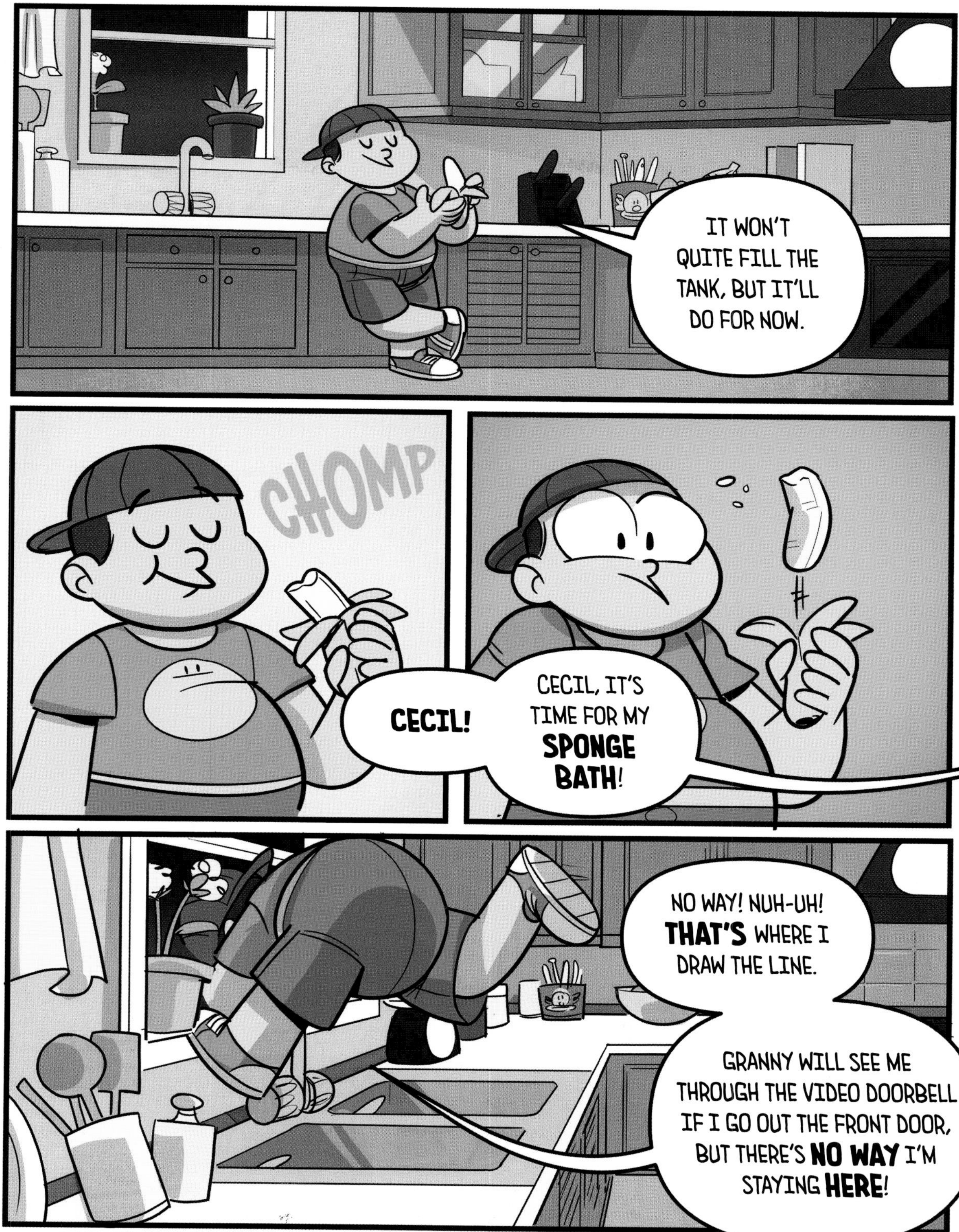
IT WON'T QUITE FILL THE TANK, BUT IT'LL DO FOR NOW.
CHOMP
CECIL!
CECIL, IT'S TIME FOR MY **SPONGE BATH**!
NO WAY! NUH-UH! **THAT'S** WHERE I DRAW THE LINE.
GRANNY WILL SEE ME THROUGH THE VIDEO DOORBELL IF I GO OUT THE FRONT DOOR, BUT THERE'S **NO WAY** I'M STAYING **HERE**!

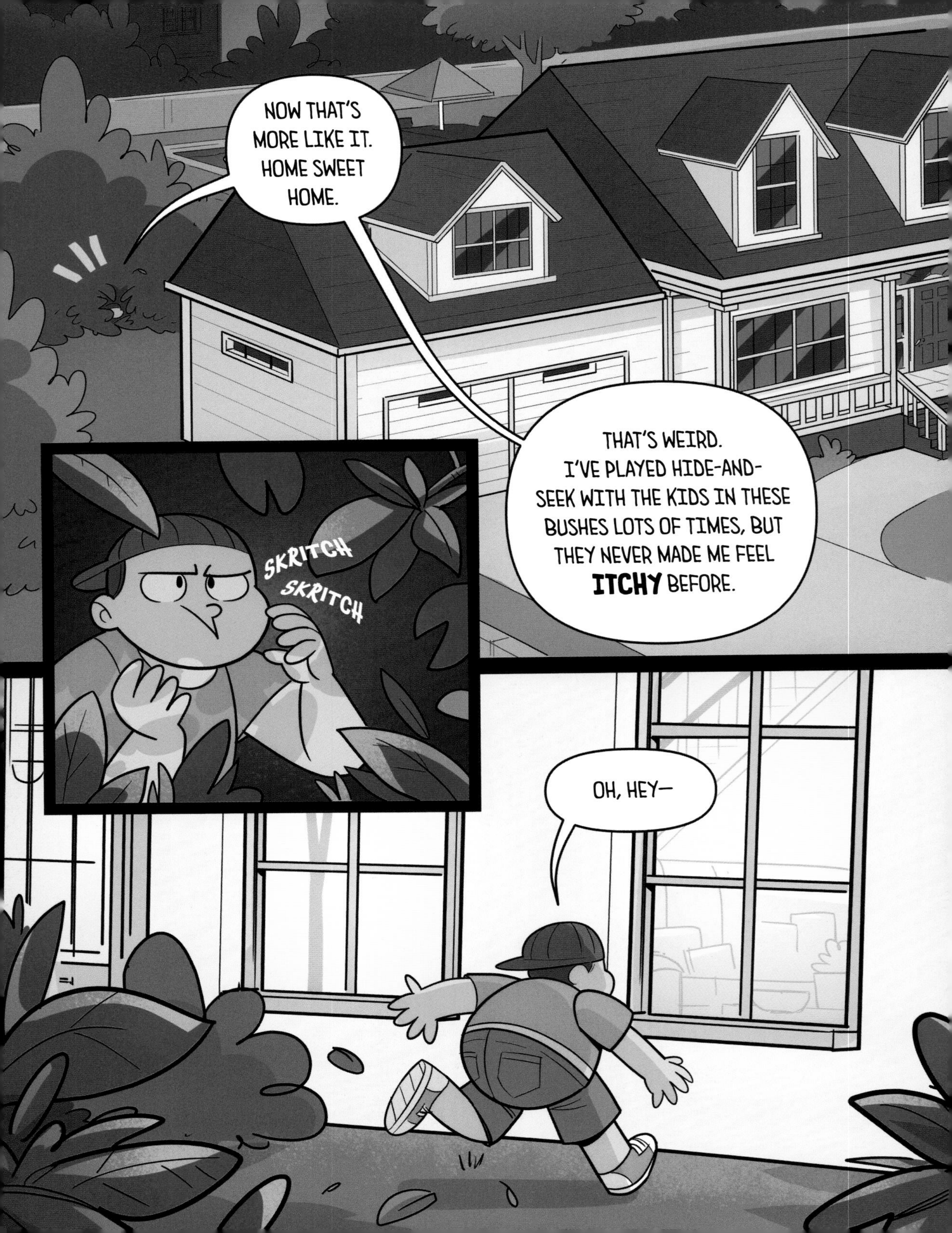
NOW THAT'S MORE LIKE IT. HOME SWEET HOME.
THAT'S WEIRD. I'VE PLAYED HIDE-AND-SEEK WITH THE KIDS IN THESE BUSHES LOTS OF TIMES, BUT THEY NEVER MADE ME FEEL **ITCHY** BEFORE.
SKRITCH
SKRITCH
OH, HEY—

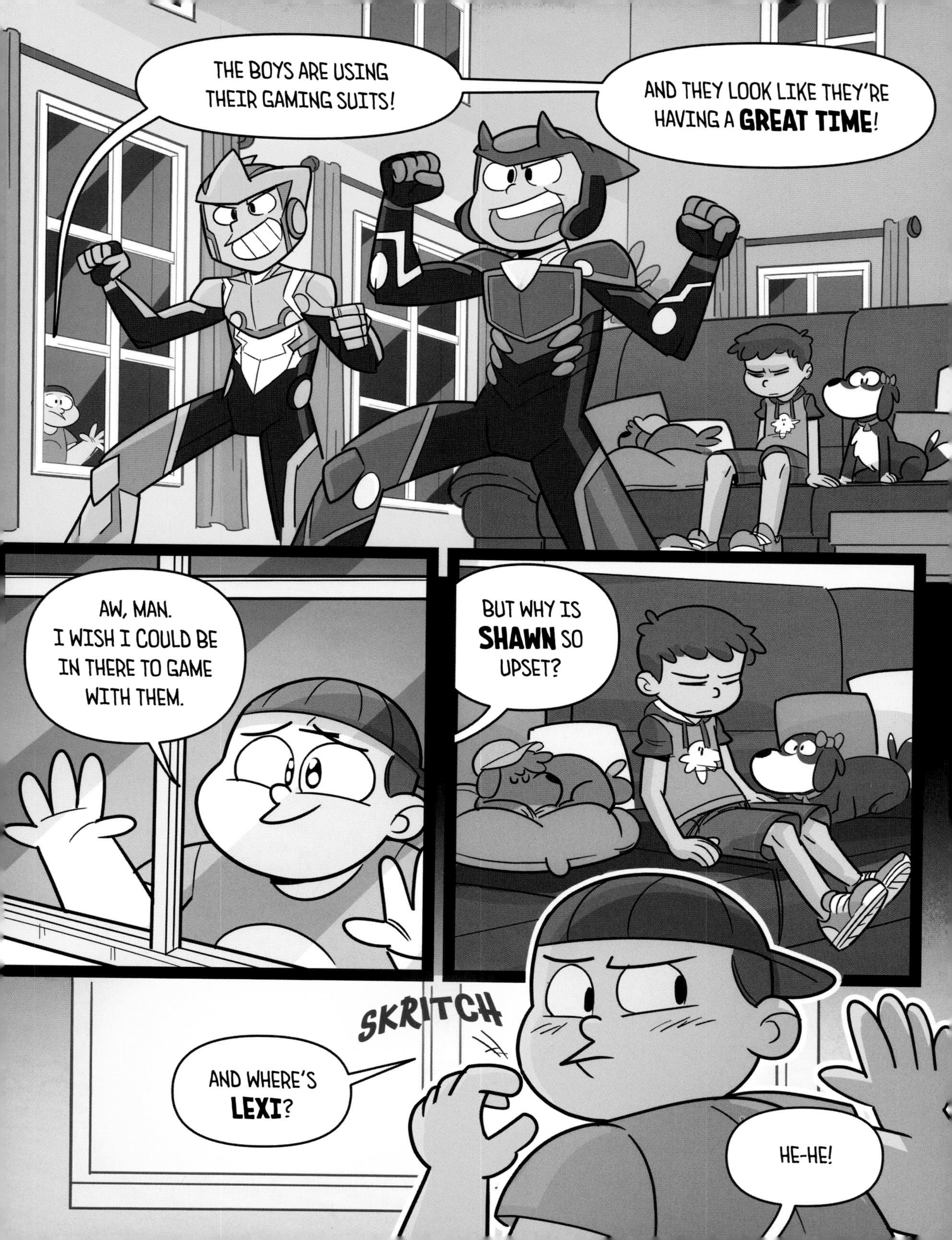

THE BOYS ARE USING THEIR GAMING SUITS!
AND THEY LOOK LIKE THEY'RE HAVING A **GREAT TIME**!
AW, MAN. I WISH I COULD BE IN THERE TO GAME WITH THEM.
BUT WHY IS **SHAWN** SO UPSET?
SKRITCH
AND WHERE'S **LEXI**?
HE-HE!

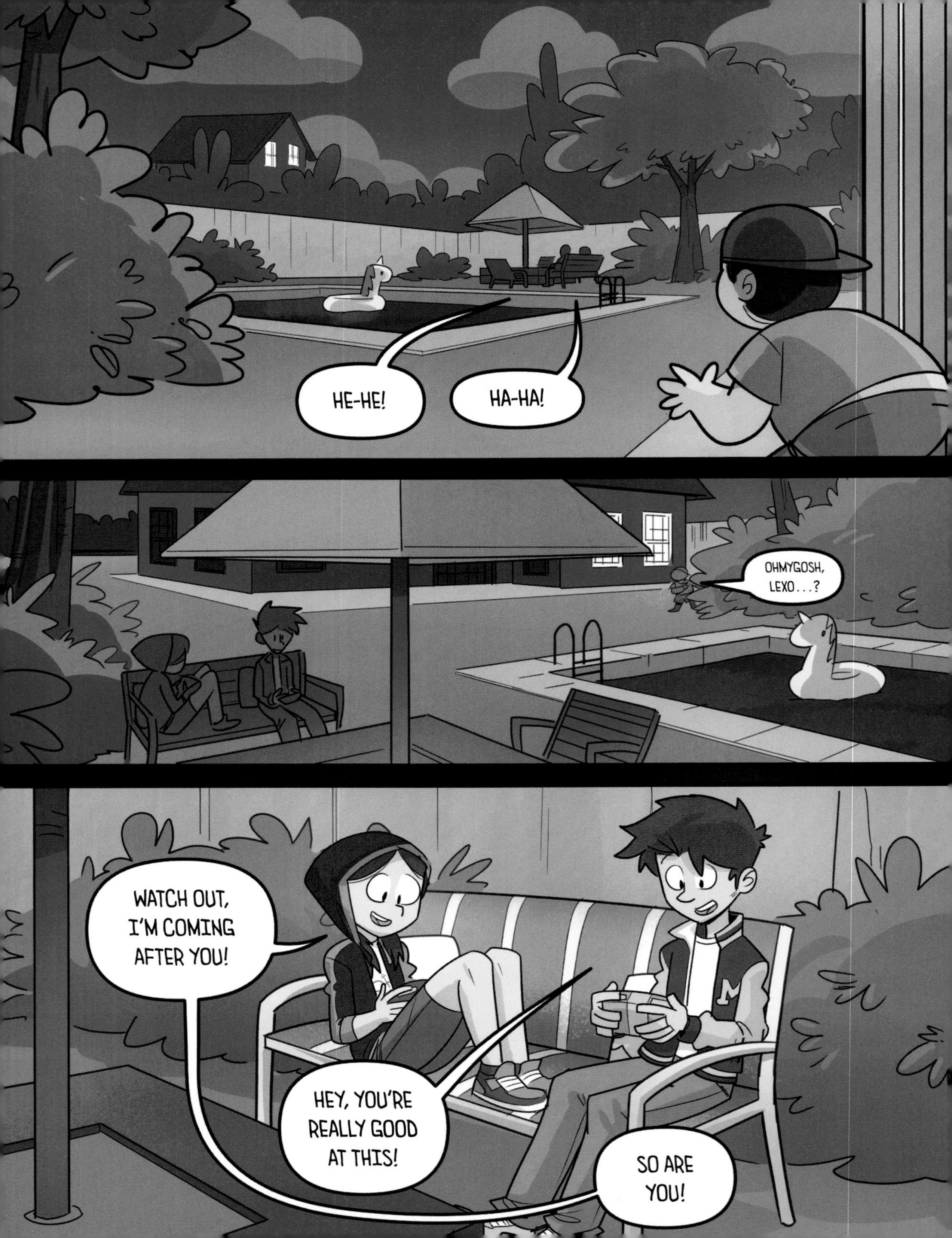
HE-HE!
HA-HA!
OHMYGOSH, LEXO . . . ?
WATCH OUT, I'M COMING AFTER YOU!
HEY, YOU'RE REALLY GOOD AT THIS!
SO ARE YOU!

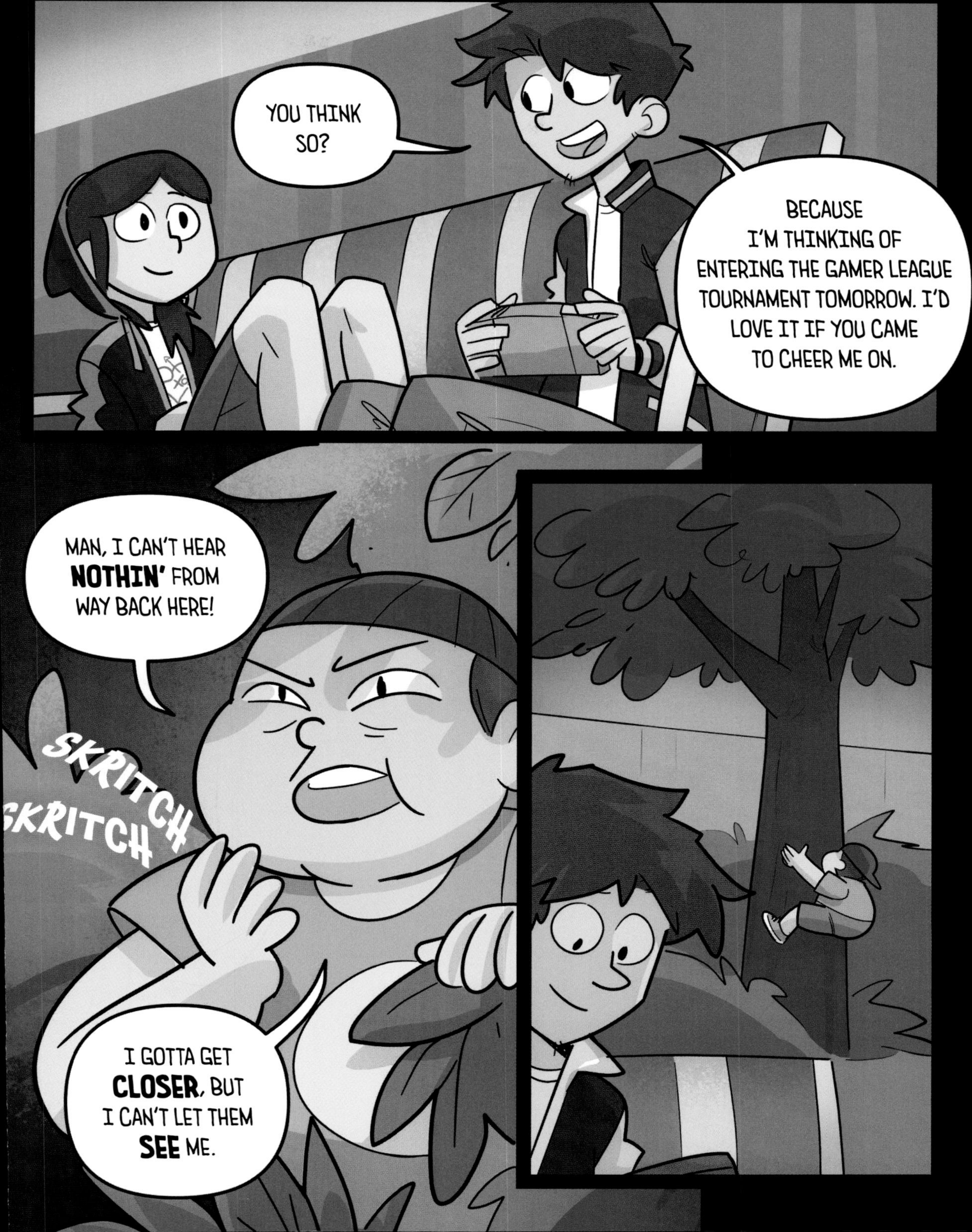
YOU THINK SO?
BECAUSE I'M THINKING OF ENTERING THE GAMER LEAGUE TOURNAMENT TOMORROW. I'D LOVE IT IF YOU CAME TO CHEER ME ON.
MAN, I CAN'T HEAR **NOTHIN'** FROM WAY BACK HERE!
SKRITCH
SKRITCH
I GOTTA GET **CLOSER**, BUT I CAN'T LET THEM **SEE** ME.

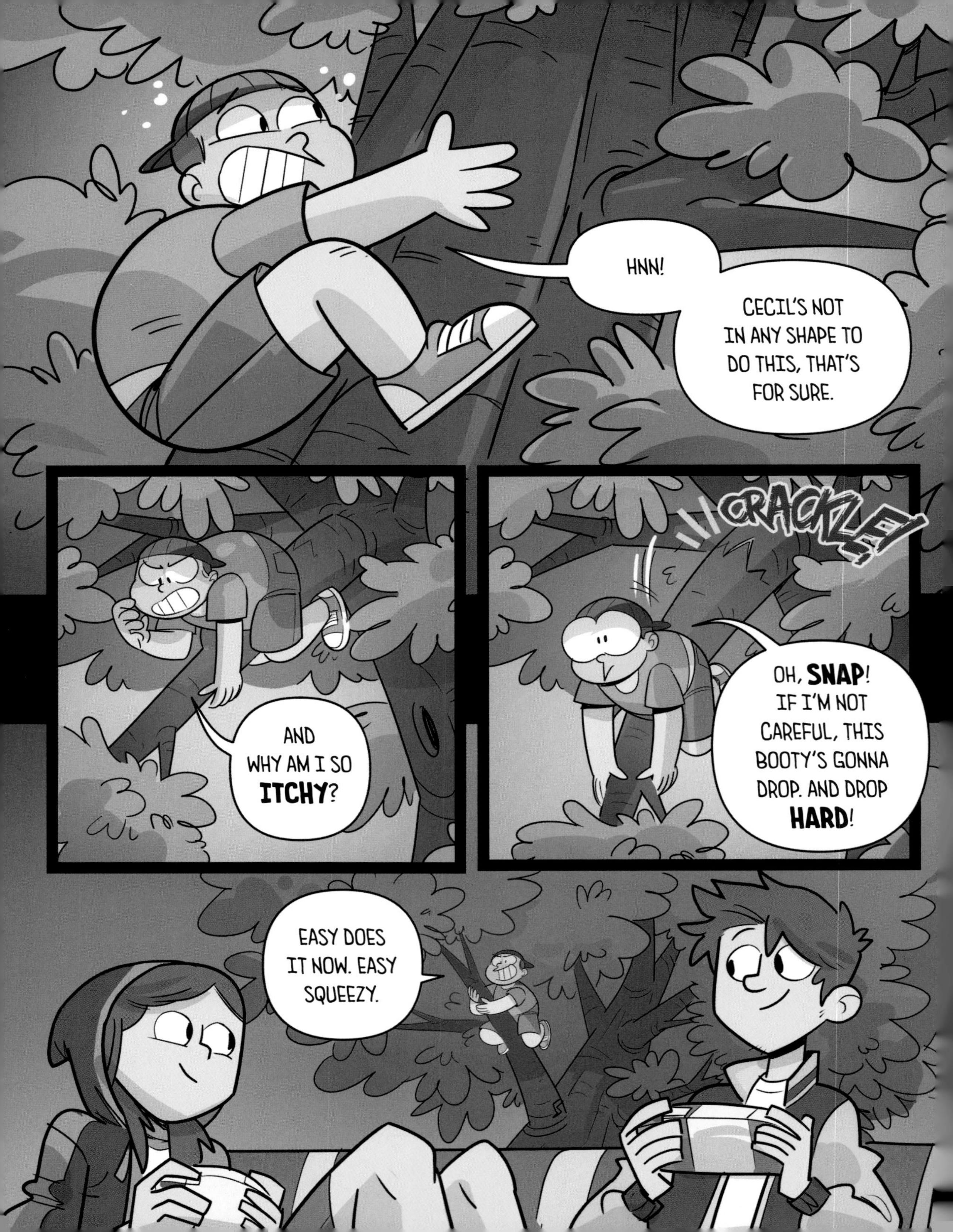
HNN!
CECIL'S NOT IN ANY SHAPE TO DO THIS, THAT'S FOR SURE.
AND WHY AM I SO **ITCHY**?
CRACKLE!
OH, **SNAP**! IF I'M NOT CAREFUL, THIS BOOTY'S GONNA DROP. AND DROP **HARD**!
EASY DOES IT NOW. EASY SQUEEZY.

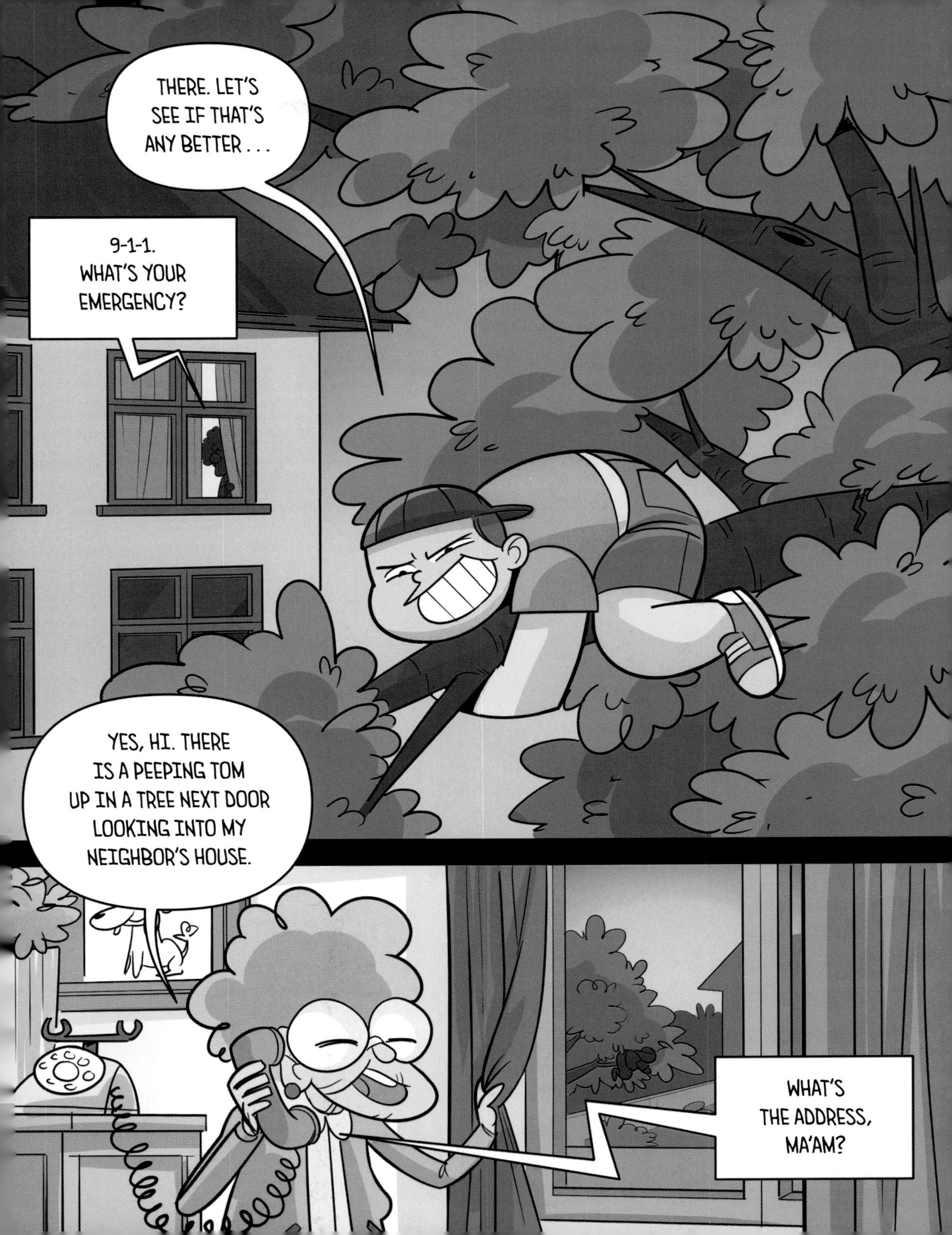
THERE. LET'S SEE IF THAT'S ANY BETTER . . .
9-1-1. WHAT'S YOUR EMERGENCY?
YES, HI. THERE IS A PEEPING TOM UP IN A TREE NEXT DOOR LOOKING INTO MY NEIGHBOR'S HOUSE.
WHAT'S THE ADDRESS, MA'AM?

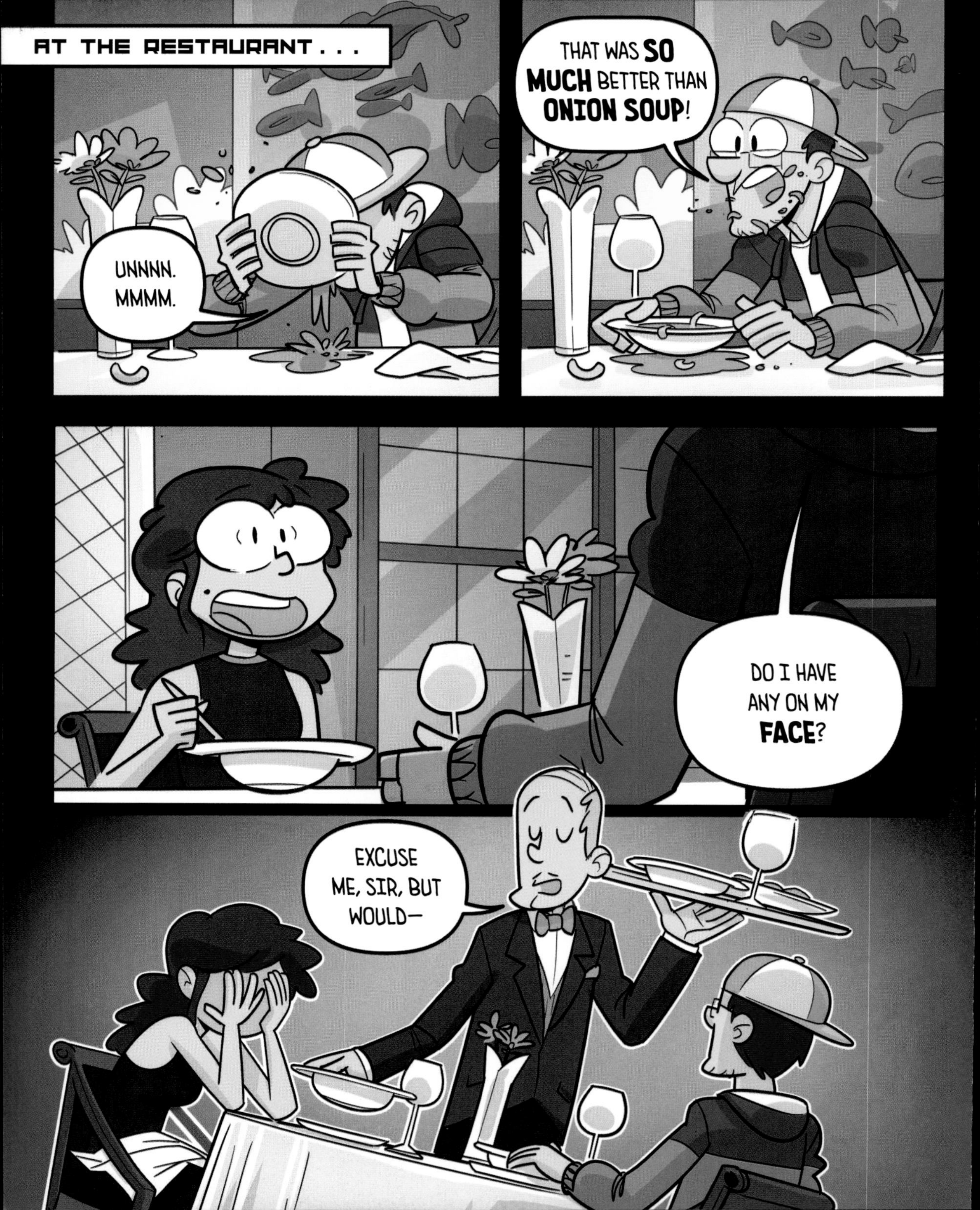
AT THE RESTAURANT . . .
UNNNN. MMMM.
THAT WAS SO MUCH BETTER THAN ONION SOUP!
DO I HAVE ANY ON MY FACE?
EXCUSE ME, SIR, BUT WOULD—

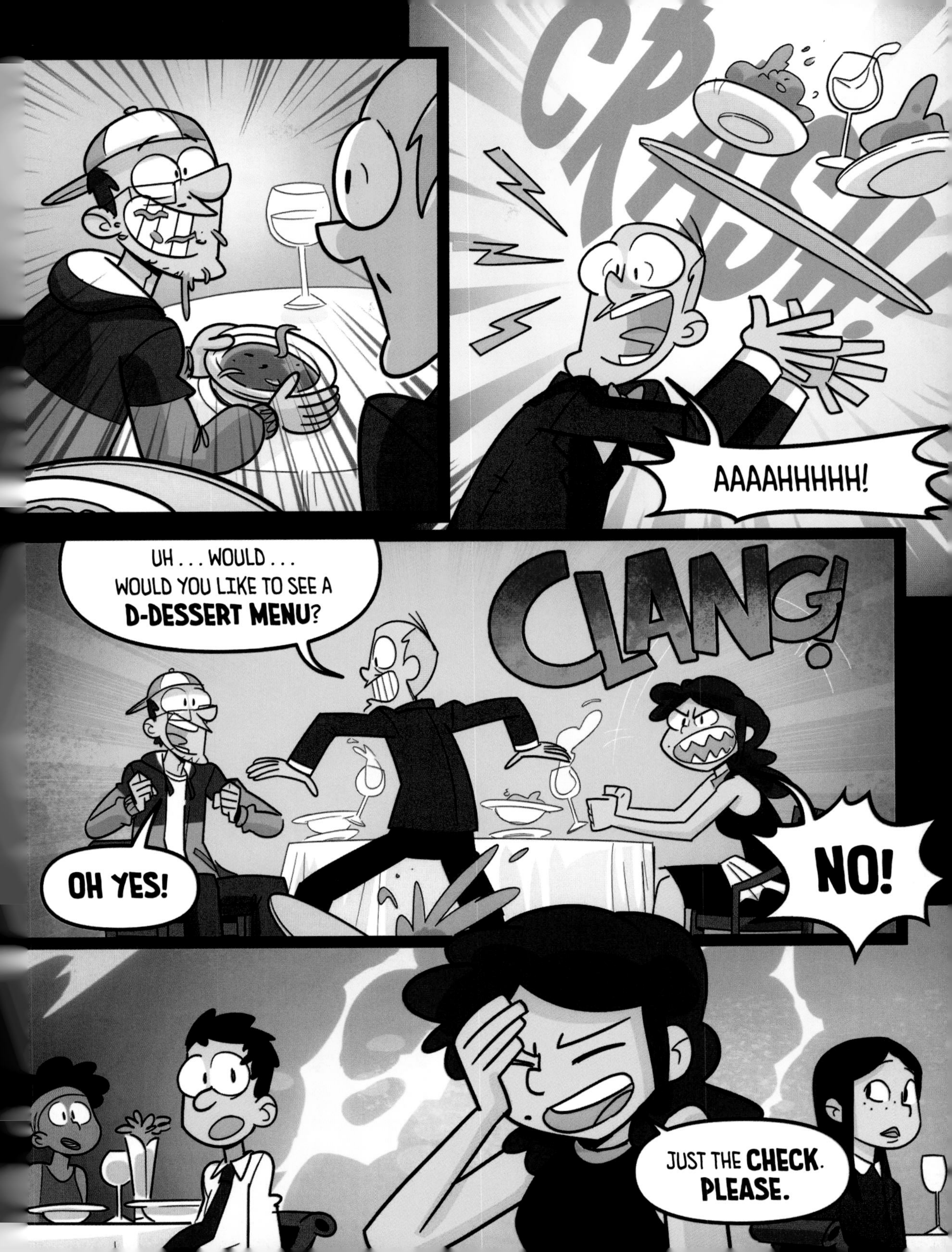
CRASH!
AAAAHHHHH!
UH . . . WOULD . . . WOULD YOU LIKE TO SEE A D-DESSERT MENU?
CLANG!
OH YES!
NO!
JUST THE CHECK. PLEASE.

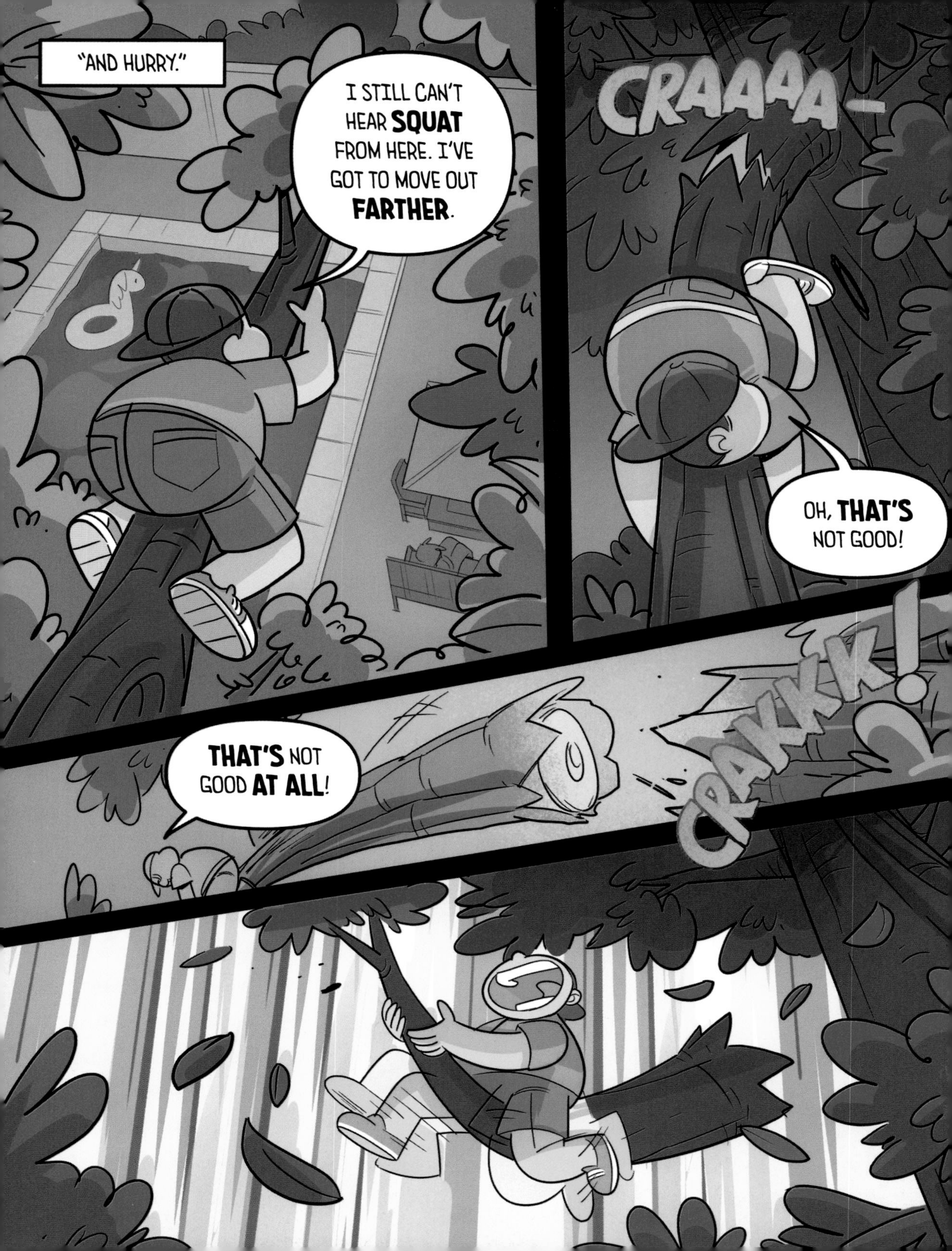
"AND HURRY."
I STILL CAN'T HEAR SQUAT FROM HERE. I'VE GOT TO MOVE OUT FARTHER.
CRAAAA-
OH, THAT'S NOT GOOD!
CRAKKK!
THAT'S NOT GOOD AT ALL!

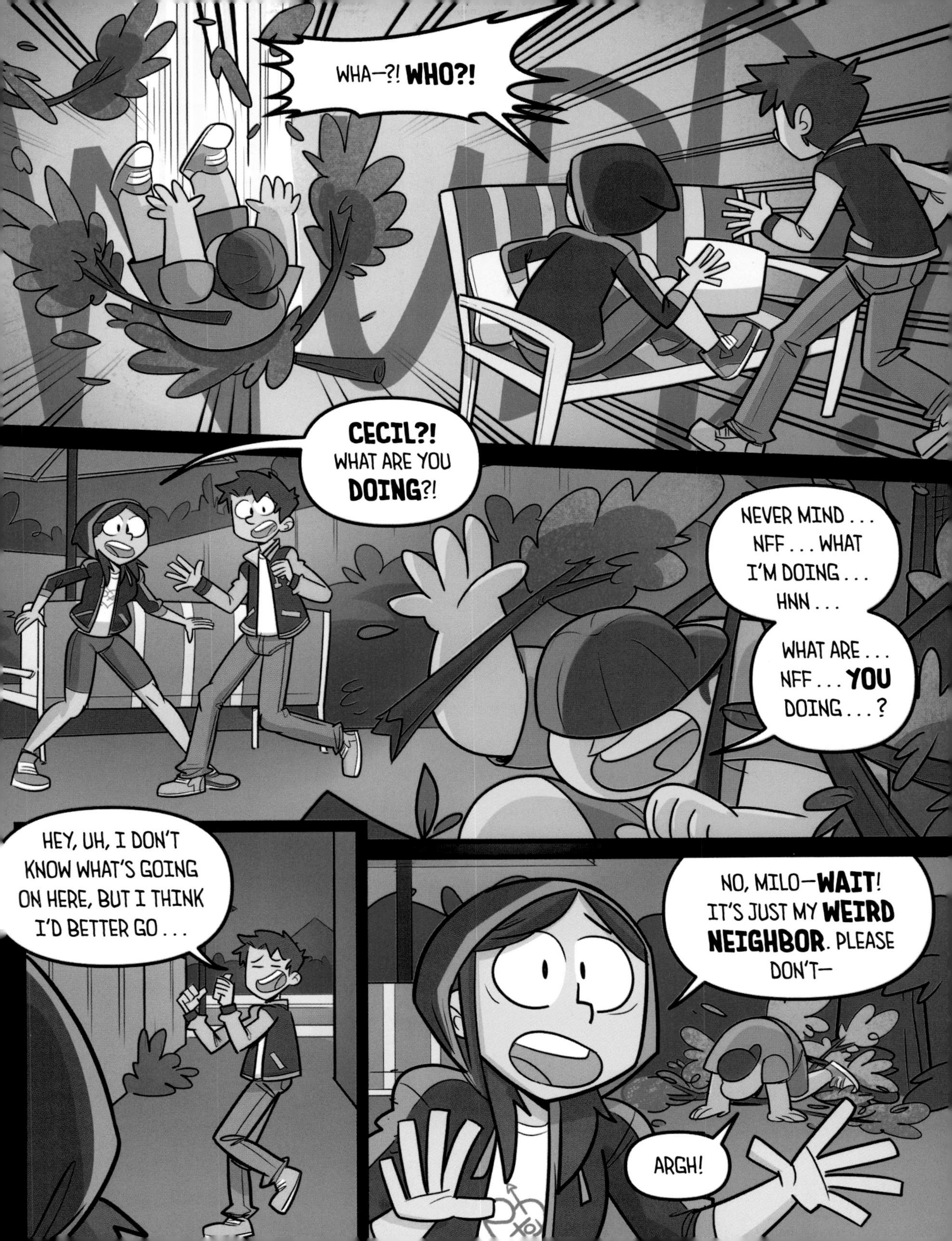
WHA–?! **WHO?!**
**CECIL?!** WHAT ARE YOU **DOING**?!
NEVER MIND . . . NFF . . . WHAT I'M DOING . . . HNN . . .
WHAT ARE . . . NFF . . . **YOU** DOING . . . ?
HEY, UH, I DON'T KNOW WHAT'S GOING ON HERE, BUT I THINK I'D BETTER GO . . .
NO, MILO—**WAIT**! IT'S JUST MY **WEIRD NEIGHBOR**. PLEASE DON'T—
ARGH!

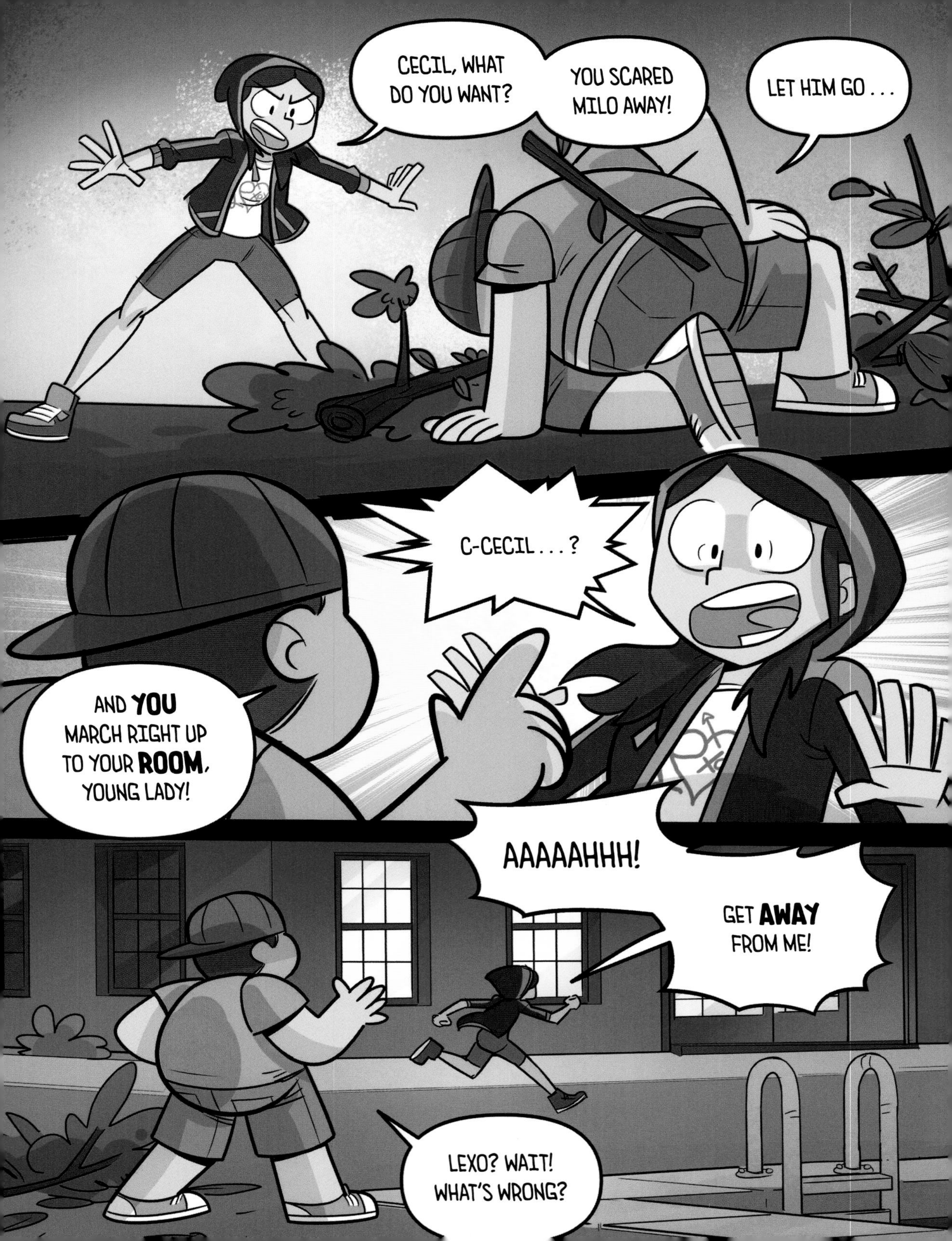
CECIL, WHAT DO YOU WANT?
YOU SCARED MILO AWAY!
LET HIM GO . . .
C-CECIL . . . ?
AND **YOU** MARCH RIGHT UP TO YOUR **ROOM**, YOUNG LADY!
AAAAAHHH!
GET **AWAY** FROM ME!
LEXO? WAIT! WHAT'S WRONG?

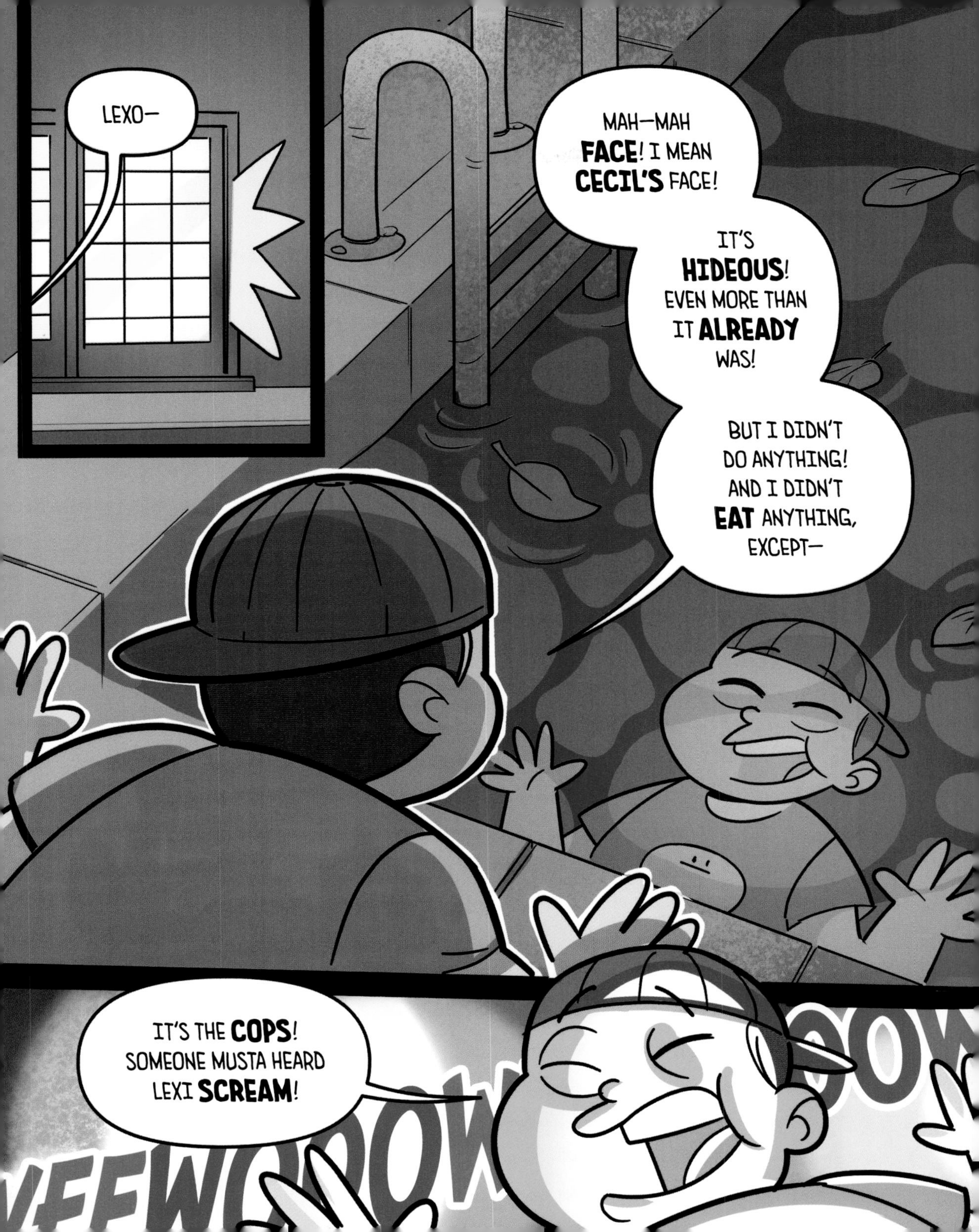
LEXO—
MAH—MAH FACE! I MEAN CECIL'S FACE!
IT'S HIDEOUS! EVEN MORE THAN IT ALREADY WAS!
BUT I DIDN'T DO ANYTHING! AND I DIDN'T EAT ANYTHING, EXCEPT—
IT'S THE COPS! SOMEONE MUSTA HEARD LEXI SCREAM!

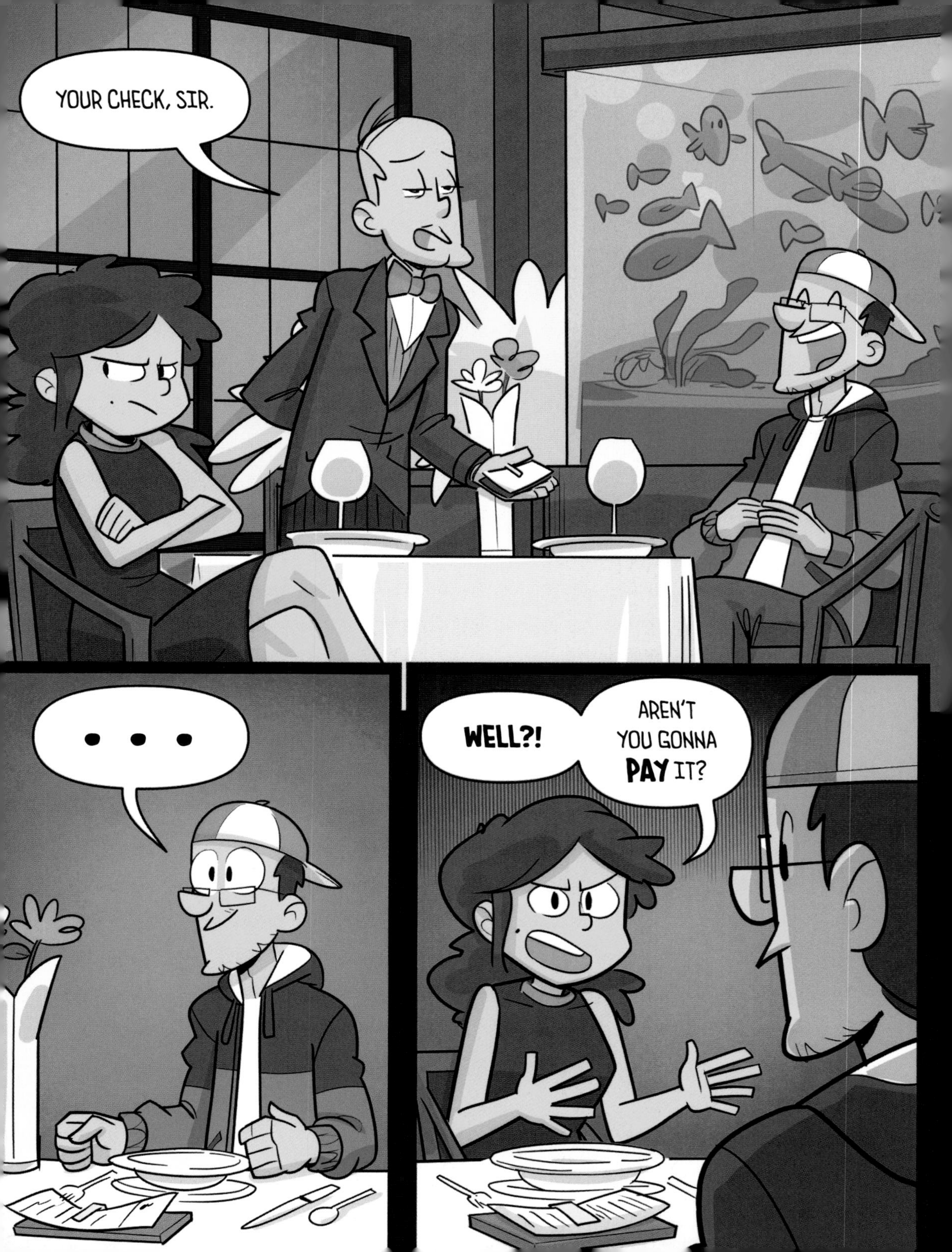
YOUR CHECK, SIR.
...
WELL?!
AREN'T YOU GONNA PAY IT?

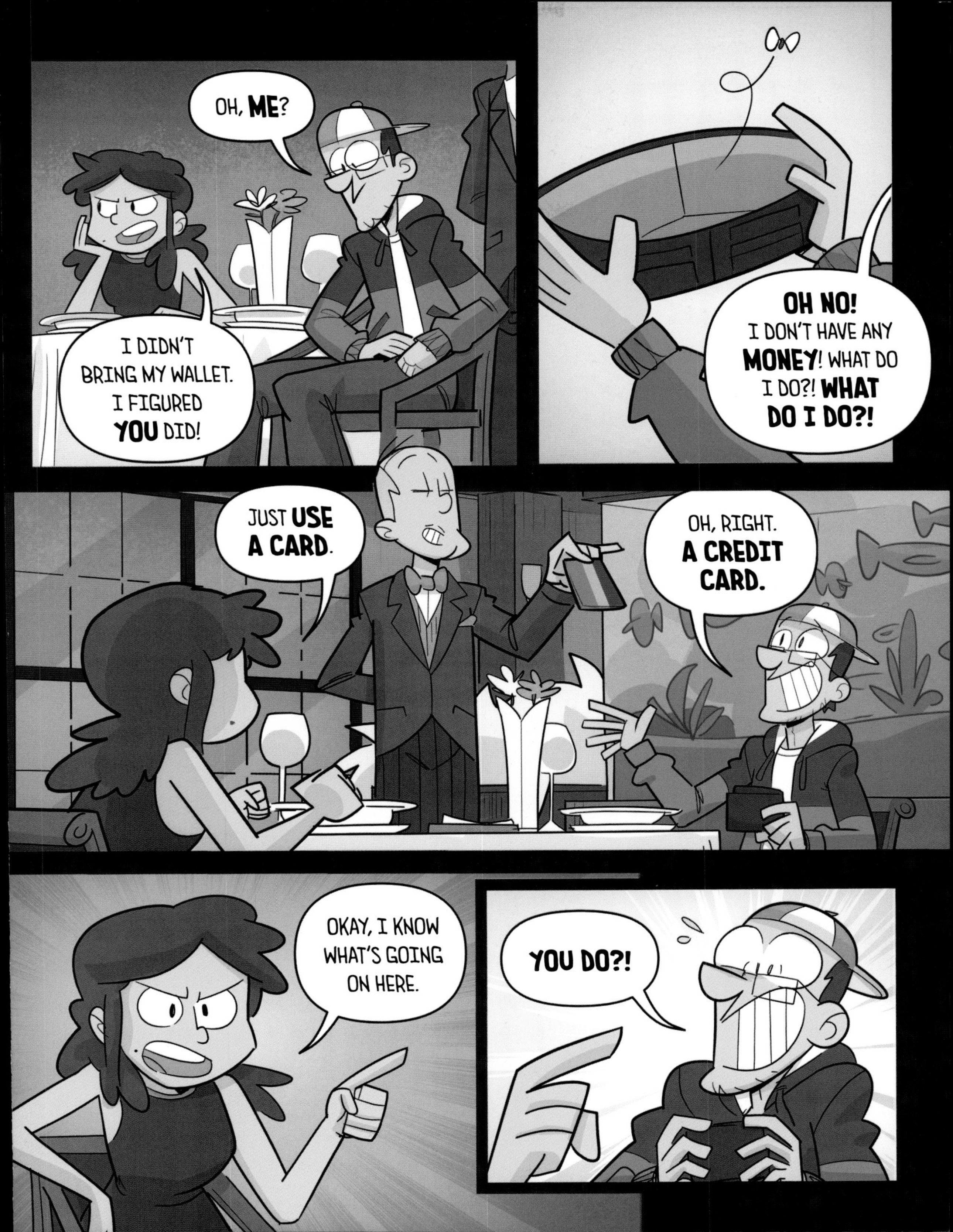
OH, ME?
I DIDN'T BRING MY WALLET. I FIGURED YOU DID!
OH NO! I DON'T HAVE ANY MONEY! WHAT DO I DO?! WHAT DO I DO?!
JUST USE A CARD.
OH, RIGHT. A CREDIT CARD.
OKAY, I KNOW WHAT'S GOING ON HERE.
YOU DO?!

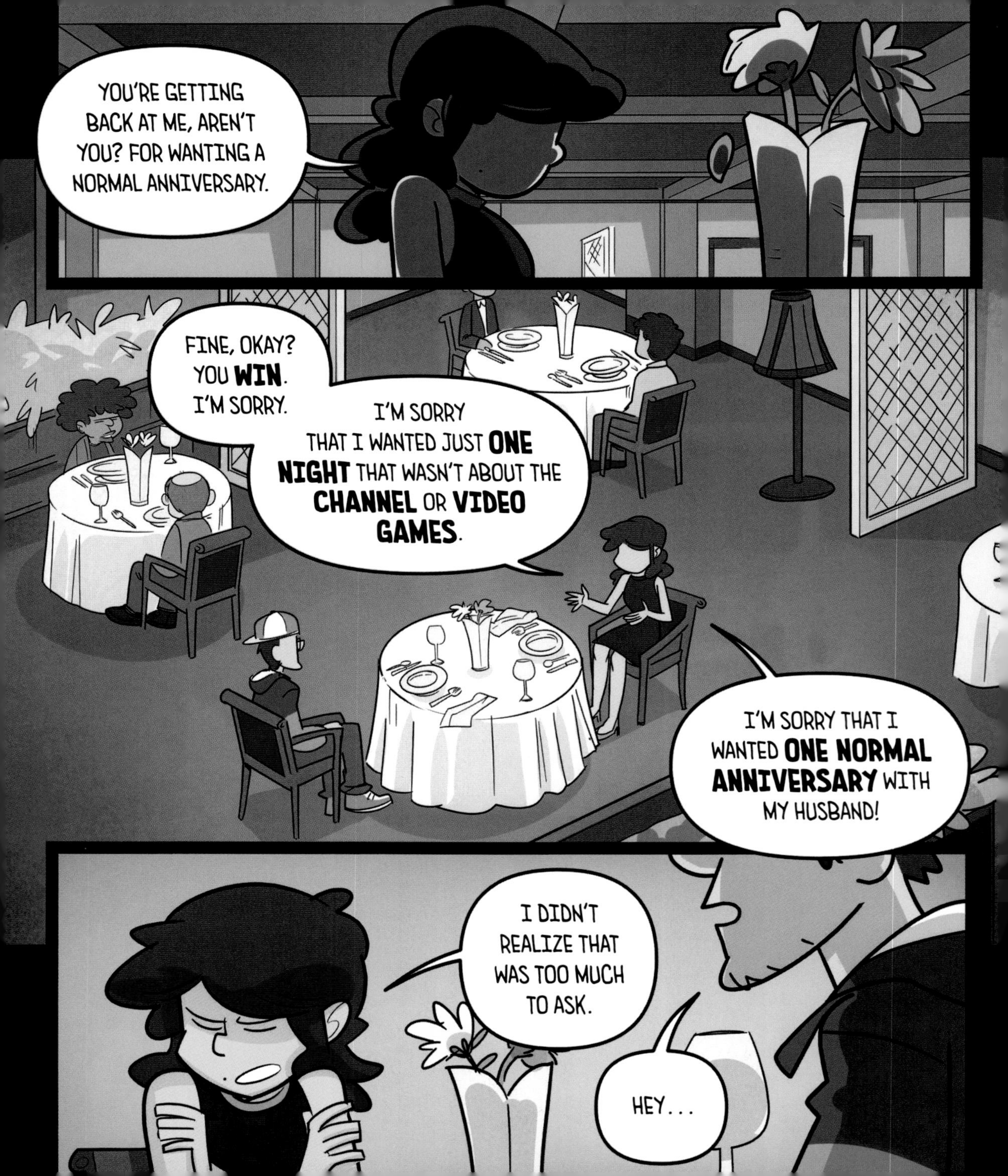

YOU'RE GETTING BACK AT ME, AREN'T YOU? FOR WANTING A NORMAL ANNIVERSARY.
FINE, OKAY? YOU **WIN**. I'M SORRY.
I'M SORRY THAT I WANTED JUST **ONE NIGHT** THAT WASN'T ABOUT THE **CHANNEL** OR **VIDEO GAMES**.
I'M SORRY THAT I WANTED **ONE NORMAL ANNIVERSARY** WITH MY HUSBAND!
I DIDN'T REALIZE THAT WAS TOO MUCH TO ASK.
HEY...

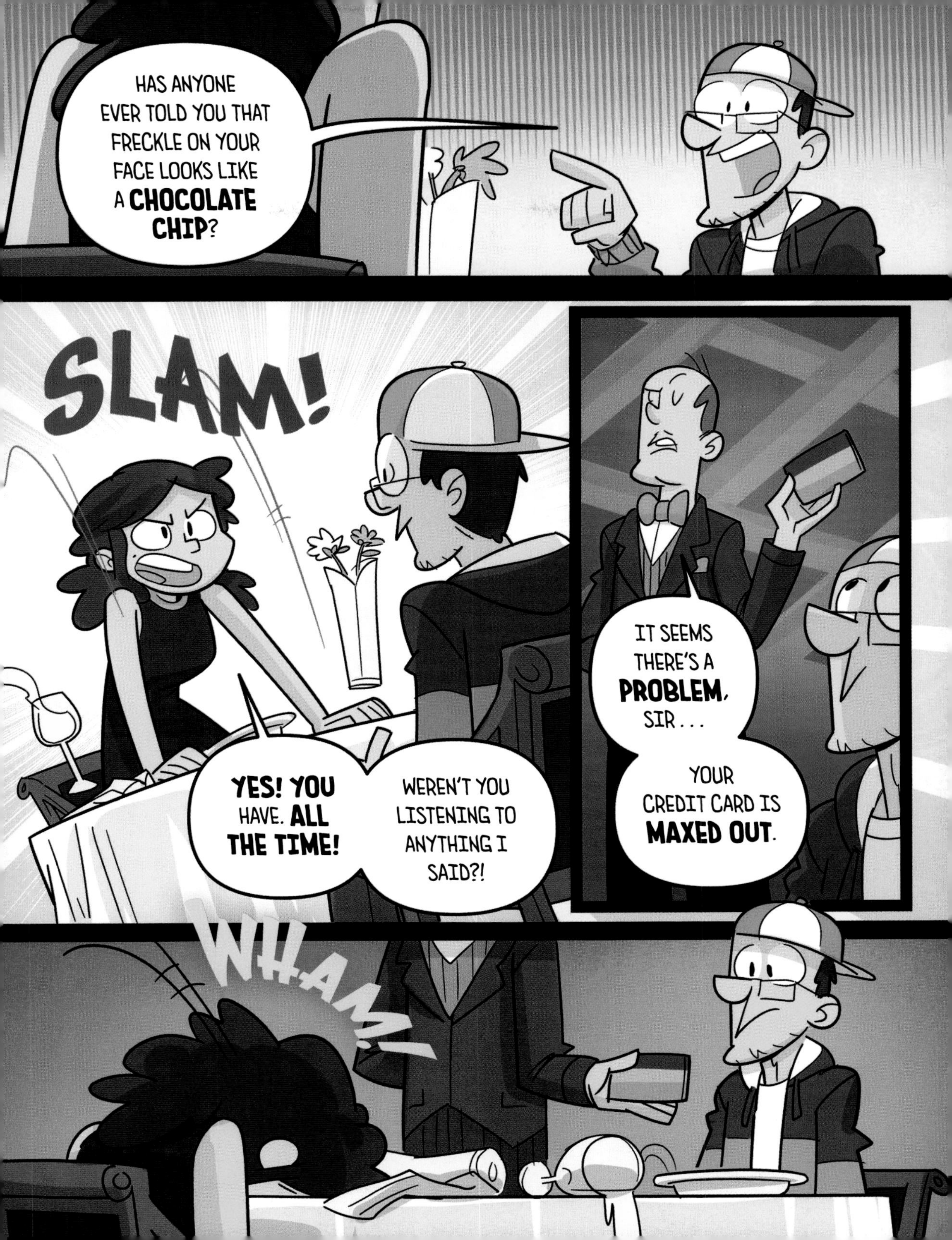
HAS ANYONE EVER TOLD YOU THAT FRECKLE ON YOUR FACE LOOKS LIKE A **CHOCOLATE CHIP**?
SLAM!
**YES! YOU** HAVE. **ALL THE TIME!**
WEREN'T YOU LISTENING TO ANYTHING I SAID?!
IT SEEMS THERE'S A **PROBLEM**, SIR . . .
YOUR CREDIT CARD IS **MAXED OUT**.
WHAM!

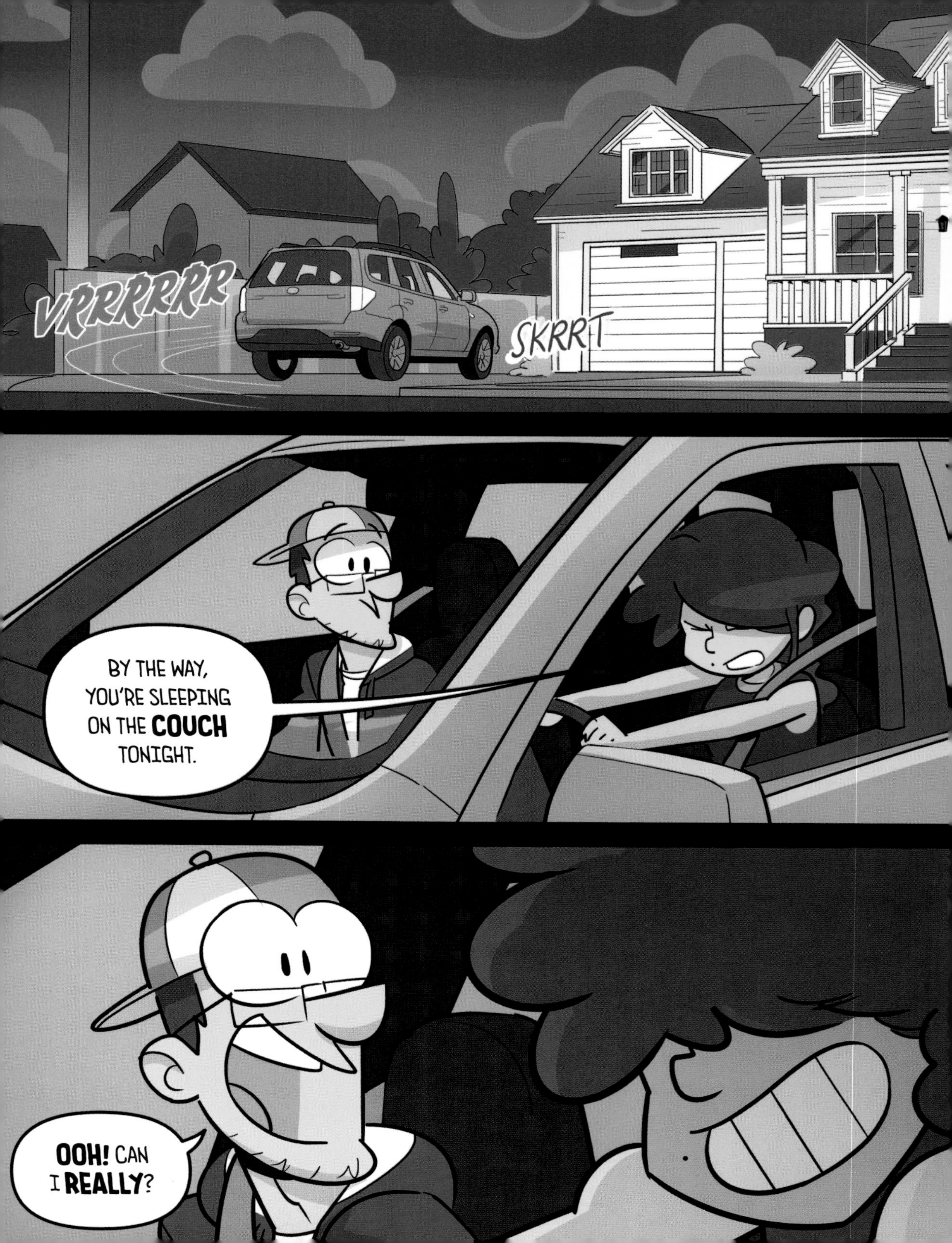
VRRRRRR
SKRRT
BY THE WAY, YOU'RE SLEEPING ON THE COUCH TONIGHT.
OOH! CAN I REALLY?

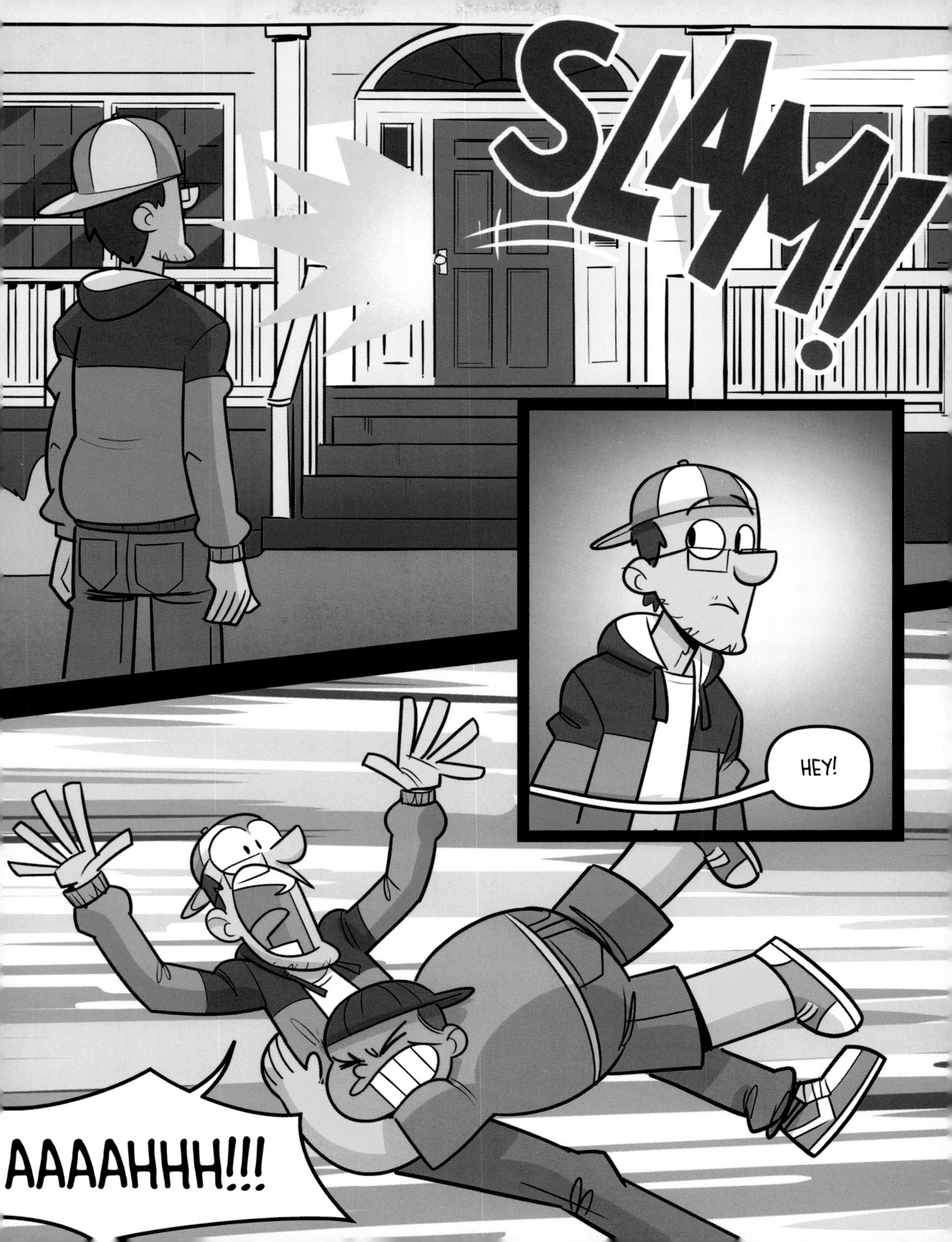
SLAM!
HEY!
AAAAHHH!!!

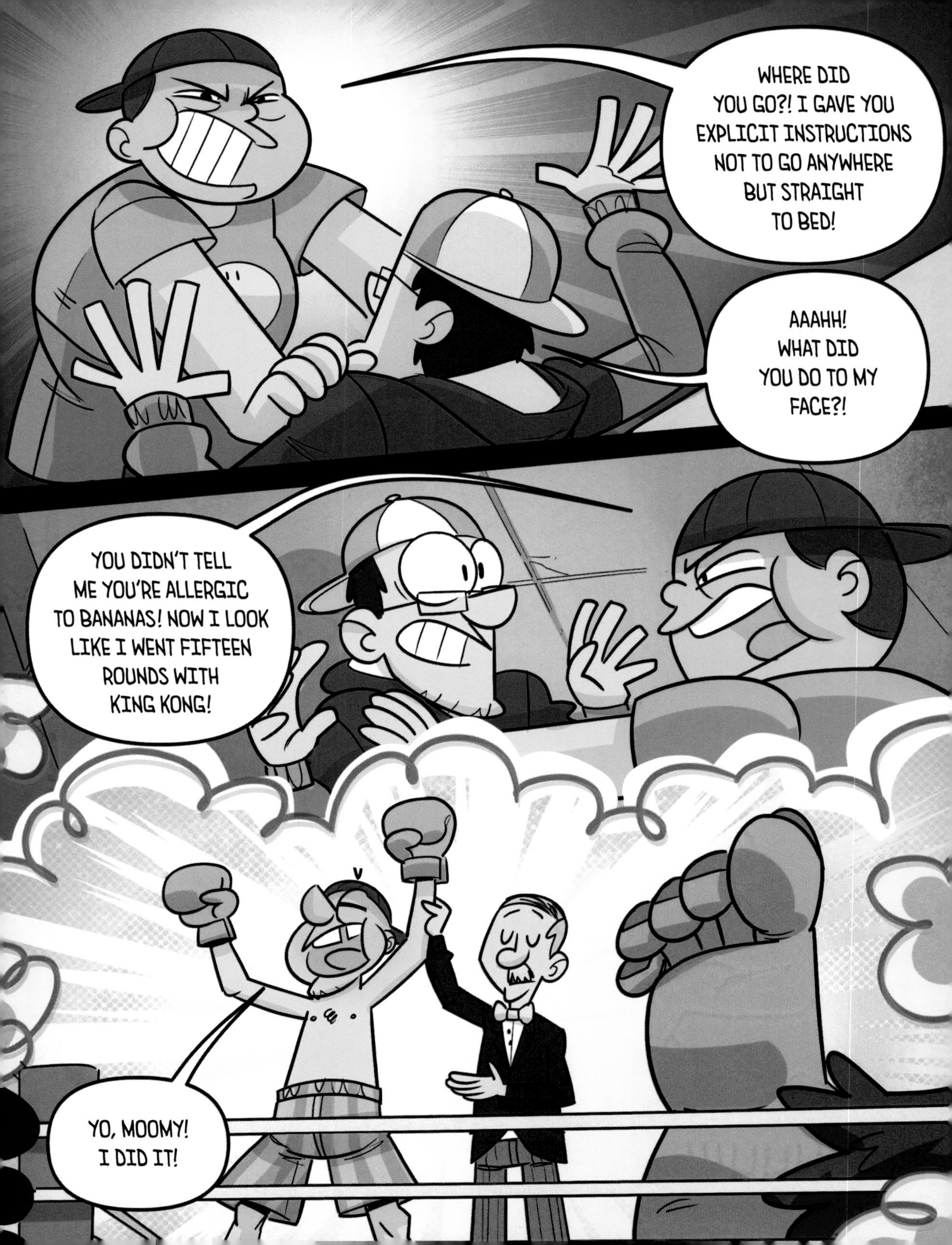
WHERE DID YOU GO?! I GAVE YOU EXPLICIT INSTRUCTIONS NOT TO GO ANYWHERE BUT STRAIGHT TO BED!
AAAHH! WHAT DID YOU DO TO MY FACE?!
YOU DIDN'T TELL ME YOU'RE ALLERGIC TO BANANAS! NOW I LOOK LIKE I WENT FIFTEEN ROUNDS WITH KING KONG!
YO, MOOMY! I DID IT!

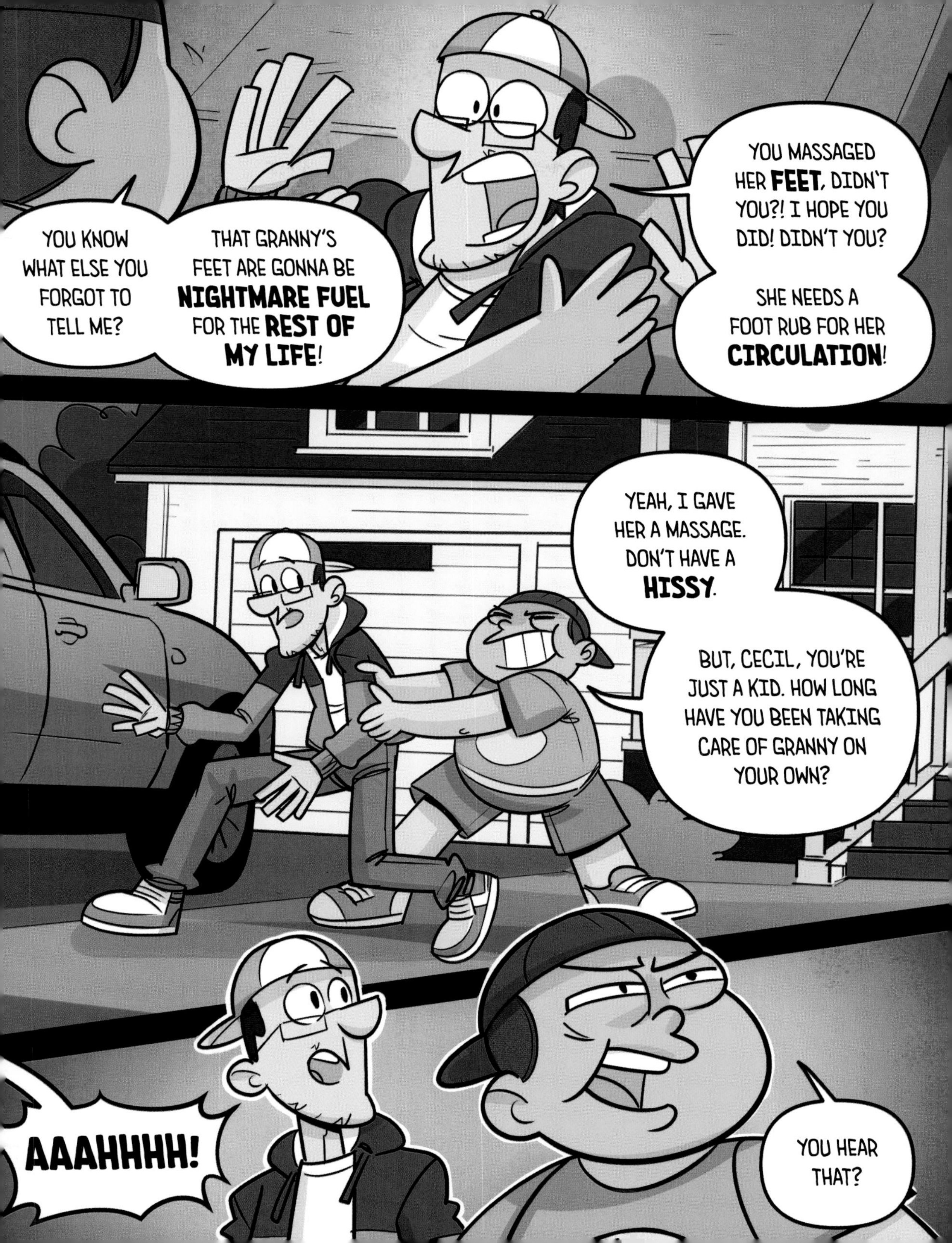
YOU KNOW WHAT ELSE YOU FORGOT TO TELL ME?
THAT GRANNY'S FEET ARE GONNA BE **NIGHTMARE FUEL** FOR THE **REST OF MY LIFE**!
YOU MASSAGED HER **FEET**, DIDN'T YOU?! I HOPE YOU DID! DIDN'T YOU?
SHE NEEDS A FOOT RUB FOR HER **CIRCULATION**!
YEAH, I GAVE HER A MASSAGE. DON'T HAVE A **HISSY**.
BUT, CECIL, YOU'RE JUST A KID. HOW LONG HAVE YOU BEEN TAKING CARE OF GRANNY ON YOUR OWN?
AAAHHHH!
YOU HEAR THAT?

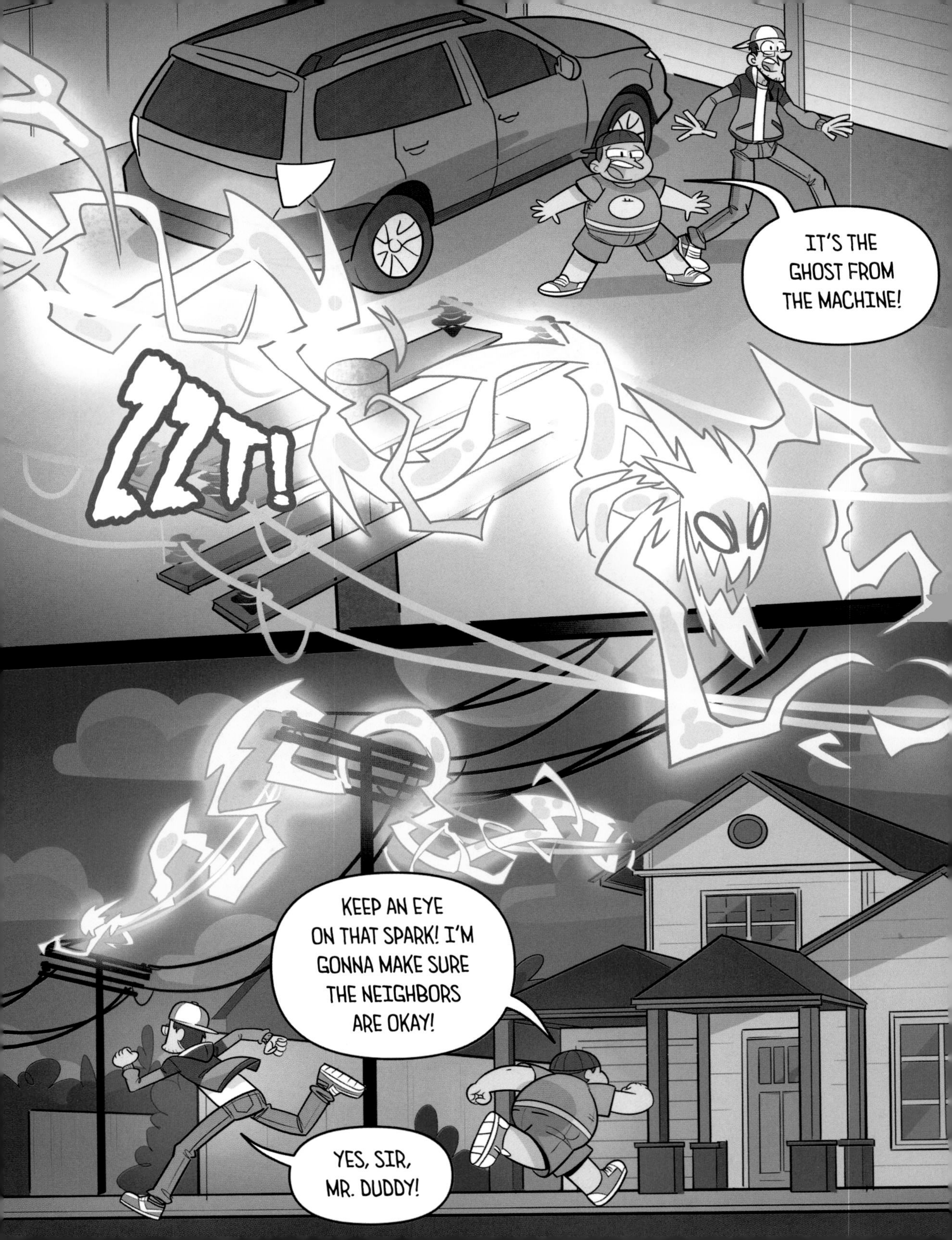
IT'S THE GHOST FROM THE MACHINE!
ZZT!
KEEP AN EYE ON THAT SPARK! I'M GONNA MAKE SURE THE NEIGHBORS ARE OKAY!
YES, SIR, MR. DUDDY!

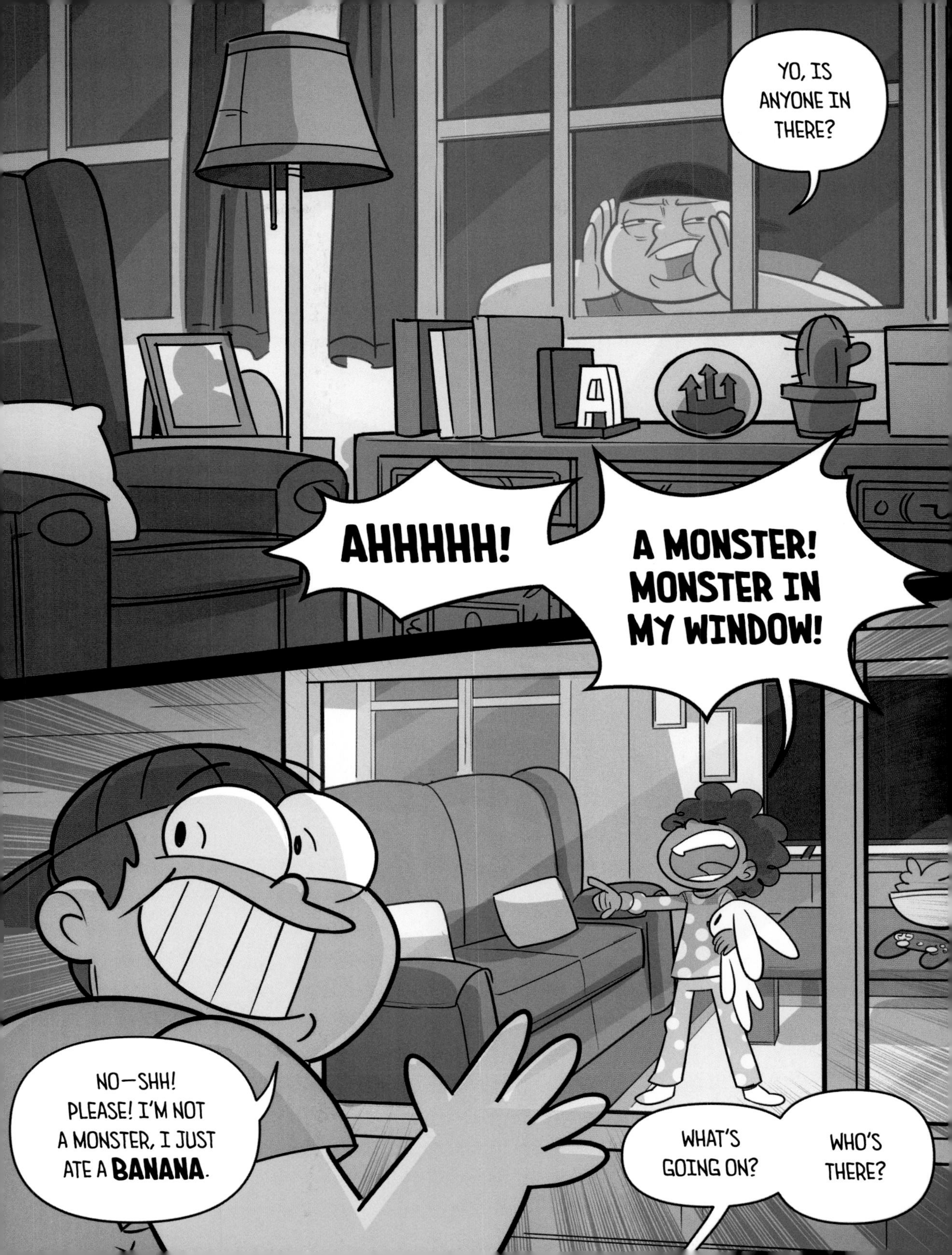
YO, IS ANYONE IN THERE?
AHHHHH!
A MONSTER! MONSTER IN MY WINDOW!
NO—SHH! PLEASE! I'M NOT A MONSTER, I JUST ATE A **BANANA**.
WHAT'S GOING ON?
WHO'S THERE?

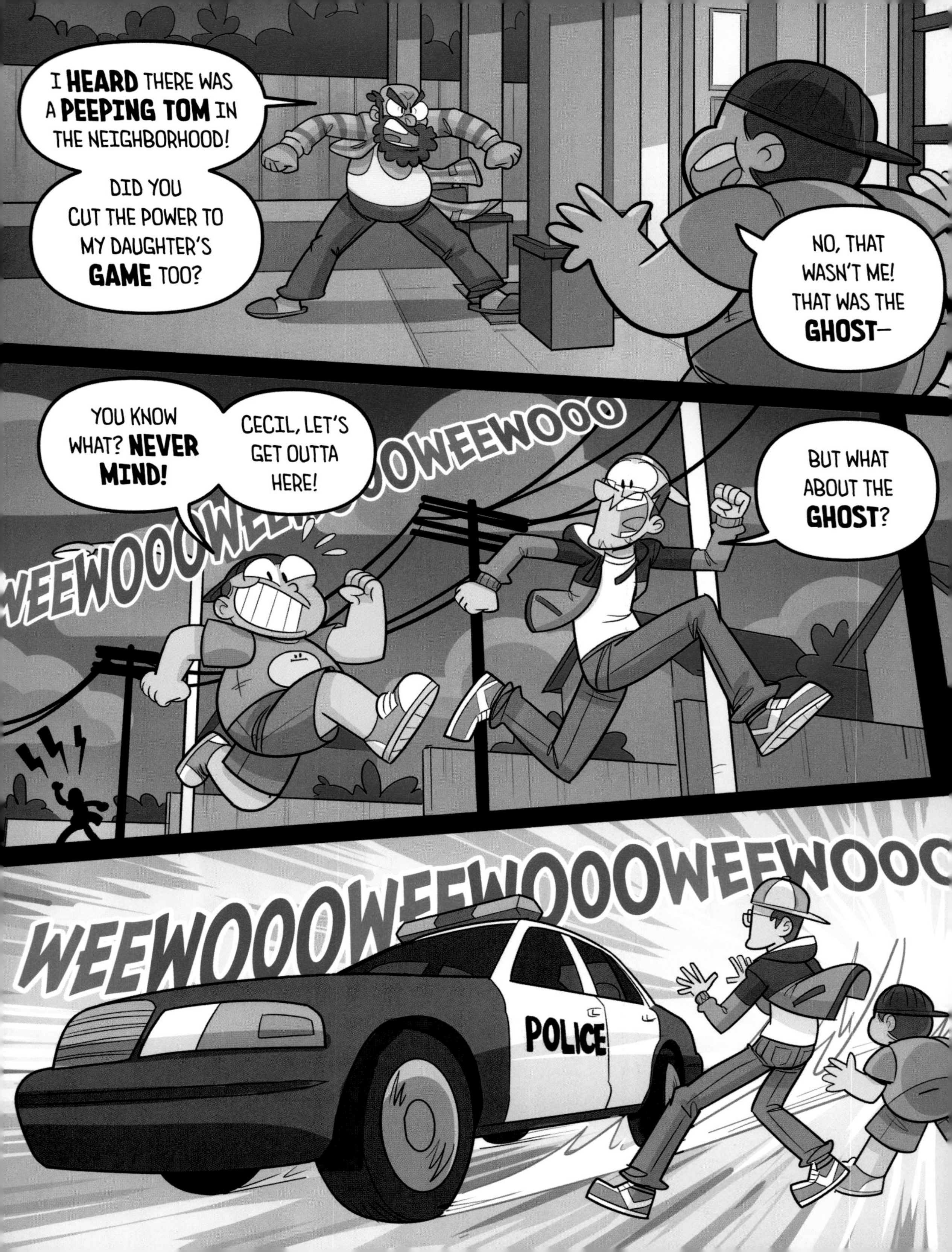
I **HEARD** THERE WAS A **PEEPING TOM** IN THE NEIGHBORHOOD!
DID YOU CUT THE POWER TO MY DAUGHTER'S **GAME** TOO?
NO, THAT WASN'T ME! THAT WAS THE **GHOST**—
YOU KNOW WHAT? **NEVER MIND!**
CECIL, LET'S GET OUTTA HERE!
BUT WHAT ABOUT THE **GHOST**?
WEEWOOOWEEWOOOWEEWOOO
WEEWOOOWEEWOOOWEEWOOO
POLICE

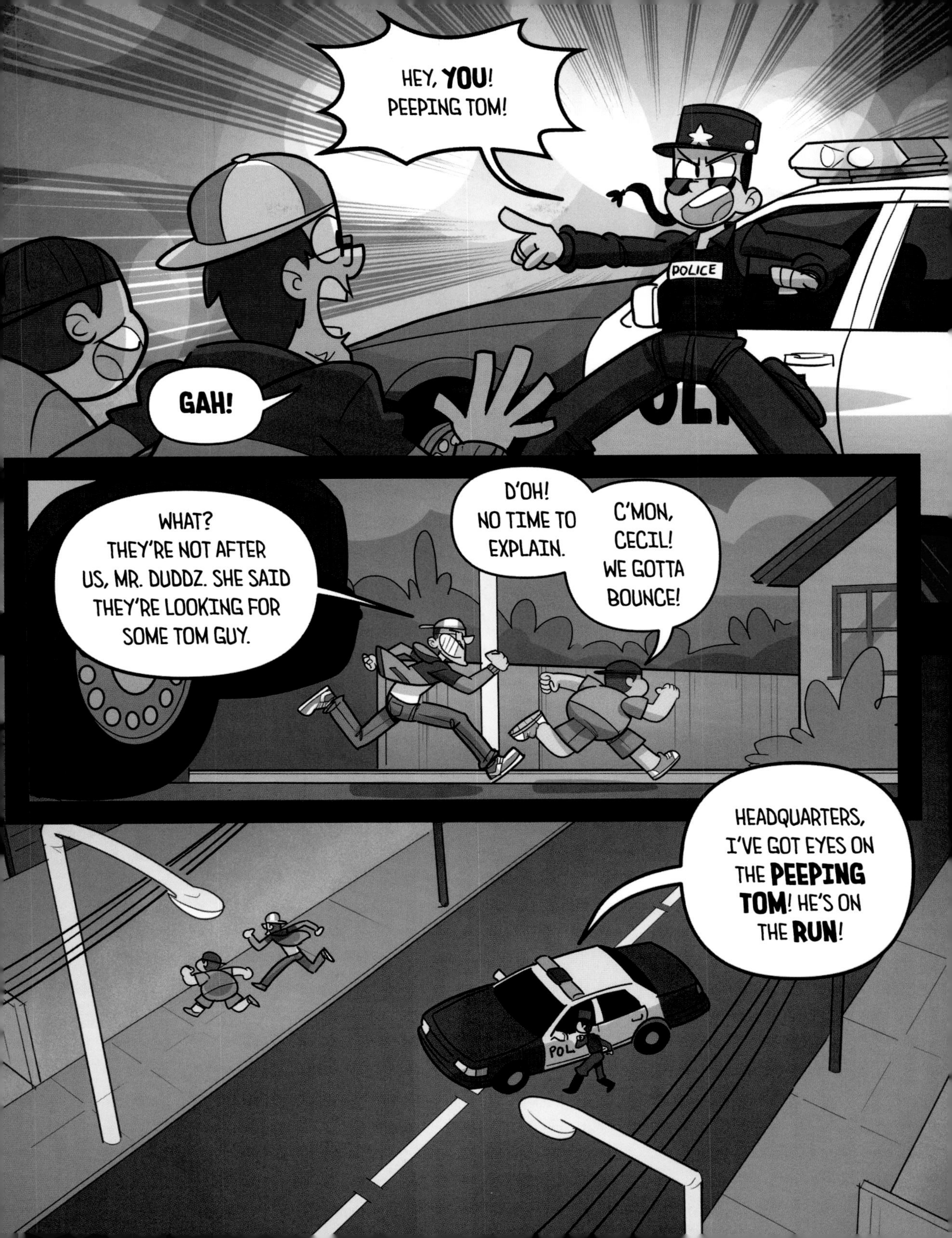
HEY, **YOU**! PEEPING TOM!
GAH!
WHAT? THEY'RE NOT AFTER US, MR. DUDDZ. SHE SAID THEY'RE LOOKING FOR SOME TOM GUY.
D'OH! NO TIME TO EXPLAIN.
C'MON, CECIL! WE GOTTA BOUNCE!
HEADQUARTERS, I'VE GOT EYES ON THE **PEEPING TOM**! HE'S ON THE **RUN**!

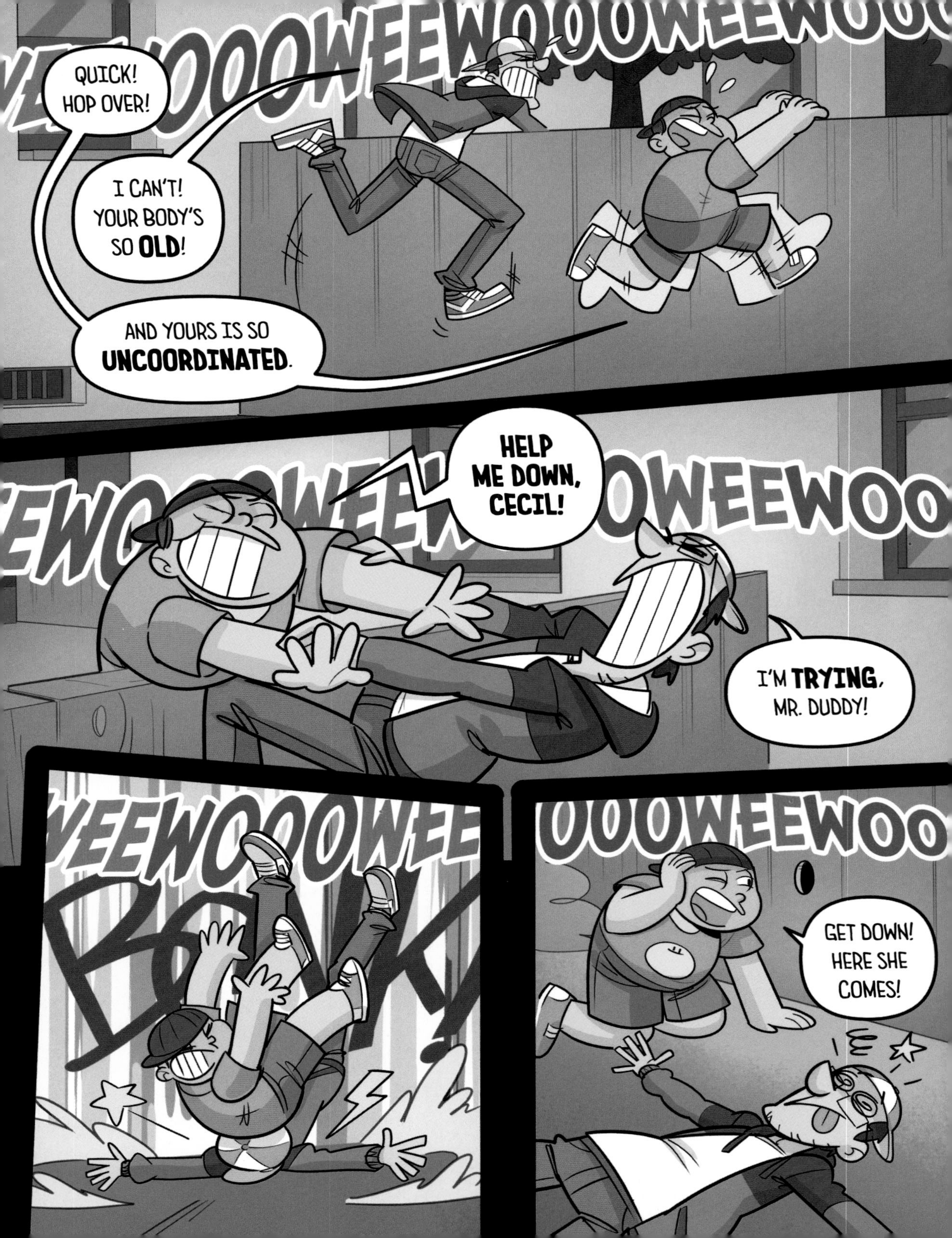
QUICK! HOP OVER!
I CAN'T! YOUR BODY'S SO **OLD**!
AND YOURS IS SO **UNCOORDINATED**.
HELP ME DOWN, CECIL!
I'M **TRYING**, MR. DUDDY!
GET DOWN! HERE SHE COMES!

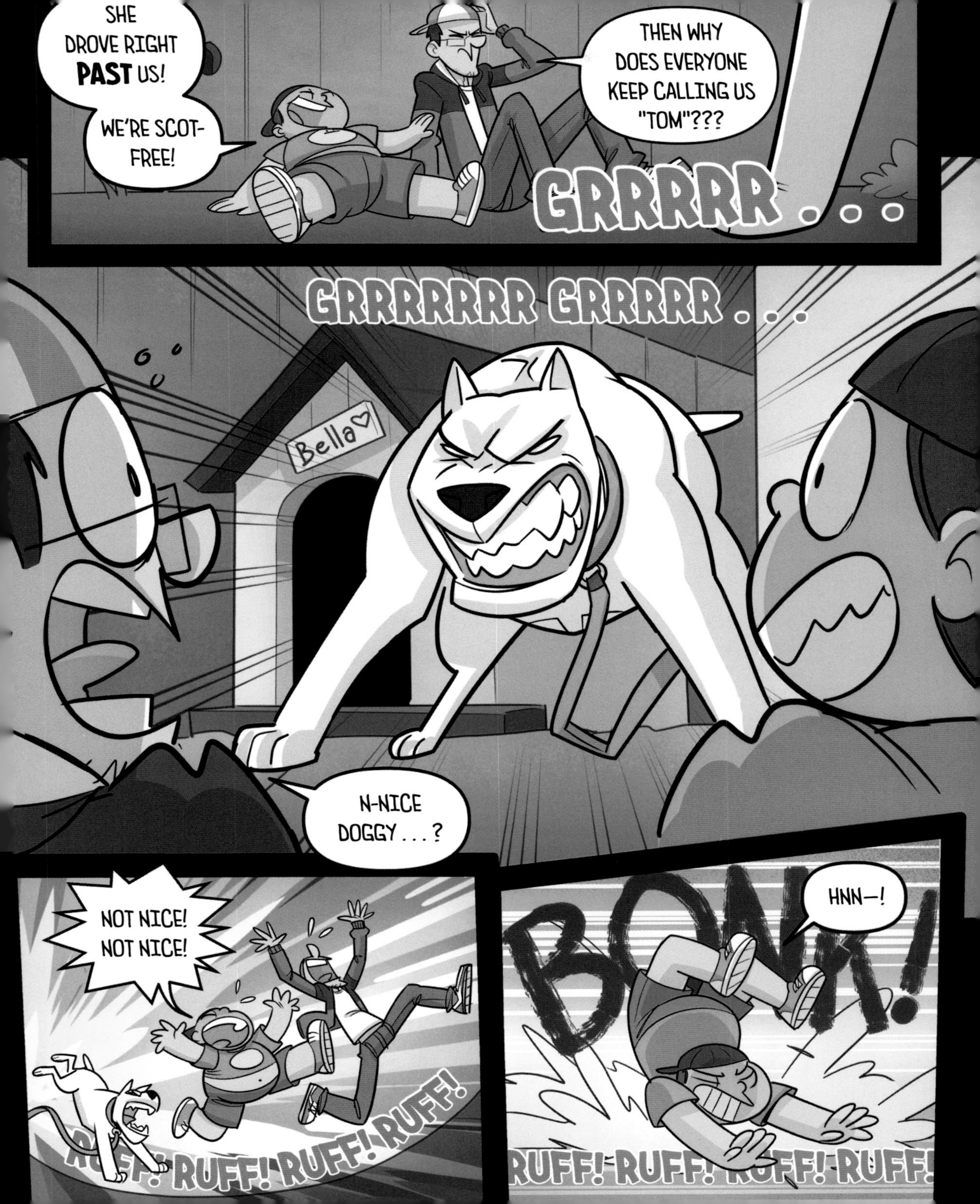
SHE DROVE RIGHT **PAST** US!
WE'RE SCOT-FREE!
THEN WHY DOES EVERYONE KEEP CALLING US "TOM"???
GRRRRR . . .
GRRRRRRR GRRRRR . . .
Bella
N-NICE DOGGY . . . ?
NOT NICE! NOT NICE!
RUFF! RUFF! RUFF! RUFF!
BONK!
HNN—!
RUFF! RUFF! RUFF! RUFF!

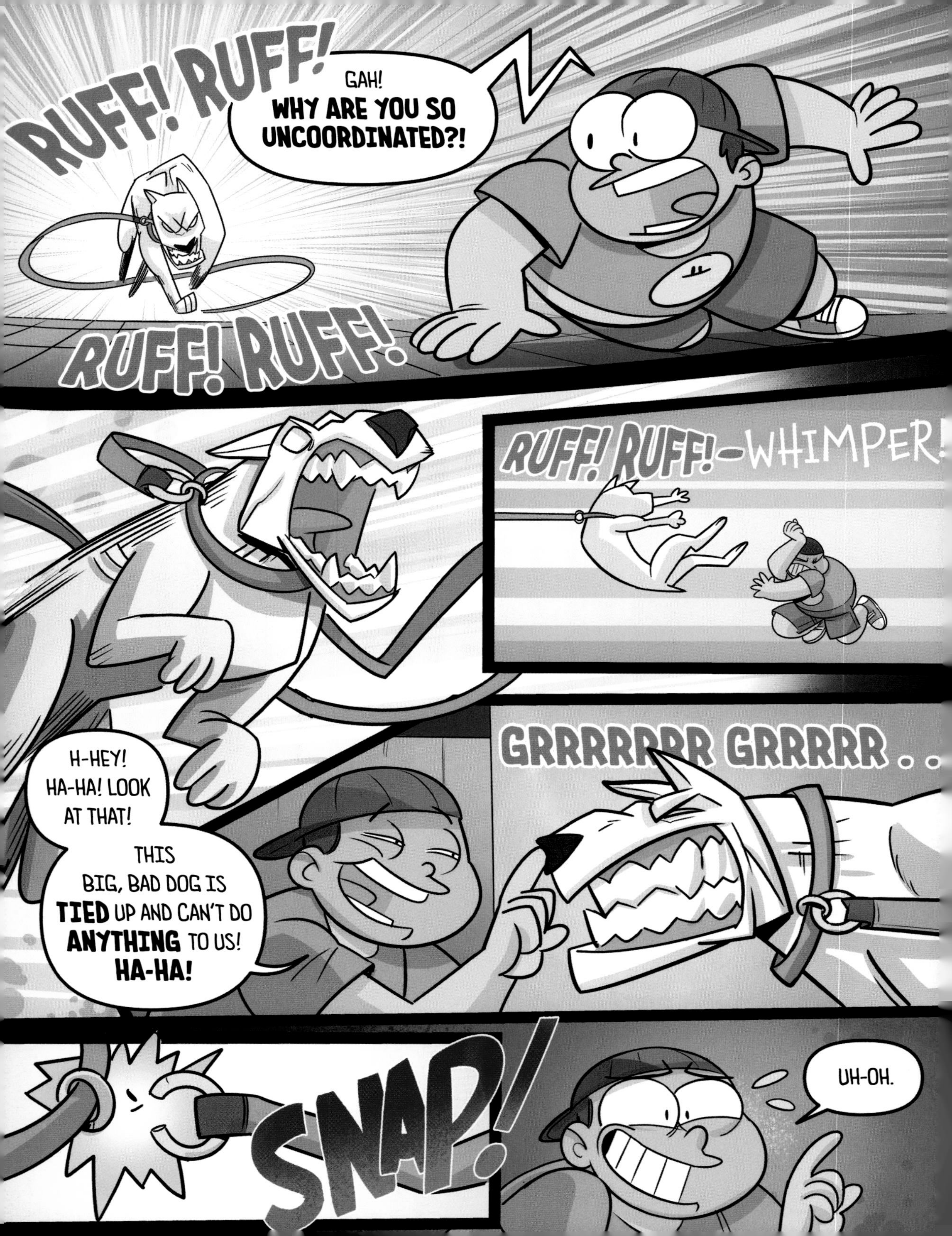
RUFF! RUFF!
GAH! WHY ARE YOU SO UNCOORDINATED?!
RUFF! RUFF!
RUFF! RUFF!-WHIMPER!
GRRRRRRR GRRRRRR . . .
H-HEY! HA-HA! LOOK AT THAT!
THIS BIG, BAD DOG IS TIED UP AND CAN'T DO ANYTHING TO US! HA-HA!
SNAP!
UH-OH.

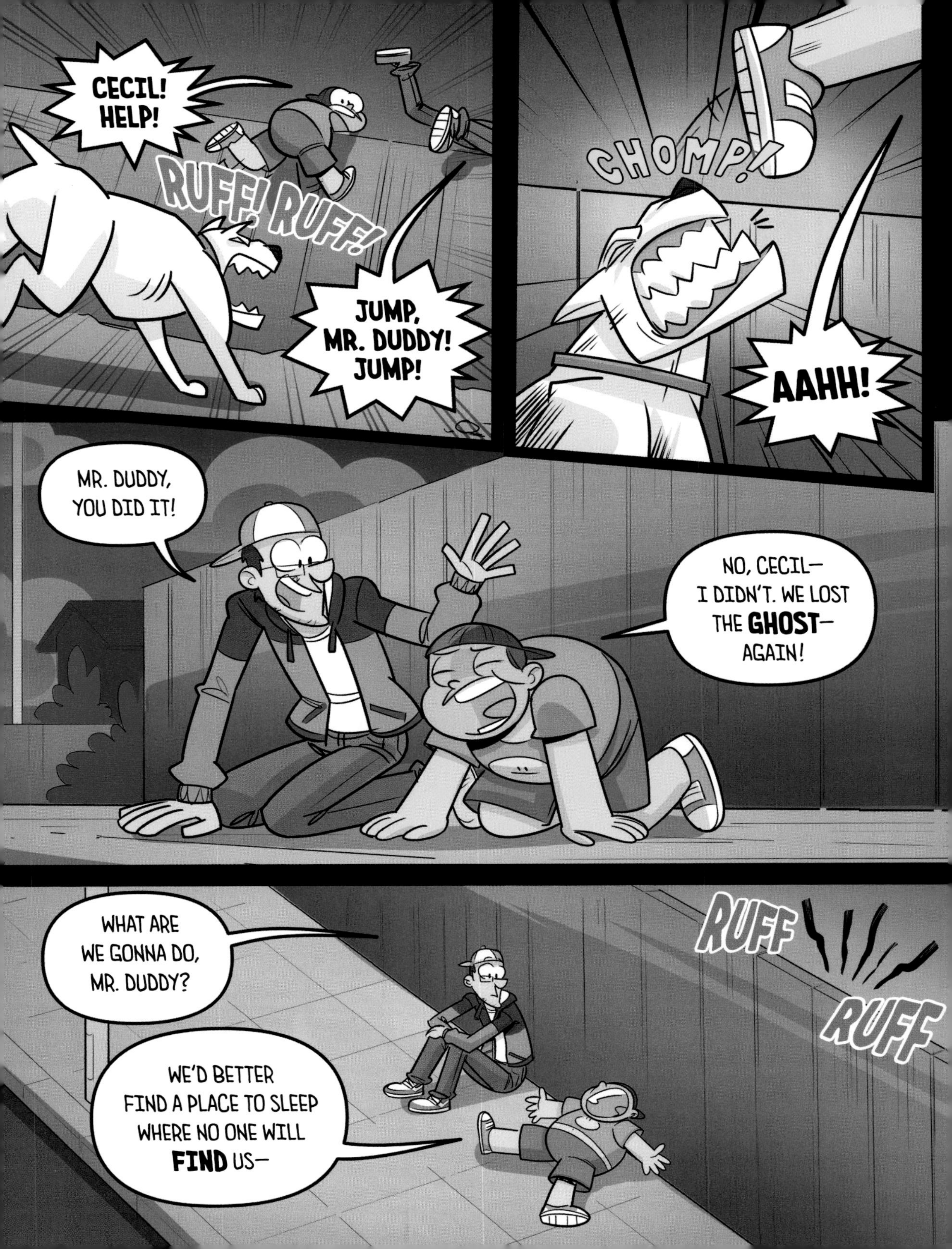
CECIL! HELP!
RUFF! RUFF!
JUMP, MR. DUDDY! JUMP!
CHOMP!
AAHH!
MR. DUDDY, YOU DID IT!
NO, CECIL— I DIDN'T. WE LOST THE **GHOST**— AGAIN!
WHAT ARE WE GONNA DO, MR. DUDDY?
WE'D BETTER FIND A PLACE TO SLEEP WHERE NO ONE WILL **FIND** US—
RUFF
RUFF

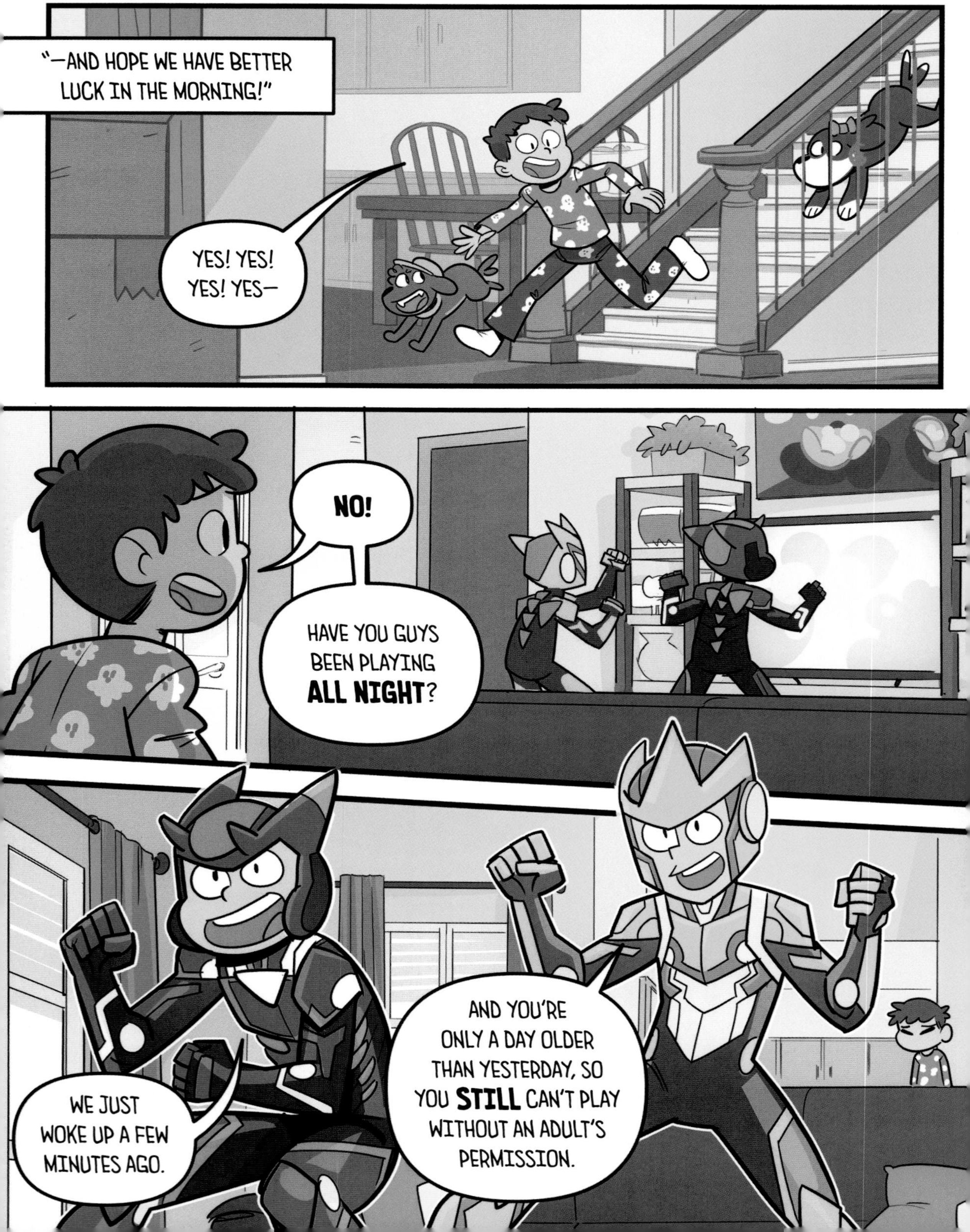
"—AND HOPE WE HAVE BETTER LUCK IN THE MORNING!"
YES! YES! YES! YES—
NO!
HAVE YOU GUYS BEEN PLAYING **ALL NIGHT**?
WE JUST WOKE UP A FEW MINUTES AGO.
AND YOU'RE ONLY A DAY OLDER THAN YESTERDAY, SO YOU **STILL** CAN'T PLAY WITHOUT AN ADULT'S PERMISSION.

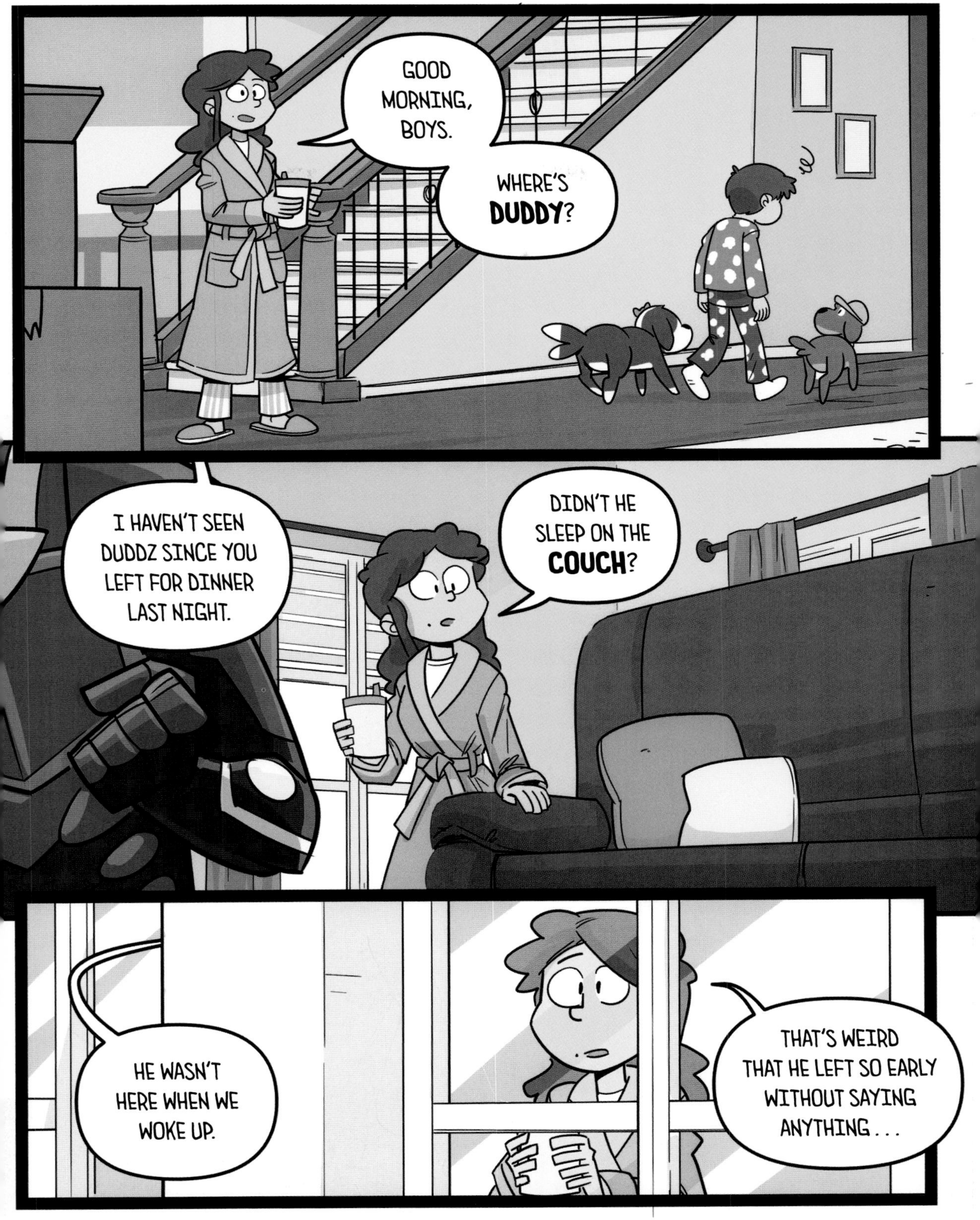
GOOD MORNING, BOYS.
WHERE'S **DUDDY**?
I HAVEN'T SEEN DUDDZ SINCE YOU LEFT FOR DINNER LAST NIGHT.
DIDN'T HE SLEEP ON THE **COUCH**?
HE WASN'T HERE WHEN WE WOKE UP.
THAT'S WEIRD THAT HE LEFT SO EARLY WITHOUT SAYING ANYTHING . . .

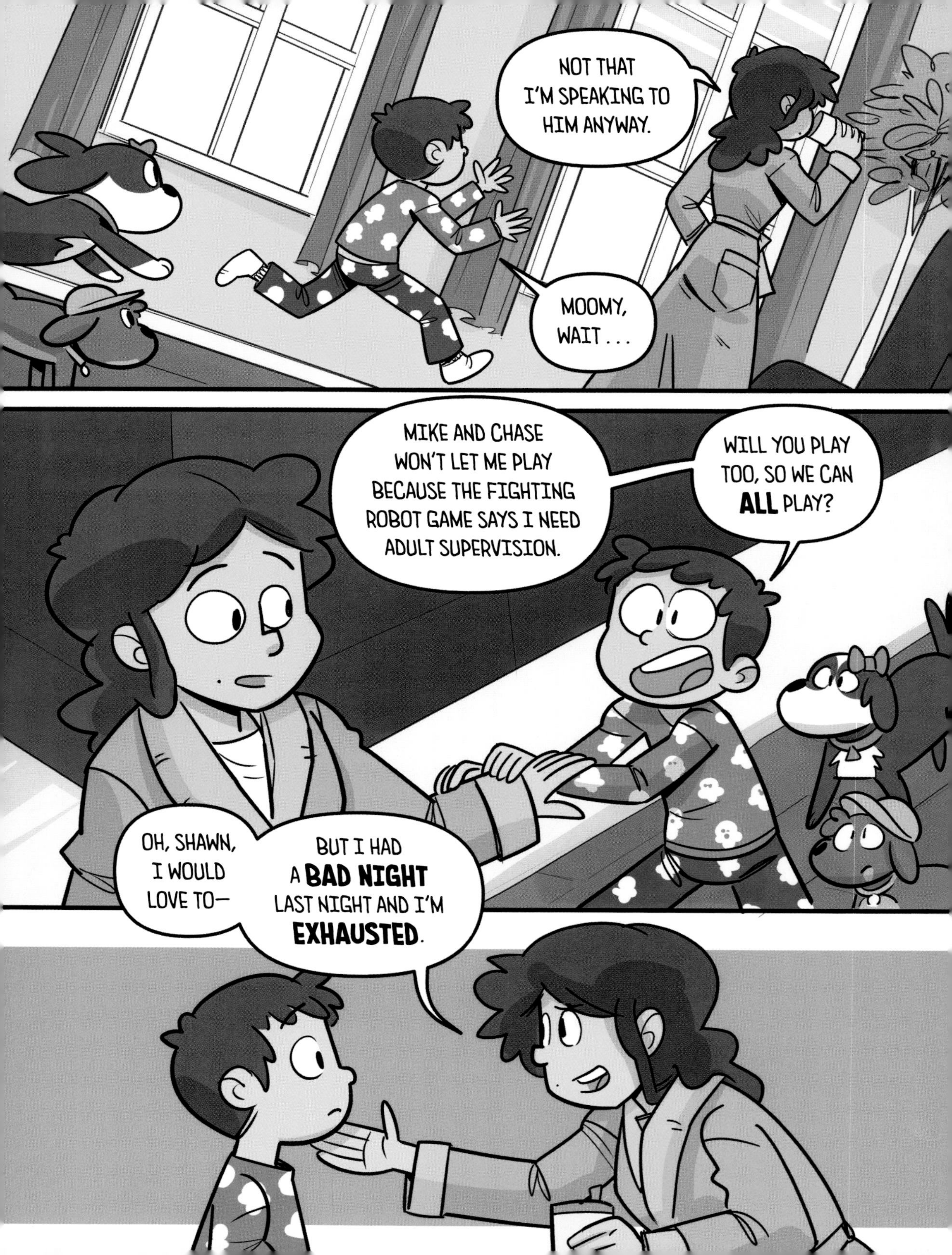
NOT THAT I'M SPEAKING TO HIM ANYWAY.
MOOMY, WAIT . . .
MIKE AND CHASE WON'T LET ME PLAY BECAUSE THE FIGHTING ROBOT GAME SAYS I NEED ADULT SUPERVISION.
WILL YOU PLAY TOO, SO WE CAN **ALL** PLAY?
OH, SHAWN, I WOULD LOVE TO—
BUT I HAD A **BAD NIGHT** LAST NIGHT AND I'M **EXHAUSTED**.

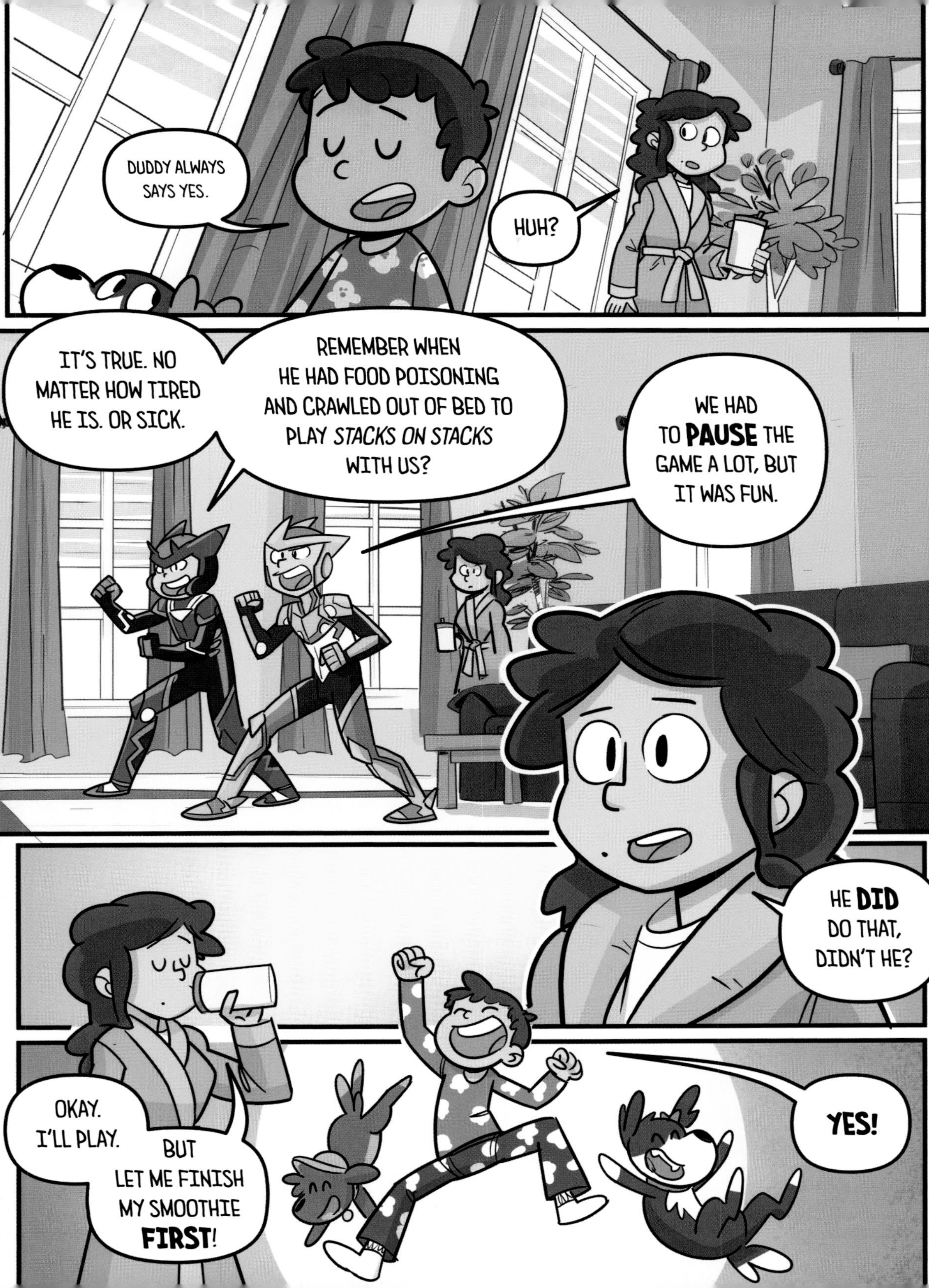
DUDDY ALWAYS SAYS YES.
HUH?
IT'S TRUE. NO MATTER HOW TIRED HE IS. OR SICK.
REMEMBER WHEN HE HAD FOOD POISONING AND CRAWLED OUT OF BED TO PLAY *STACKS ON STACKS* WITH US?
WE HAD TO **PAUSE** THE GAME A LOT, BUT IT WAS FUN.
HE **DID** DO THAT, DIDN'T HE?
OKAY. I'LL PLAY.
BUT LET ME FINISH MY SMOOTHIE **FIRST**!
YES!

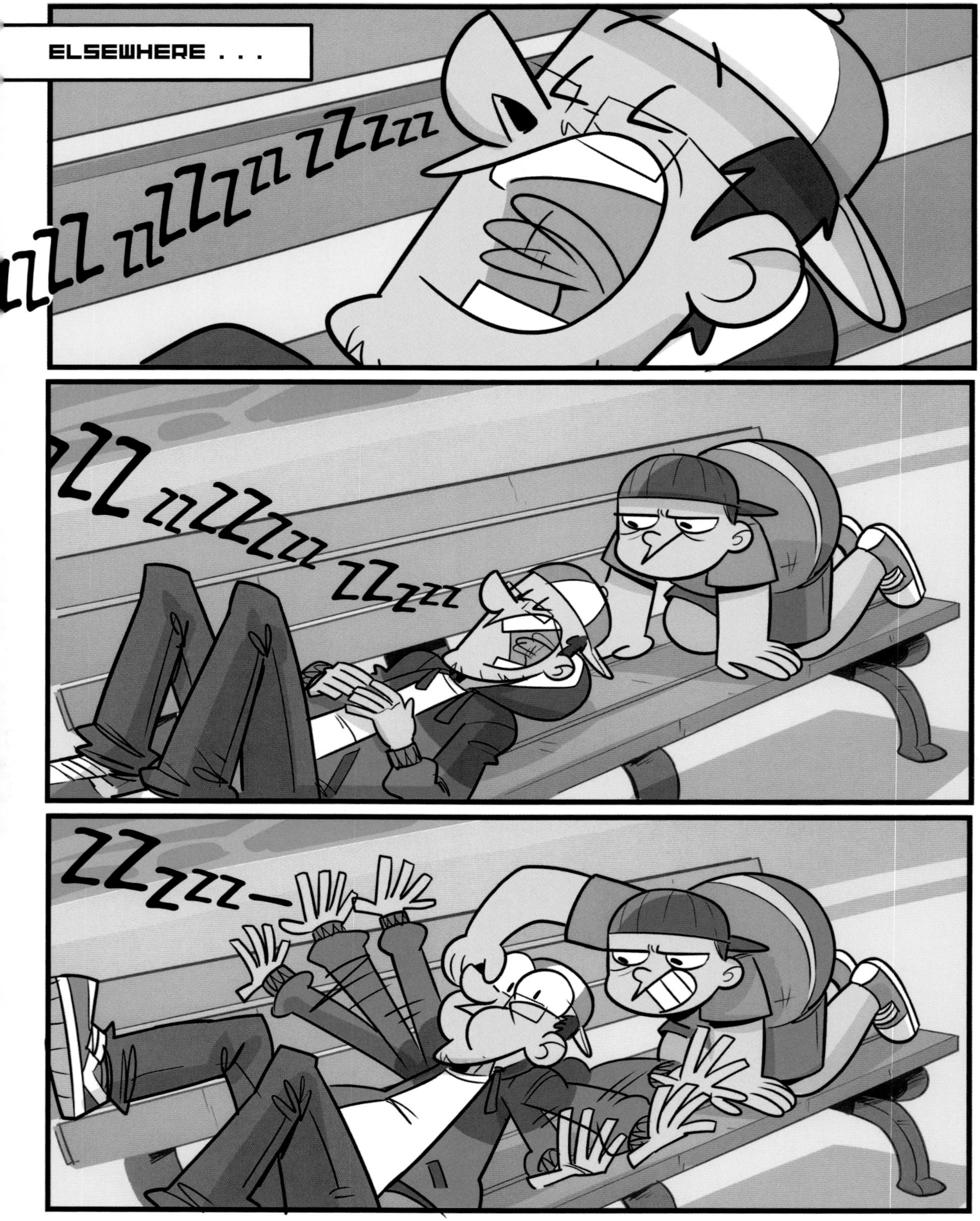
ELSEWHERE . . .
ZZZ zzZZzzz ZZzzz
ZZ zzZZZzz ZZzzz
ZZzzz—

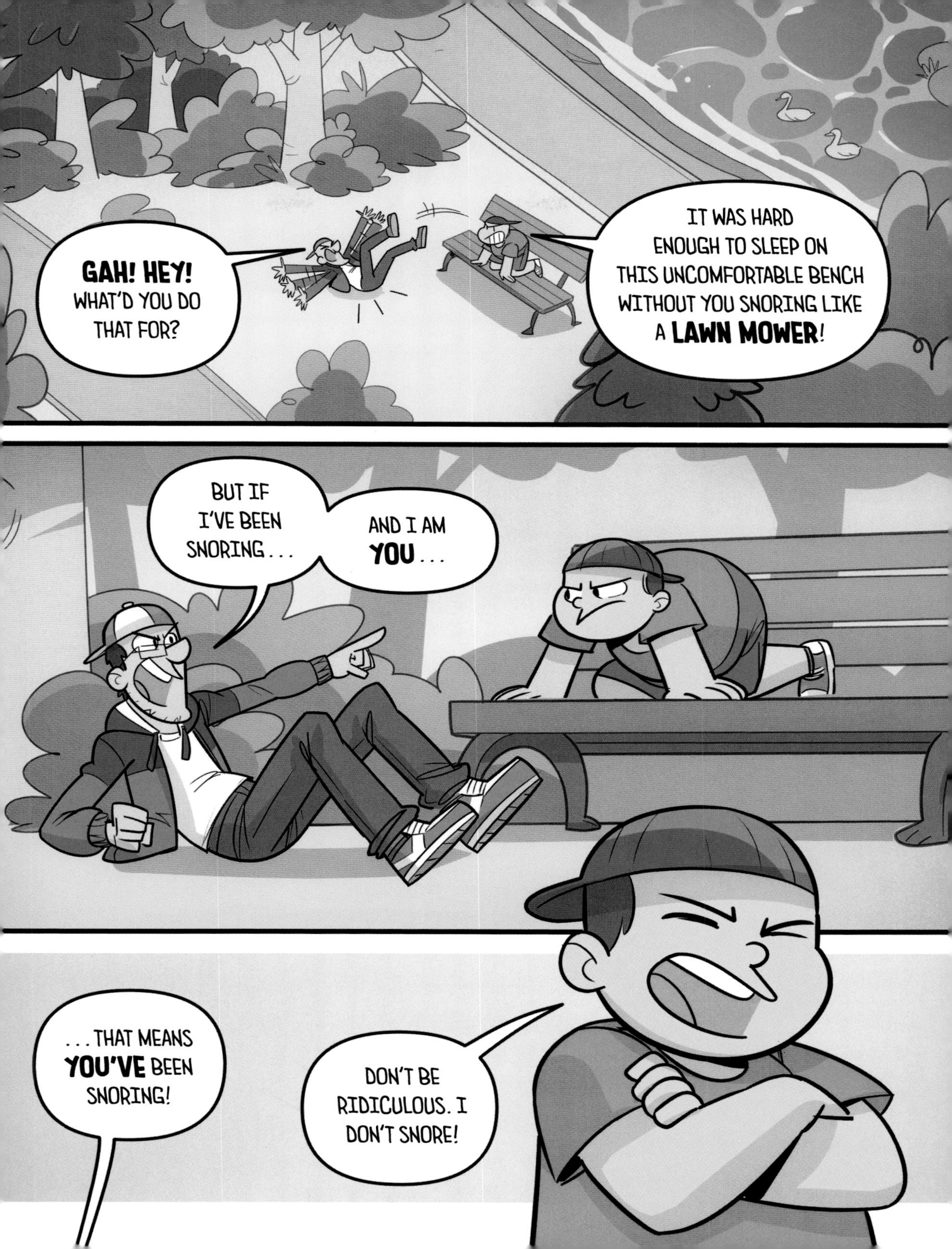
GAH! HEY! WHAT'D YOU DO THAT FOR?
IT WAS HARD ENOUGH TO SLEEP ON THIS UNCOMFORTABLE BENCH WITHOUT YOU SNORING LIKE A LAWN MOWER!
BUT IF I'VE BEEN SNORING . . .
AND I AM YOU . . .
. . . THAT MEANS YOU'VE BEEN SNORING!
DON'T BE RIDICULOUS. I DON'T SNORE!

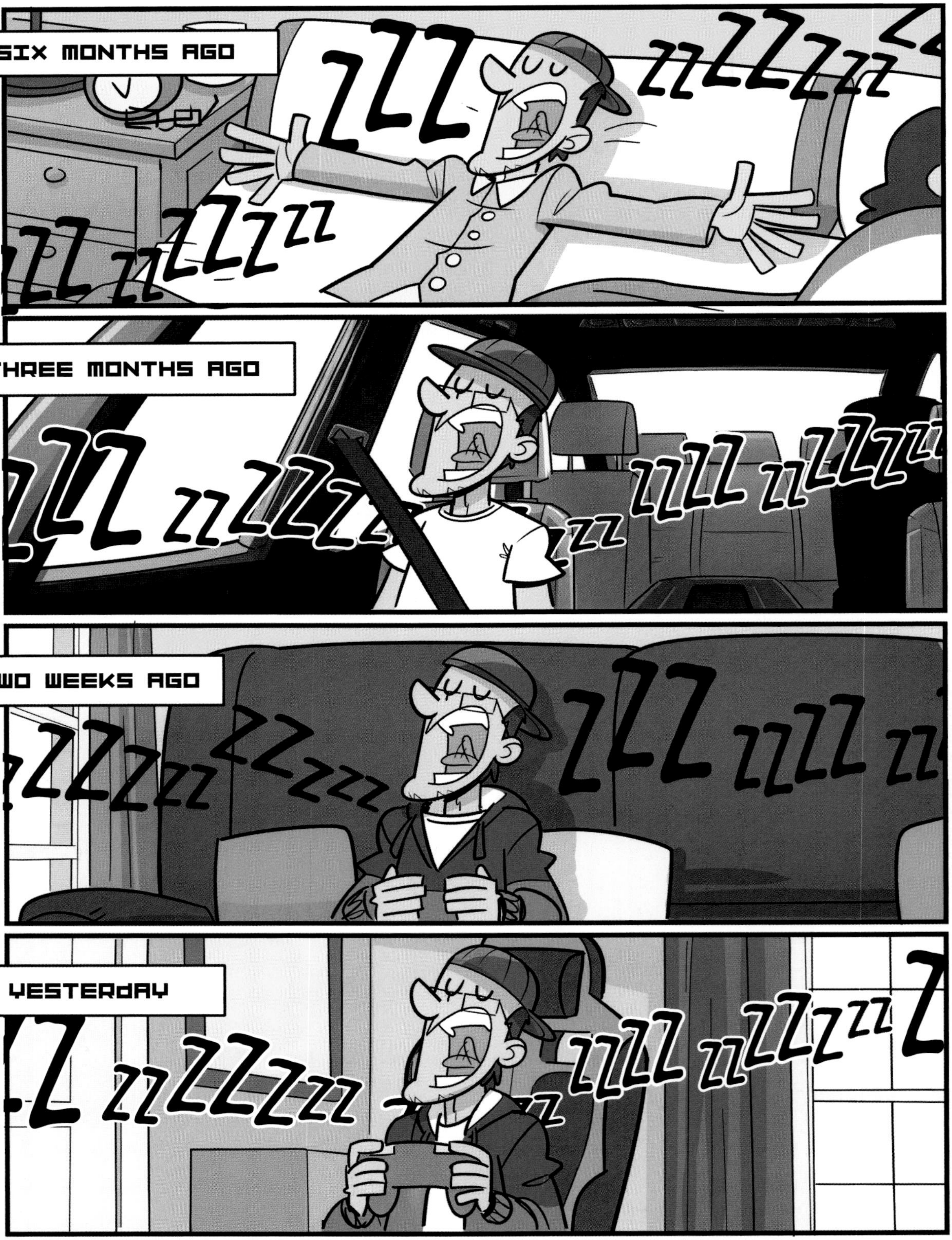

SIX MONTHS AGO
ZZZ
zzZZZzzz
zzZZZzzz
THREE MONTHS AGO
zzZZZZ
zzzZZZZ zzZZZzzz
TWO WEEKS AGO
ZZZzzz ZZzzzz
ZZZ zzzZZ
YESTERDAY
zzZZZzzz
zzZZZ zzZZZzzz

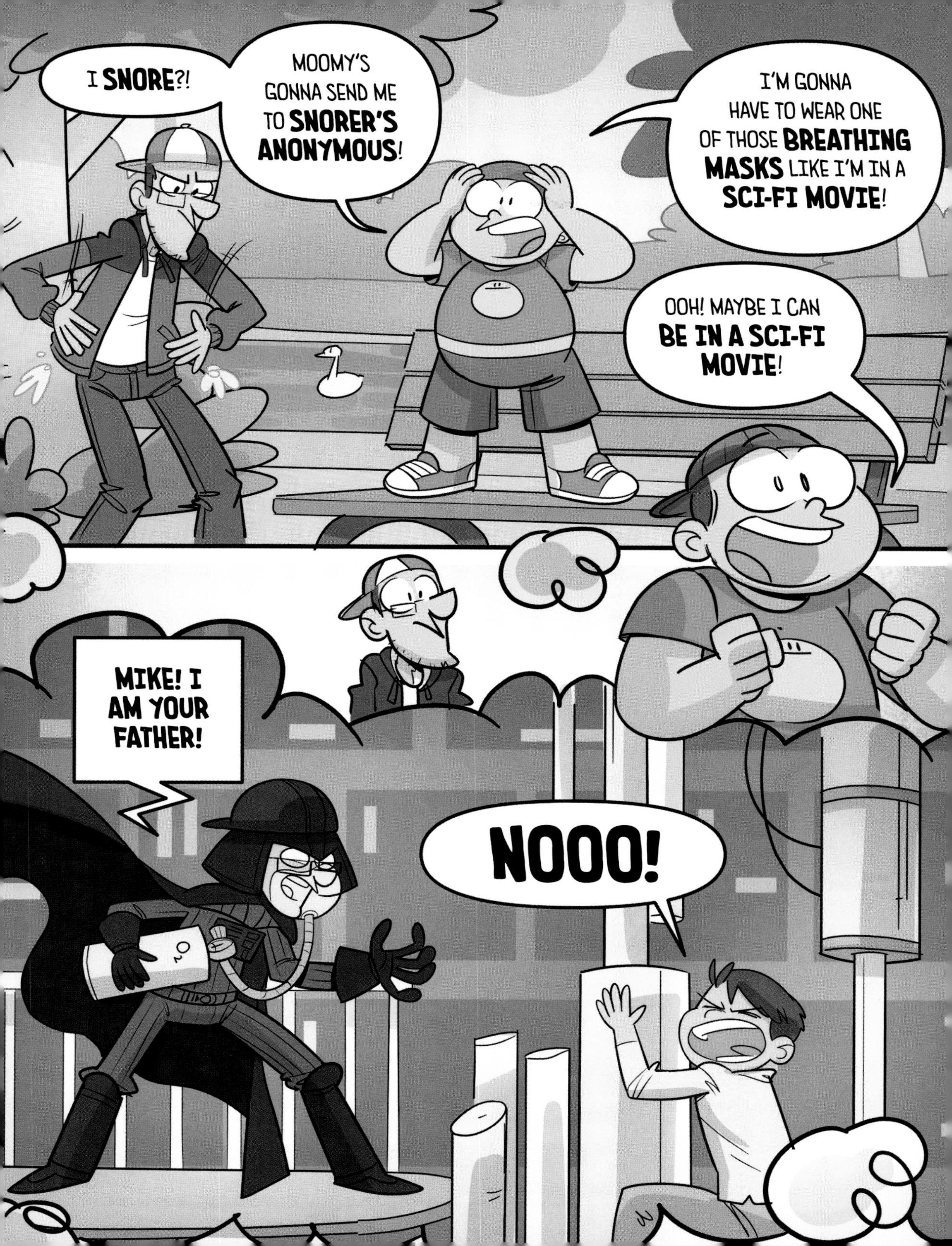
I SNORE?!
MOOMY'S GONNA SEND ME TO SNORER'S ANONYMOUS!
I'M GONNA HAVE TO WEAR ONE OF THOSE BREATHING MASKS LIKE I'M IN A SCI-FI MOVIE!
OOH! MAYBE I CAN BE IN A SCI-FI MOVIE!
MIKE! I AM YOUR FATHER!
$O_2$
NOOO!

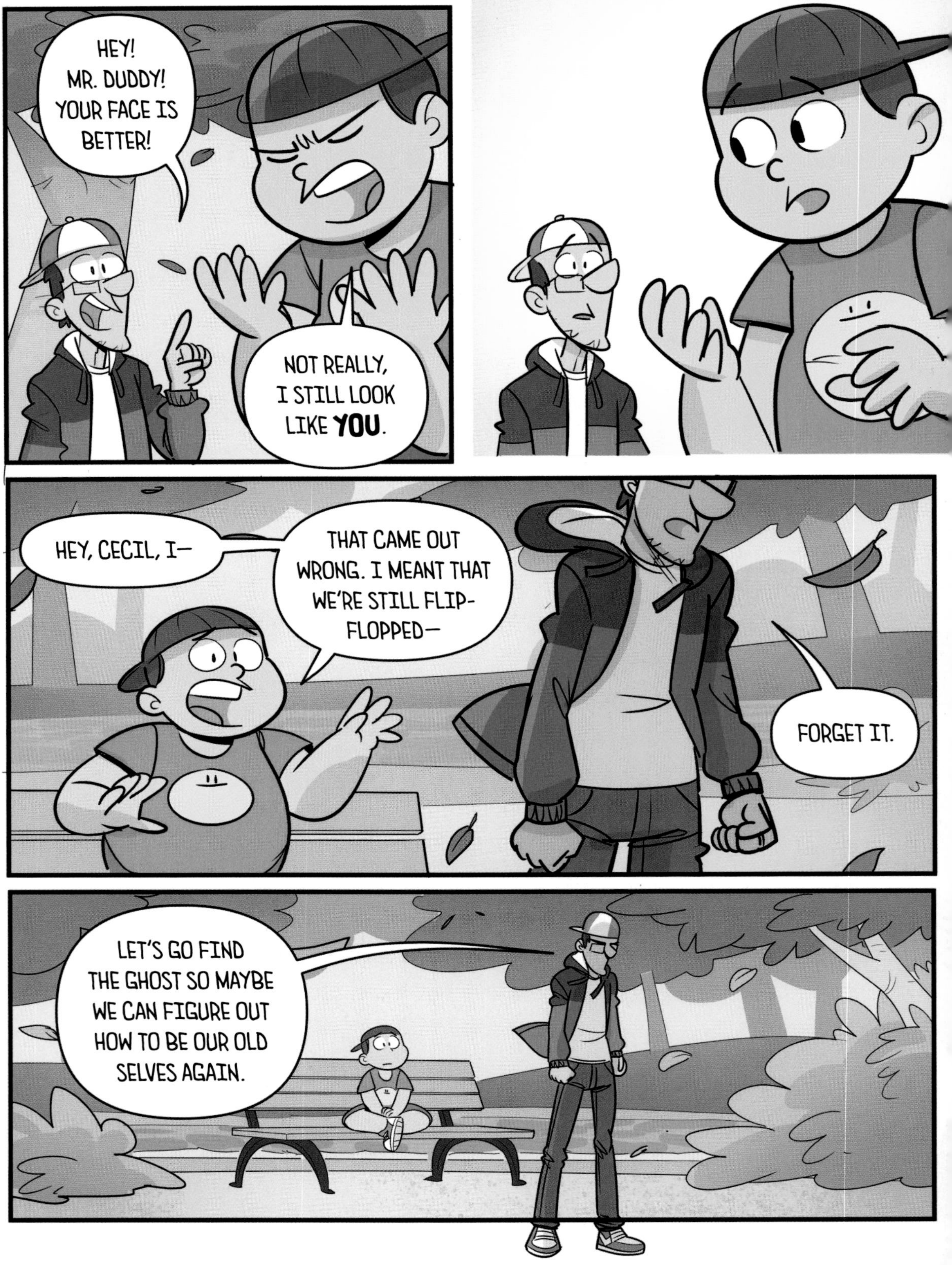
HEY! MR. DUDDY! YOUR FACE IS BETTER!
NOT REALLY, I STILL LOOK LIKE **YOU**.
HEY, CECIL, I—
THAT CAME OUT WRONG. I MEANT THAT WE'RE STILL FLIP-FLOPPED—
FORGET IT.
LET'S GO FIND THE GHOST SO MAYBE WE CAN FIGURE OUT HOW TO BE OUR OLD SELVES AGAIN.

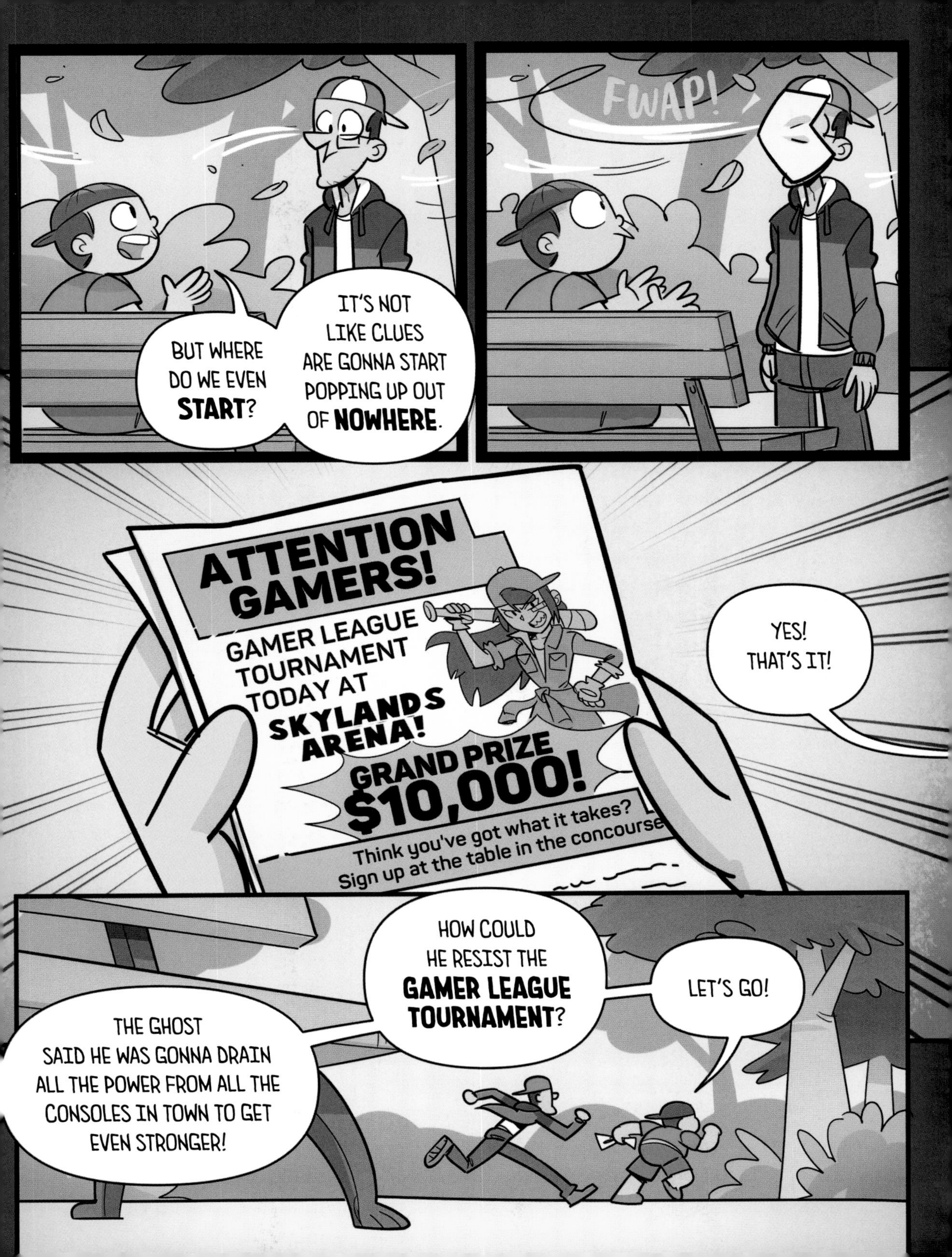
BUT WHERE DO WE EVEN START?
IT'S NOT LIKE CLUES ARE GONNA START POPPING UP OUT OF NOWHERE.
FWAP!
ATTENTION GAMERS!
GAMER LEAGUE TOURNAMENT TODAY AT SKYLANDS ARENA!
GRAND PRIZE $10,000!
Think you've got what it takes? Sign up at the table in the concourse
YES! THAT'S IT!
THE GHOST SAID HE WAS GONNA DRAIN ALL THE POWER FROM ALL THE CONSOLES IN TOWN TO GET EVEN STRONGER!
HOW COULD HE RESIST THE GAMER LEAGUE TOURNAMENT?
LET'S GO!

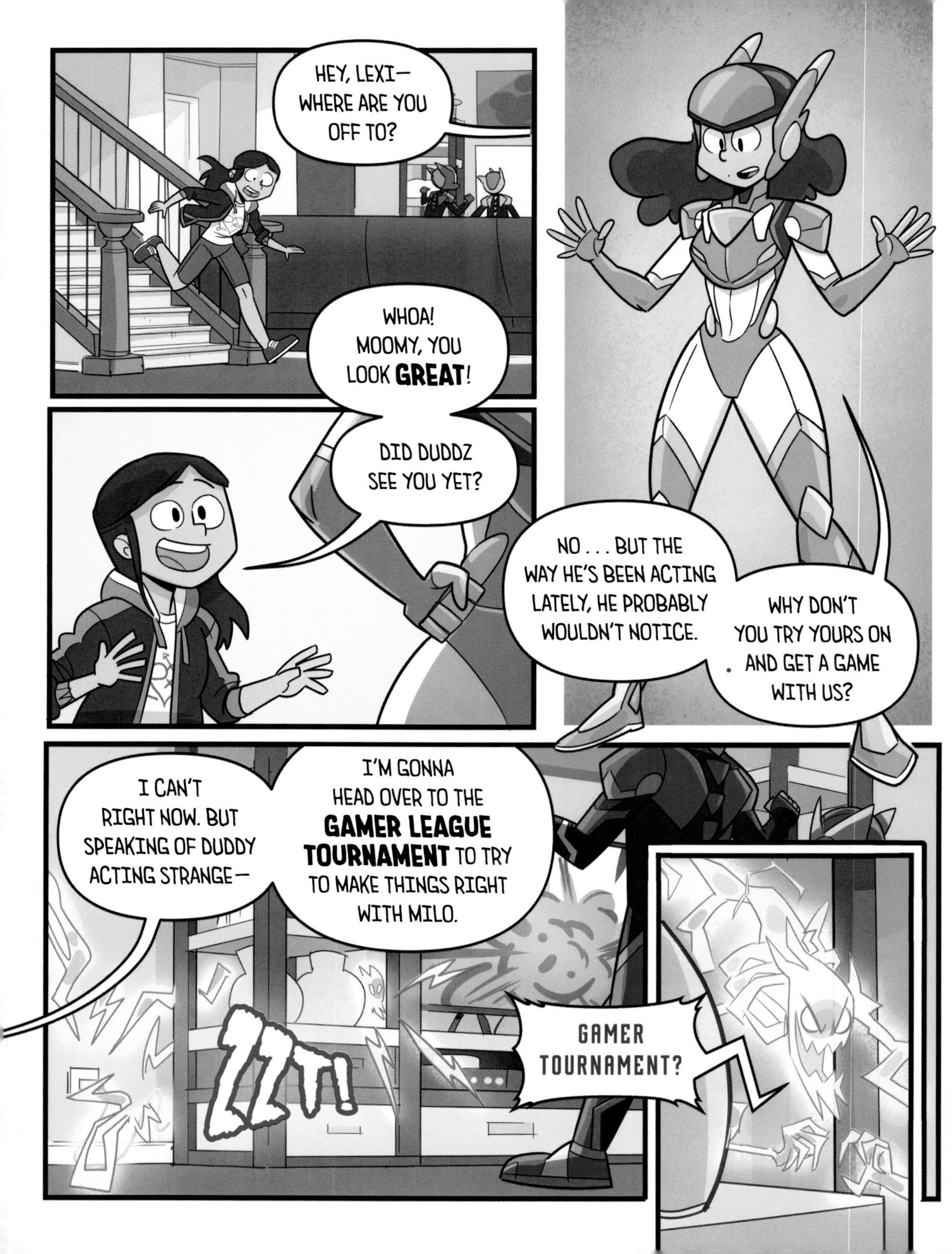
HEY, LEXI—
WHERE ARE YOU
OFF TO?
WHOA!
MOOMY, YOU
LOOK **GREAT**!
DID DUDDZ
SEE YOU YET?
NO . . . BUT THE
WAY HE'S BEEN ACTING
LATELY, HE PROBABLY
WOULDN'T NOTICE.
WHY DON'T
YOU TRY YOURS ON
AND GET A GAME
WITH US?
I CAN'T
RIGHT NOW. BUT
SPEAKING OF DUDDY
ACTING STRANGE—
I'M GONNA
HEAD OVER TO THE
**GAMER LEAGUE**
**TOURNAMENT** TO TRY
TO MAKE THINGS RIGHT
WITH MILO.
ZZT!
GAMER
TOURNAMENT?

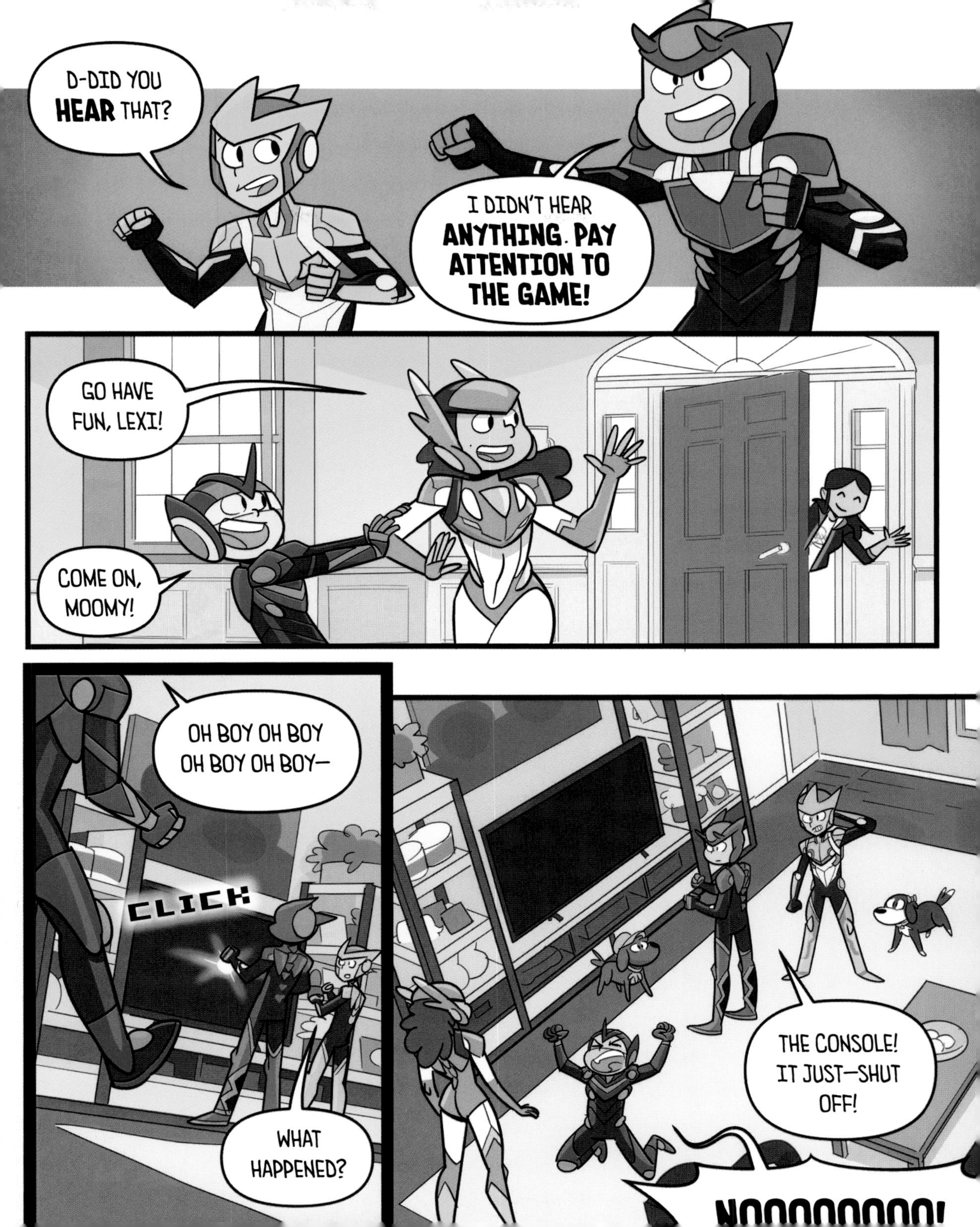
D-DID YOU HEAR THAT?
I DIDN'T HEAR ANYTHING. PAY ATTENTION TO THE GAME!
GO HAVE FUN, LEXI!
COME ON, MOOMY!
OH BOY OH BOY OH BOY OH BOY—
CLICK
WHAT HAPPENED?
THE CONSOLE! IT JUST—SHUT OFF!
NOOOOOOOO!

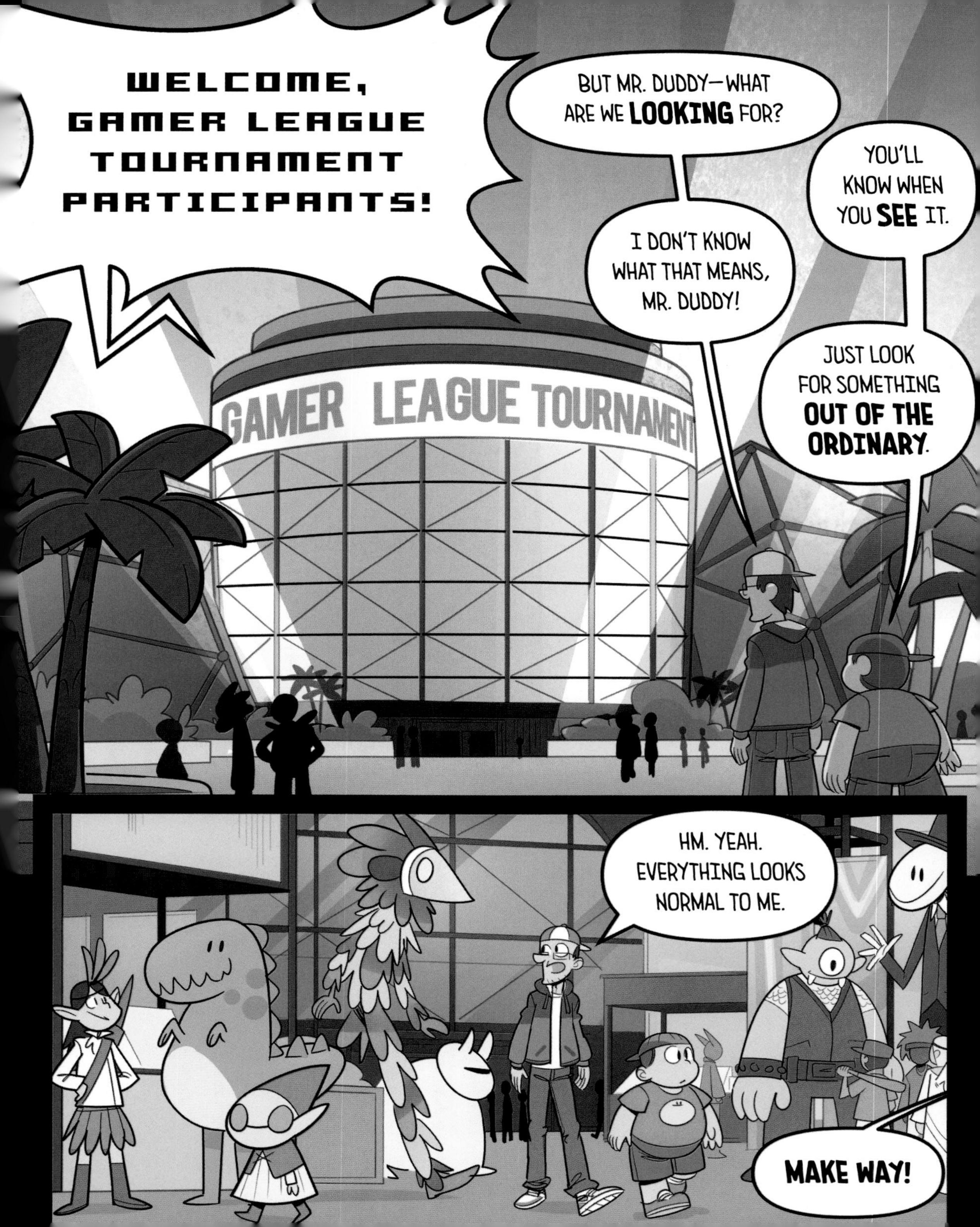
WELCOME, GAMER LEAGUE TOURNAMENT PARTICIPANTS!
BUT MR. DUDDY—WHAT ARE WE LOOKING FOR?
YOU'LL KNOW WHEN YOU SEE IT.
I DON'T KNOW WHAT THAT MEANS, MR. DUDDY!
JUST LOOK FOR SOMETHING OUT OF THE ORDINARY.
GAMER LEAGUE TOURNAMENT
HM. YEAH. EVERYTHING LOOKS NORMAL TO ME.
MAKE WAY!

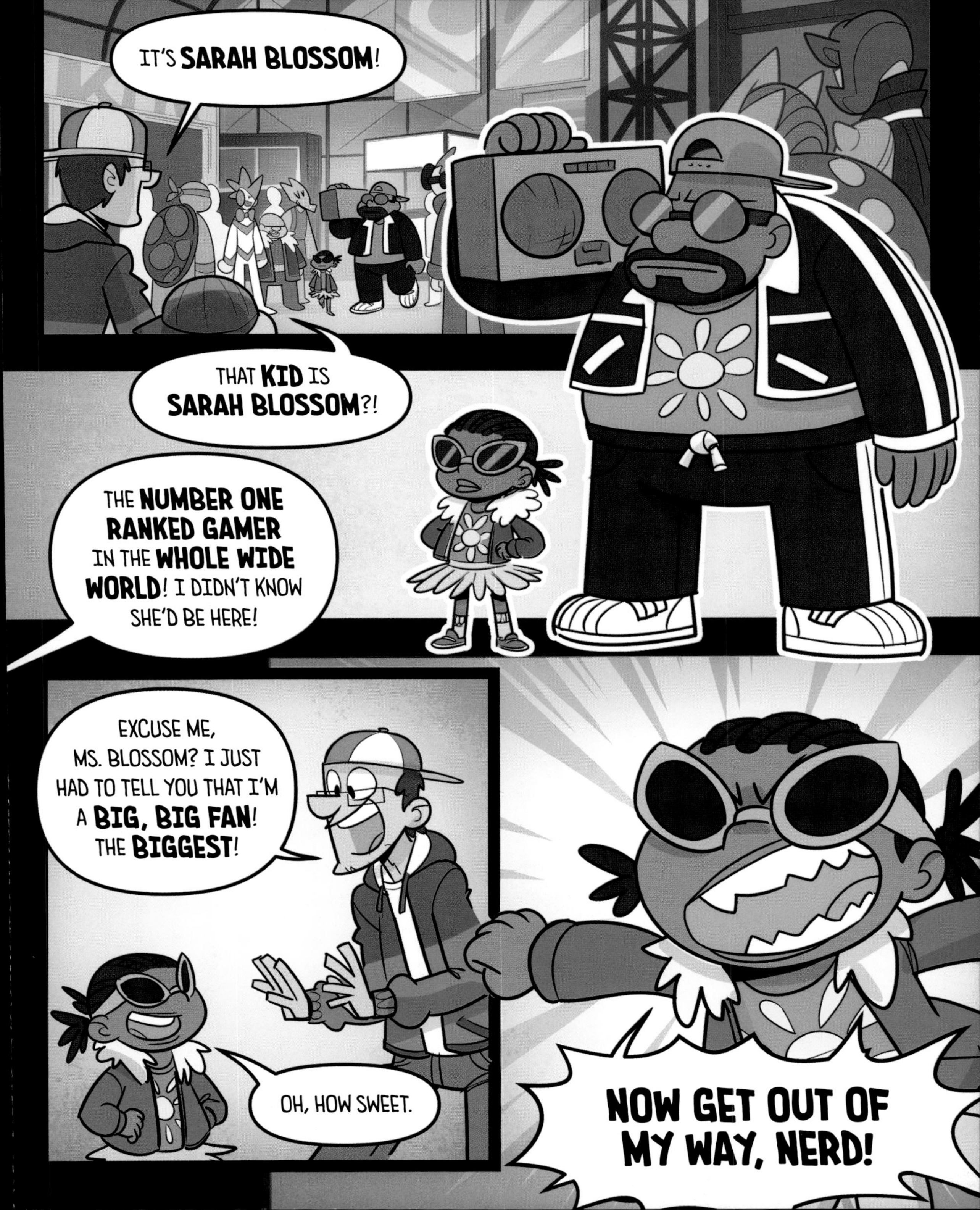
IT'S SARAH BLOSSOM!
THAT KID IS SARAH BLOSSOM?!
THE NUMBER ONE RANKED GAMER IN THE WHOLE WIDE WORLD! I DIDN'T KNOW SHE'D BE HERE!
EXCUSE ME, MS. BLOSSOM? I JUST HAD TO TELL YOU THAT I'M A BIG, BIG FAN! THE BIGGEST!
OH, HOW SWEET.
NOW GET OUT OF MY WAY, NERD!

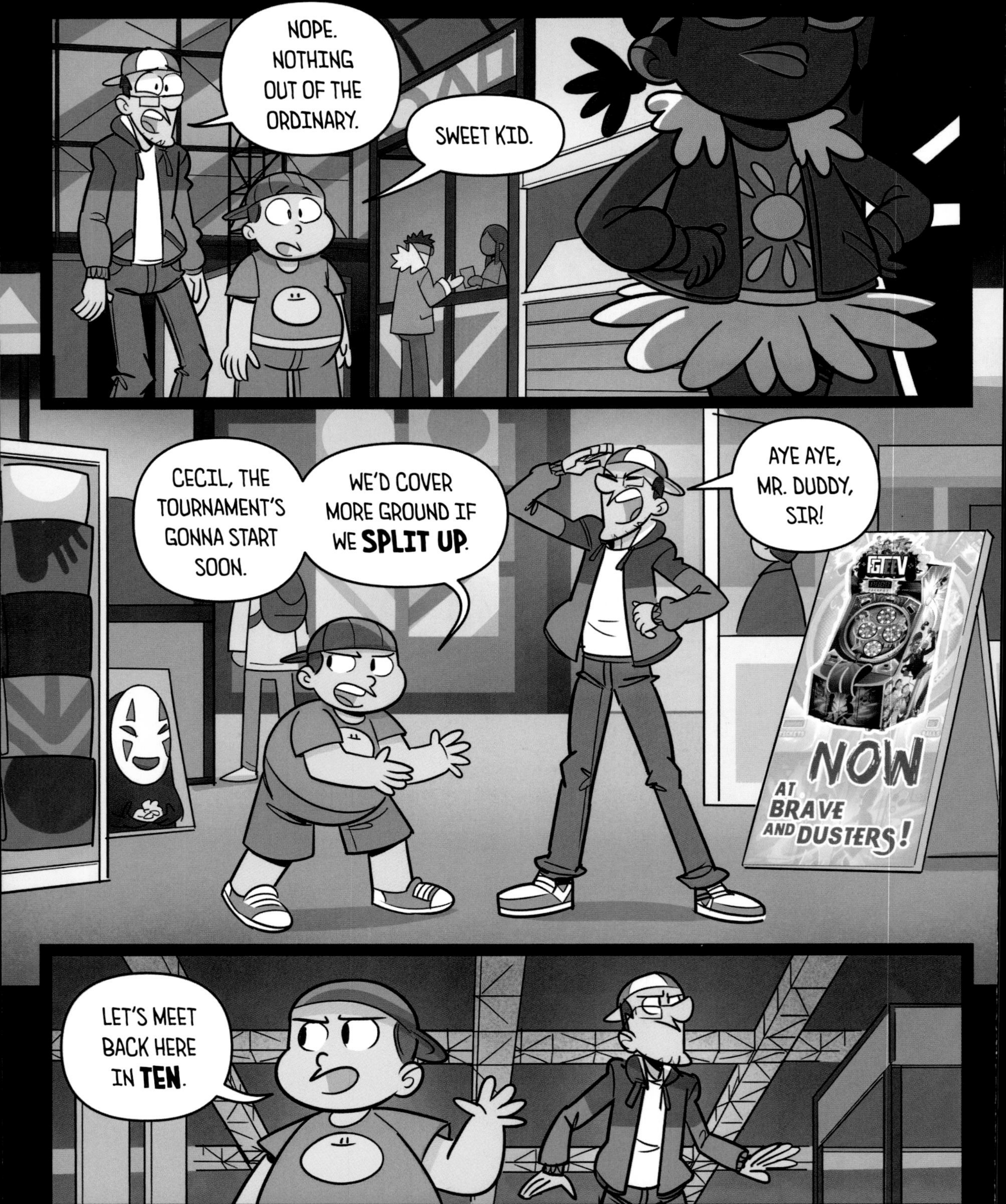
NOPE. NOTHING OUT OF THE ORDINARY.
SWEET KID.
CECIL, THE TOURNAMENT'S GONNA START SOON.
WE'D COVER MORE GROUND IF WE **SPLIT UP**.
AYE AYE, MR. DUDDY, SIR!
NOW AT BRAVE AND DUSTERS!
LET'S MEET BACK HERE IN **TEN**.

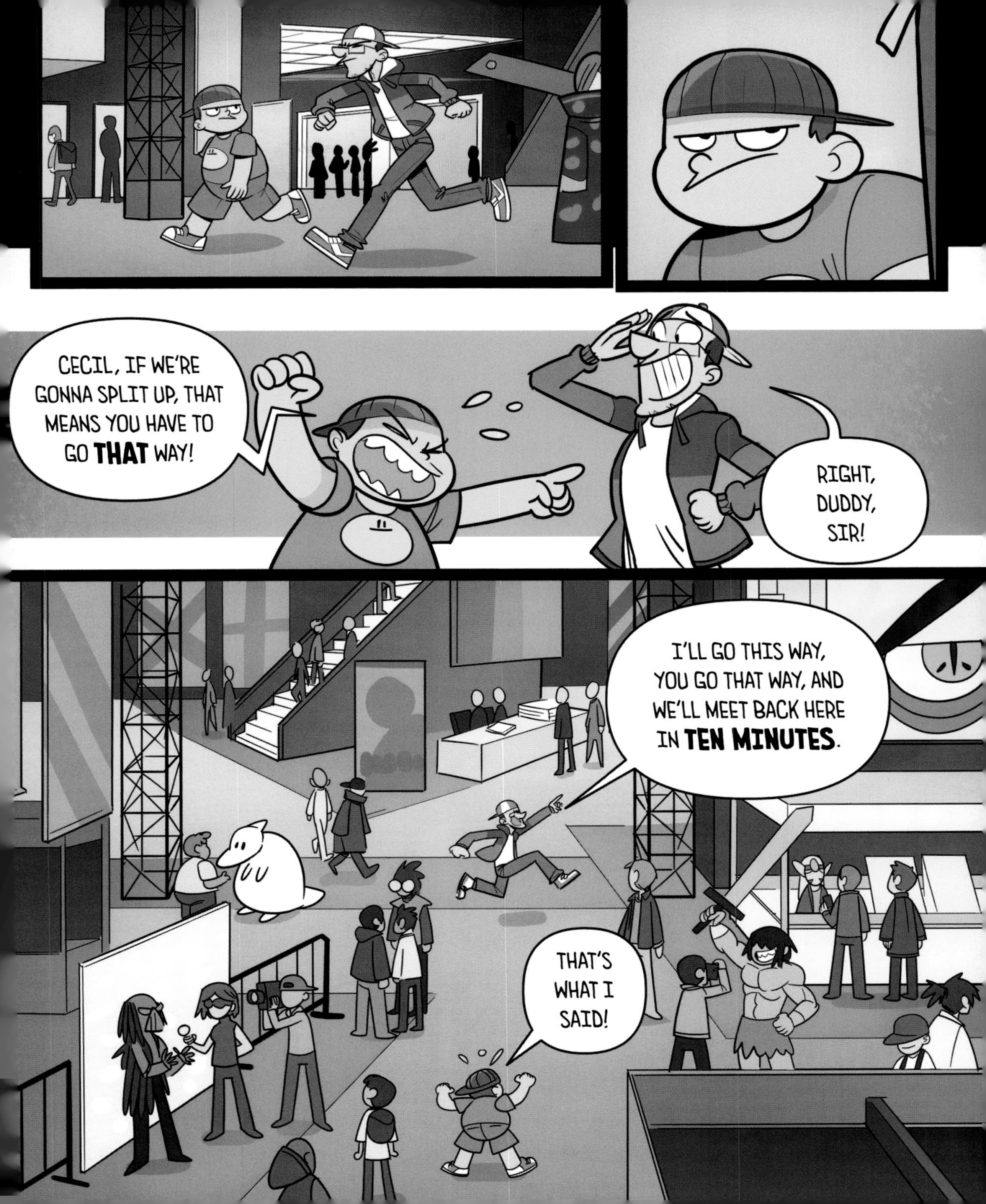
CECIL, IF WE'RE GONNA SPLIT UP, THAT MEANS YOU HAVE TO GO **THAT** WAY!
RIGHT, DUDDY, SIR!
I'LL GO THIS WAY, YOU GO THAT WAY, AND WE'LL MEET BACK HERE IN **TEN MINUTES**.
THAT'S WHAT I SAID!

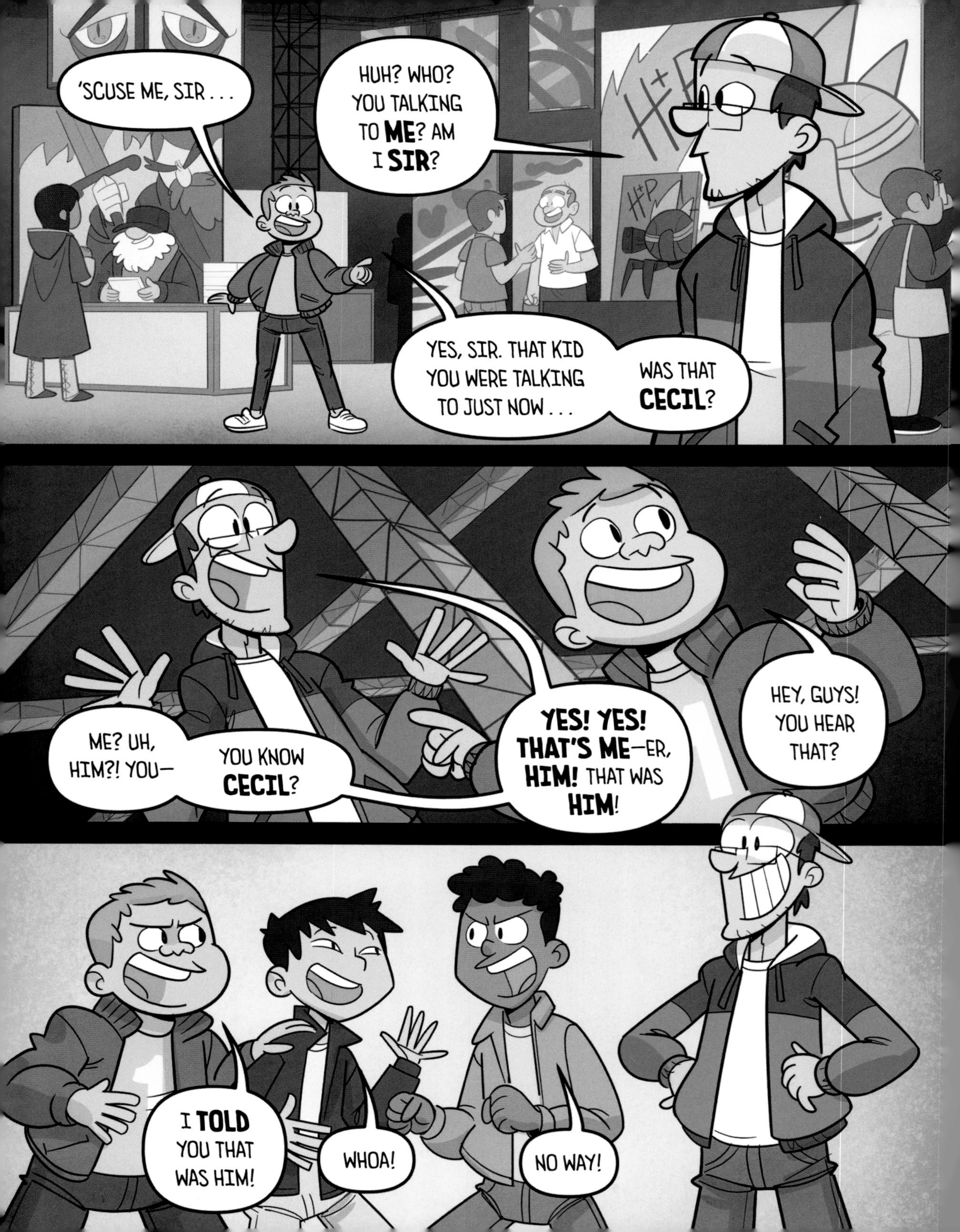

'SCUSE ME, SIR . . .
HUH? WHO? YOU TALKING TO **ME**? AM I **SIR**?
YES, SIR. THAT KID YOU WERE TALKING TO JUST NOW . . .
WAS THAT **CECIL**?
ME? UH, HIM?! YOU—
YOU KNOW **CECIL**?
**YES! YES! THAT'S ME**—ER, **HIM!** THAT WAS **HIM**!
HEY, GUYS! YOU HEAR THAT?
I **TOLD** YOU THAT WAS HIM!
WHOA!
NO WAY!

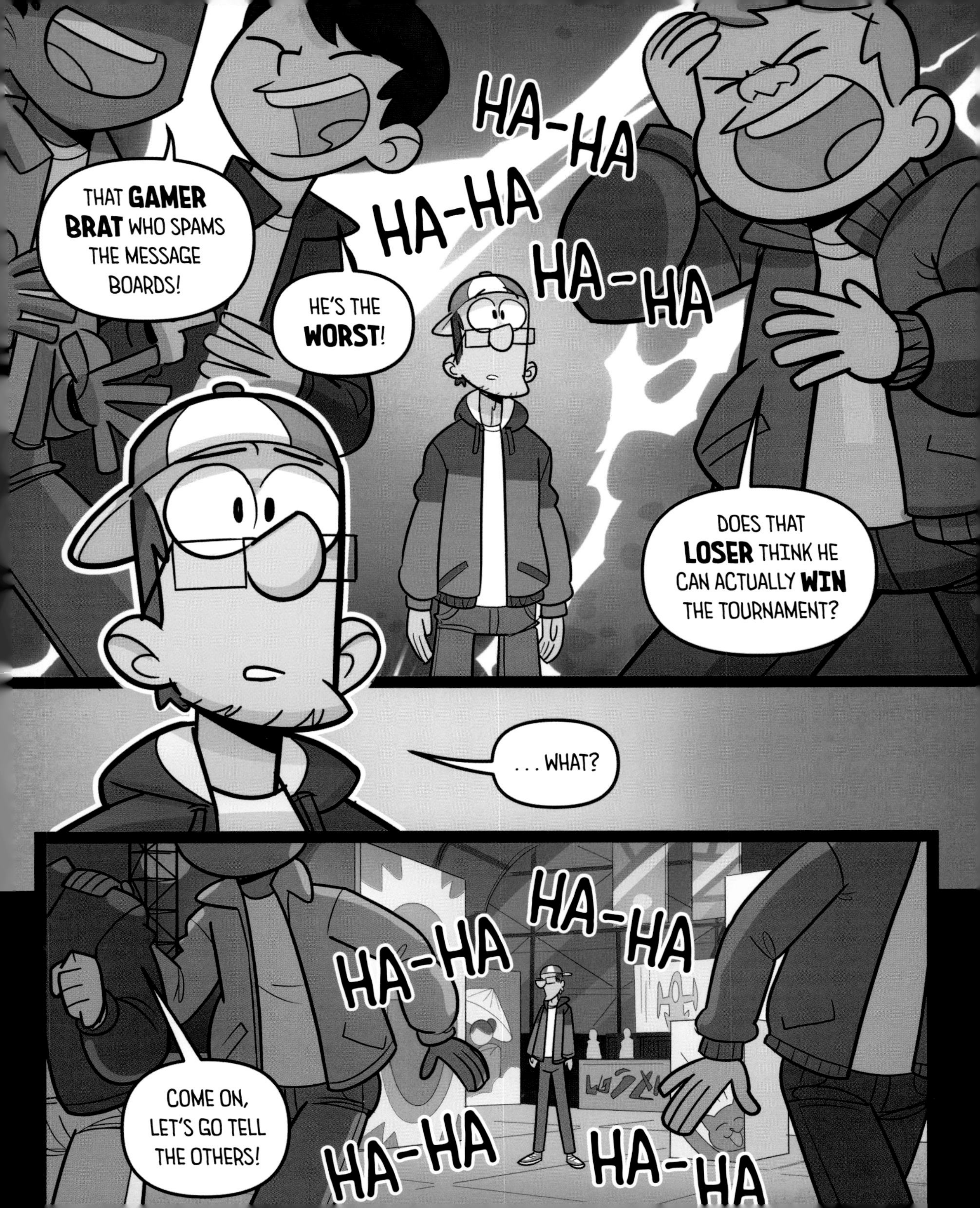
THAT **GAMER BRAT** WHO SPAMS THE MESSAGE BOARDS!
HE'S THE **WORST**!
HA-HA
HA-HA
HA-HA
DOES THAT **LOSER** THINK HE CAN ACTUALLY **WIN** THE TOURNAMENT?
. . . WHAT?
HA-HA
HA-HA
COME ON, LET'S GO TELL THE OTHERS!
HA-HA
HA-HA

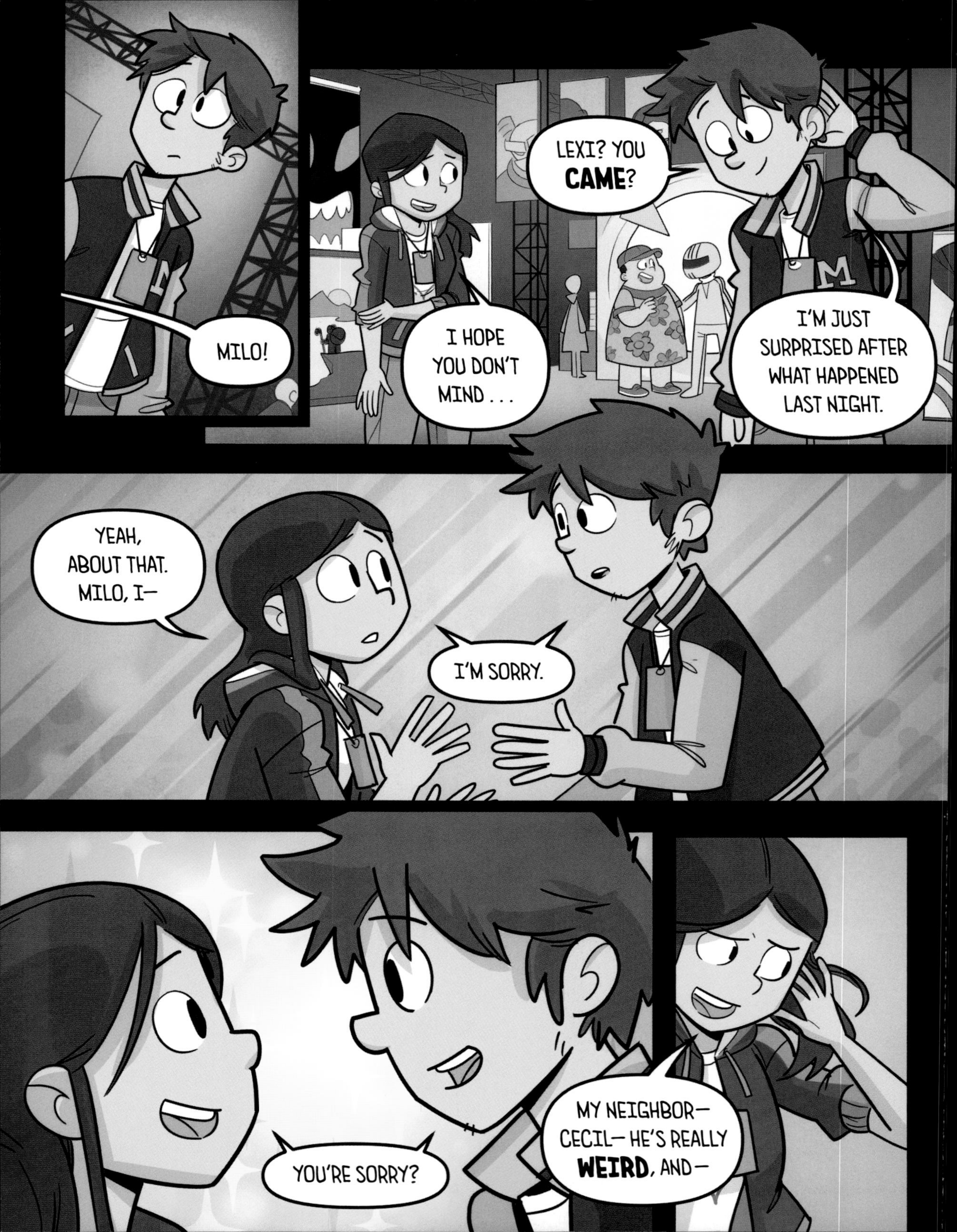
MILO!
I HOPE YOU DON'T MIND . . .
LEXI? YOU **CAME**?
I'M JUST SURPRISED AFTER WHAT HAPPENED LAST NIGHT.
YEAH, ABOUT THAT. MILO, I—
I'M SORRY.
YOU'RE SORRY?
MY NEIGHBOR— CECIL— HE'S REALLY **WEIRD**, AND—

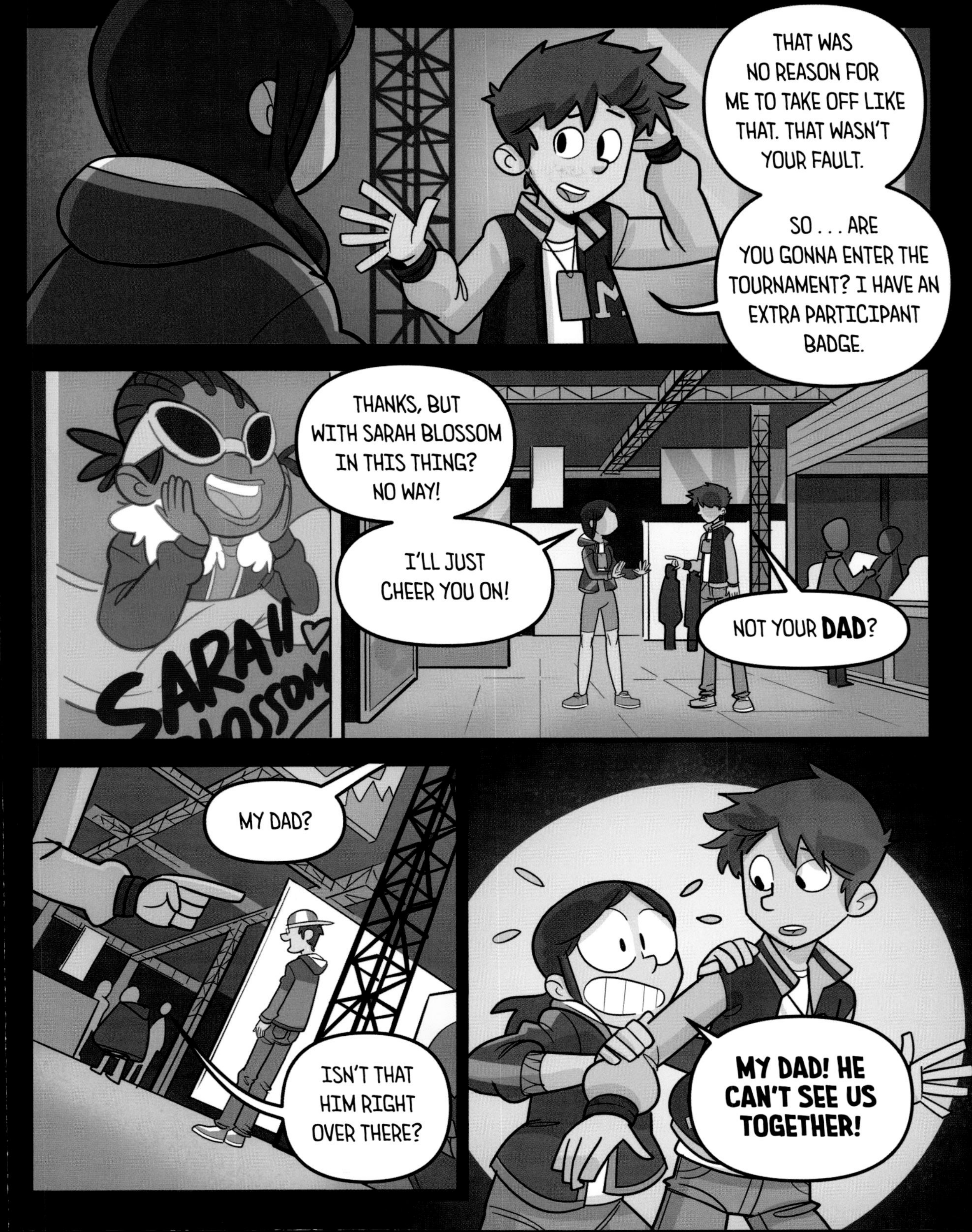
THAT WAS NO REASON FOR ME TO TAKE OFF LIKE THAT. THAT WASN'T YOUR FAULT.
SO . . . ARE YOU GONNA ENTER THE TOURNAMENT? I HAVE AN EXTRA PARTICIPANT BADGE.
SARAH BLOSSOM
THANKS, BUT WITH SARAH BLOSSOM IN THIS THING? NO WAY!
I'LL JUST CHEER YOU ON!
NOT YOUR **DAD**?
MY DAD?
ISN'T THAT HIM RIGHT OVER THERE?
**MY DAD! HE CAN'T SEE US TOGETHER!**

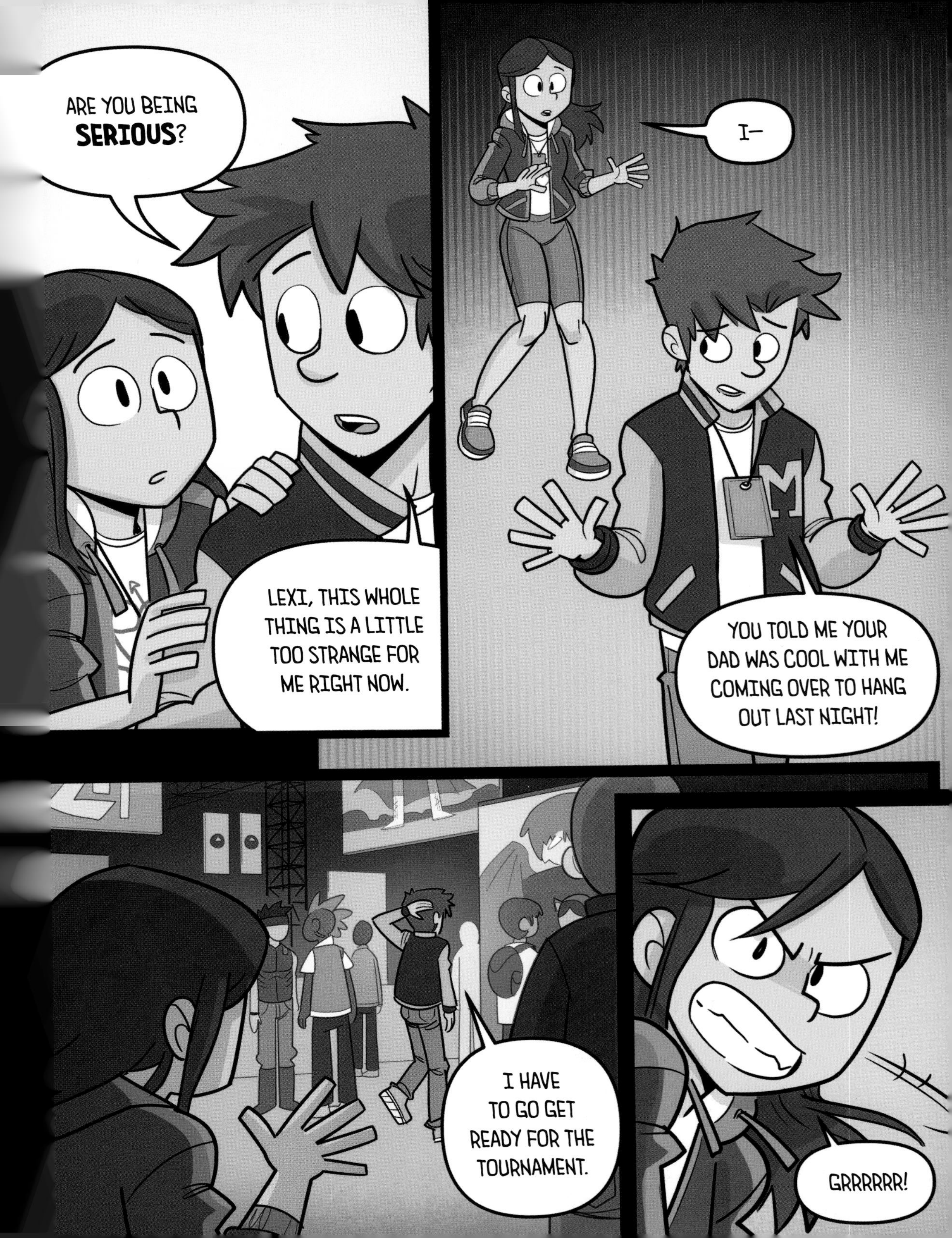
ARE YOU BEING **SERIOUS**?
LEXI, THIS WHOLE THING IS A LITTLE TOO STRANGE FOR ME RIGHT NOW.
I—
YOU TOLD ME YOUR DAD WAS COOL WITH ME COMING OVER TO HANG OUT LAST NIGHT!
I HAVE TO GO GET READY FOR THE TOURNAMENT.
GRRRRRR!

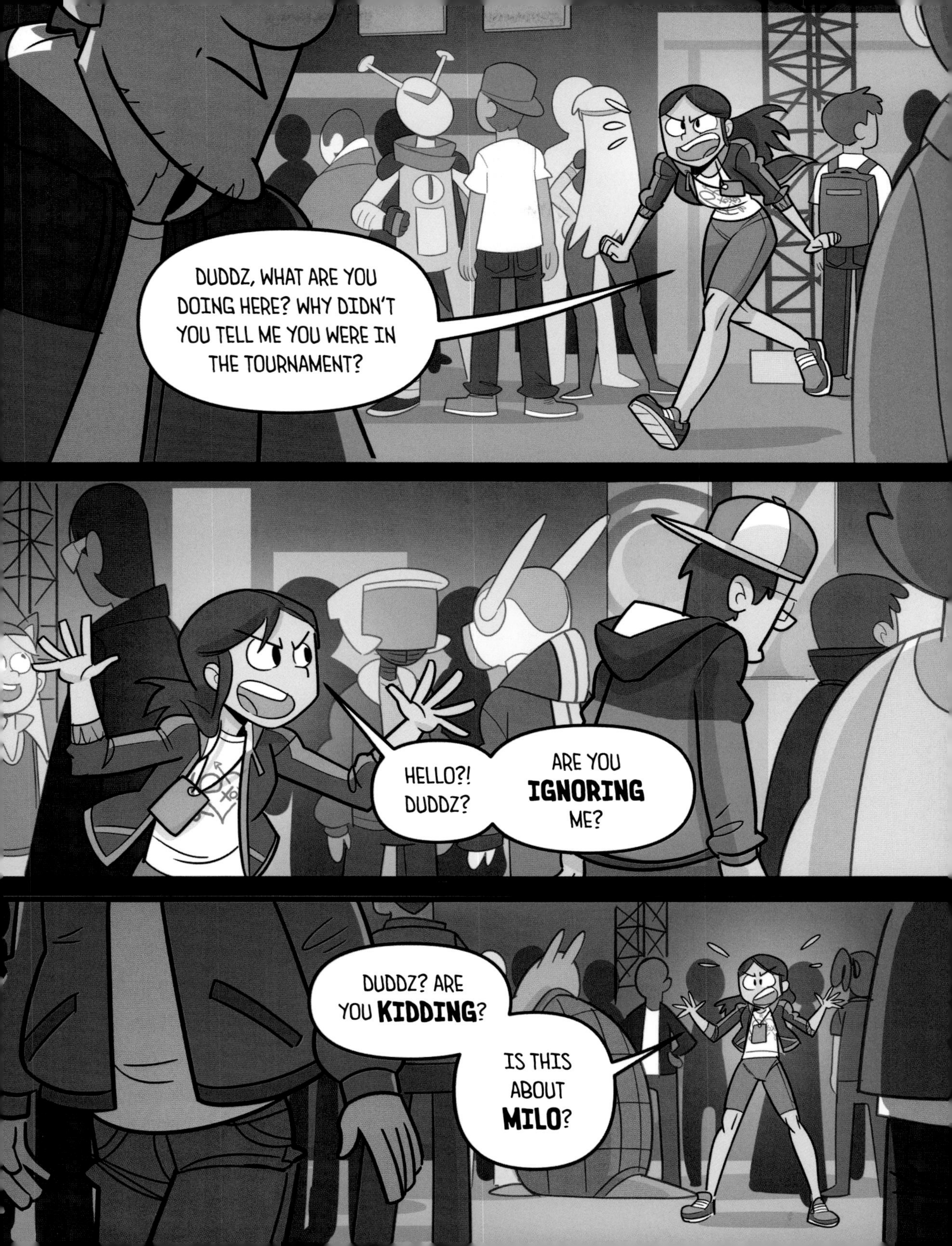
DUDDZ, WHAT ARE YOU DOING HERE? WHY DIDN'T YOU TELL ME YOU WERE IN THE TOURNAMENT?
HELLO?! DUDDZ?
ARE YOU **IGNORING** ME?
DUDDZ? ARE YOU **KIDDING**?
IS THIS ABOUT **MILO**?

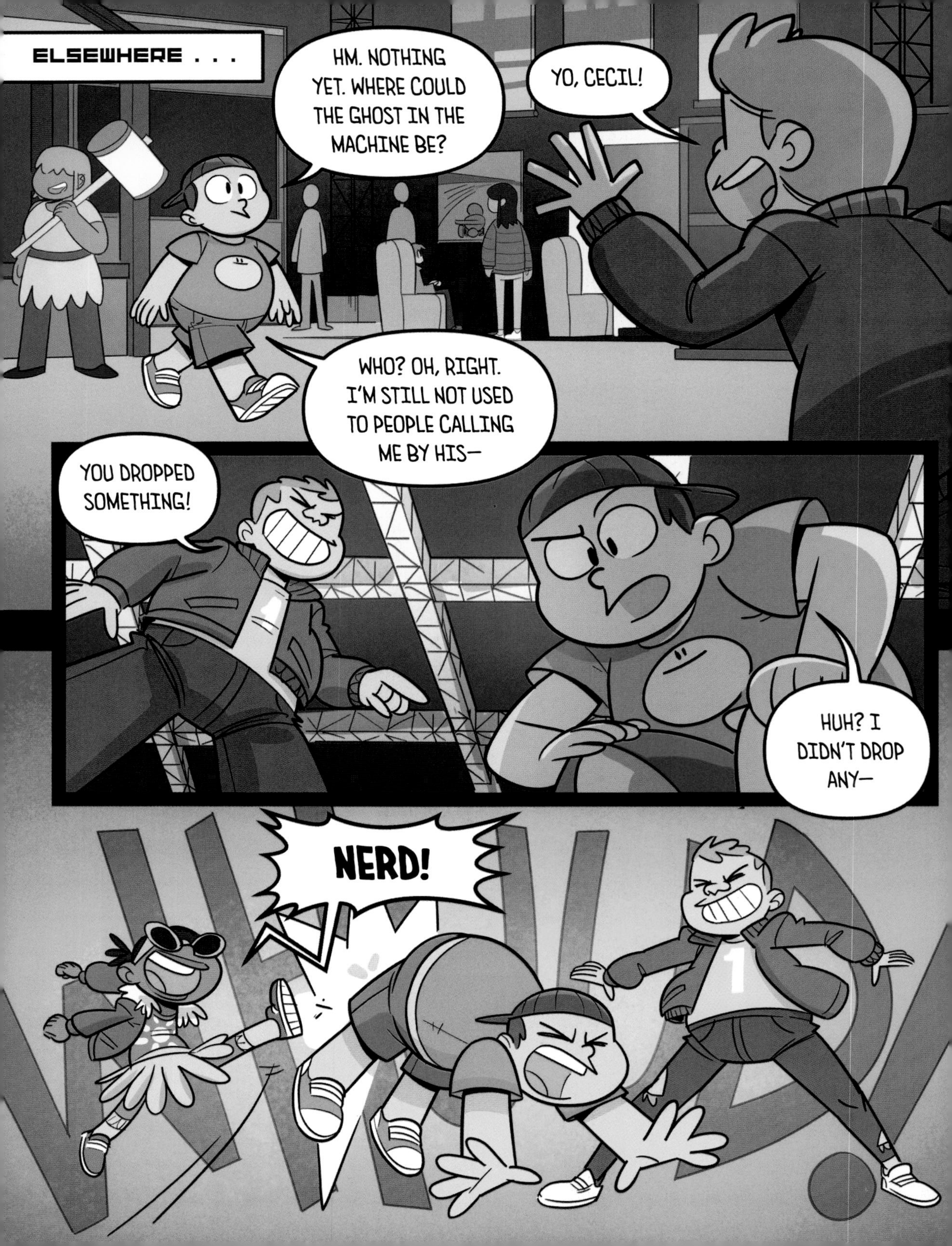
ELSEWHERE . . .
HM. NOTHING YET. WHERE COULD THE GHOST IN THE MACHINE BE?
YO, CECIL!
WHO? OH, RIGHT. I'M STILL NOT USED TO PEOPLE CALLING ME BY HIS—
YOU DROPPED SOMETHING!
HUH? I DIDN'T DROP ANY—
NERD!

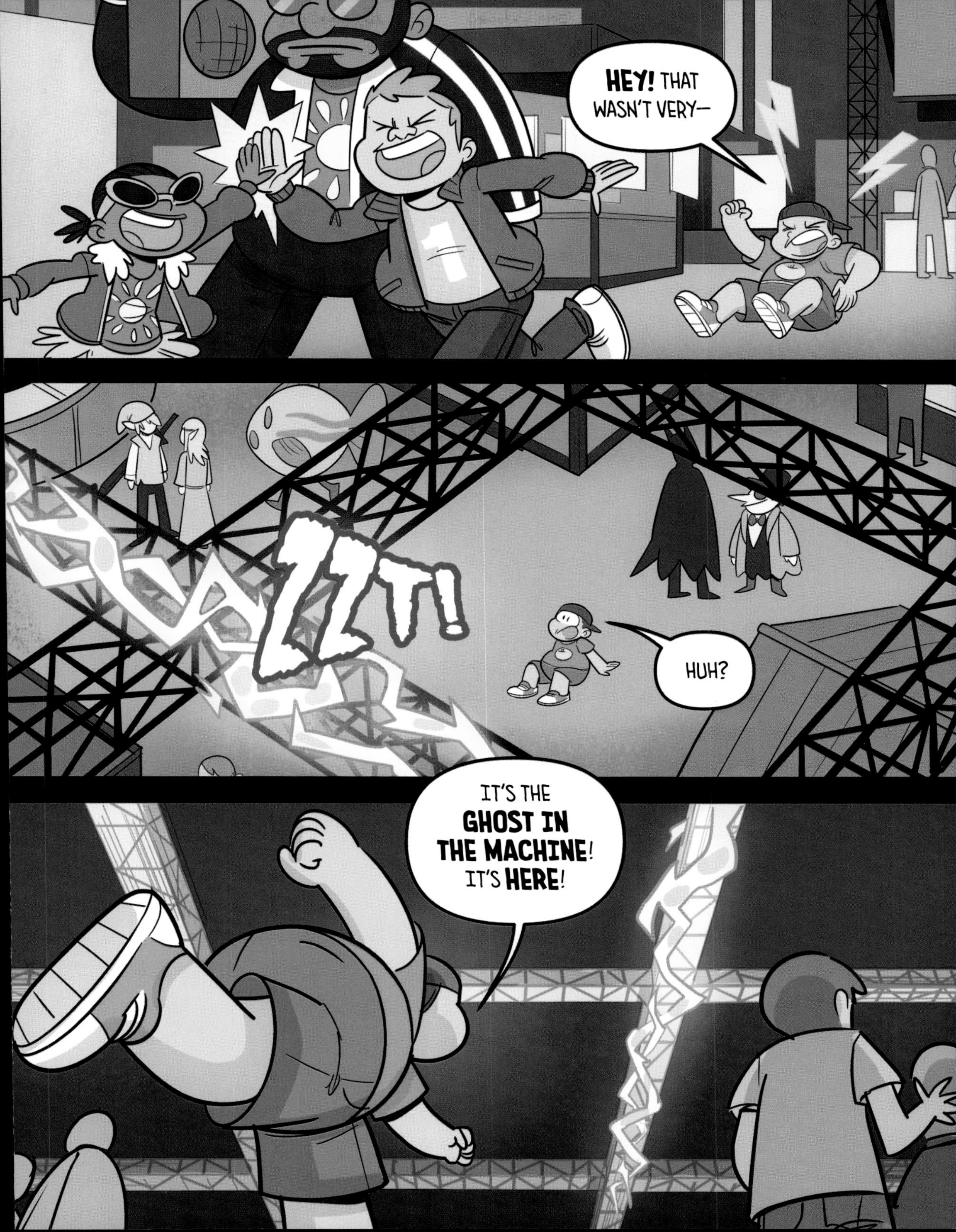
**HEY!** THAT WASN'T VERY—
ZZT!
HUH?
IT'S THE **GHOST IN THE MACHINE**! IT'S **HERE**!

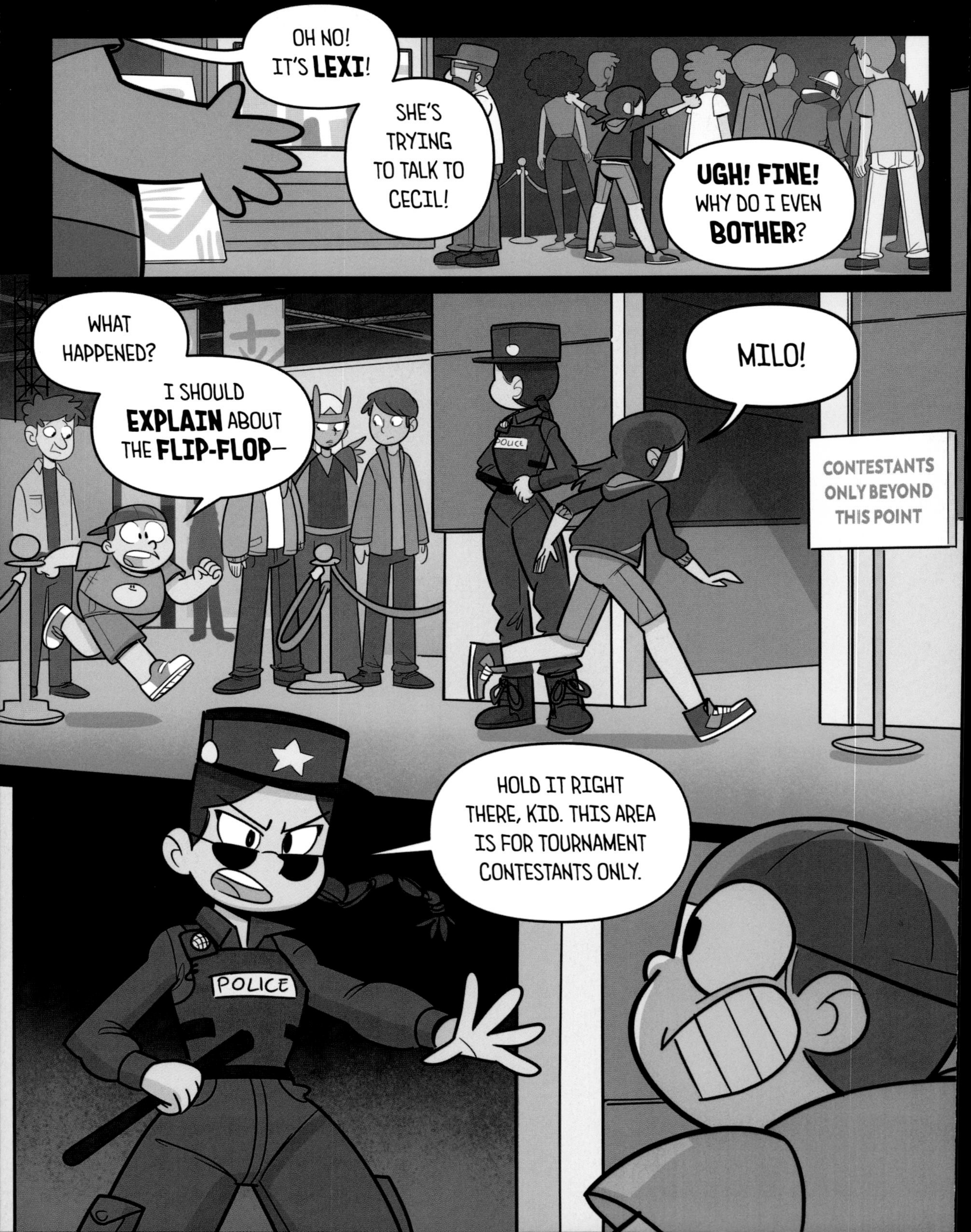
OH NO! IT'S LEXI!
SHE'S TRYING TO TALK TO CECIL!
UGH! FINE! WHY DO I EVEN BOTHER?
WHAT HAPPENED?
I SHOULD EXPLAIN ABOUT THE FLIP-FLOP—
MILO!
CONTESTANTS ONLY BEYOND THIS POINT
POLICE
HOLD IT RIGHT THERE, KID. THIS AREA IS FOR TOURNAMENT CONTESTANTS ONLY.
POLICE

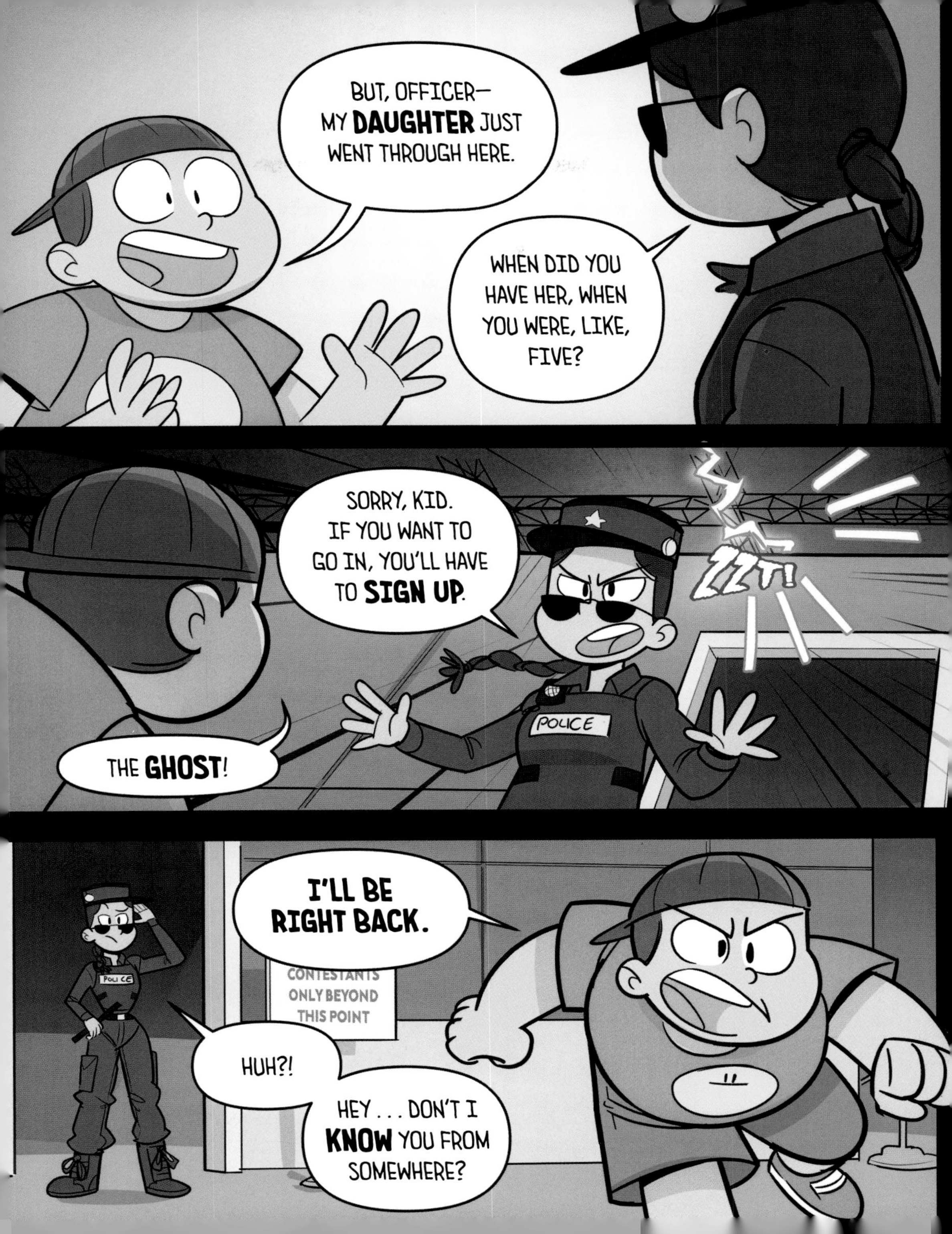
BUT, OFFICER— MY **DAUGHTER** JUST WENT THROUGH HERE.
WHEN DID YOU HAVE HER, WHEN YOU WERE, LIKE, FIVE?
SORRY, KID. IF YOU WANT TO GO IN, YOU'LL HAVE TO **SIGN UP**.
ZZT!
THE **GHOST**!
**I'LL BE RIGHT BACK.**
CONTESTANTS ONLY BEYOND THIS POINT
POLICE
HUH?!
HEY . . . DON'T I **KNOW** YOU FROM SOMEWHERE?

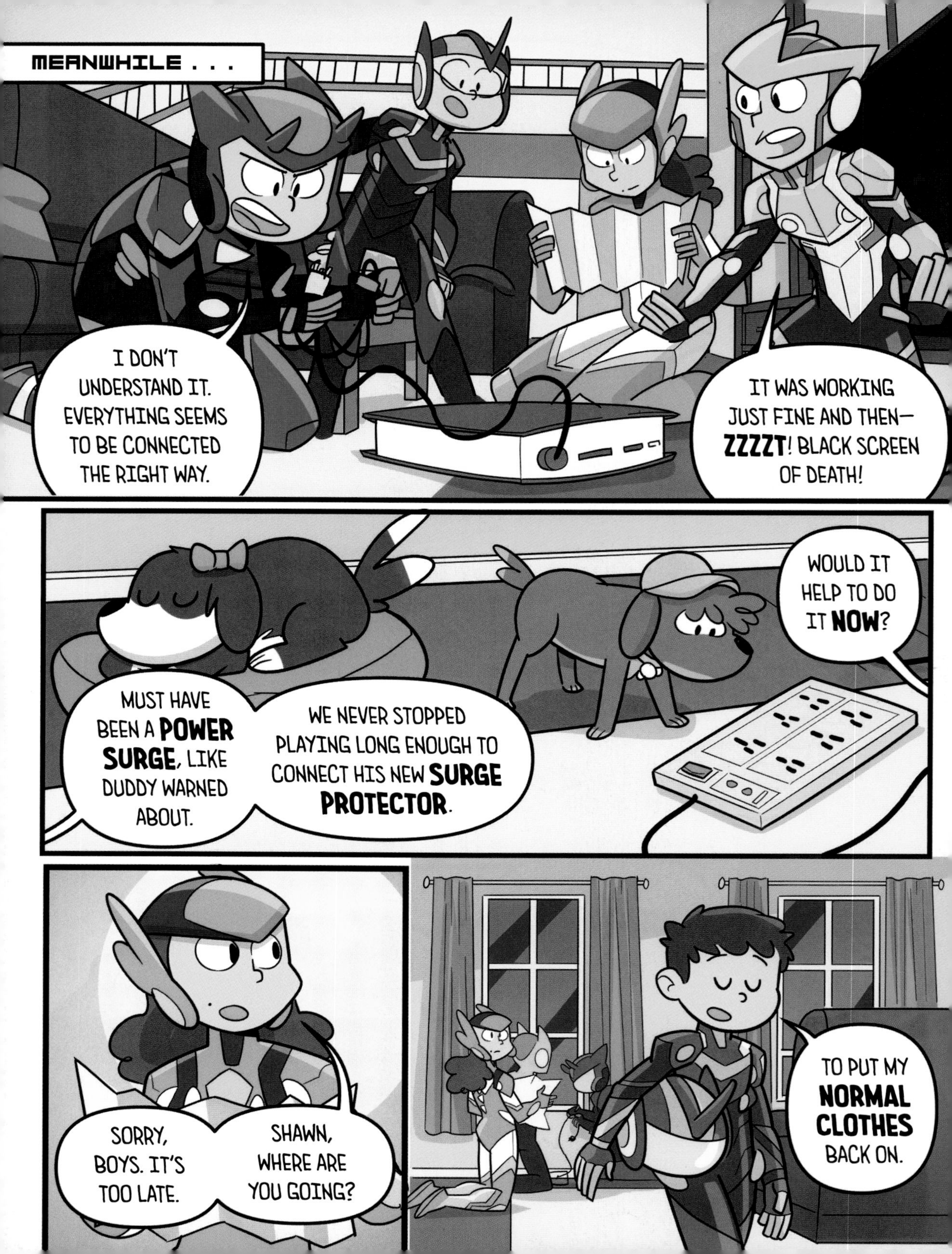
MEANWHILE . . .
I DON'T UNDERSTAND IT. EVERYTHING SEEMS TO BE CONNECTED THE RIGHT WAY.
IT WAS WORKING JUST FINE AND THEN— ZZZZT! BLACK SCREEN OF DEATH!
MUST HAVE BEEN A POWER SURGE, LIKE DUDDY WARNED ABOUT.
WE NEVER STOPPED PLAYING LONG ENOUGH TO CONNECT HIS NEW SURGE PROTECTOR.
WOULD IT HELP TO DO IT NOW?
SORRY, BOYS. IT'S TOO LATE.
SHAWN, WHERE ARE YOU GOING?
TO PUT MY NORMAL CLOTHES BACK ON.

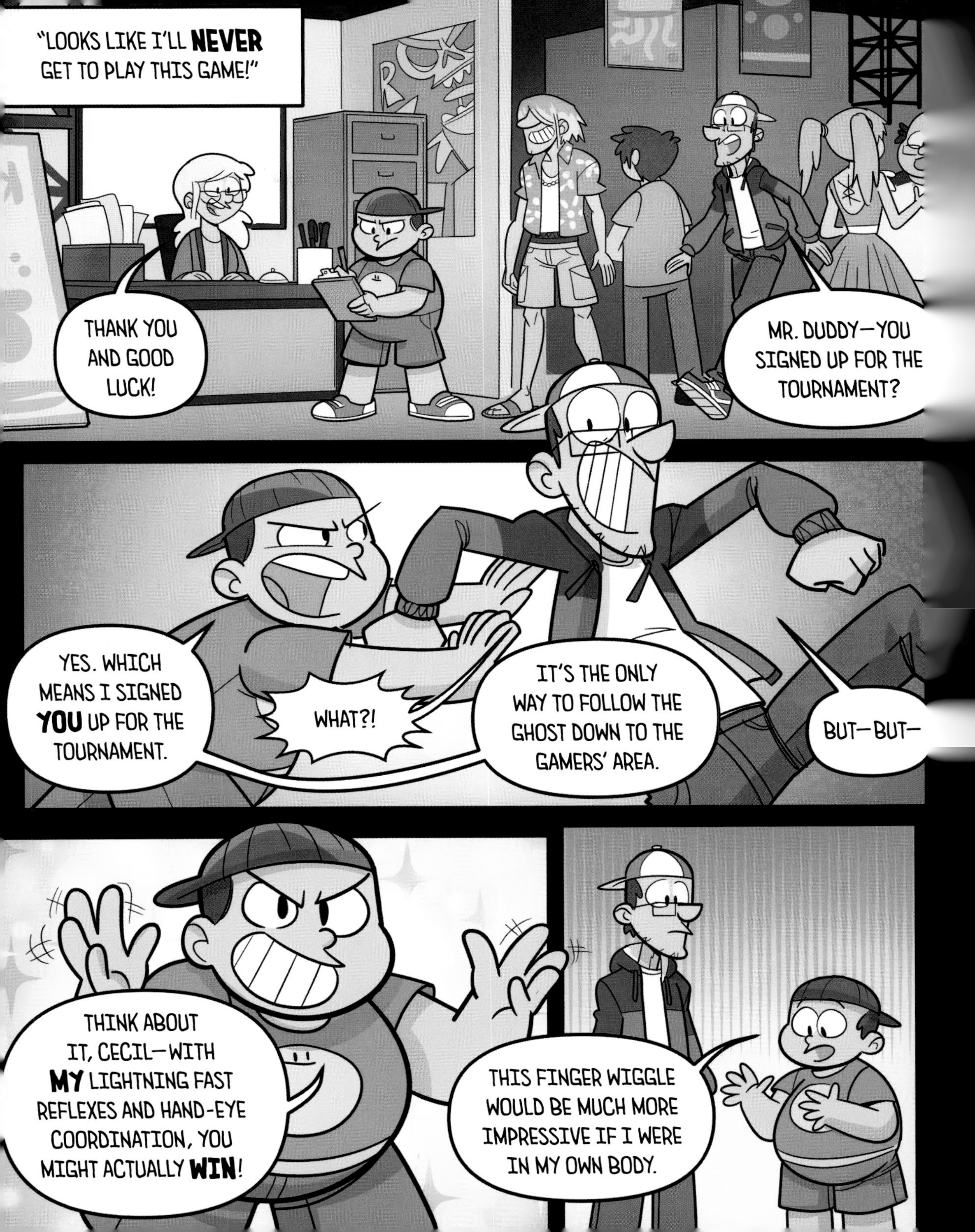
"LOOKS LIKE I'LL **NEVER** GET TO PLAY THIS GAME!"
THANK YOU AND GOOD LUCK!
MR. DUDDY—YOU SIGNED UP FOR THE TOURNAMENT?
YES. WHICH MEANS I SIGNED **YOU** UP FOR THE TOURNAMENT.
WHAT?!
IT'S THE ONLY WAY TO FOLLOW THE GHOST DOWN TO THE GAMERS' AREA.
BUT—BUT—
THINK ABOUT IT, CECIL—WITH **MY** LIGHTNING FAST REFLEXES AND HAND-EYE COORDINATION, YOU MIGHT ACTUALLY **WIN**!
THIS FINGER WIGGLE WOULD BE MUCH MORE IMPRESSIVE IF I WERE IN MY OWN BODY.

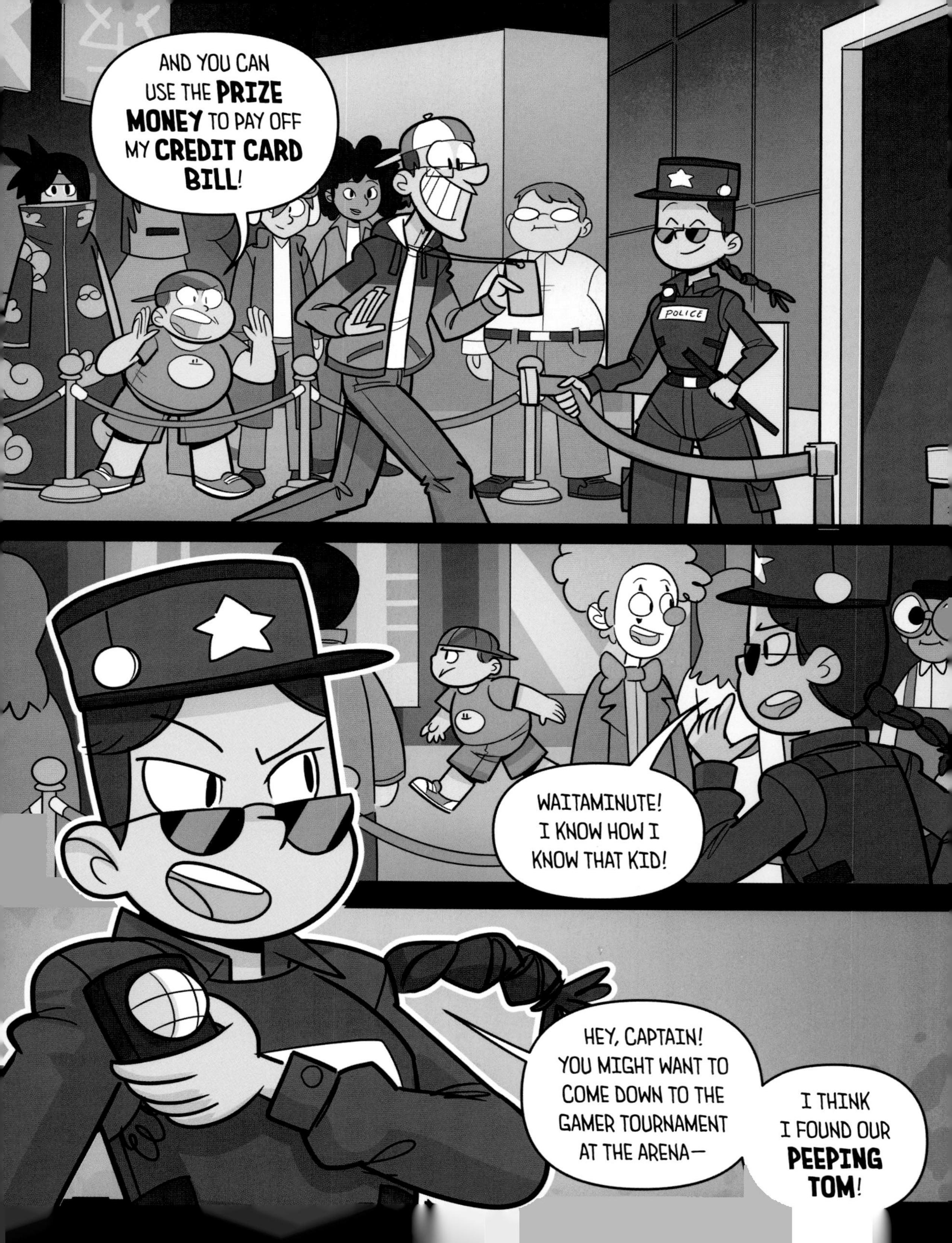
AND YOU CAN USE THE **PRIZE MONEY** TO PAY OFF MY **CREDIT CARD BILL**!
POLICE
WAITAMINUTE! I KNOW HOW I KNOW THAT KID!
HEY, CAPTAIN! YOU MIGHT WANT TO COME DOWN TO THE GAMER TOURNAMENT AT THE ARENA—
I THINK I FOUND OUR **PEEPING TOM**!

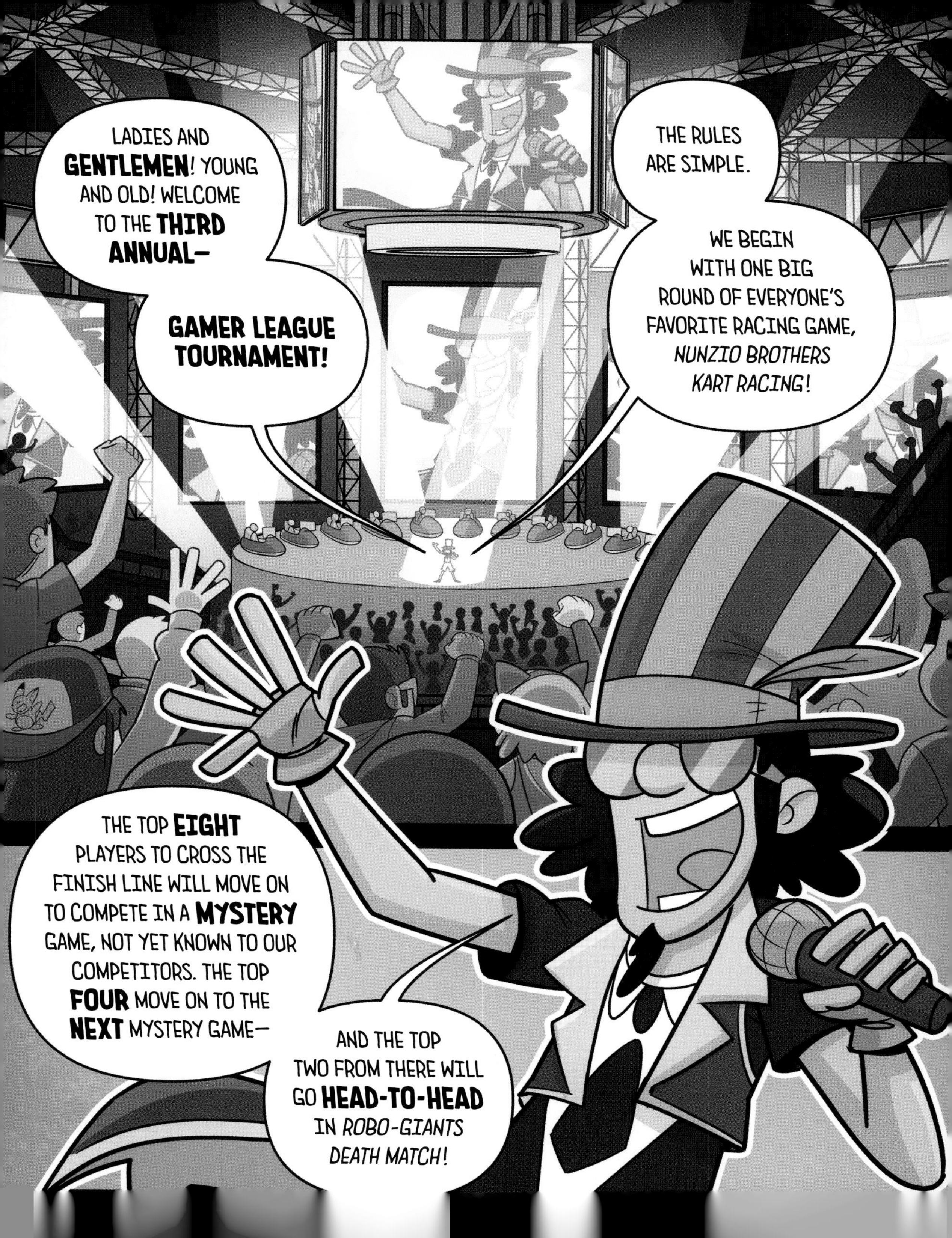
LADIES AND **GENTLEMEN**! YOUNG AND OLD! WELCOME TO THE **THIRD ANNUAL**—
**GAMER LEAGUE TOURNAMENT!**
THE RULES ARE SIMPLE.
WE BEGIN WITH ONE BIG ROUND OF EVERYONE'S FAVORITE RACING GAME, *NUNZIO BROTHERS KART RACING*!
THE TOP **EIGHT** PLAYERS TO CROSS THE FINISH LINE WILL MOVE ON TO COMPETE IN A **MYSTERY** GAME, NOT YET KNOWN TO OUR COMPETITORS. THE TOP **FOUR** MOVE ON TO THE **NEXT** MYSTERY GAME—
AND THE TOP TWO FROM THERE WILL GO **HEAD-TO-HEAD** IN *ROBO-GIANTS DEATH MATCH*!

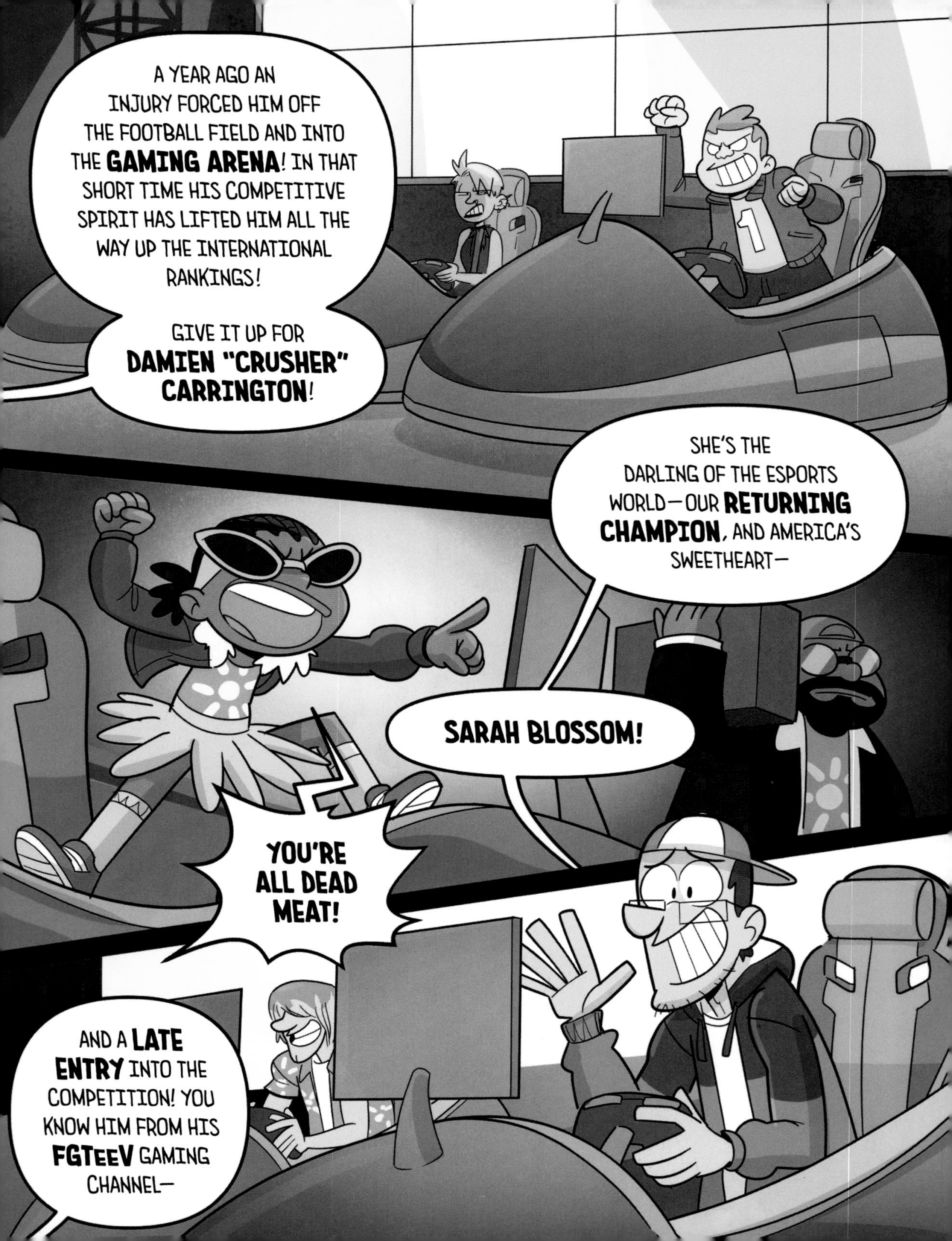
A YEAR AGO AN INJURY FORCED HIM OFF THE FOOTBALL FIELD AND INTO THE **GAMING ARENA**! IN THAT SHORT TIME HIS COMPETITIVE SPIRIT HAS LIFTED HIM ALL THE WAY UP THE INTERNATIONAL RANKINGS!
GIVE IT UP FOR **DAMIEN "CRUSHER" CARRINGTON**!
SHE'S THE DARLING OF THE ESPORTS WORLD—OUR **RETURNING CHAMPION**, AND AMERICA'S SWEETHEART—
SARAH BLOSSOM!
YOU'RE ALL DEAD MEAT!
AND A **LATE ENTRY** INTO THE COMPETITION! YOU KNOW HIM FROM HIS **FGTeeV** GAMING CHANNEL—

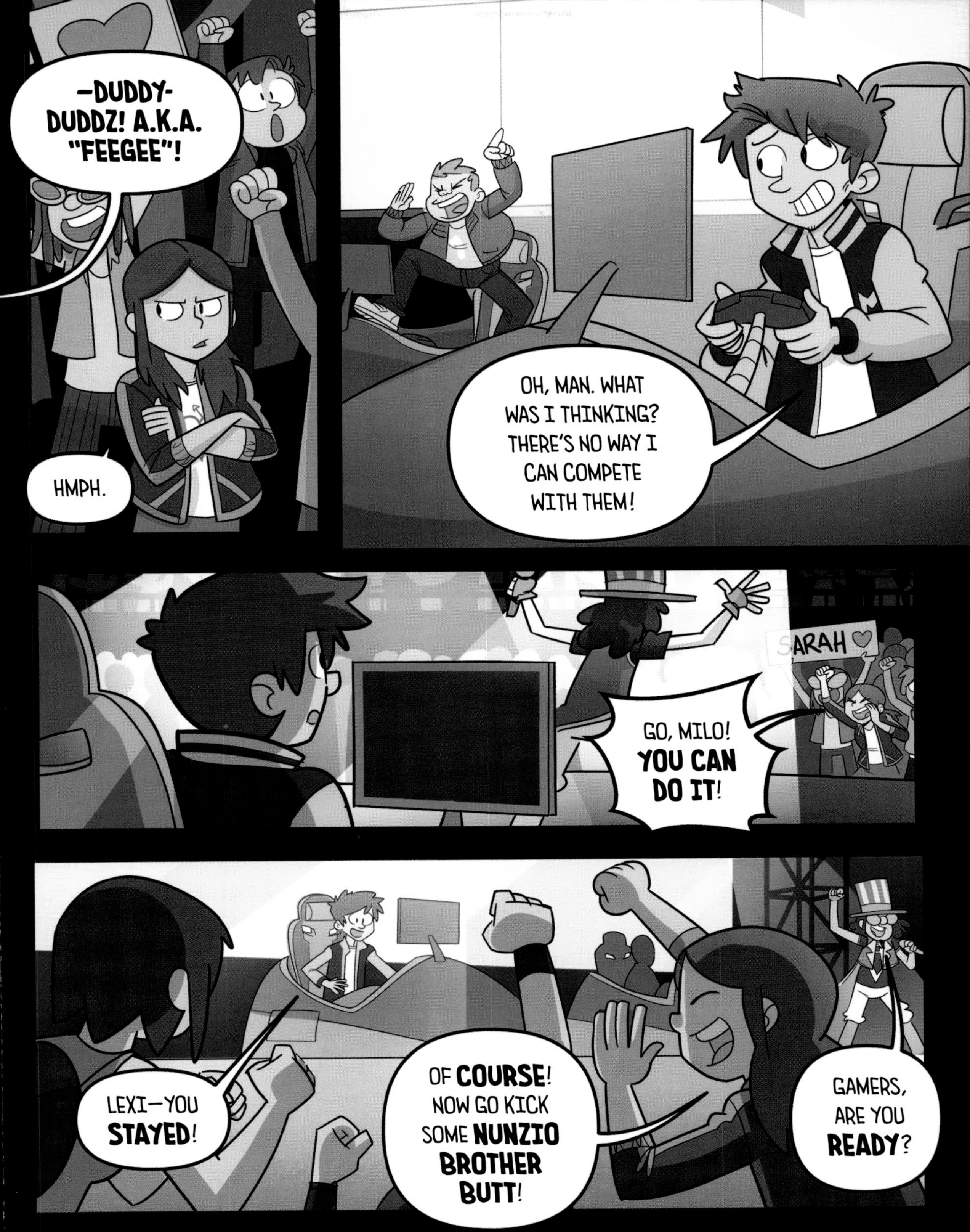

—DUDDY-DUDDZ! A.K.A. "FEEGEE"!
HMPH.
OH, MAN. WHAT WAS I THINKING? THERE'S NO WAY I CAN COMPETE WITH THEM!
SARAH
GO, MILO! **YOU CAN DO IT**!
LEXI—YOU **STAYED**!
OF **COURSE**! NOW GO KICK SOME **NUNZIO BROTHER BUTT**!
GAMERS, ARE YOU **READY**?

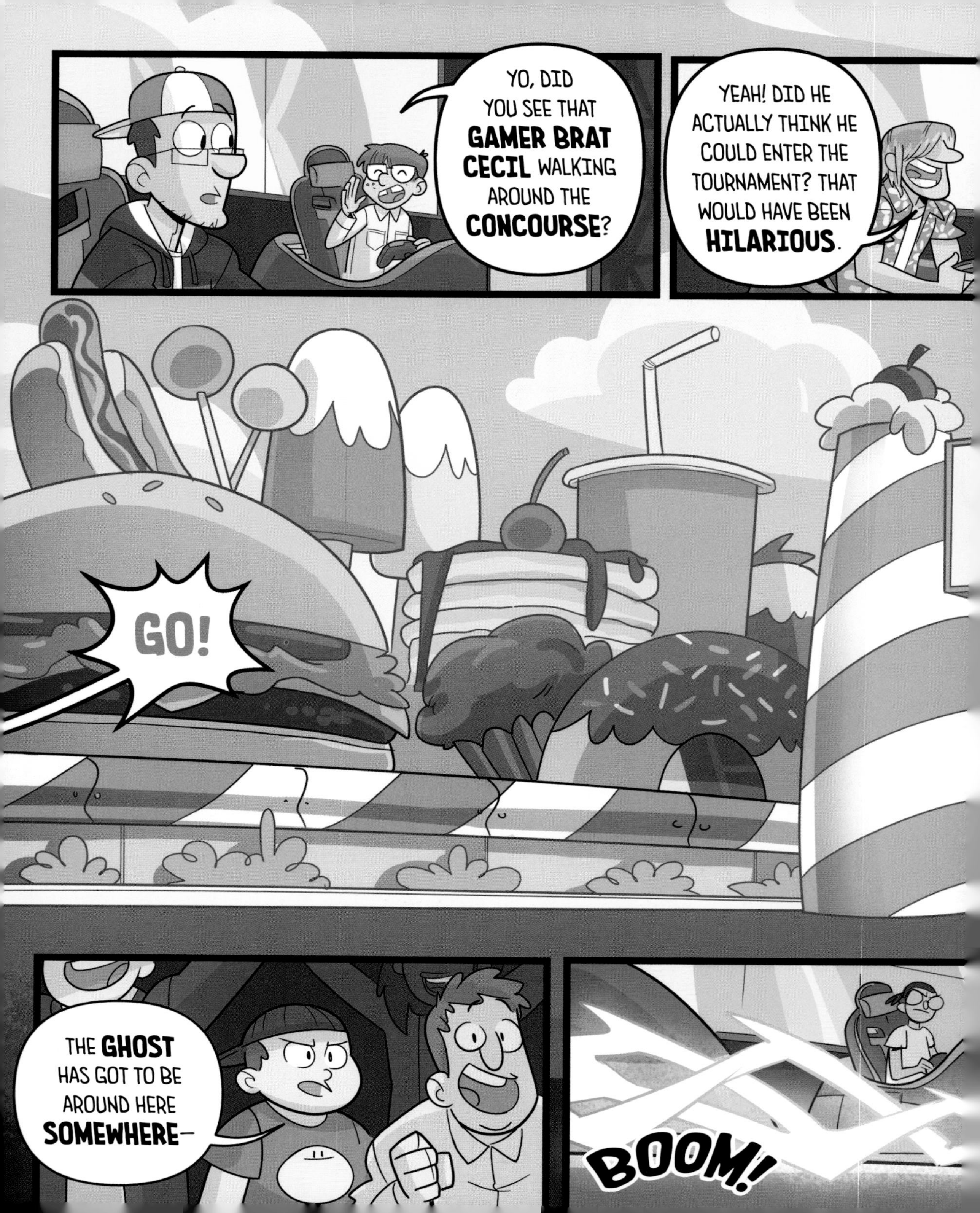
YO, DID YOU SEE THAT **GAMER BRAT CECIL** WALKING AROUND THE **CONCOURSE**?
YEAH! DID HE ACTUALLY THINK HE COULD ENTER THE TOURNAMENT? THAT WOULD HAVE BEEN **HILARIOUS**.
GO!
THE **GHOST** HAS GOT TO BE AROUND HERE **SOMEWHERE**—
BOOM!

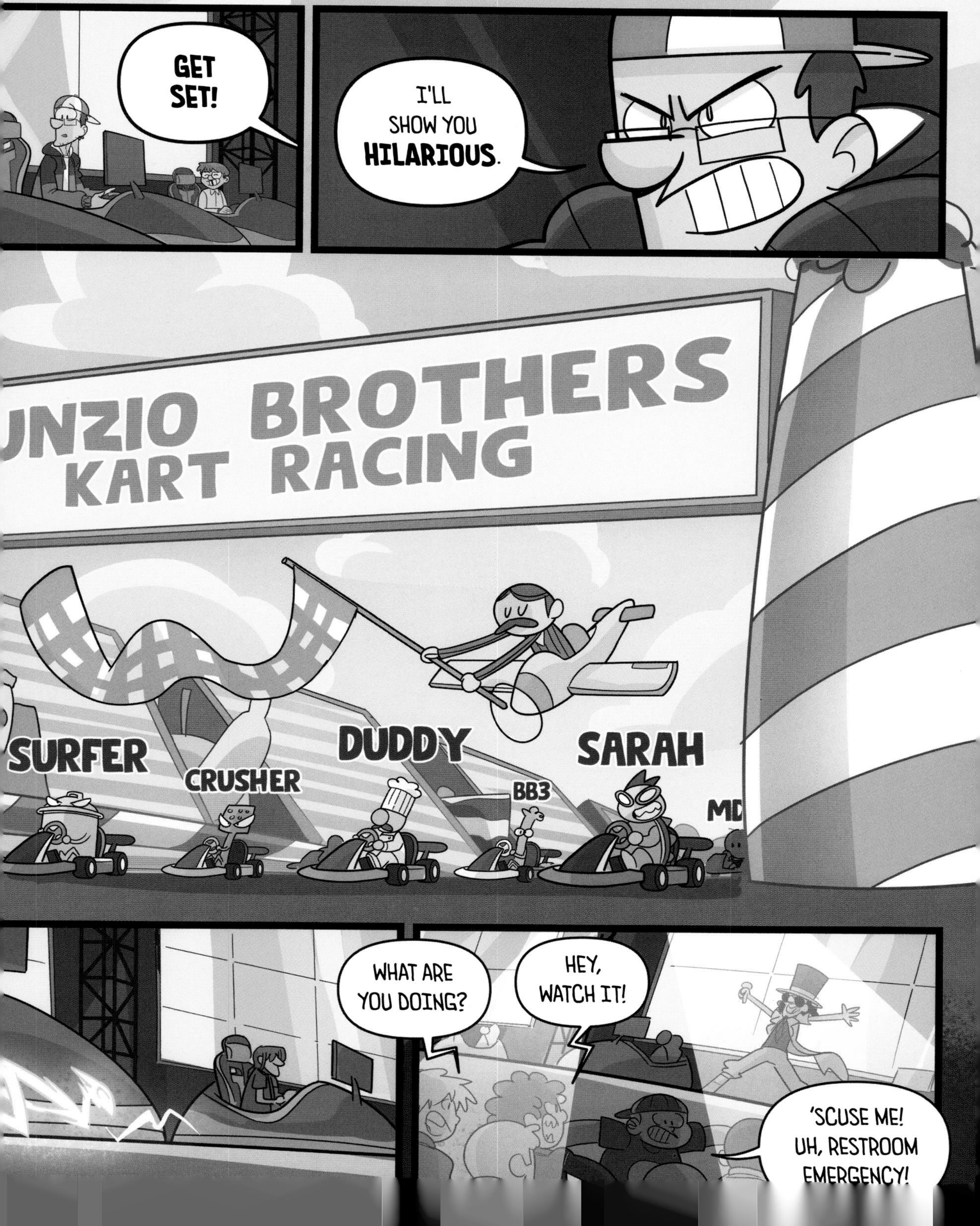
GET SET!
I'LL SHOW YOU HILARIOUS.
UNZIO BROTHERS KART RACING
SURFER
CRUSHER
DUDDY
BB3
SARAH
MD
WHAT ARE YOU DOING?
HEY, WATCH IT!
'SCUSE ME! UH, RESTROOM EMERGENCY!

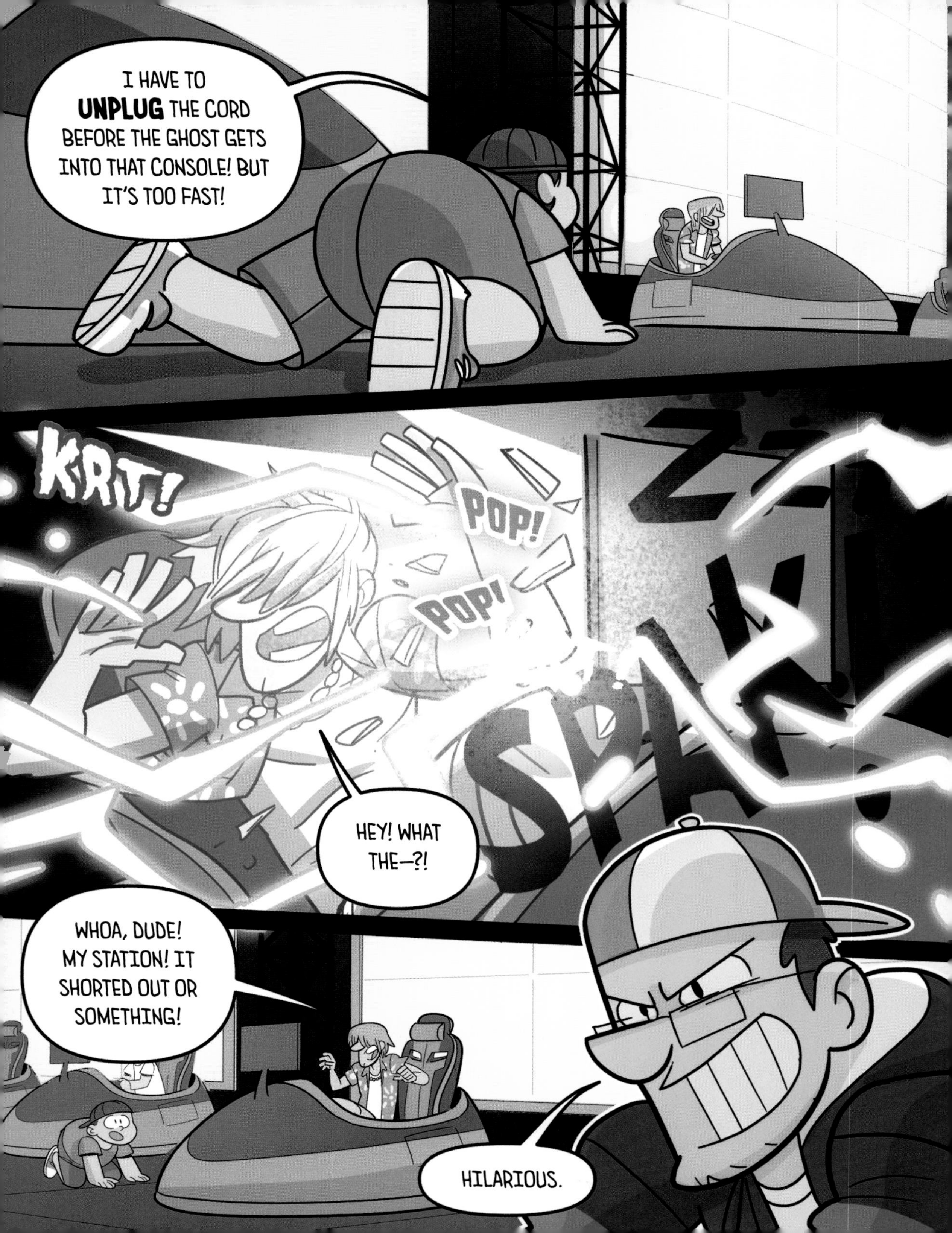
I HAVE TO **UNPLUG** THE CORD BEFORE THE GHOST GETS INTO THAT CONSOLE! BUT IT'S TOO FAST!
KRT!
POP!
POP!
HEY! WHAT THE—?!
WHOA, DUDE! MY STATION! IT SHORTED OUT OR SOMETHING!
HILARIOUS.

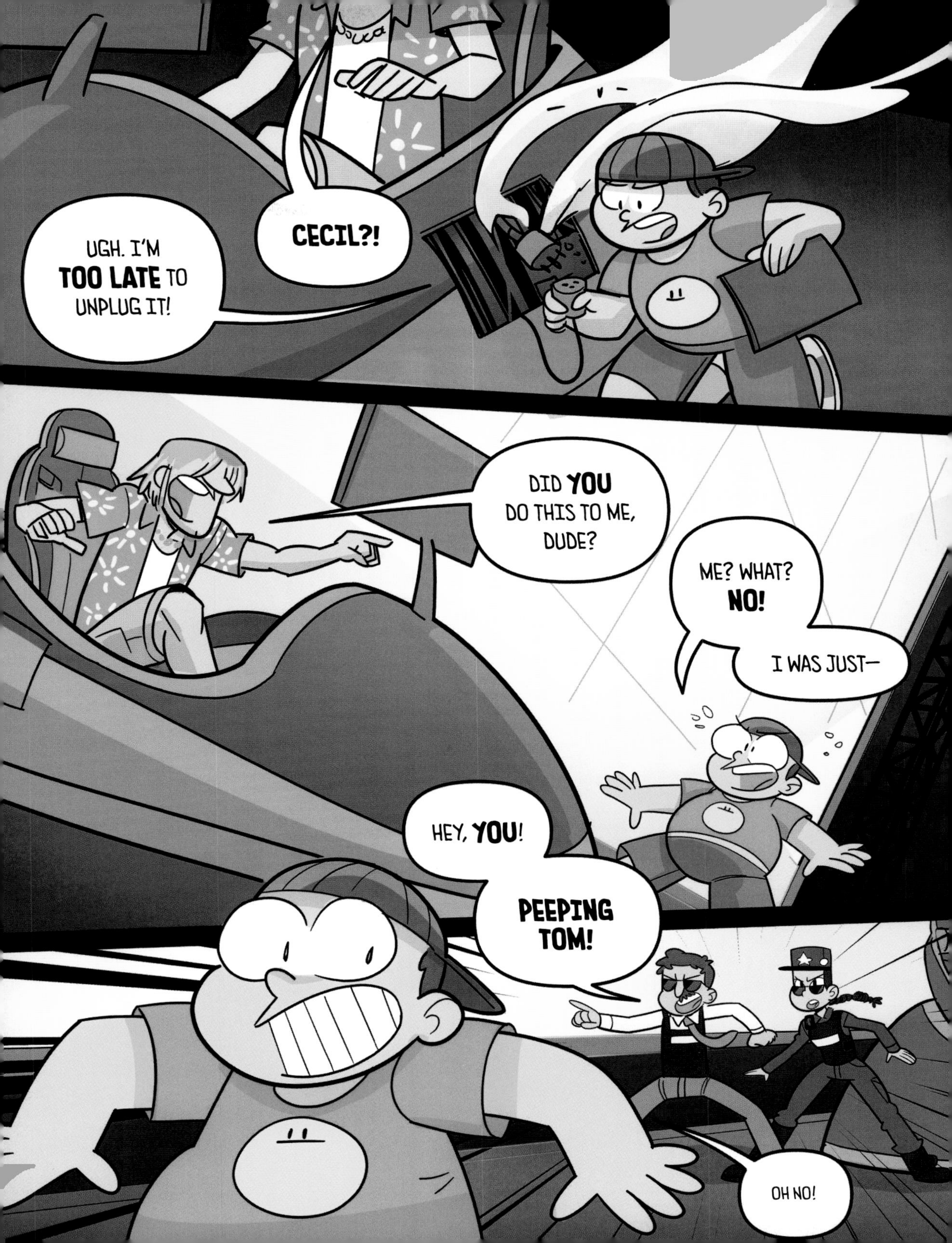
CECIL?!
UGH. I'M TOO LATE TO UNPLUG IT!
DID YOU DO THIS TO ME, DUDE?
ME? WHAT? NO!
I WAS JUST—
HEY, YOU!
PEEPING TOM!
OH NO!

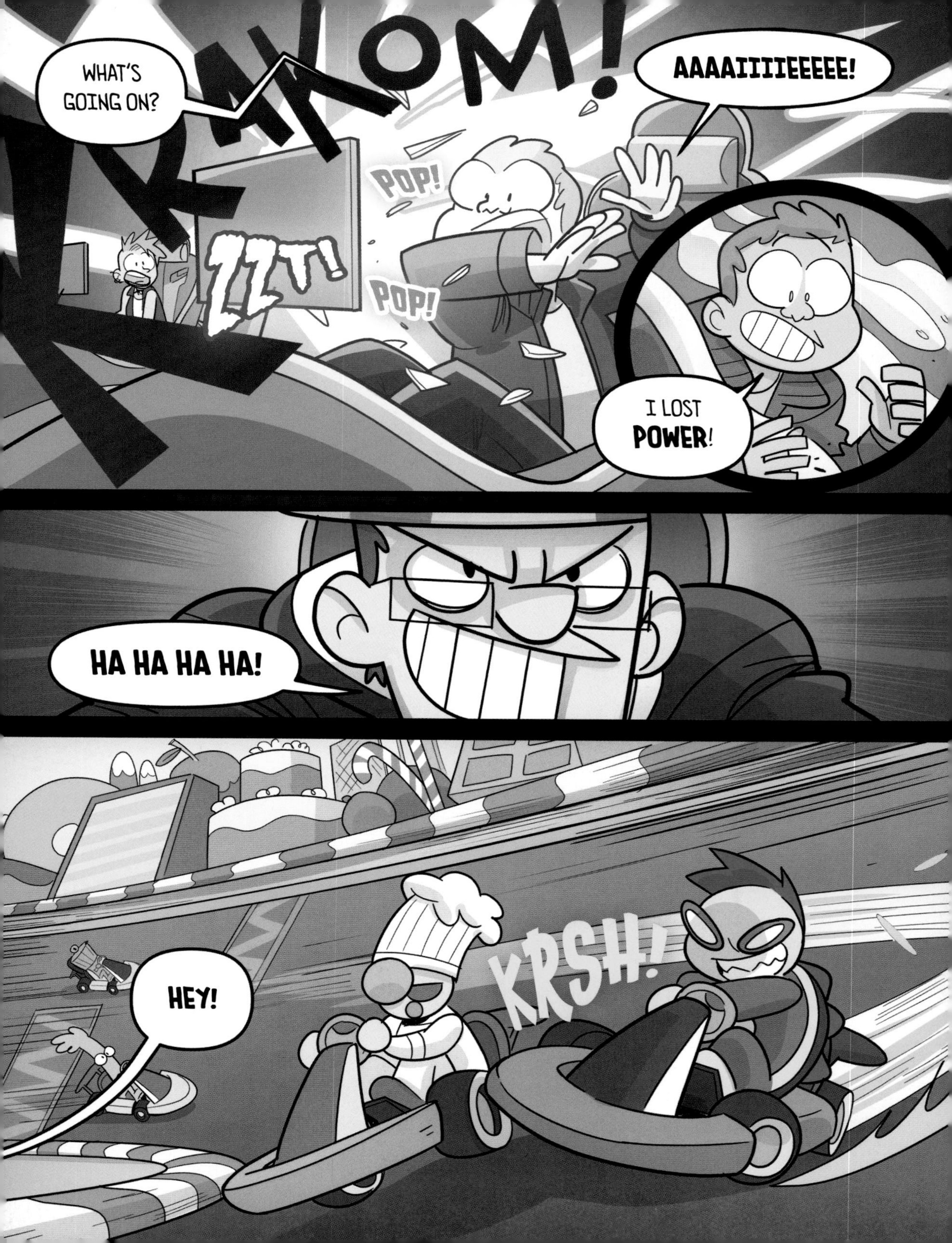
KRAKOOM!
WHAT'S GOING ON?
AAAAIIIIEEEEE!
POP!
ZZT!
POP!
I LOST POWER!
HA HA HA HA!
HEY!
KRSH!

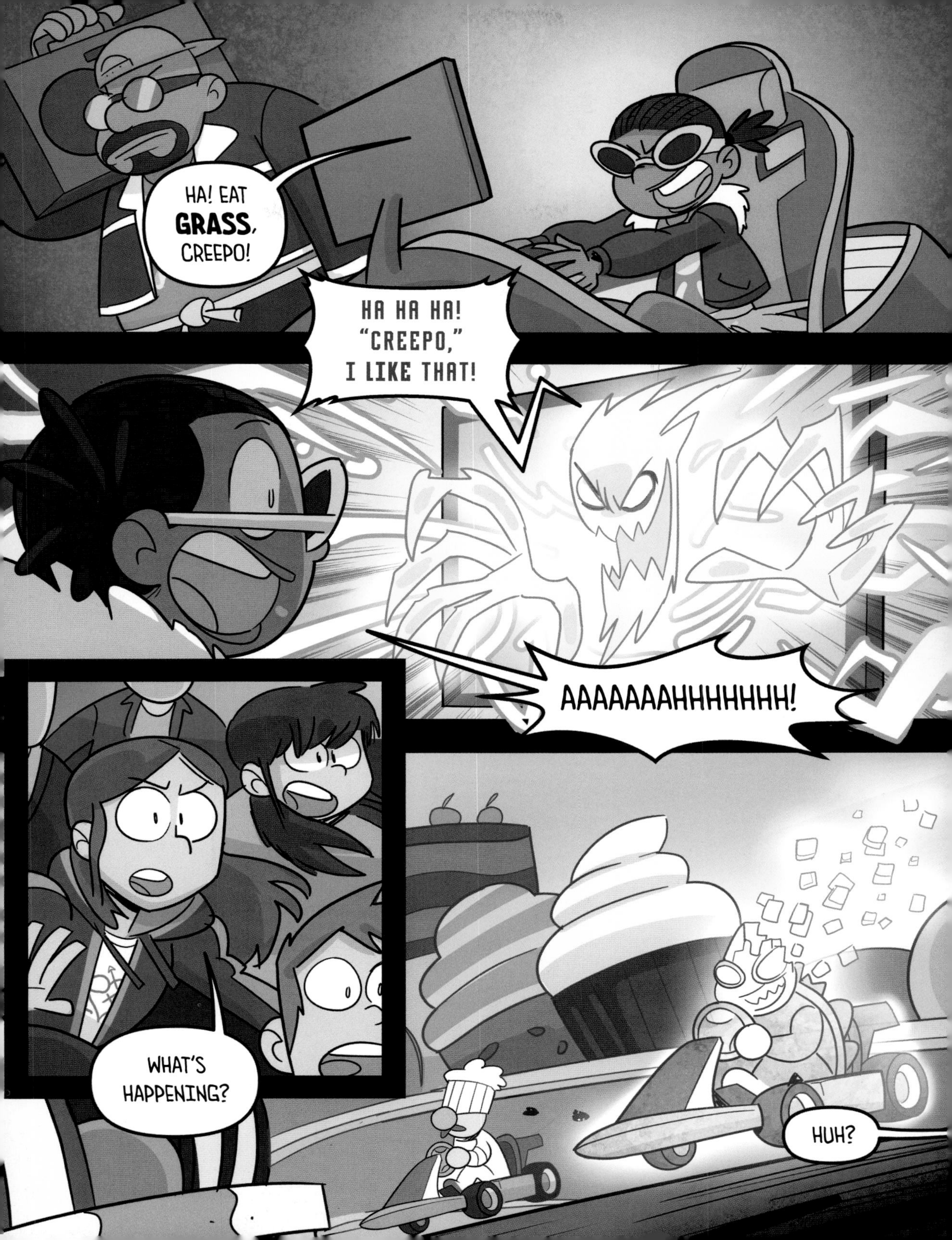
HA! EAT **GRASS**, CREEPO!
HA HA HA! "CREEPO," I **LIKE** THAT!
AAAAAAAHHHHHHH!
WHAT'S HAPPENING?
HUH?

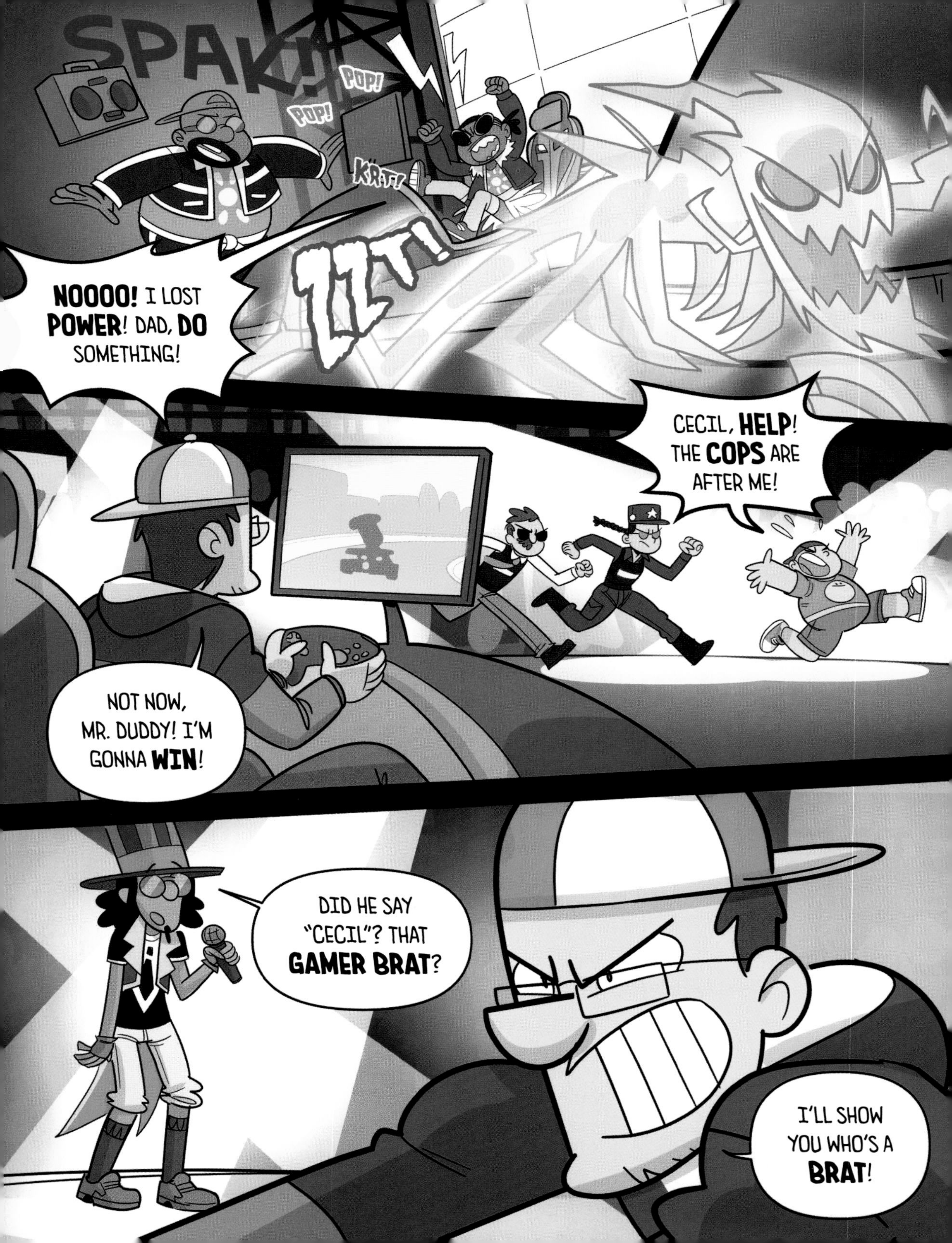
SPAK!!
POP!
POP!
KRTT!
ZZT!
NOOOO! I LOST POWER! DAD, DO SOMETHING!
CECIL, HELP! THE COPS ARE AFTER ME!
NOT NOW, MR. DUDDY! I'M GONNA WIN!
DID HE SAY "CECIL"? THAT GAMER BRAT?
I'LL SHOW YOU WHO'S A BRAT!

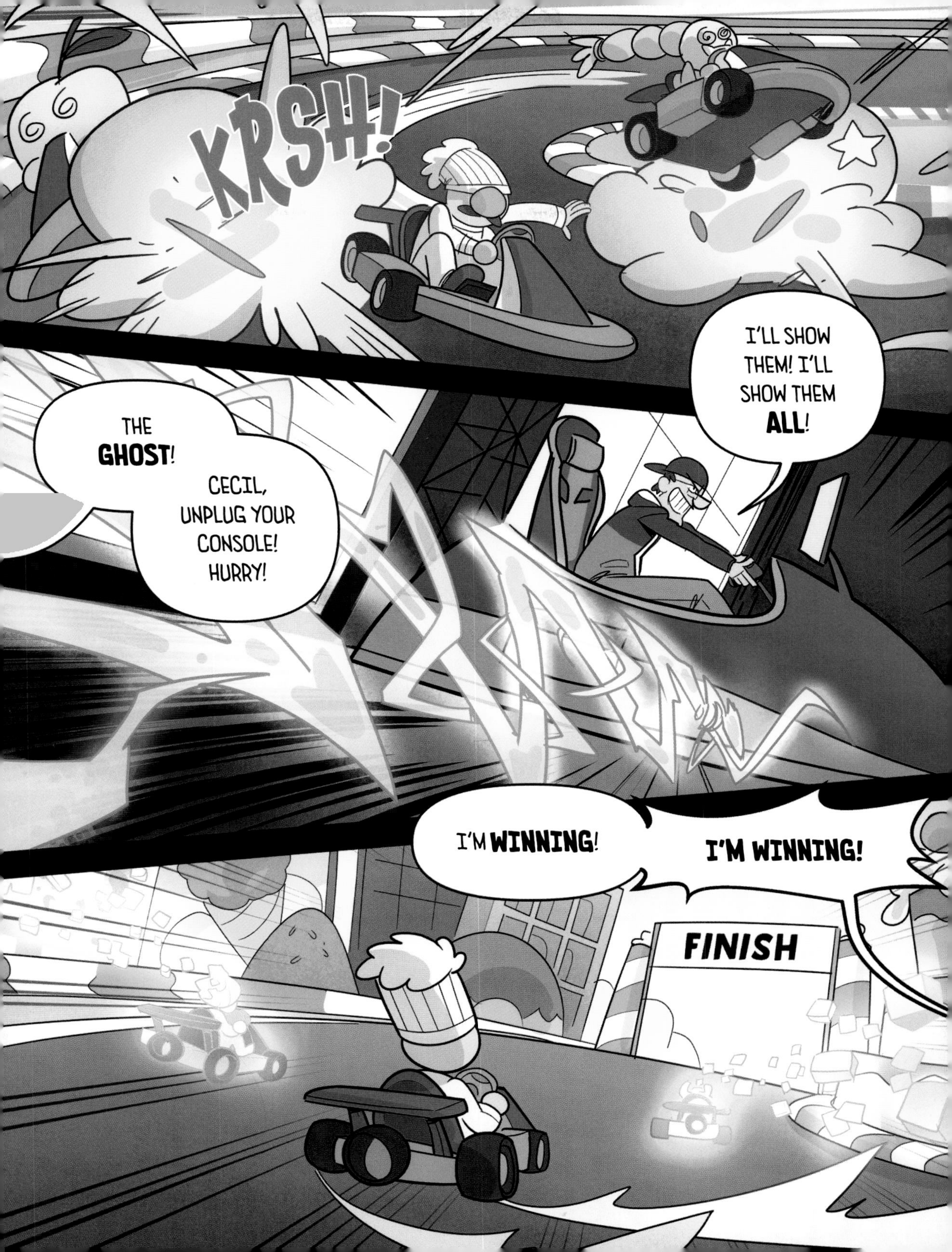
KRSH!
I'LL SHOW THEM! I'LL SHOW THEM ALL!
THE GHOST!
CECIL, UNPLUG YOUR CONSOLE! HURRY!
I'M WINNING!
I'M WINNING!
FINISH

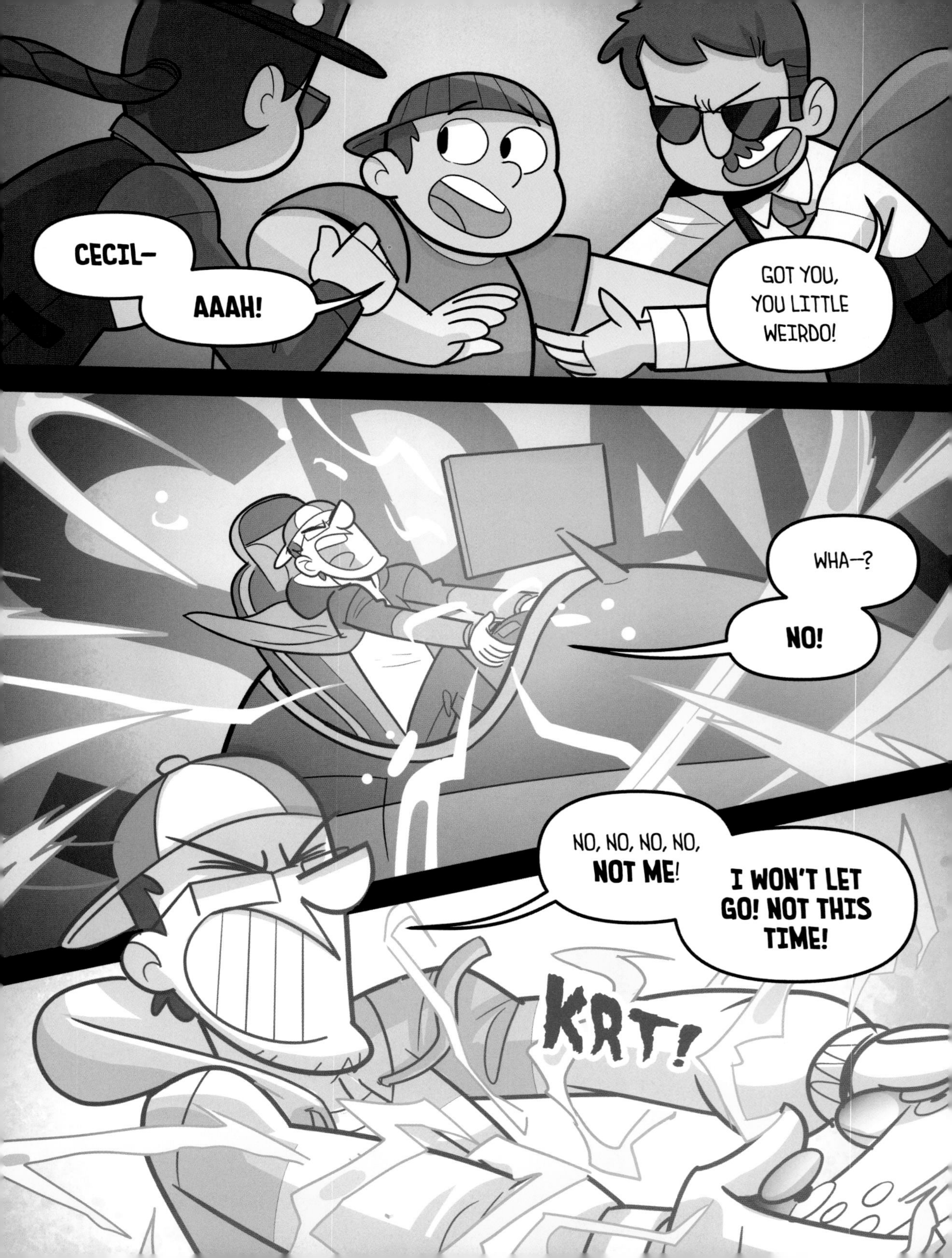
CECIL—
AAAH!
GOT YOU, YOU LITTLE WEIRDO!
WHA—?
NO!
NO, NO, NO, NO, NOT ME!
I WON'T LET GO! NOT THIS TIME!
KRT!

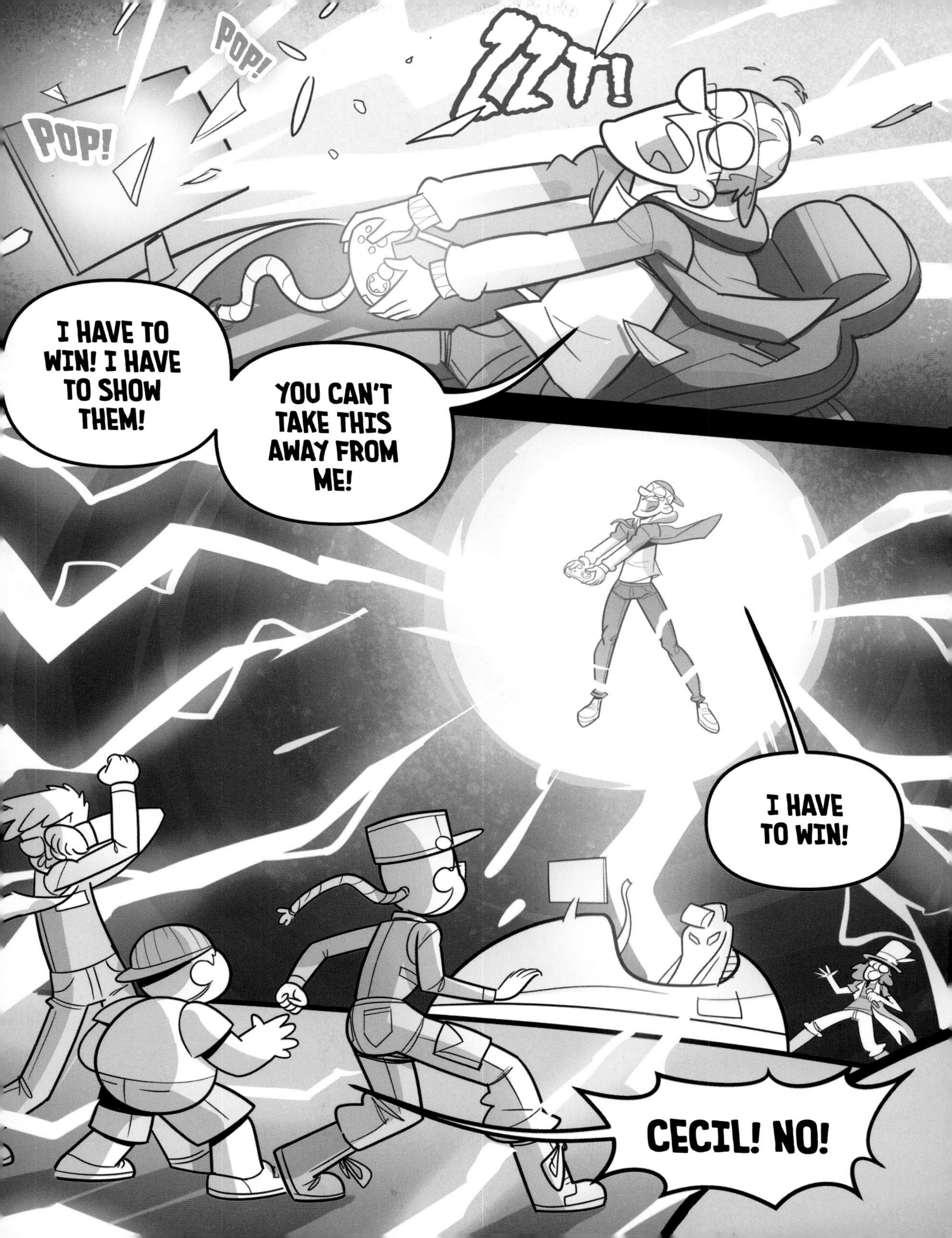
POP!
POP!
ZZZT!
I HAVE TO WIN! I HAVE TO SHOW THEM!
YOU CAN'T TAKE THIS AWAY FROM ME!
I HAVE TO WIN!
CECIL! NO!

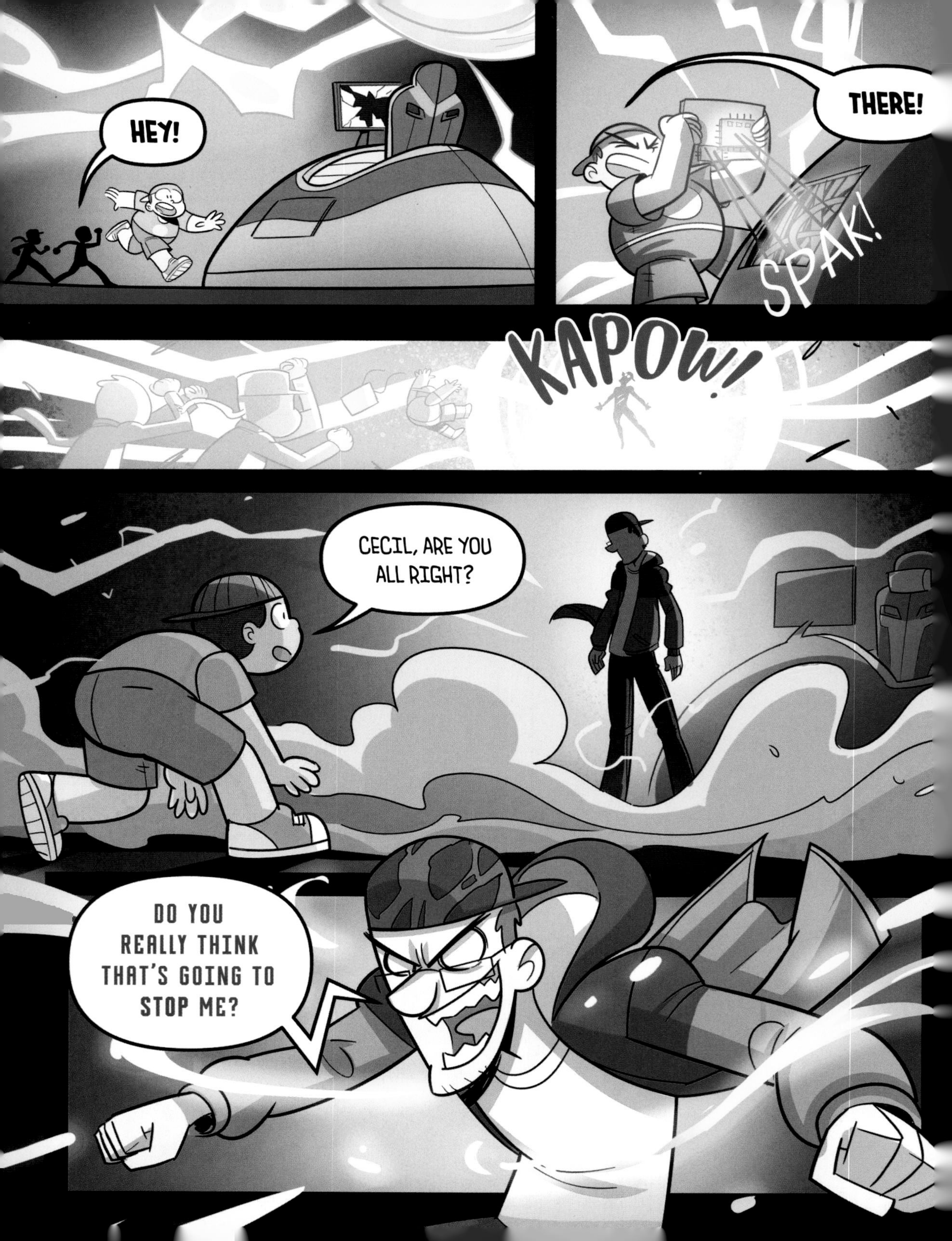
HEY!
THERE!
SPAK!
KAPOW!
CECIL, ARE YOU ALL RIGHT?
DO YOU REALLY THINK THAT'S GOING TO STOP ME?

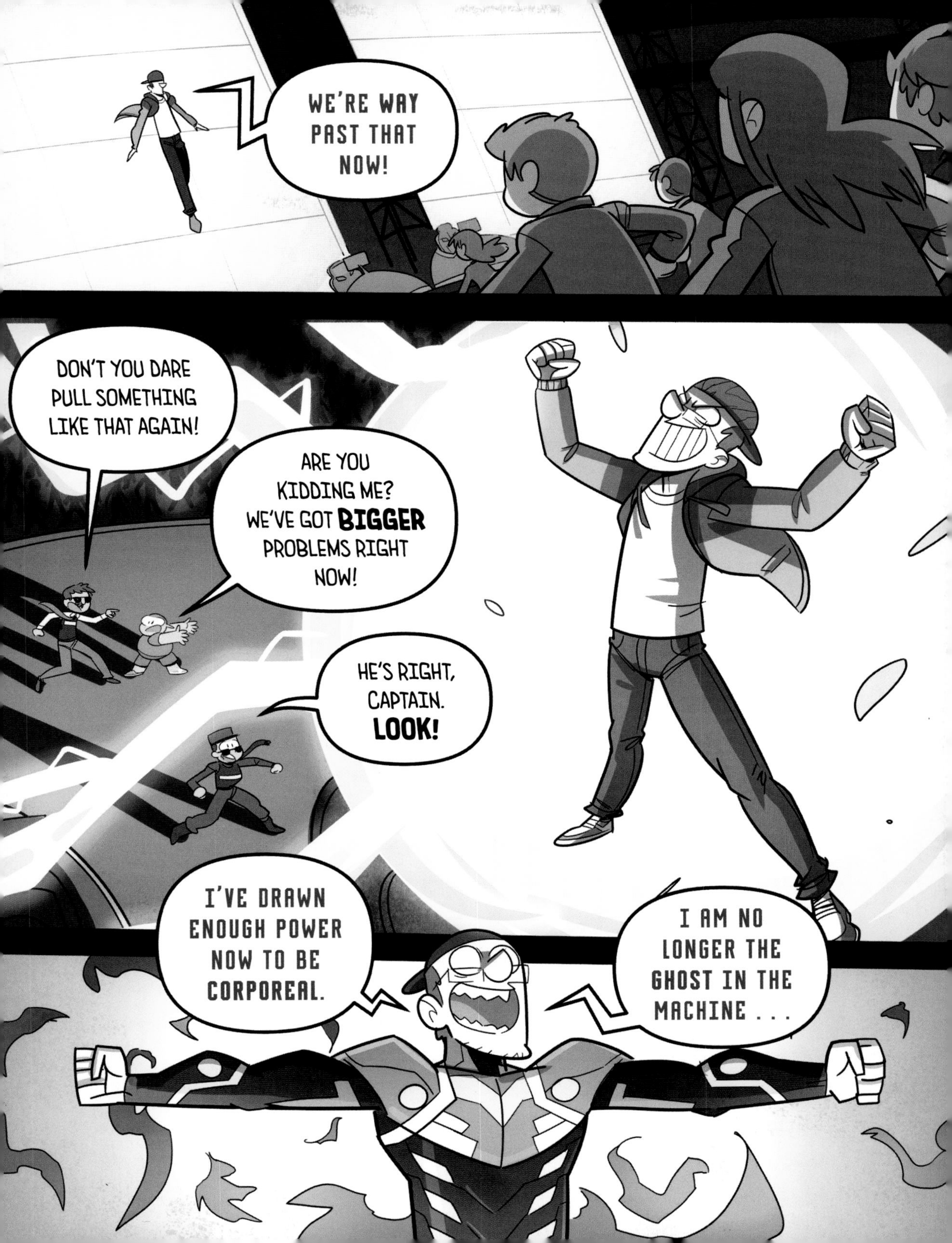
WE'RE WAY PAST THAT NOW!
DON'T YOU DARE PULL SOMETHING LIKE THAT AGAIN!
ARE YOU KIDDING ME? WE'VE GOT **BIGGER** PROBLEMS RIGHT NOW!
HE'S RIGHT, CAPTAIN. **LOOK!**
I'VE DRAWN ENOUGH POWER NOW TO BE CORPOREAL.
I AM NO LONGER THE GHOST IN THE MACHINE . . .

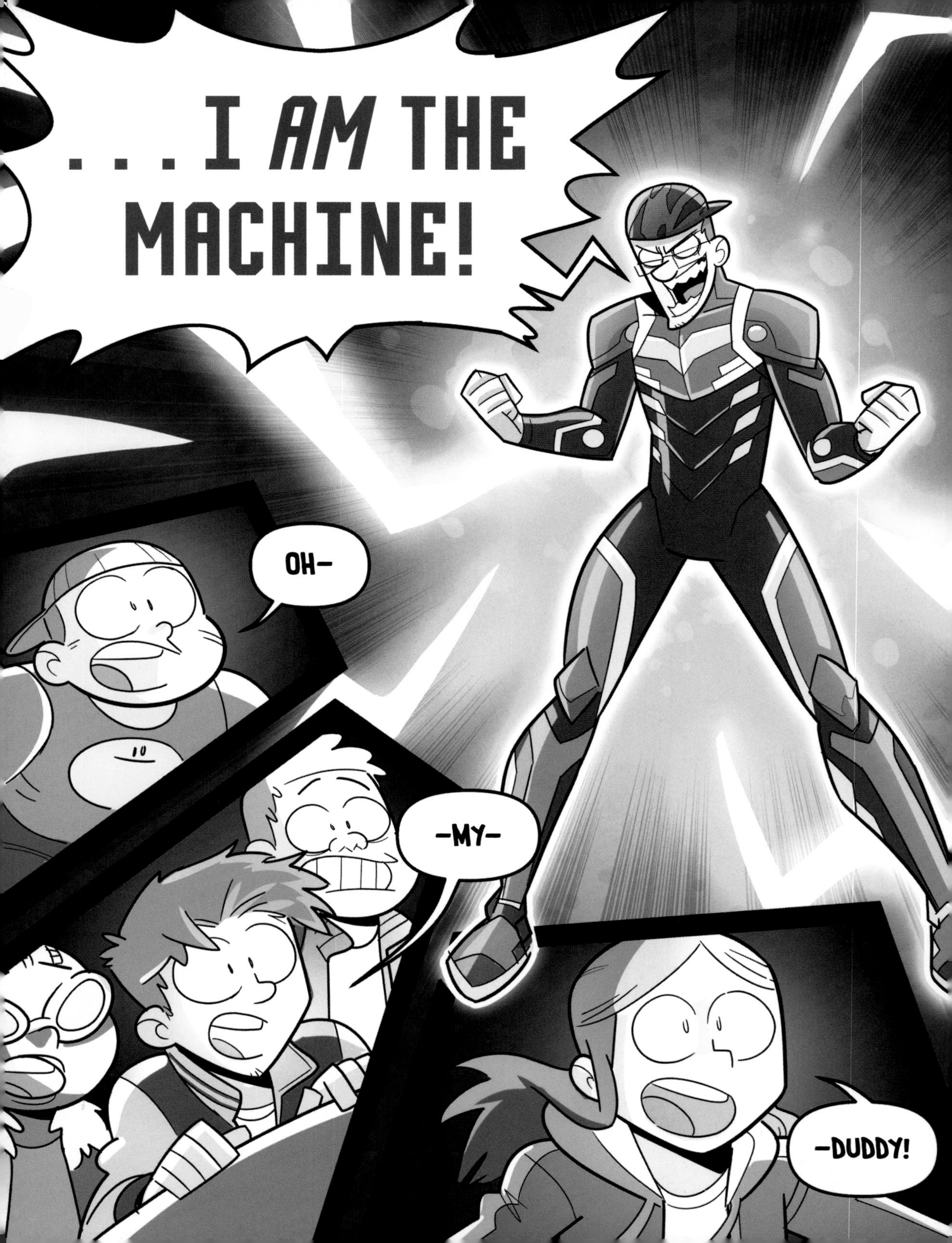
. . . I *AM* THE MACHINE!
OH-
-MY-
-DUDDY!

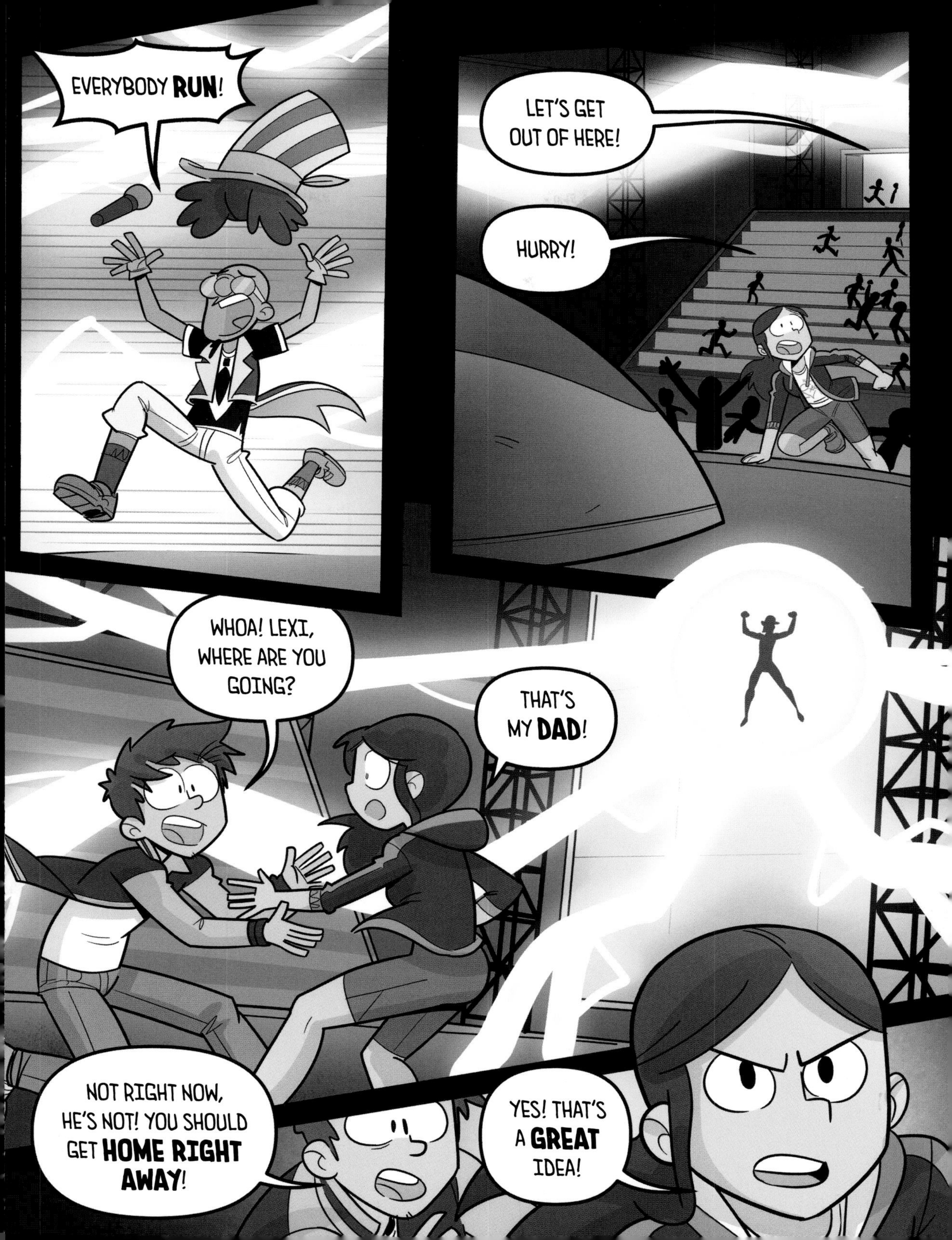
EVERYBODY **RUN**!
LET'S GET OUT OF HERE!
HURRY!
WHOA! LEXI, WHERE ARE YOU GOING?
THAT'S MY **DAD**!
NOT RIGHT NOW, HE'S NOT! YOU SHOULD GET **HOME RIGHT AWAY**!
YES! THAT'S A **GREAT** IDEA!

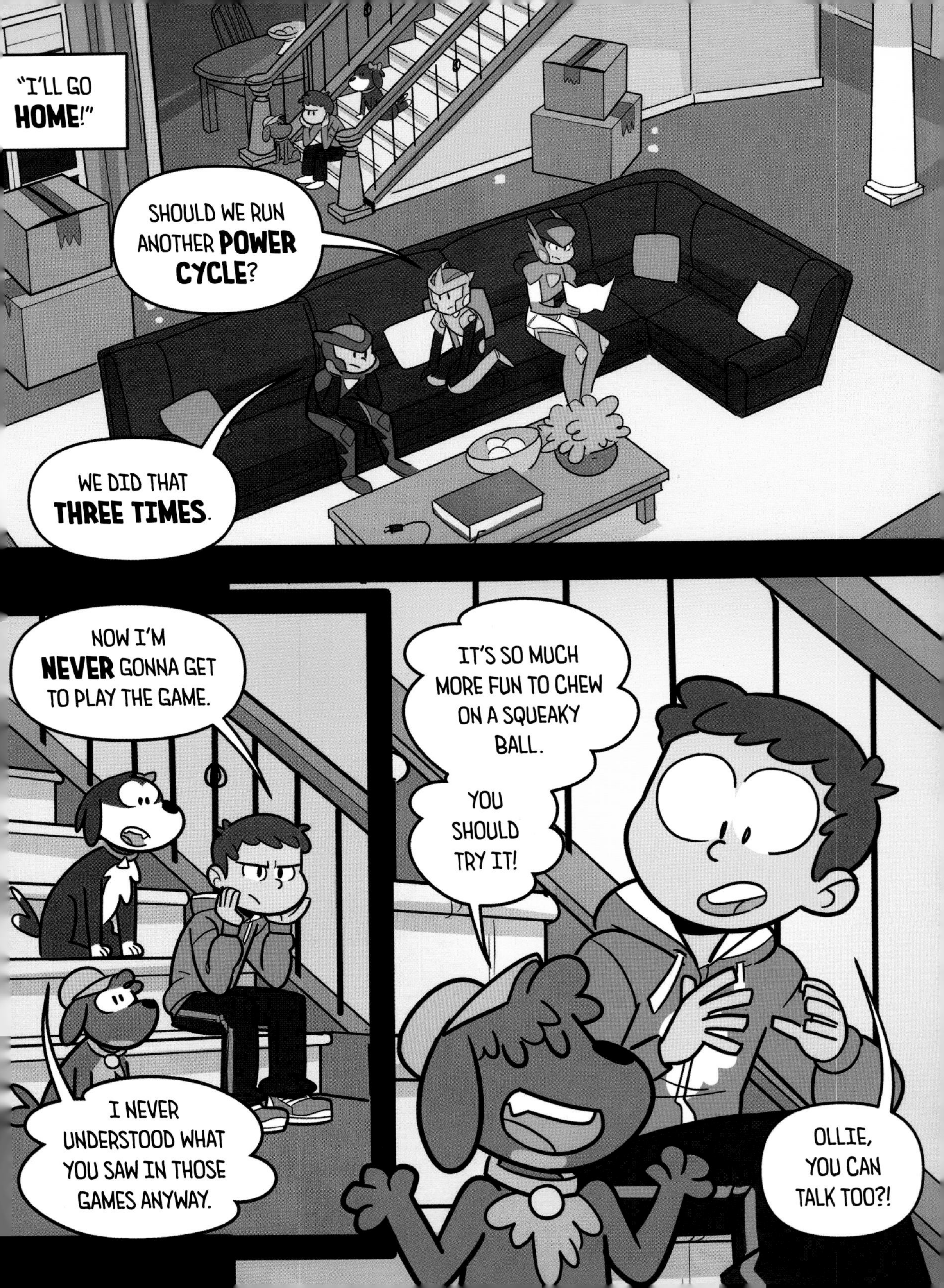
"I'LL GO **HOME**!"
SHOULD WE RUN ANOTHER **POWER CYCLE**?
WE DID THAT **THREE TIMES**.
NOW I'M **NEVER** GONNA GET TO PLAY THE GAME.
I NEVER UNDERSTOOD WHAT YOU SAW IN THOSE GAMES ANYWAY.
IT'S SO MUCH MORE FUN TO CHEW ON A SQUEAKY BALL.
YOU SHOULD TRY IT!
OLLIE, YOU CAN TALK TOO?!

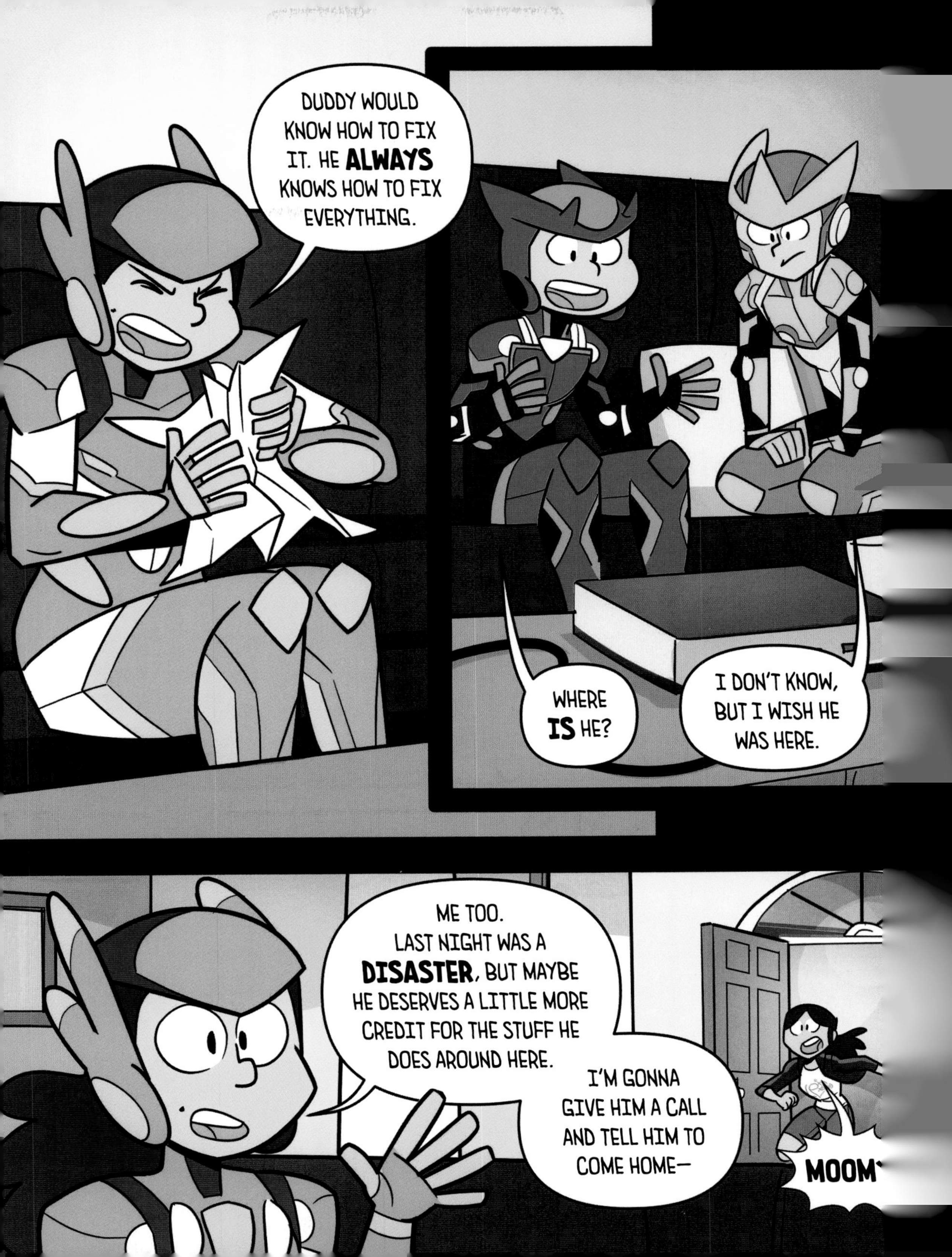
DUDDY WOULD KNOW HOW TO FIX IT. HE **ALWAYS** KNOWS HOW TO FIX EVERYTHING.
WHERE **IS** HE?
I DON'T KNOW, BUT I WISH HE WAS HERE.
ME TOO. LAST NIGHT WAS A **DISASTER**, BUT MAYBE HE DESERVES A LITTLE MORE CREDIT FOR THE STUFF HE DOES AROUND HERE.
I'M GONNA GIVE HIM A CALL AND TELL HIM TO COME HOME—
MOOM

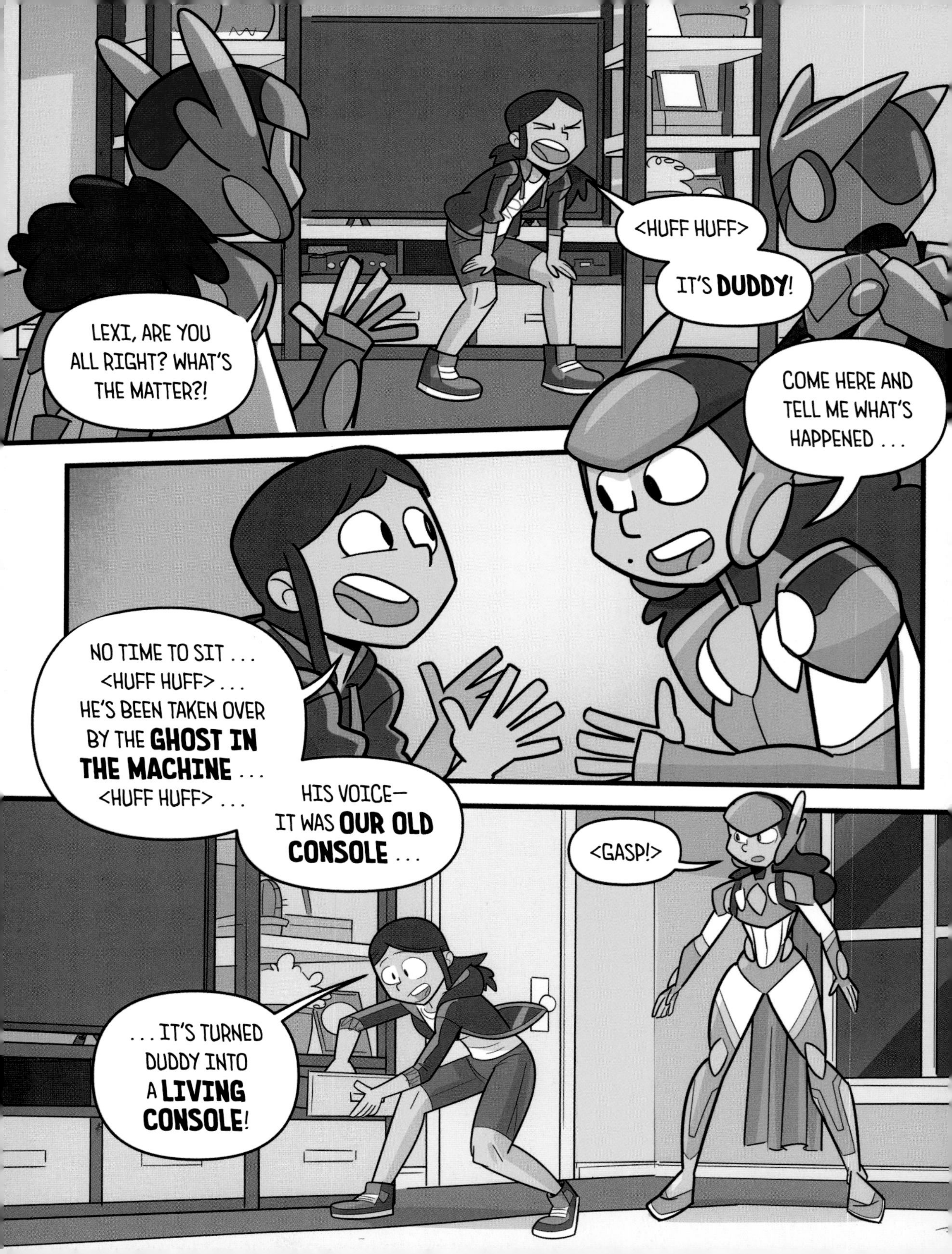
LEXI, ARE YOU ALL RIGHT? WHAT'S THE MATTER?!
<HUFF HUFF>
IT'S **DUDDY**!
COME HERE AND TELL ME WHAT'S HAPPENED . . .
NO TIME TO SIT . . . <HUFF HUFF> . . . HE'S BEEN TAKEN OVER BY THE **GHOST IN THE MACHINE** . . . <HUFF HUFF> . . .
HIS VOICE— IT WAS **OUR OLD CONSOLE** . . .
<GASP!>
. . . IT'S TURNED DUDDY INTO A **LIVING CONSOLE**!

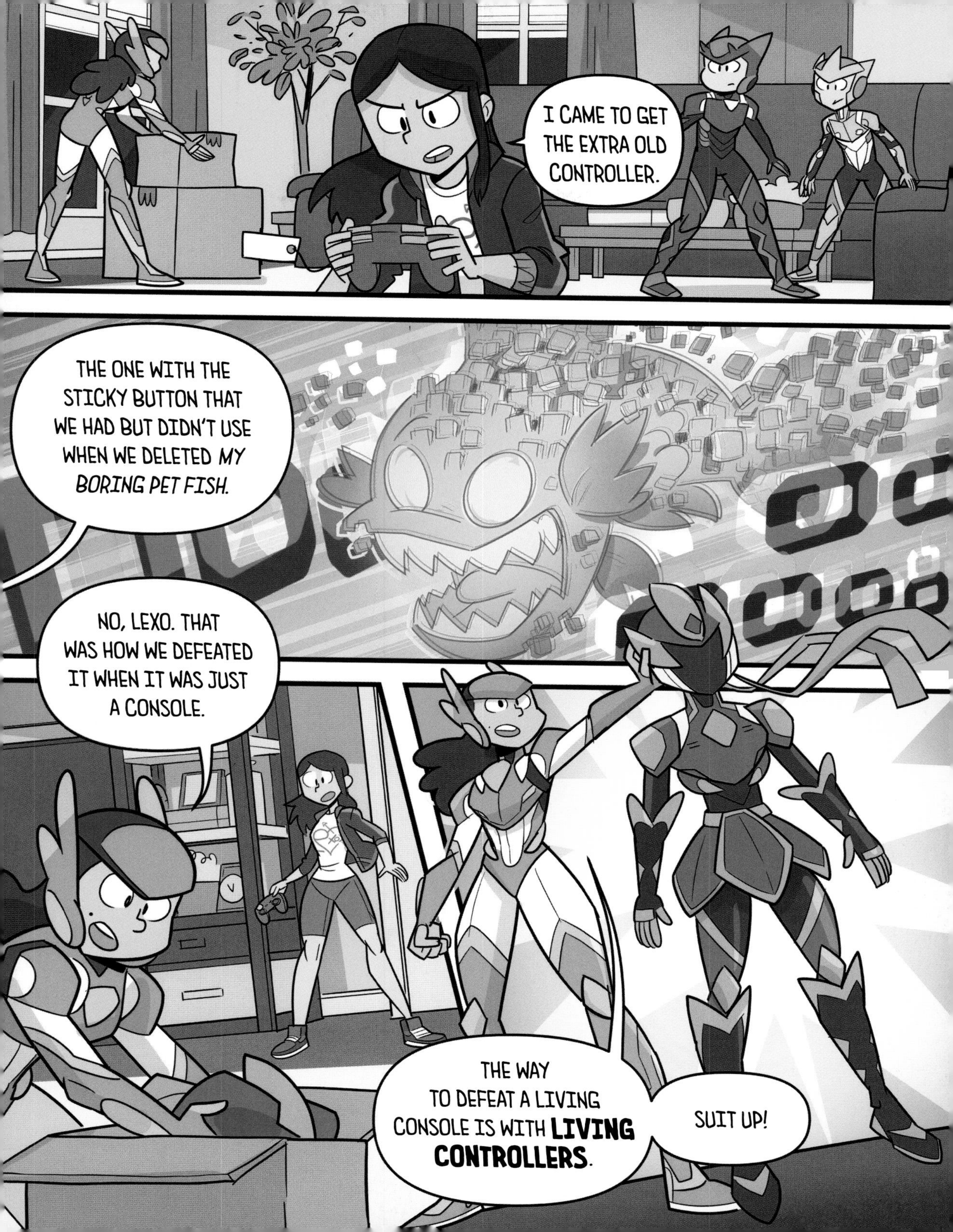
I CAME TO GET THE EXTRA OLD CONTROLLER.
THE ONE WITH THE STICKY BUTTON THAT WE HAD BUT DIDN'T USE WHEN WE DELETED *MY BORING PET FISH.*
NO, LEXO. THAT WAS HOW WE DEFEATED IT WHEN IT WAS JUST A CONSOLE.
THE WAY TO DEFEAT A LIVING CONSOLE IS WITH **LIVING CONTROLLERS**.
SUIT UP!

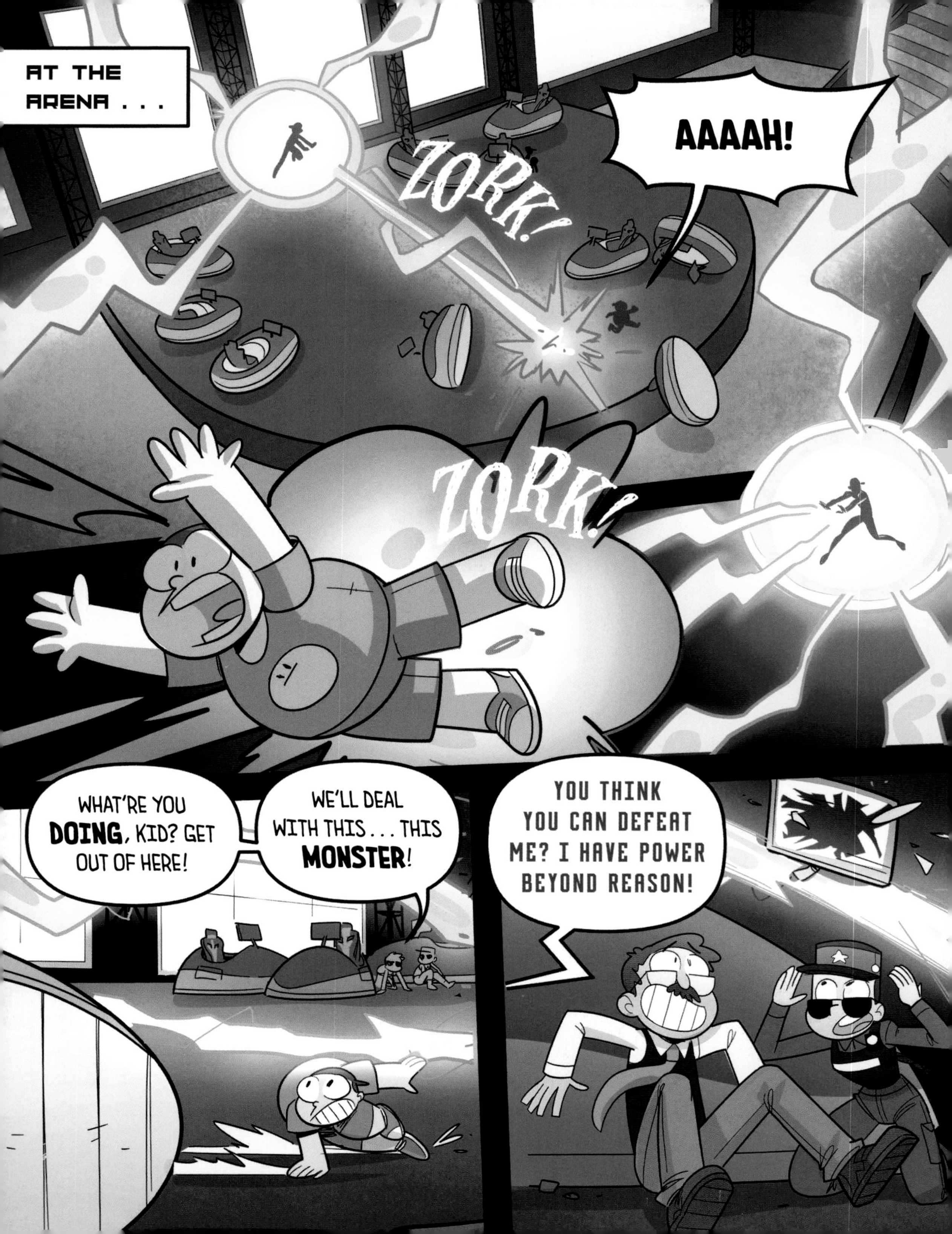
AT THE ARENA . . .
ZORK!
AAAAH!
ZORK!
WHAT'RE YOU DOING, KID? GET OUT OF HERE!
WE'LL DEAL WITH THIS . . . THIS MONSTER!
YOU THINK YOU CAN DEFEAT ME? I HAVE POWER BEYOND REASON!

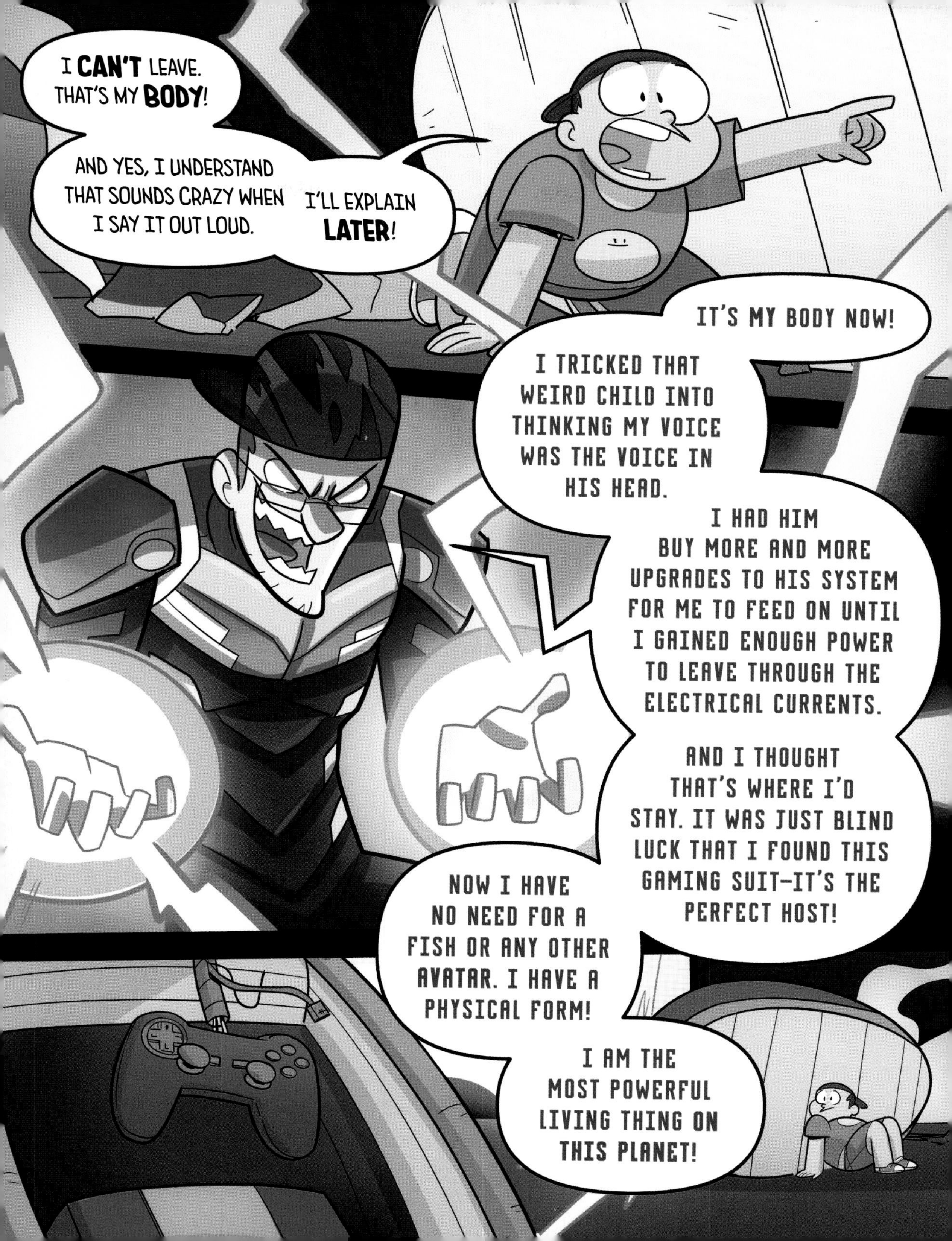

I CAN'T LEAVE. THAT'S MY BODY!
AND YES, I UNDERSTAND THAT SOUNDS CRAZY WHEN I SAY IT OUT LOUD.
I'LL EXPLAIN LATER!
IT'S MY BODY NOW!
I TRICKED THAT WEIRD CHILD INTO THINKING MY VOICE WAS THE VOICE IN HIS HEAD.
I HAD HIM BUY MORE AND MORE UPGRADES TO HIS SYSTEM FOR ME TO FEED ON UNTIL I GAINED ENOUGH POWER TO LEAVE THROUGH THE ELECTRICAL CURRENTS.
AND I THOUGHT THAT'S WHERE I'D STAY. IT WAS JUST BLIND LUCK THAT I FOUND THIS GAMING SUIT—IT'S THE PERFECT HOST!
NOW I HAVE NO NEED FOR A FISH OR ANY OTHER AVATAR. I HAVE A PHYSICAL FORM!
I AM THE MOST POWERFUL LIVING THING ON THIS PLANET!

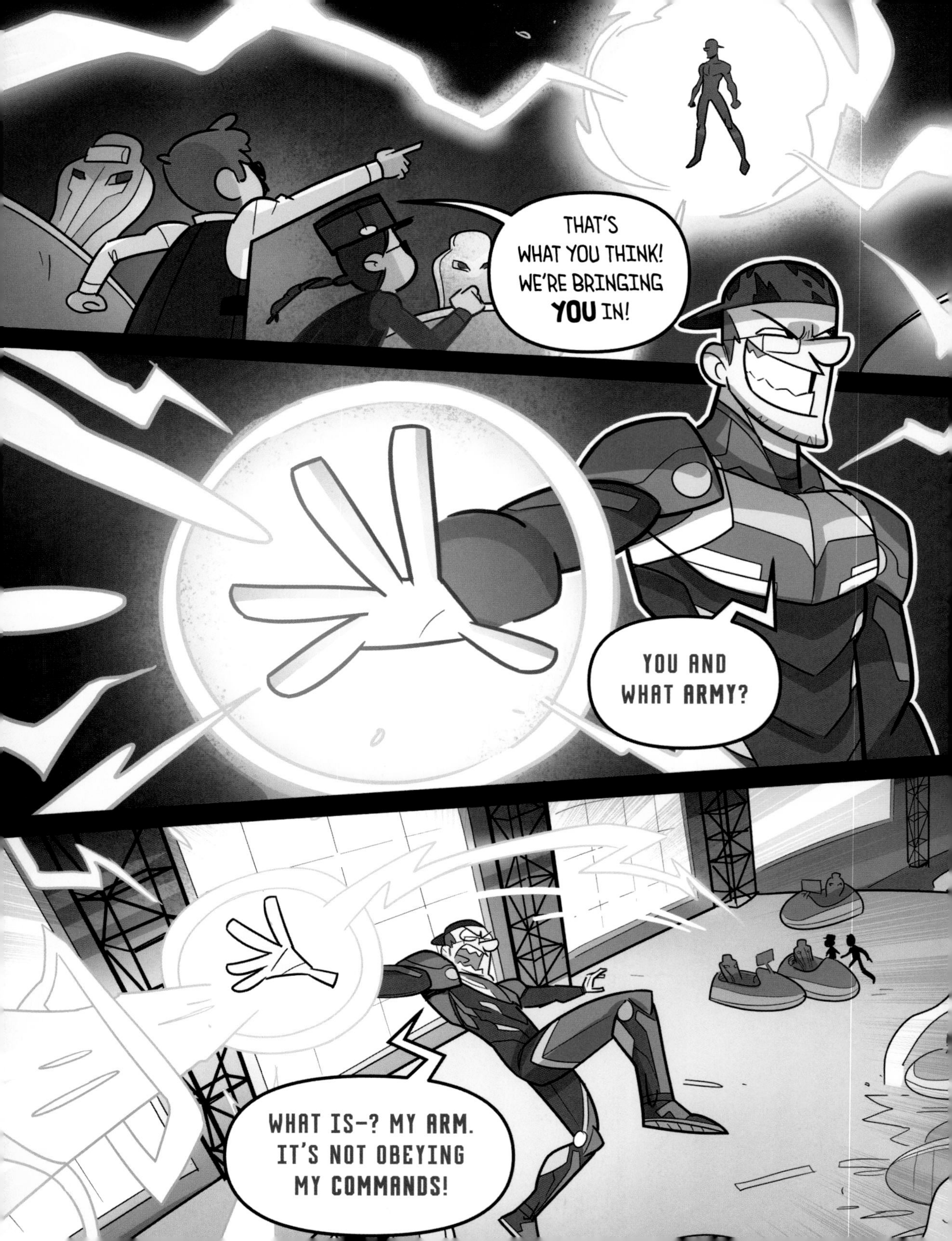
THAT'S WHAT YOU THINK! WE'RE BRINGING **YOU** IN!
YOU AND WHAT ARMY?
WHAT IS—? MY ARM. IT'S NOT OBEYING MY COMMANDS!

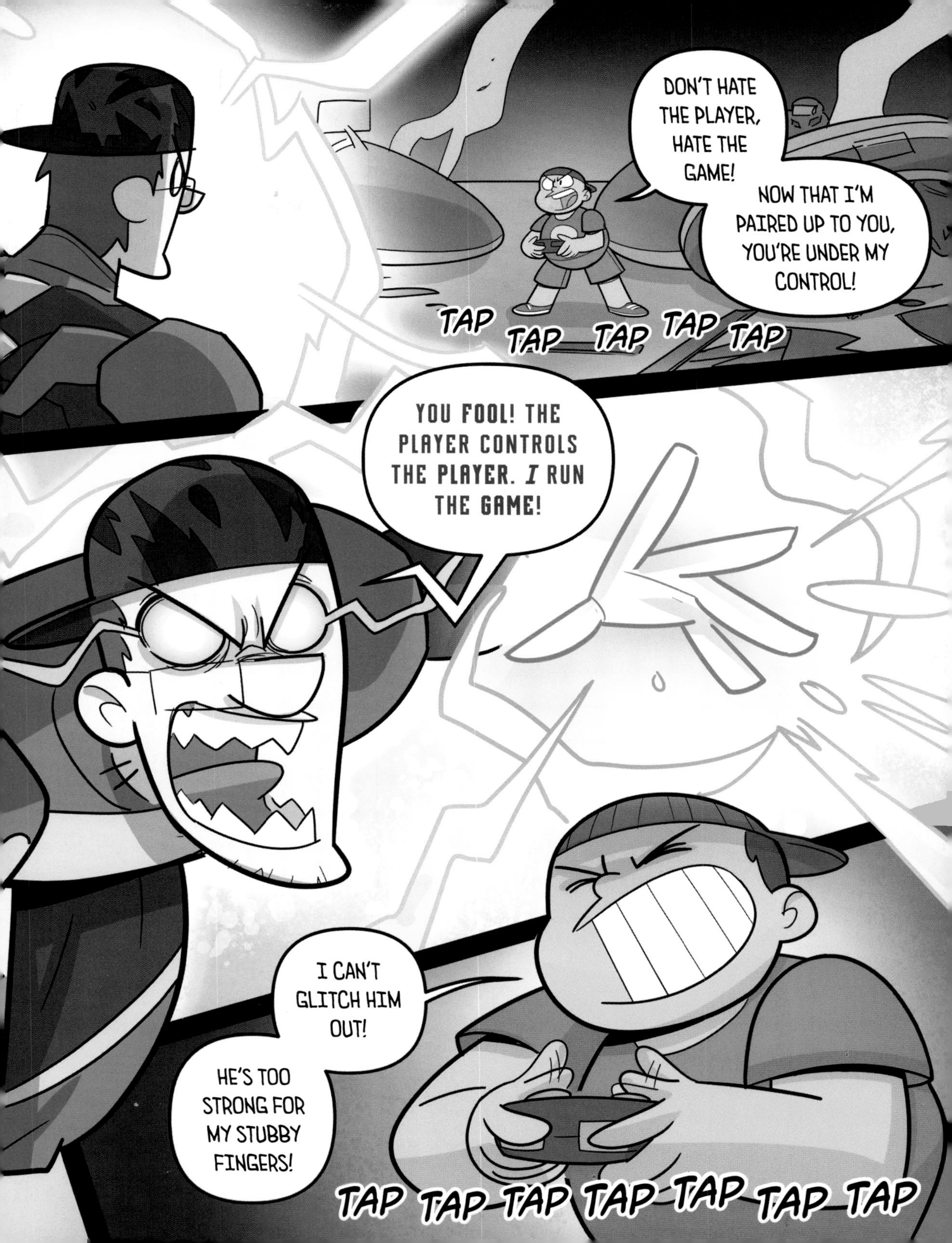

DON'T HATE THE PLAYER, HATE THE GAME!
NOW THAT I'M PAIRED UP TO YOU, YOU'RE UNDER MY CONTROL!
TAP TAP TAP TAP TAP
YOU FOOL! THE PLAYER CONTROLS THE PLAYER. *I* RUN THE GAME!
I CAN'T GLITCH HIM OUT!
HE'S TOO STRONG FOR MY STUBBY FINGERS!
TAP TAP TAP TAP TAP TAP TAP

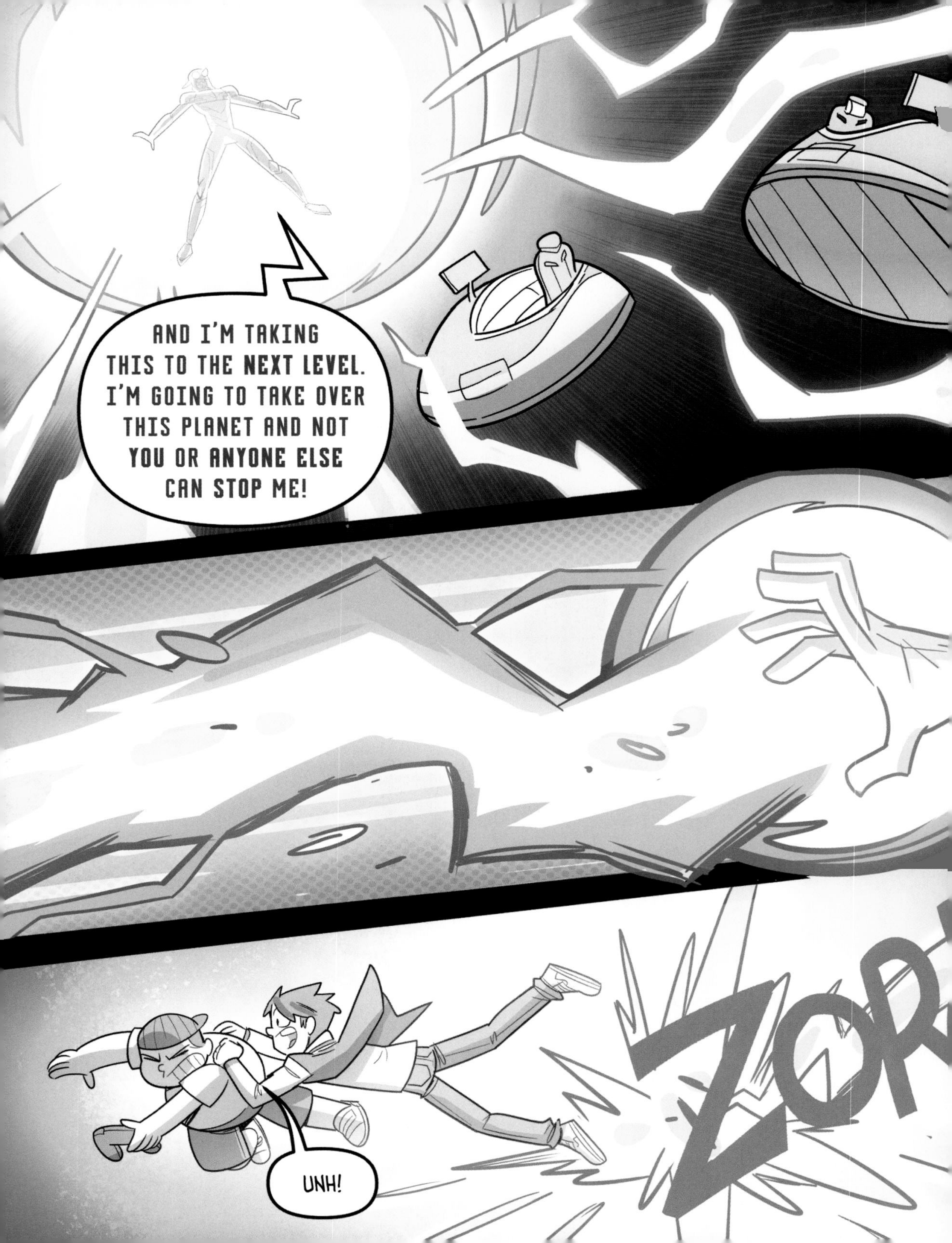
AND I'M TAKING THIS TO THE NEXT LEVEL. I'M GOING TO TAKE OVER THIS PLANET AND NOT YOU OR ANYONE ELSE CAN STOP ME!
UNH!
ZOR

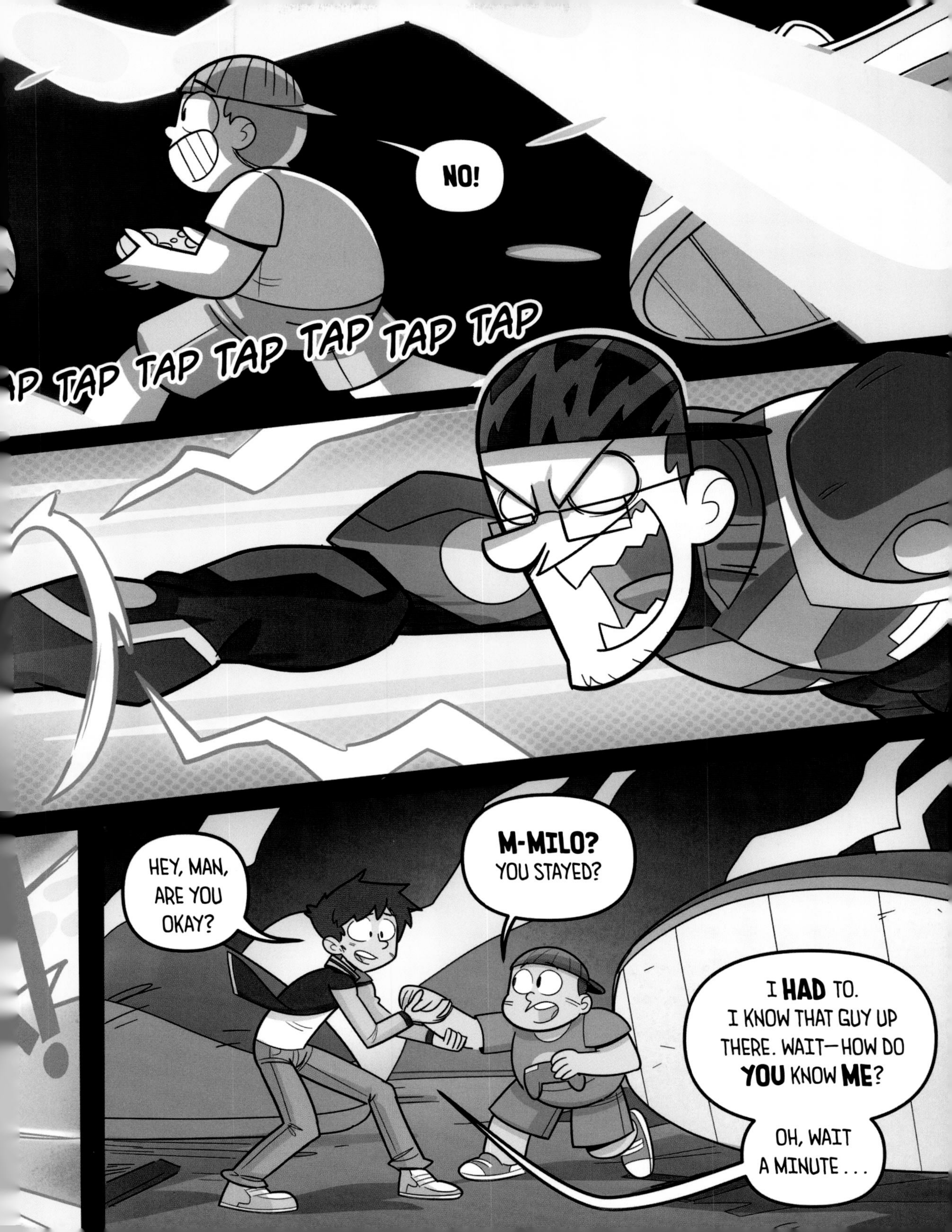
NO!
TAP TAP TAP TAP TAP TAP TAP
HEY, MAN, ARE YOU OKAY?
M-MILO? YOU STAYED?
I HAD TO. I KNOW THAT GUY UP THERE. WAIT—HOW DO YOU KNOW ME?
OH, WAIT A MINUTE . . .

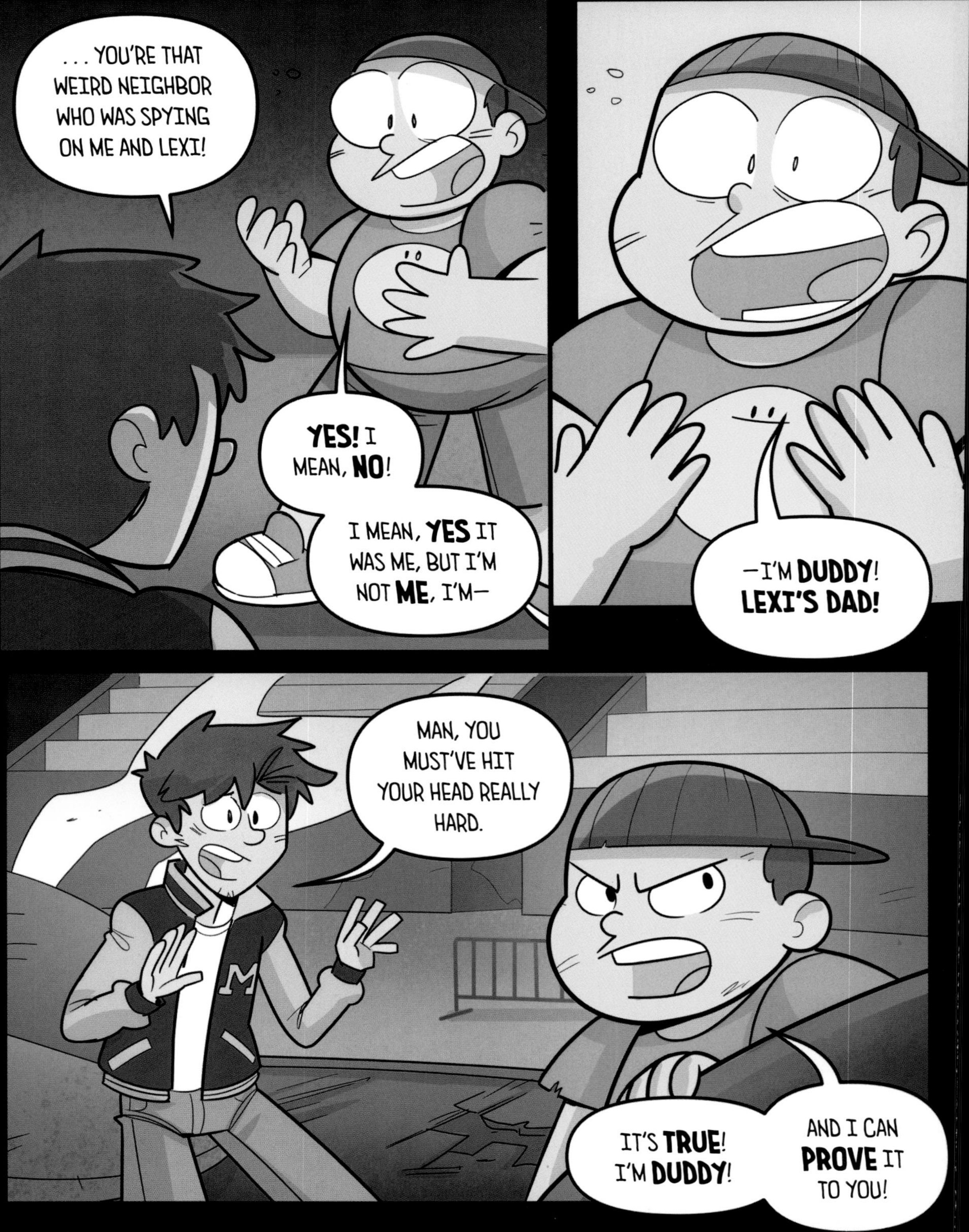
. . . YOU'RE THAT WEIRD NEIGHBOR WHO WAS SPYING ON ME AND LEXI!
YES! I MEAN, NO!
I MEAN, YES IT WAS ME, BUT I'M NOT ME, I'M—
—I'M DUDDY! LEXI'S DAD!
MAN, YOU MUST'VE HIT YOUR HEAD REALLY HARD.
IT'S TRUE! I'M DUDDY!
AND I CAN PROVE IT TO YOU!

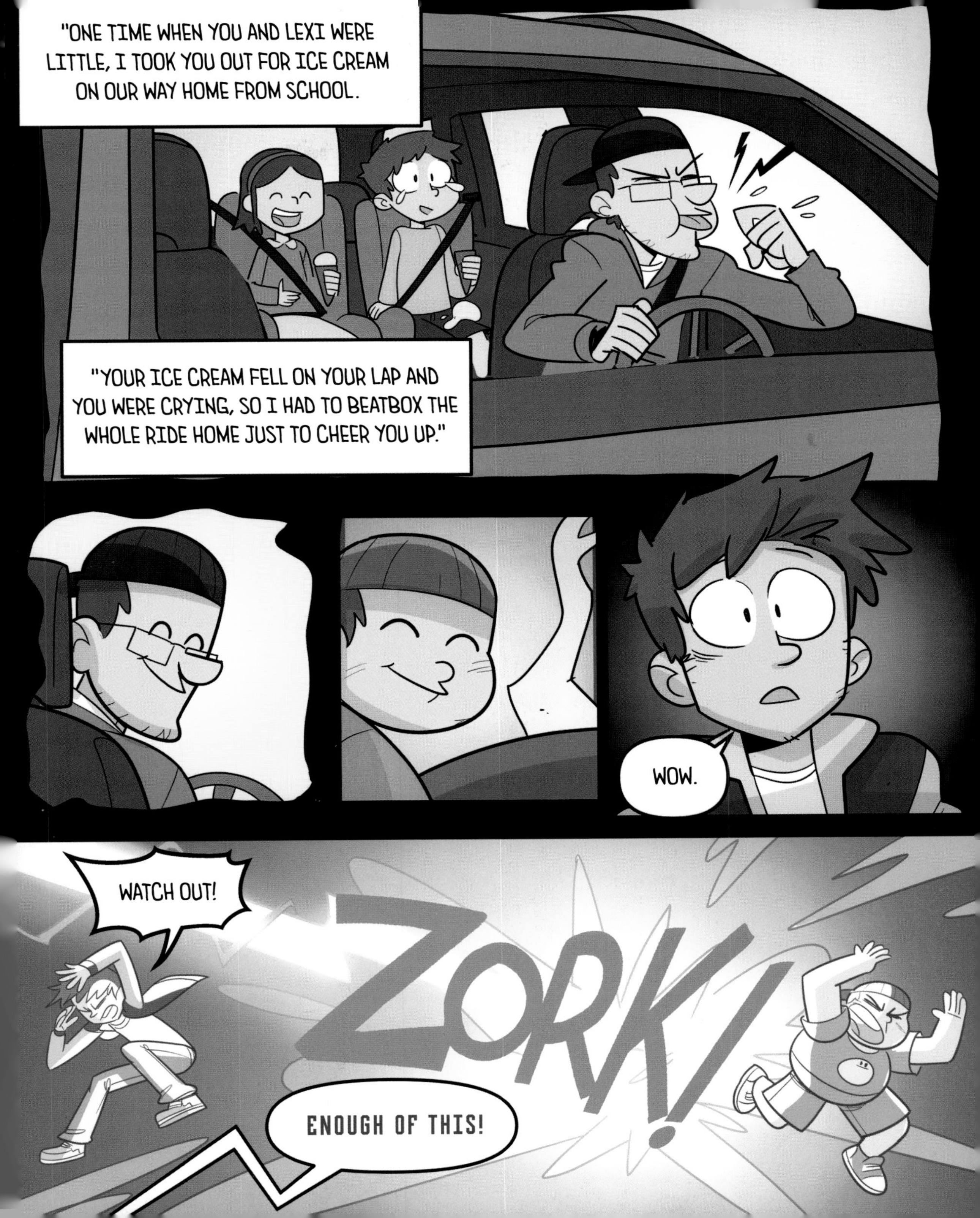
"ONE TIME WHEN YOU AND LEXI WERE LITTLE, I TOOK YOU OUT FOR ICE CREAM ON OUR WAY HOME FROM SCHOOL.
"YOUR ICE CREAM FELL ON YOUR LAP AND YOU WERE CRYING, SO I HAD TO BEATBOX THE WHOLE RIDE HOME JUST TO CHEER YOU UP."
WOW.
WATCH OUT!
ZORK!
ENOUGH OF THIS!

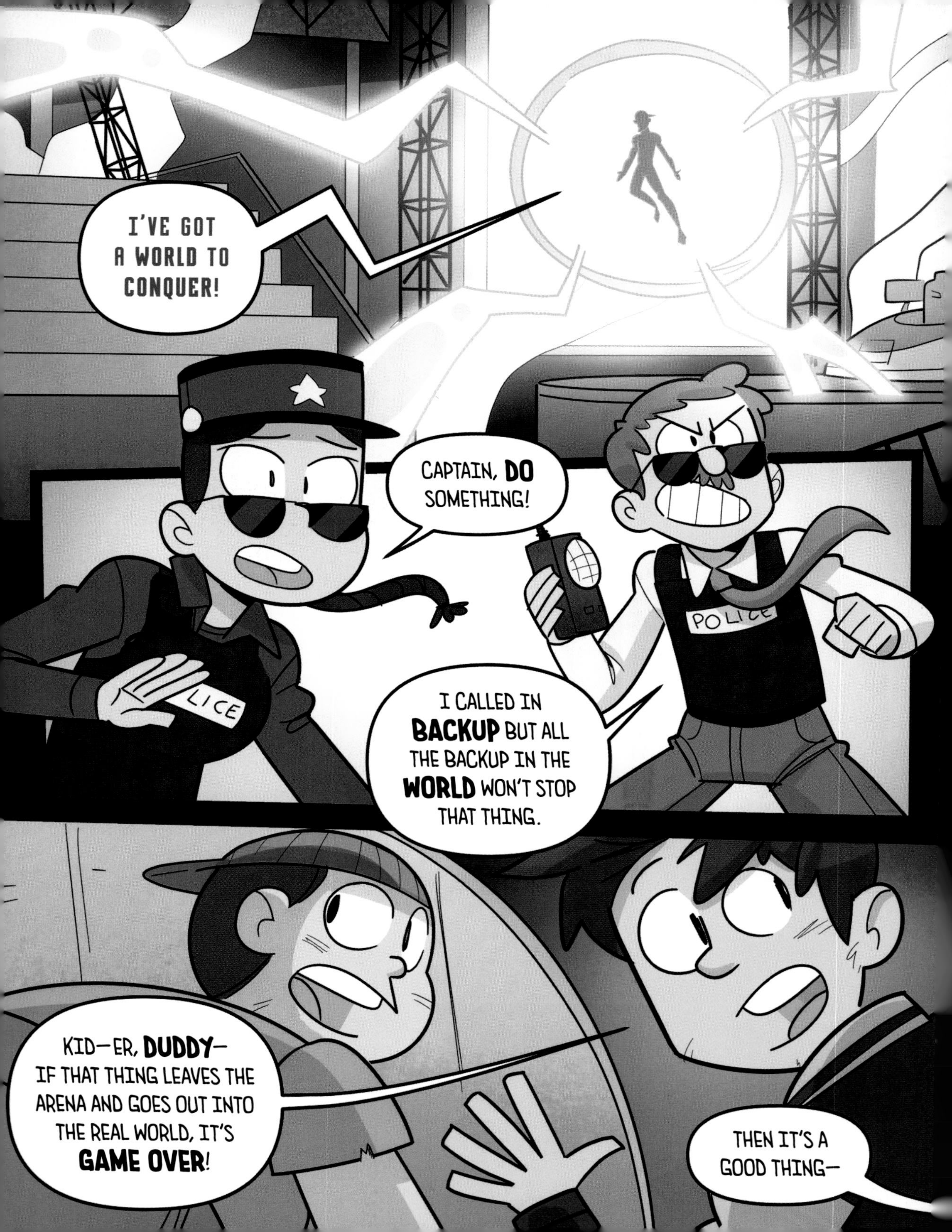
I'VE GOT A WORLD TO CONQUER!
CAPTAIN, **DO** SOMETHING!
I CALLED IN **BACKUP** BUT ALL THE BACKUP IN THE **WORLD** WON'T STOP THAT THING.
KID—ER, **DUDDY**— IF THAT THING LEAVES THE ARENA AND GOES OUT INTO THE REAL WORLD, IT'S **GAME OVER**!
THEN IT'S A GOOD THING—

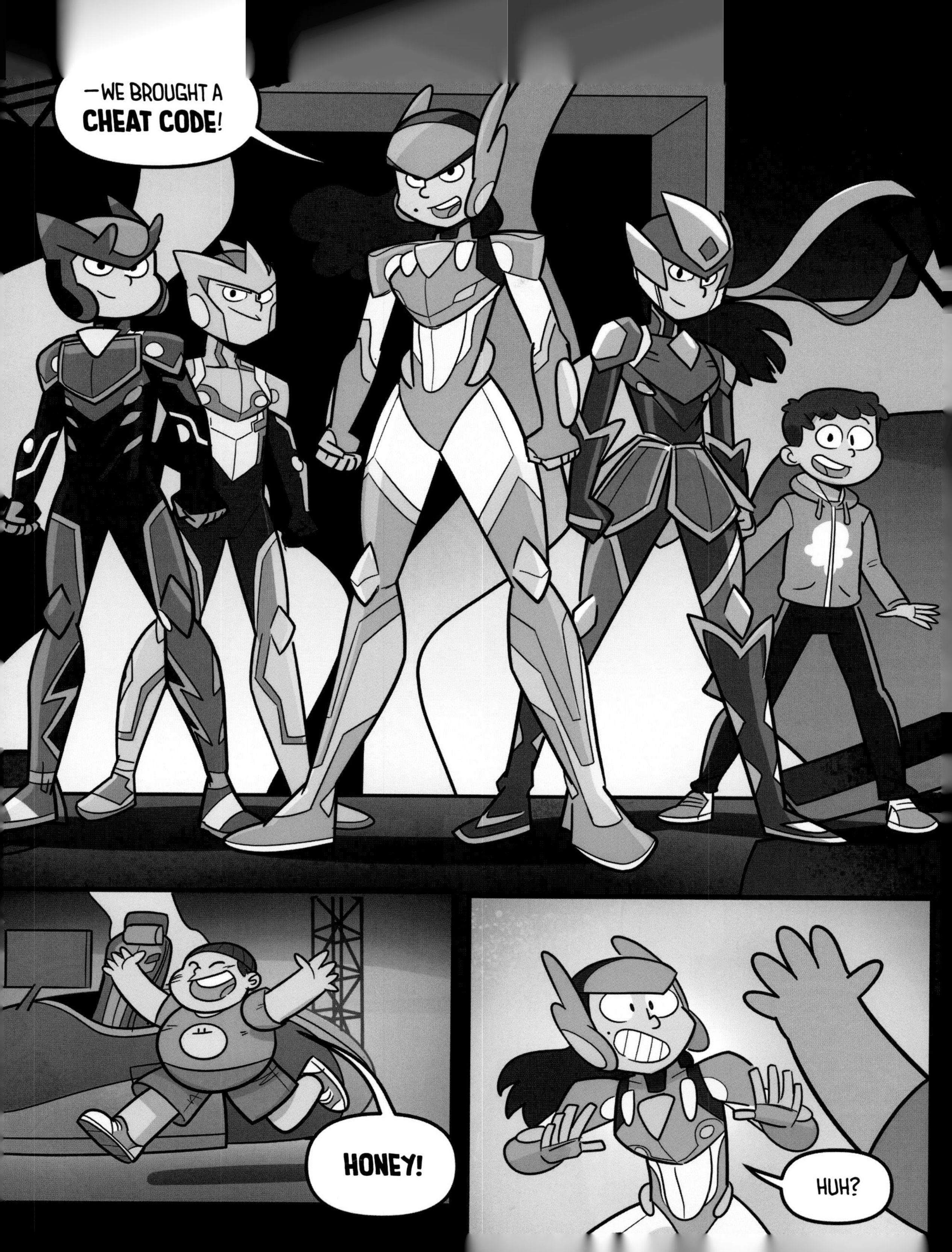
—WE BROUGHT A CHEAT CODE!
HONEY!
HUH?

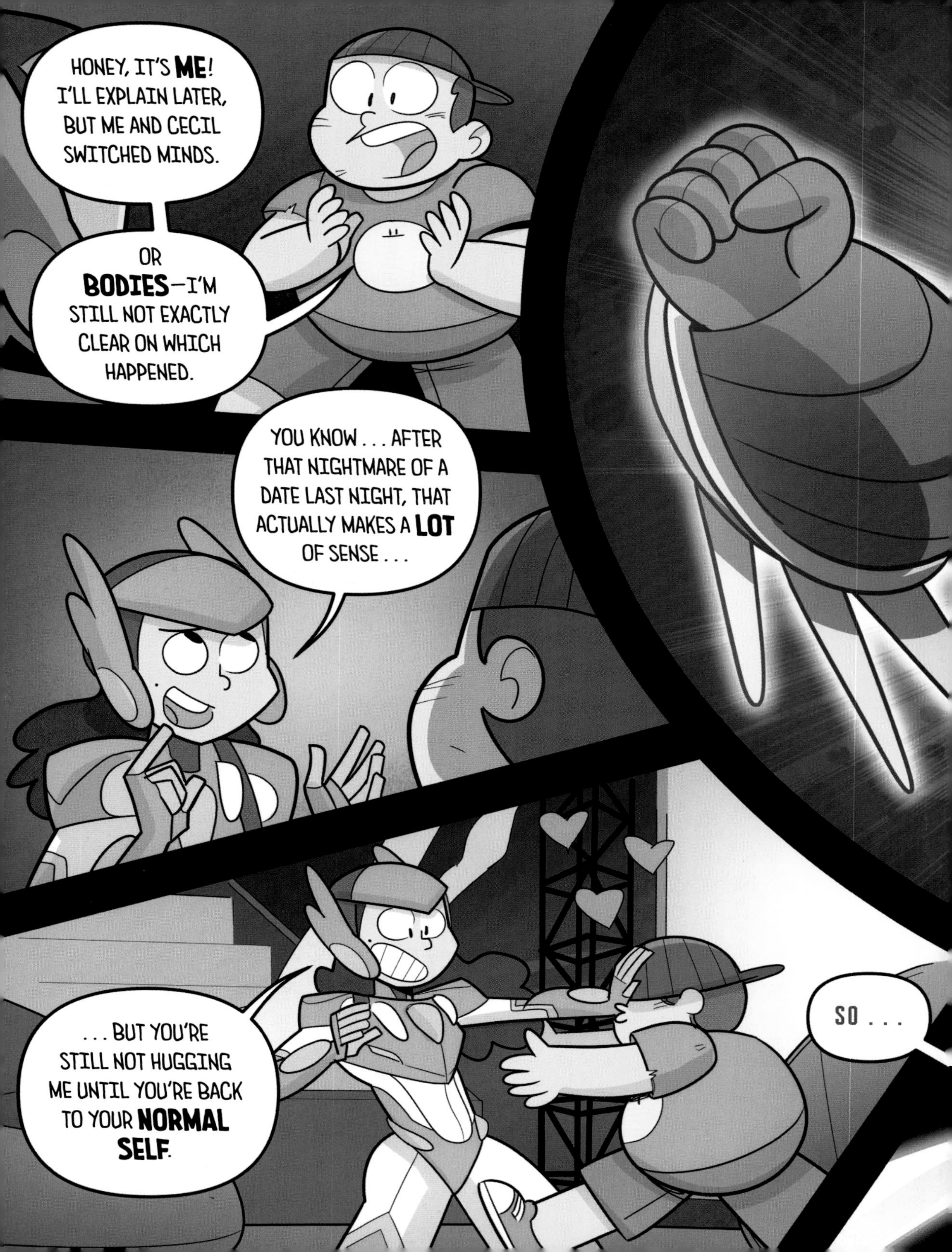

HONEY, IT'S **ME**! I'LL EXPLAIN LATER, BUT ME AND CECIL SWITCHED MINDS.
OR **BODIES**—I'M STILL NOT EXACTLY CLEAR ON WHICH HAPPENED.
YOU KNOW . . . AFTER THAT NIGHTMARE OF A DATE LAST NIGHT, THAT ACTUALLY MAKES A **LOT** OF SENSE . . .
. . . BUT YOU'RE STILL NOT HUGGING ME UNTIL YOU'RE BACK TO YOUR **NORMAL SELF**.
SO . . .

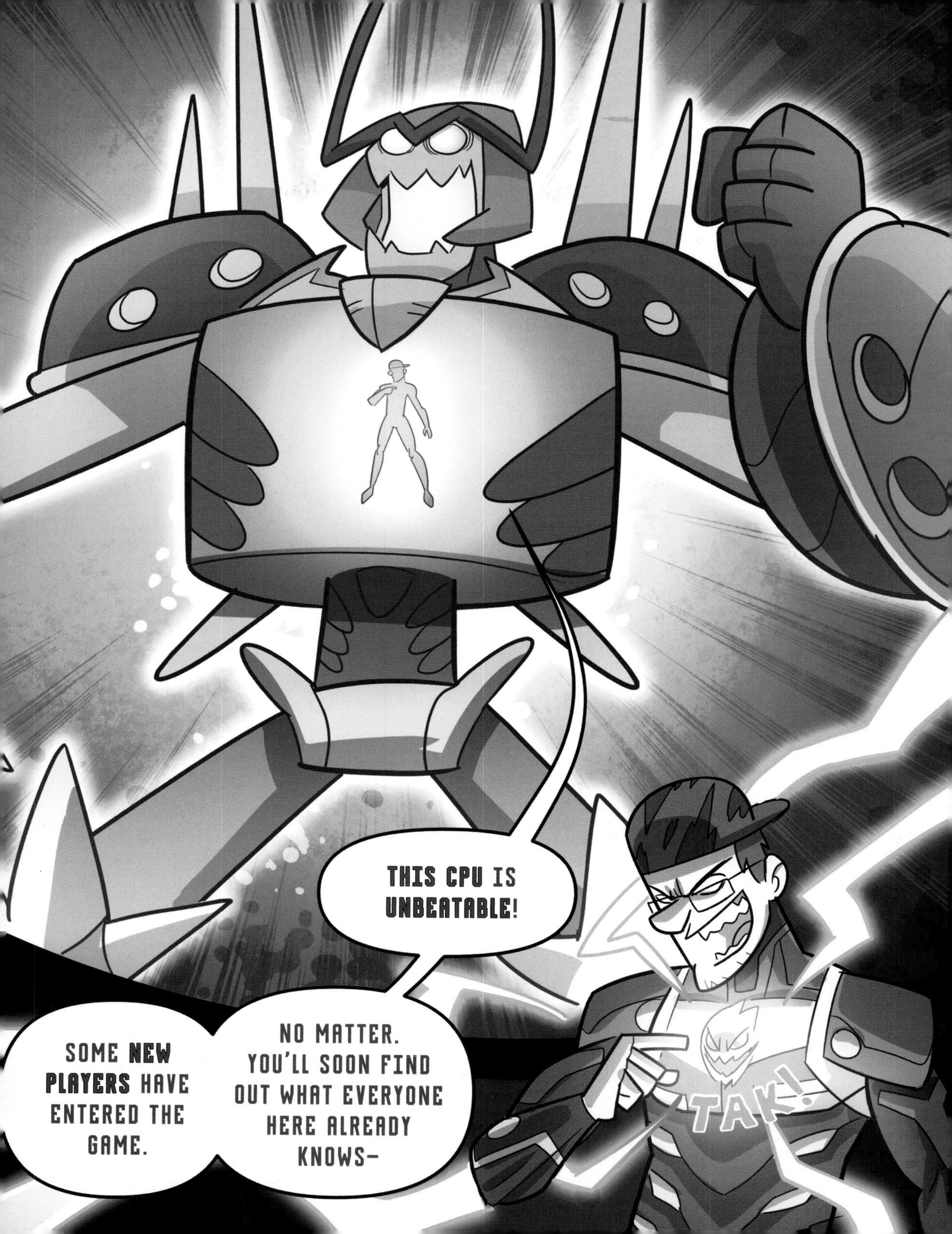
THIS CPU IS UNBEATABLE!
SOME NEW PLAYERS HAVE ENTERED THE GAME.
NO MATTER. YOU'LL SOON FIND OUT WHAT EVERYONE HERE ALREADY KNOWS—
TAK!

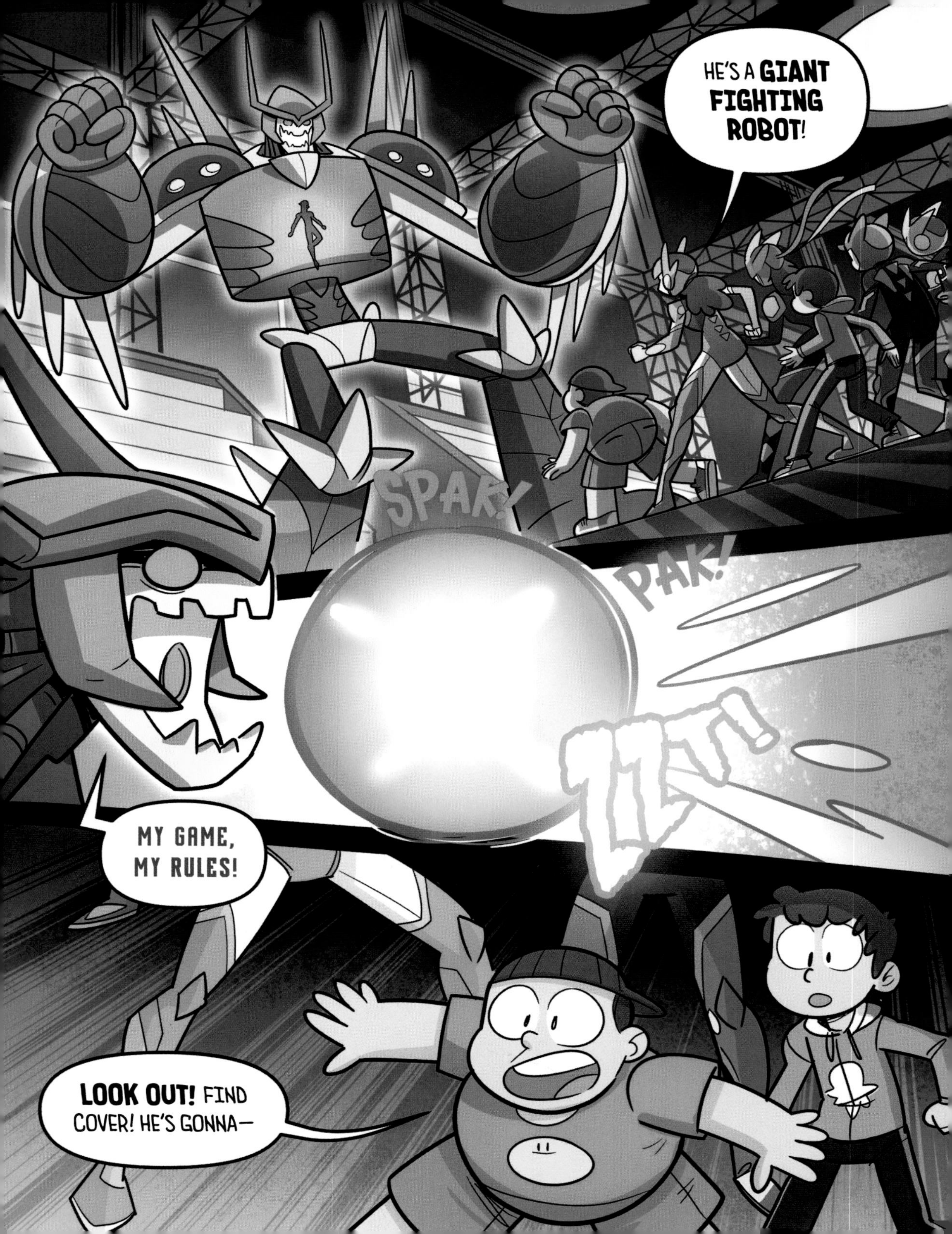
HE'S A **GIANT FIGHTING ROBOT**!
SPAK!
PAK!
ZZZT!
MY GAME, MY RULES!
**LOOK OUT!** FIND COVER! HE'S GONNA—

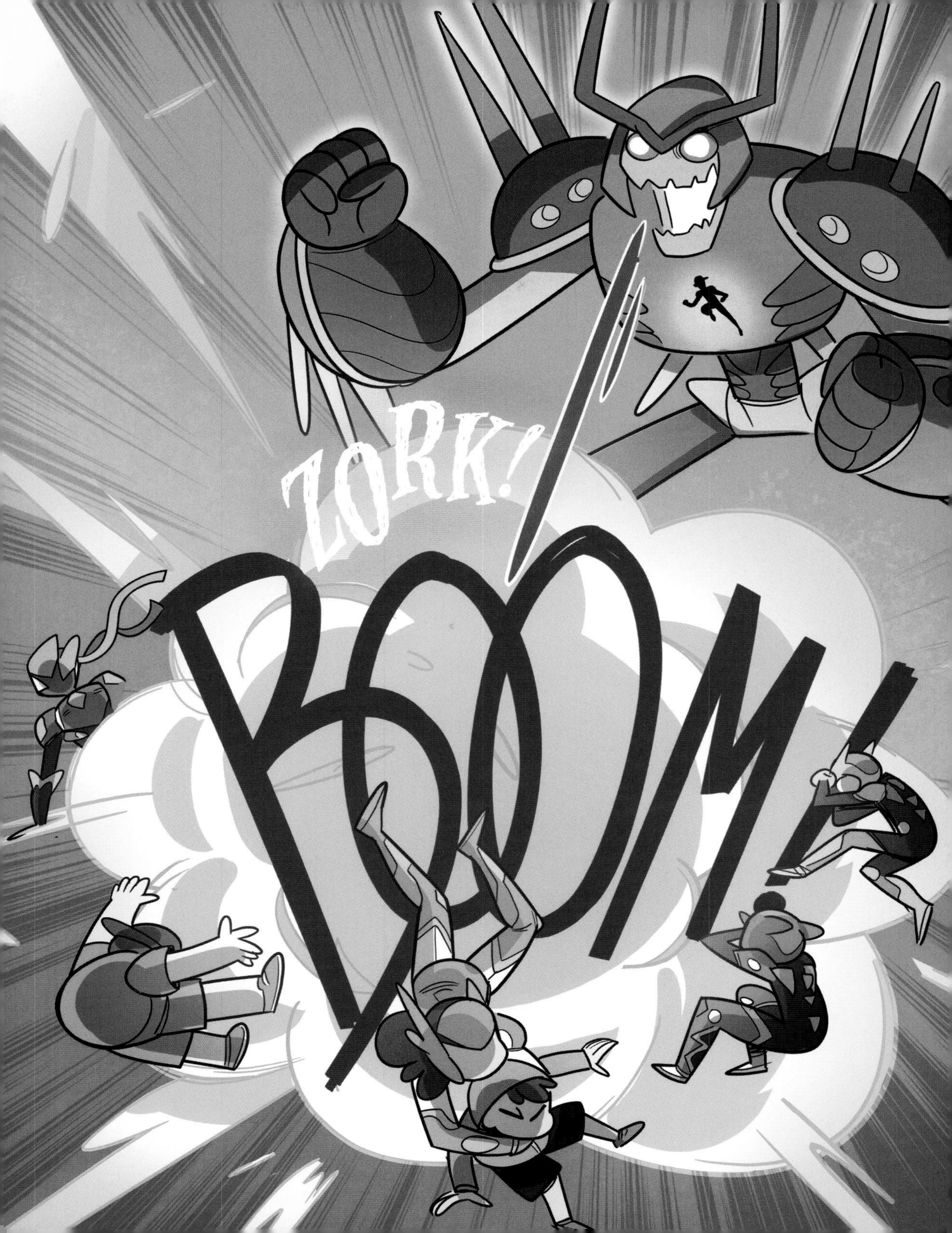
ZORK!
BOOM!

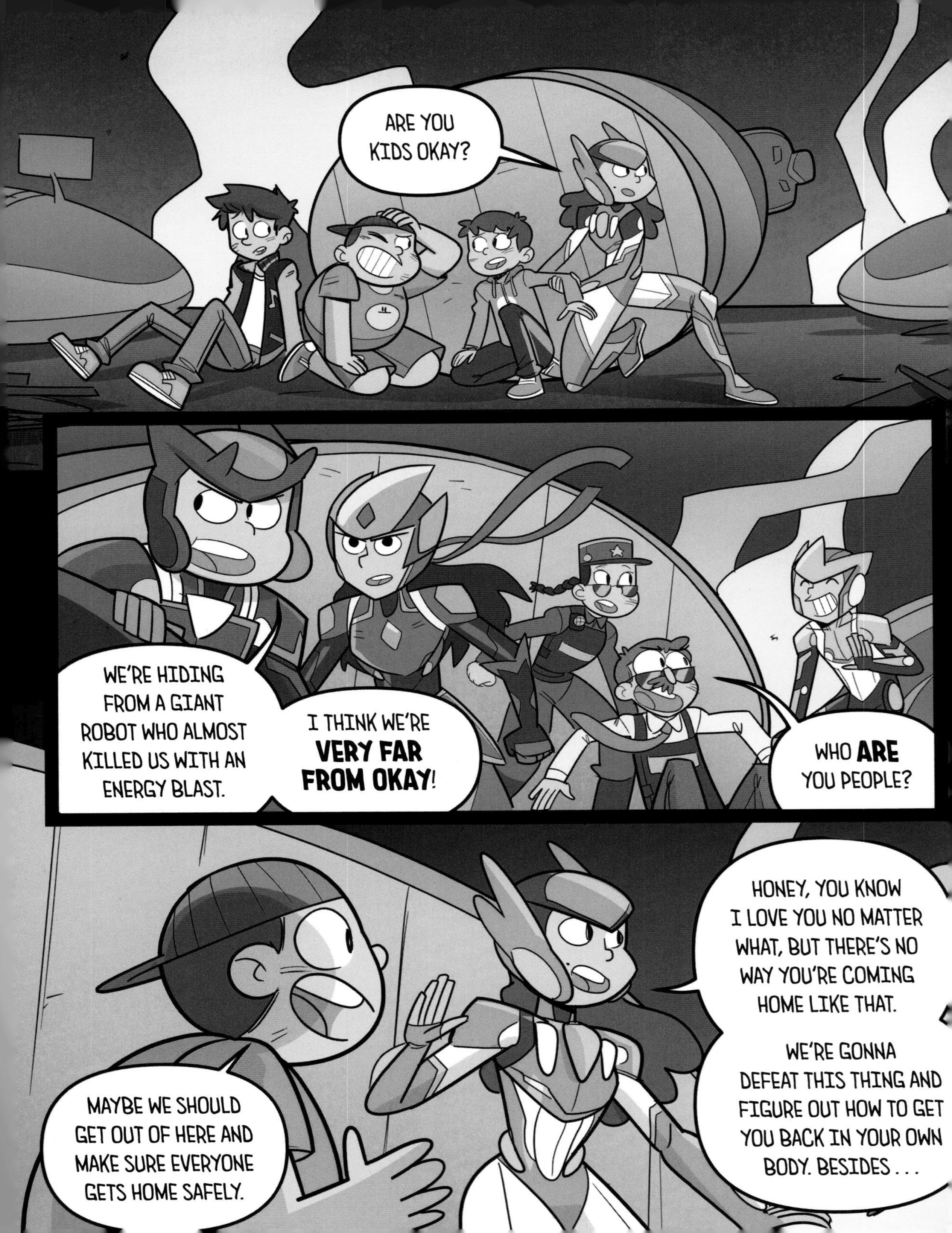
ARE YOU KIDS OKAY?
WE'RE HIDING FROM A GIANT ROBOT WHO ALMOST KILLED US WITH AN ENERGY BLAST.
I THINK WE'RE **VERY FAR FROM OKAY**!
WHO **ARE** YOU PEOPLE?
MAYBE WE SHOULD GET OUT OF HERE AND MAKE SURE EVERYONE GETS HOME SAFELY.
HONEY, YOU KNOW I LOVE YOU NO MATTER WHAT, BUT THERE'S NO WAY YOU'RE COMING HOME LIKE THAT.
WE'RE GONNA DEFEAT THIS THING AND FIGURE OUT HOW TO GET YOU BACK IN YOUR OWN BODY. BESIDES . . .

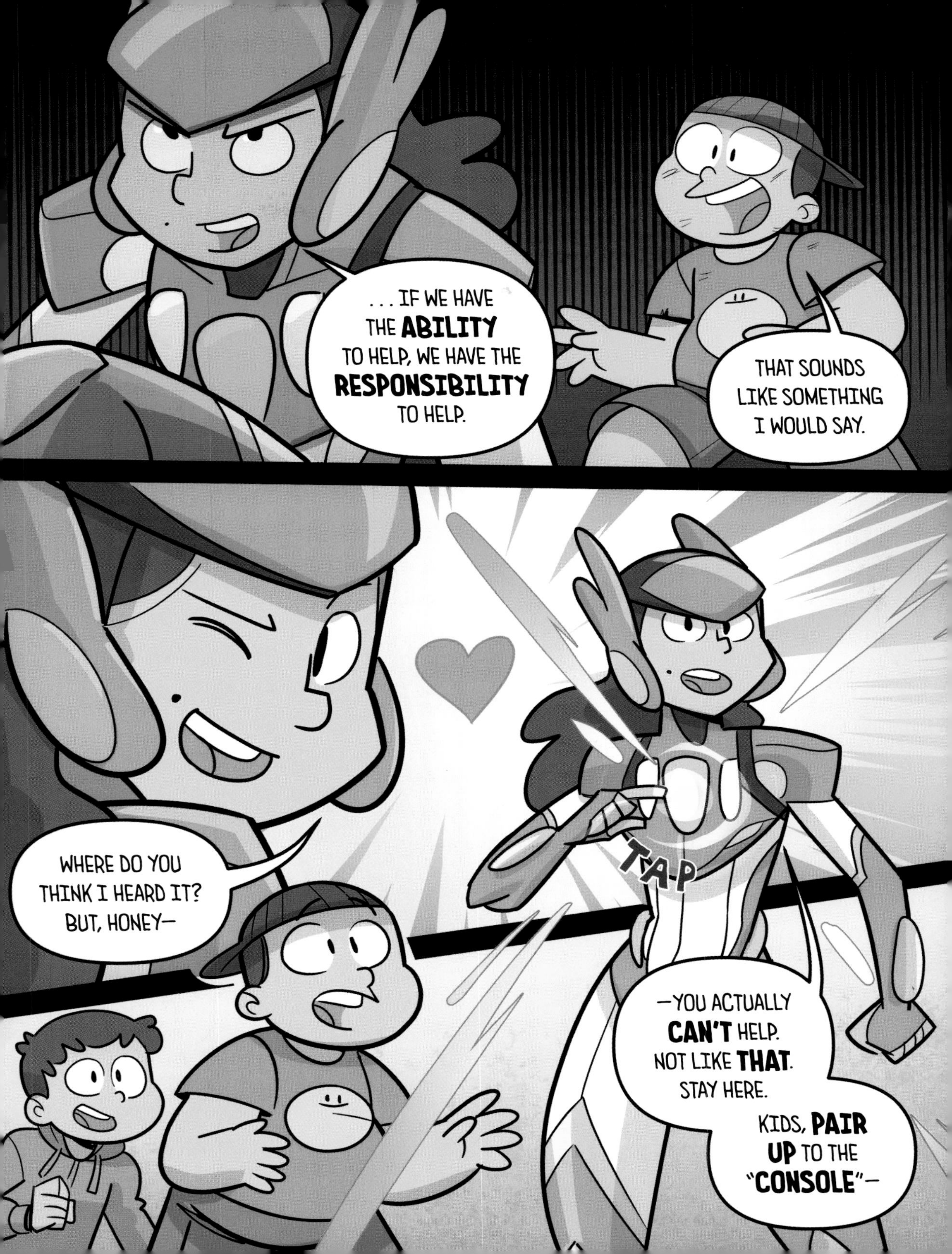

. . . IF WE HAVE THE **ABILITY** TO HELP, WE HAVE THE **RESPONSIBILITY** TO HELP.
THAT SOUNDS LIKE SOMETHING I WOULD SAY.
WHERE DO YOU THINK I HEARD IT? BUT, HONEY—
TAP
—YOU ACTUALLY **CAN'T** HELP. NOT LIKE **THAT**. STAY HERE.
KIDS, **PAIR UP** TO THE "**CONSOLE**"—

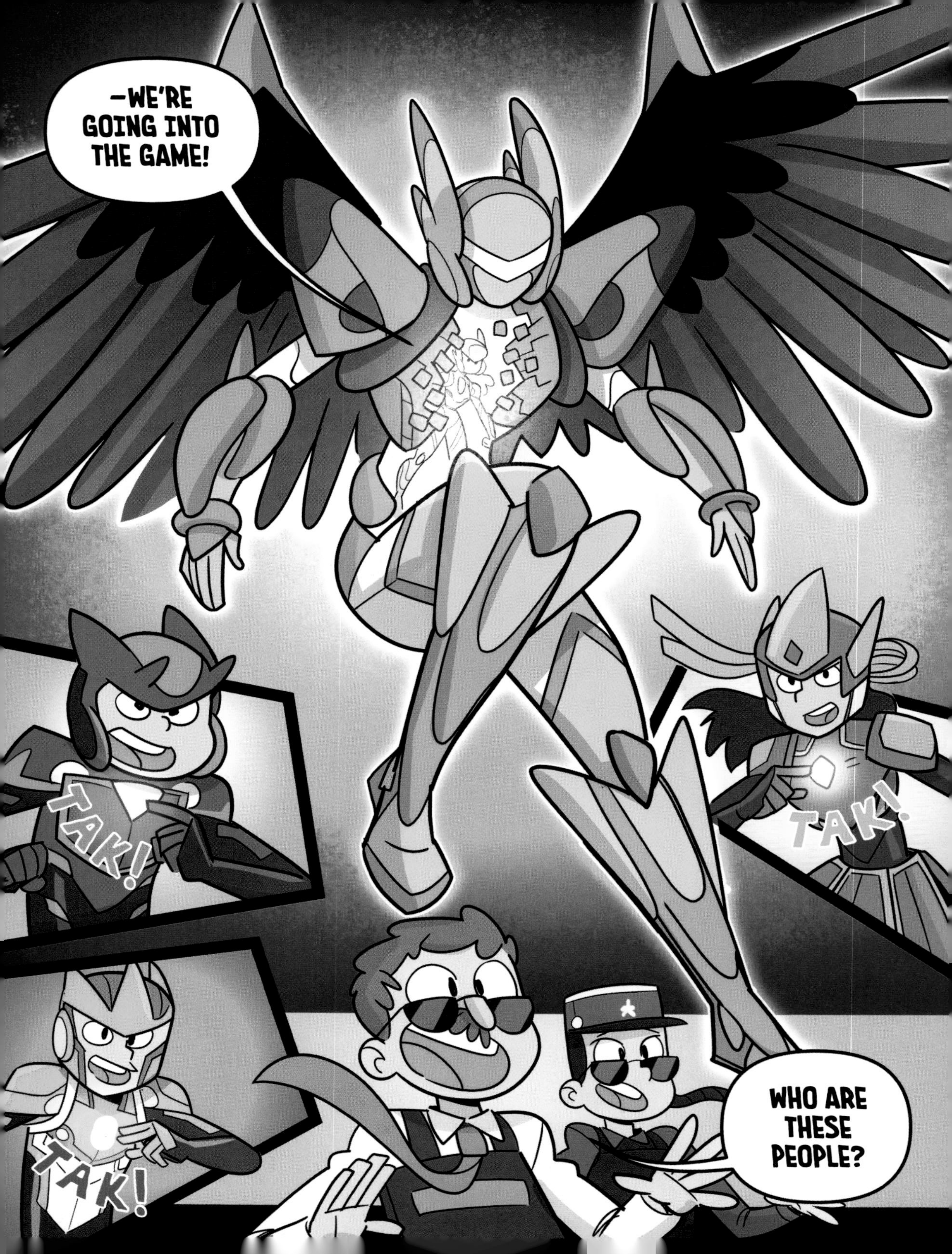
—WE'RE GOING INTO THE GAME!
TAK!
TAK!
TAK!
WHO ARE THESE PEOPLE?

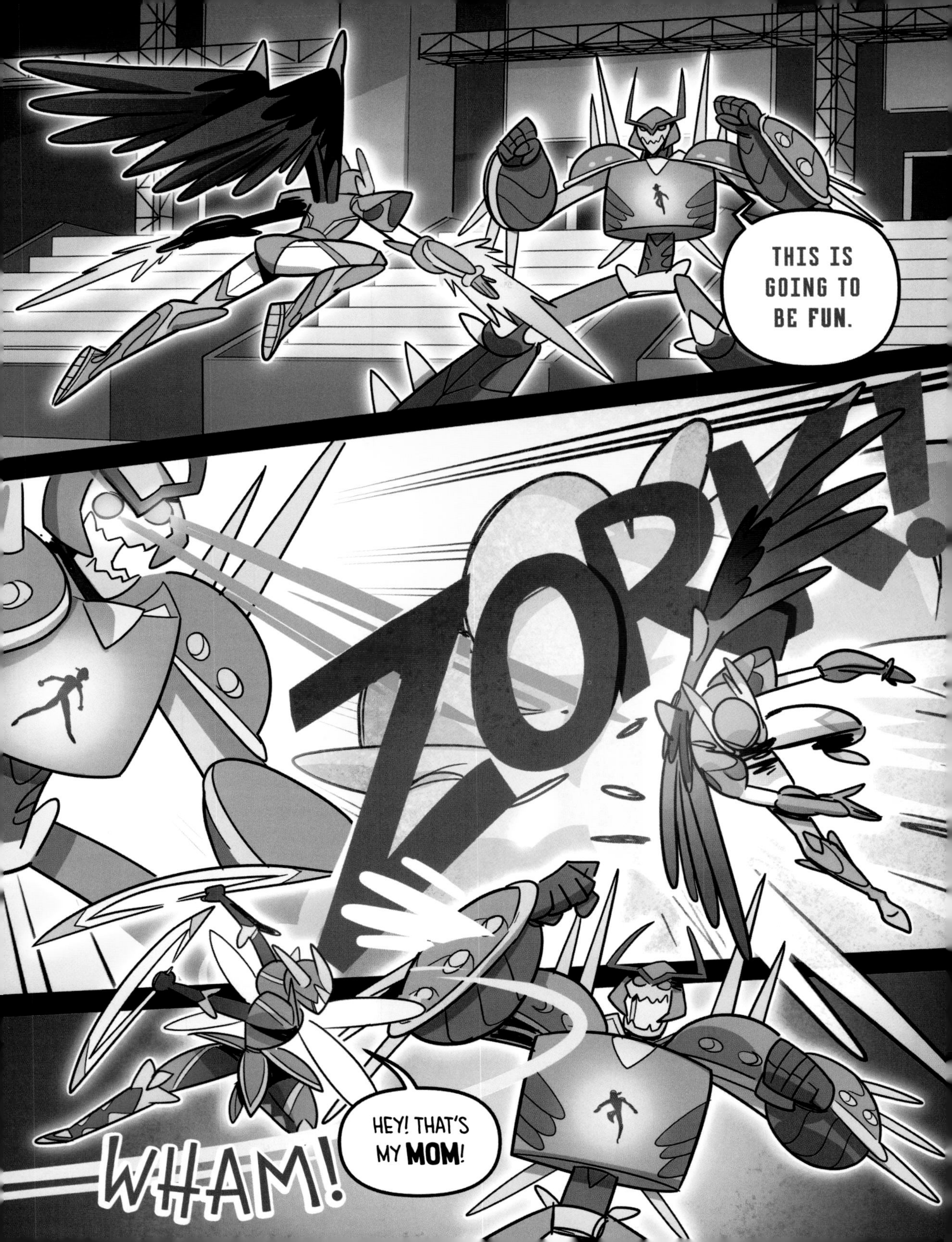
THIS IS GOING TO BE FUN.
ZORK!
HEY! THAT'S MY **MOM**!
WHAM!

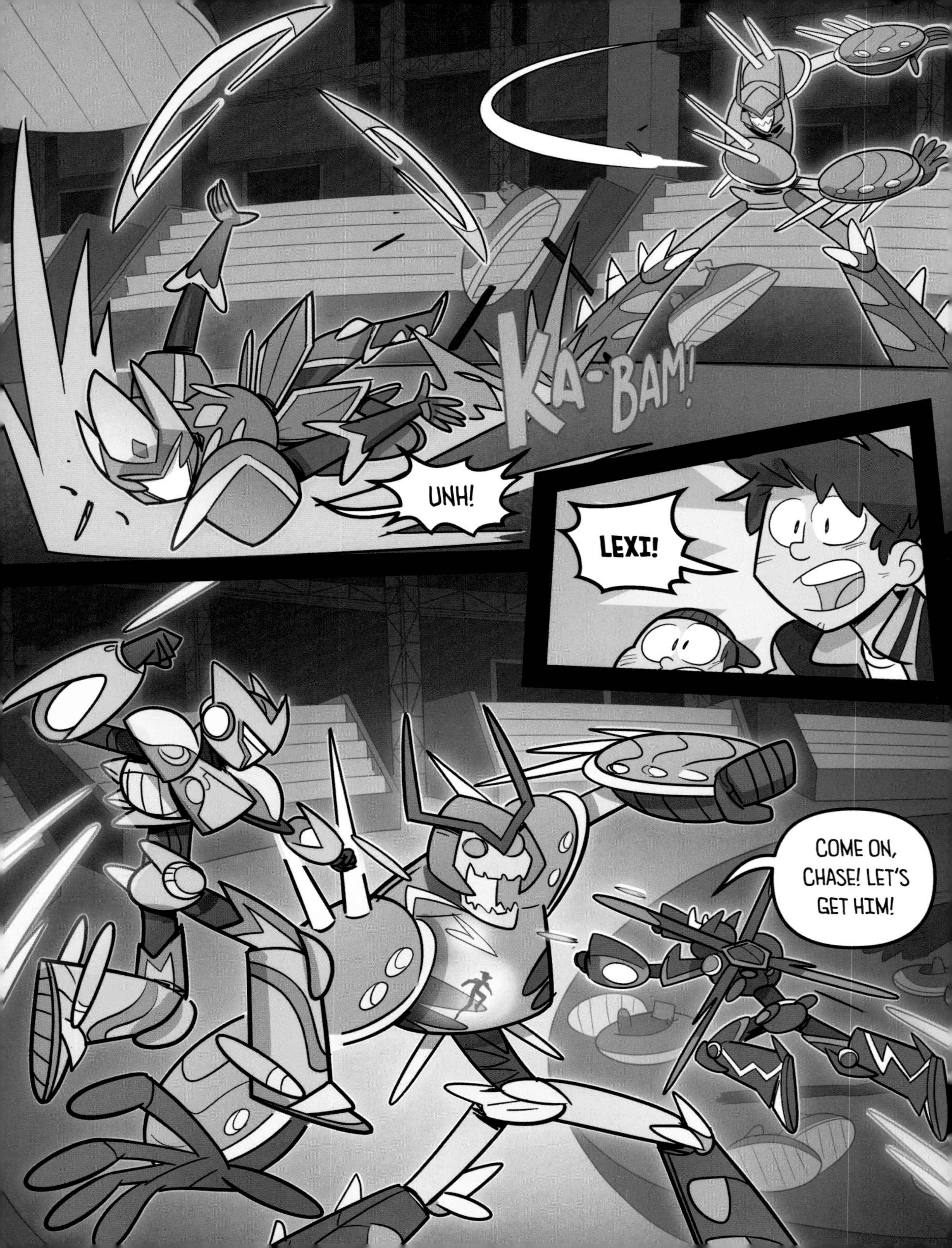
KA-BAM!
UNH!
LEXI!
COME ON, CHASE! LET'S GET HIM!

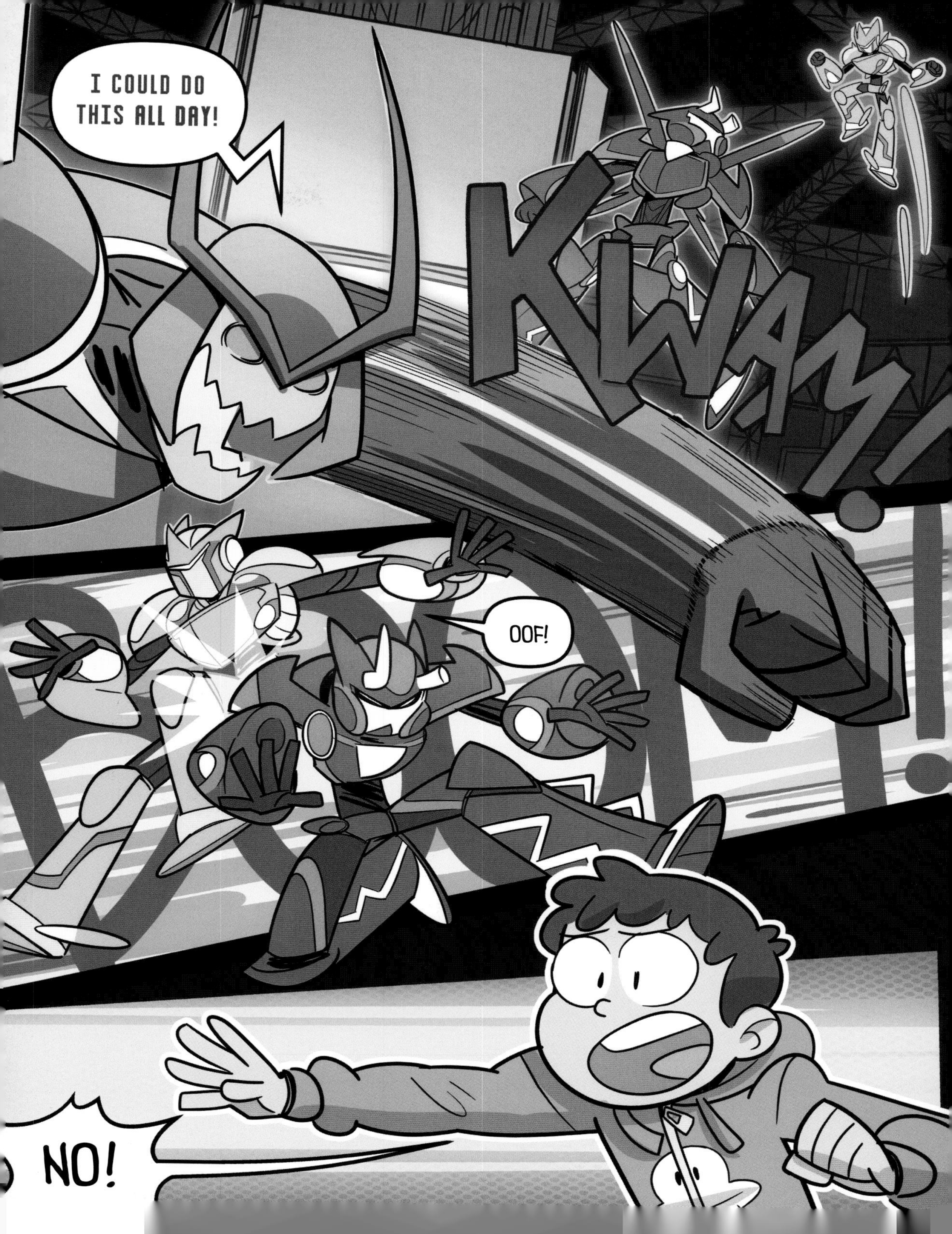
I COULD DO THIS ALL DAY!
KWAM!!
OOF!
NO!

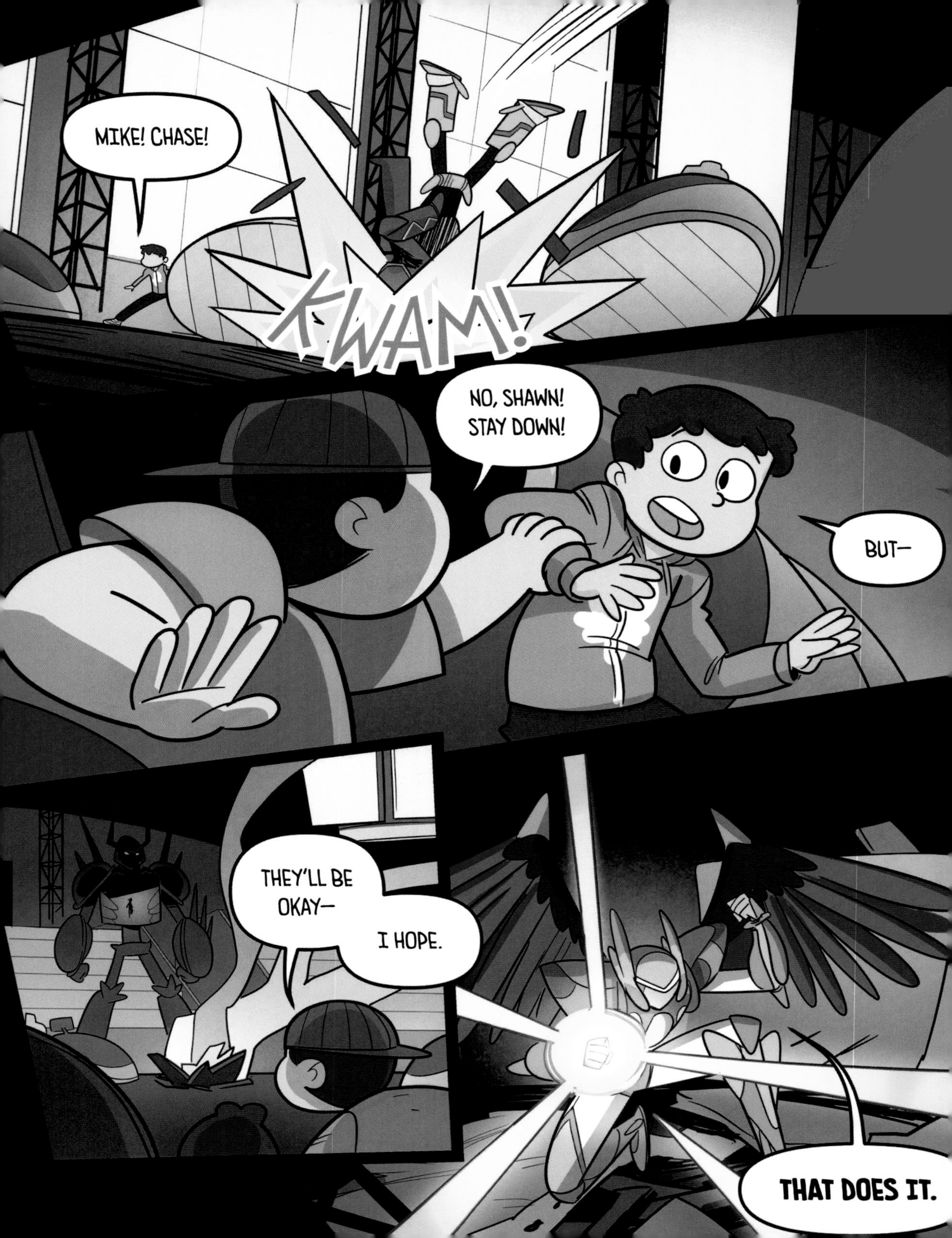
MIKE! CHASE!
KWAM!
NO, SHAWN! STAY DOWN!
BUT—
THEY'LL BE OKAY—
I HOPE.
THAT DOES IT.

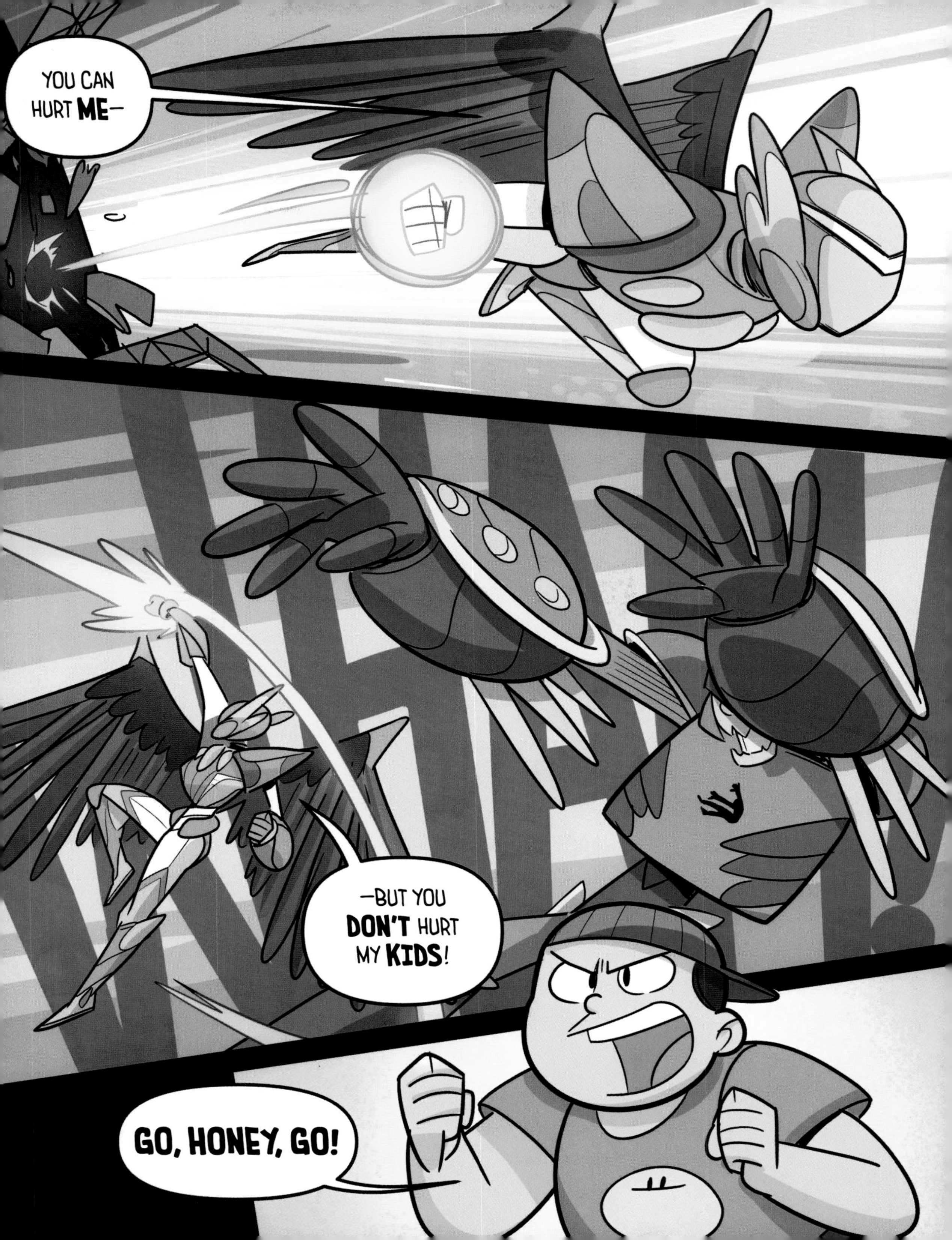
YOU CAN HURT **ME**—
—BUT YOU **DON'T** HURT MY **KIDS**!
GO, HONEY, GO!

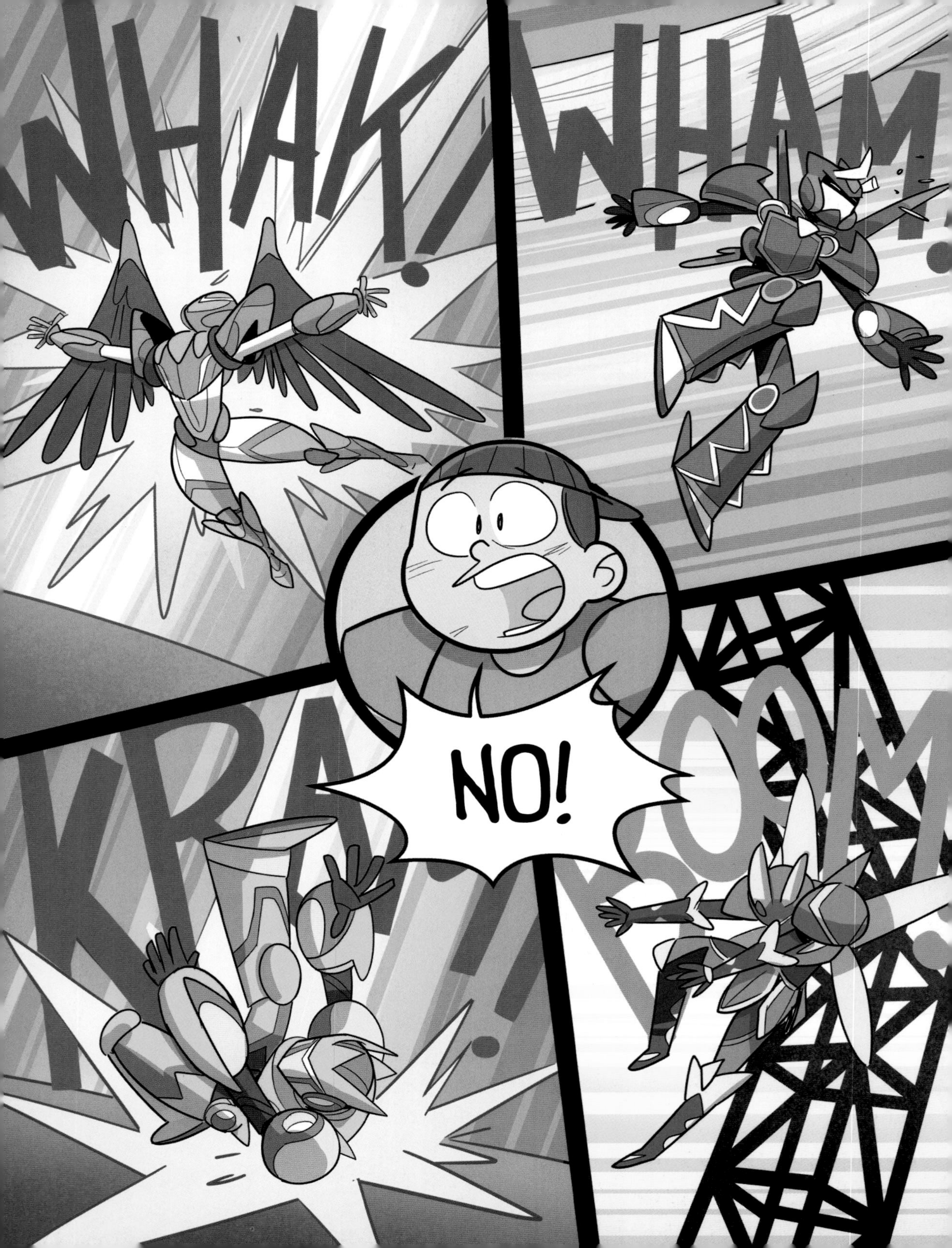
WHAK!
WHAM!
NO!

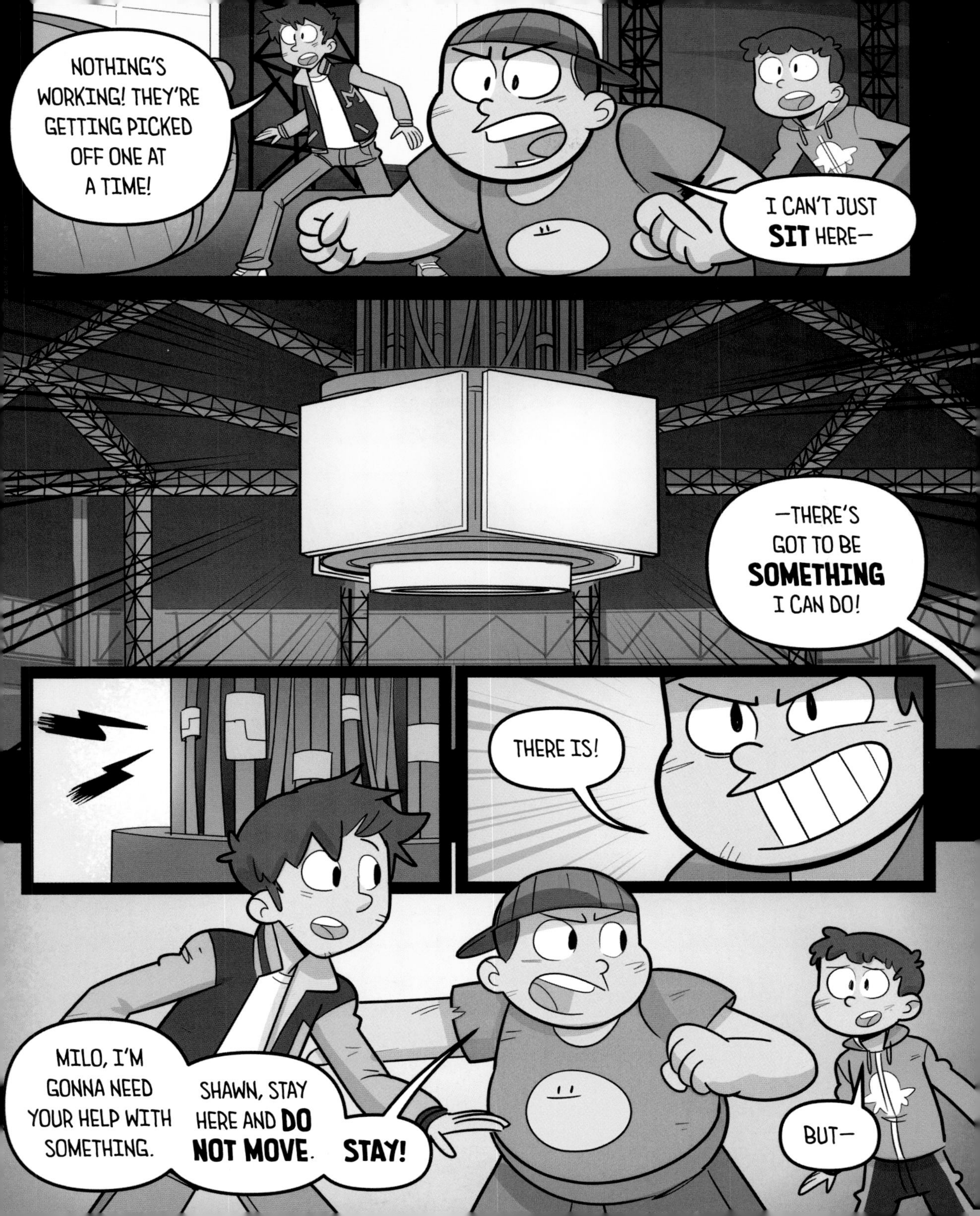
NOTHING'S WORKING! THEY'RE GETTING PICKED OFF ONE AT A TIME!
I CAN'T JUST **SIT** HERE—
—THERE'S GOT TO BE **SOMETHING** I CAN DO!
THERE IS!
MILO, I'M GONNA NEED YOUR HELP WITH SOMETHING.
SHAWN, STAY HERE AND **DO NOT MOVE**.
**STAY!**
BUT—

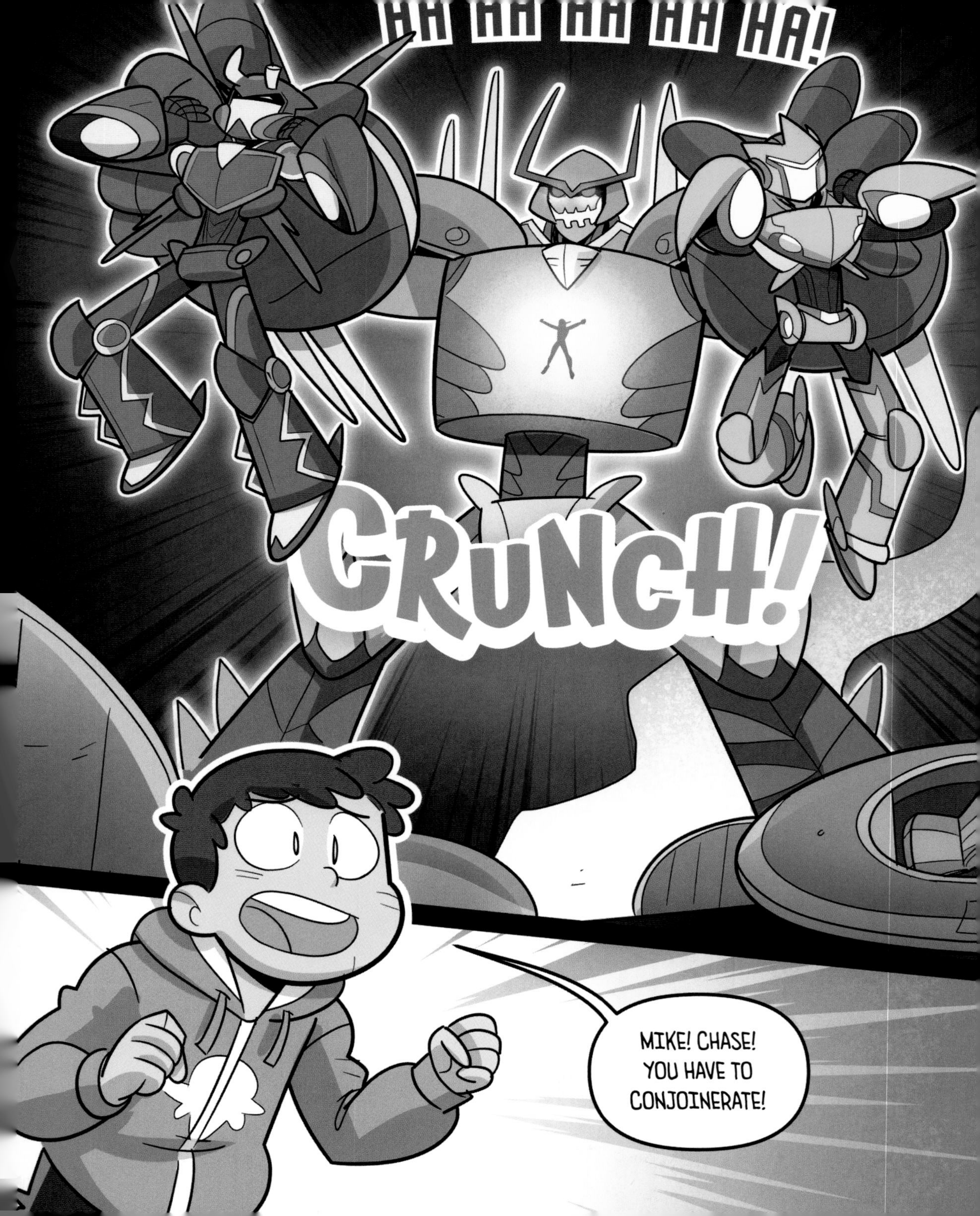
HA HA HA HA HA!
CRUNCH!
MIKE! CHASE! YOU HAVE TO CONJOINERATE!

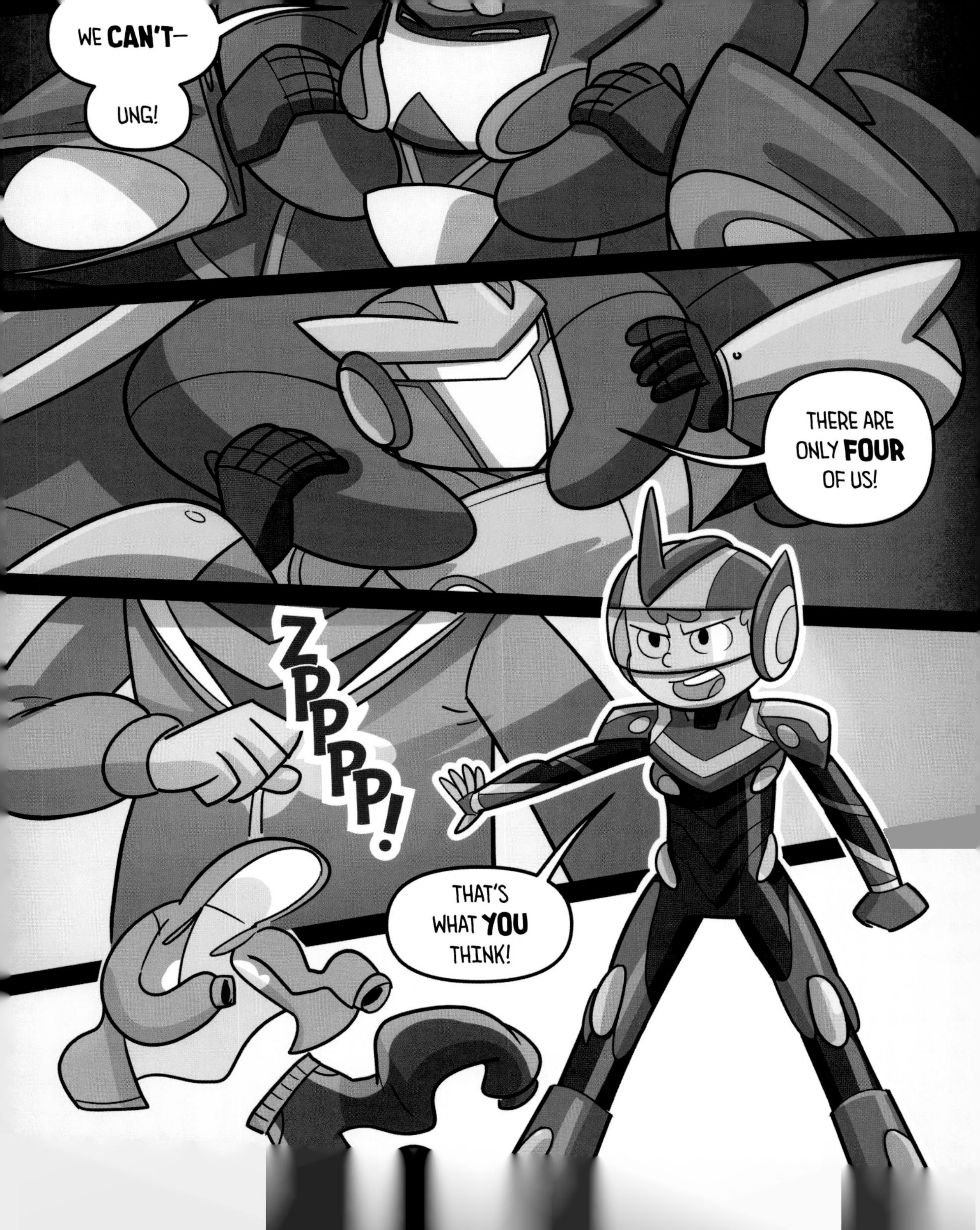
WE CAN'T—
UNG!
THERE ARE ONLY FOUR OF US!
ZPPPP!
THAT'S WHAT YOU THINK!

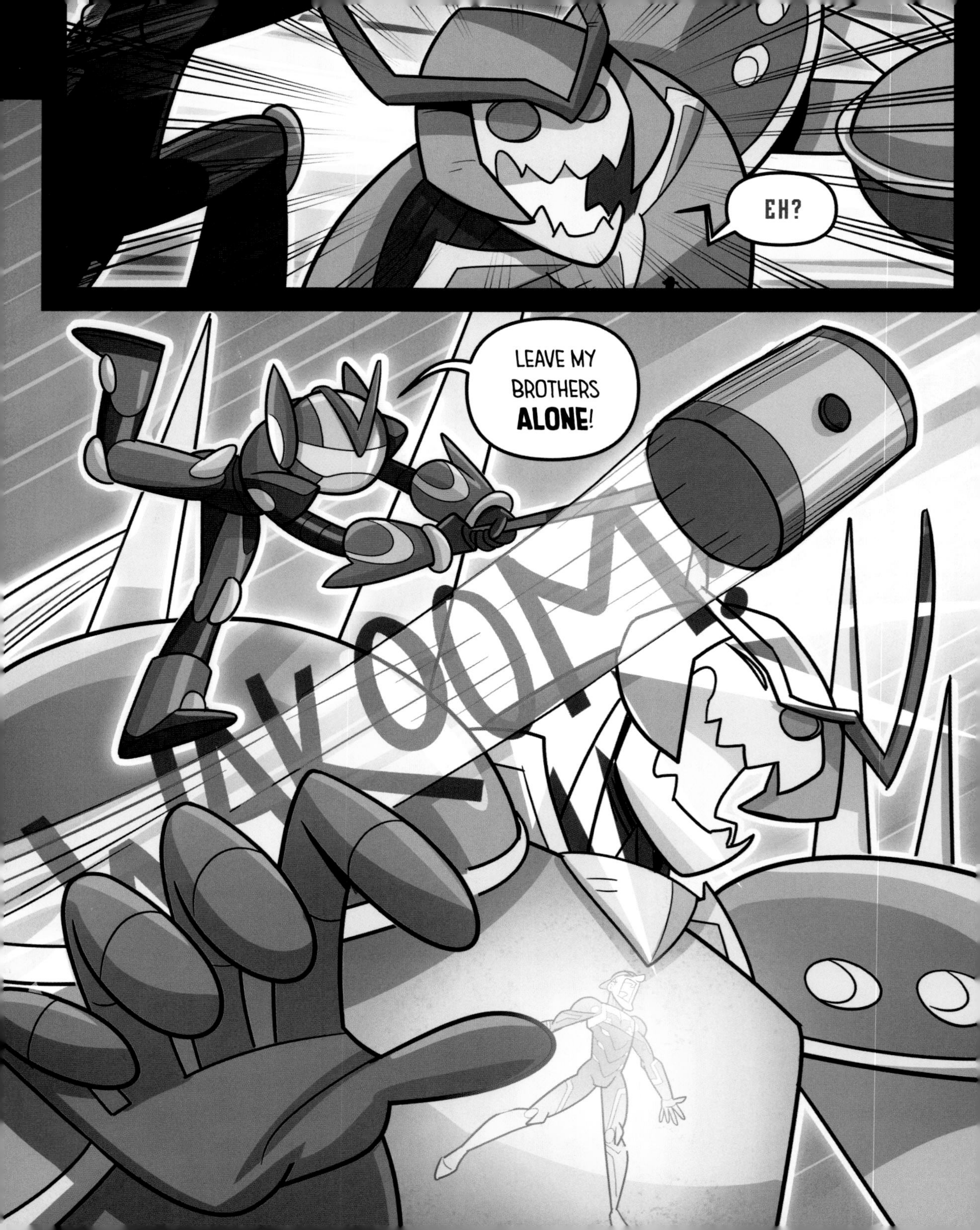
EH?
LEAVE MY BROTHERS **ALONE**!

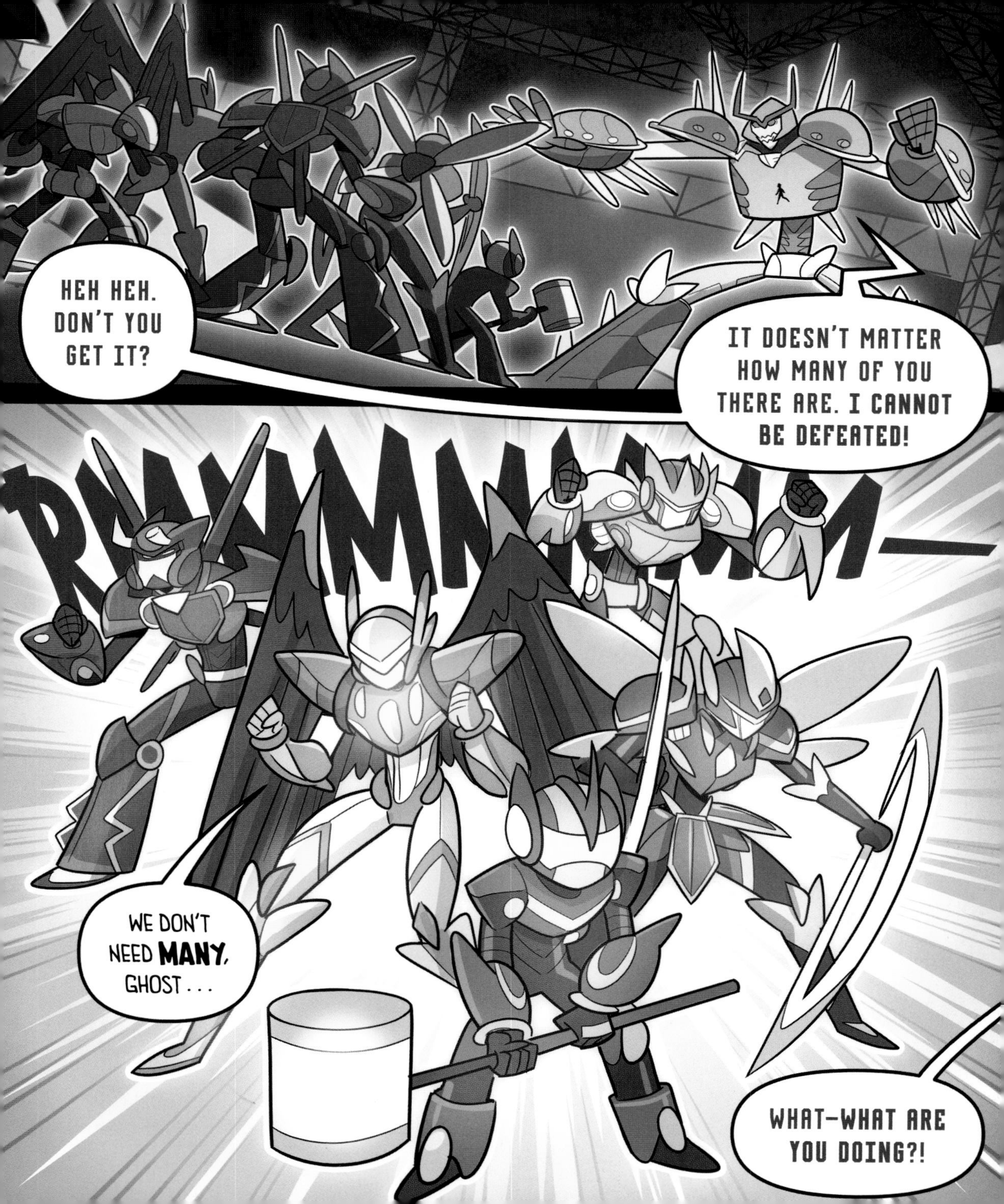
HEH HEH. DON'T YOU GET IT?
IT DOESN'T MATTER HOW MANY OF YOU THERE ARE. I CANNOT BE DEFEATED!
RMMMMMMM—
WE DON'T NEED **MANY**, GHOST . . .
WHAT—WHAT ARE YOU DOING?!

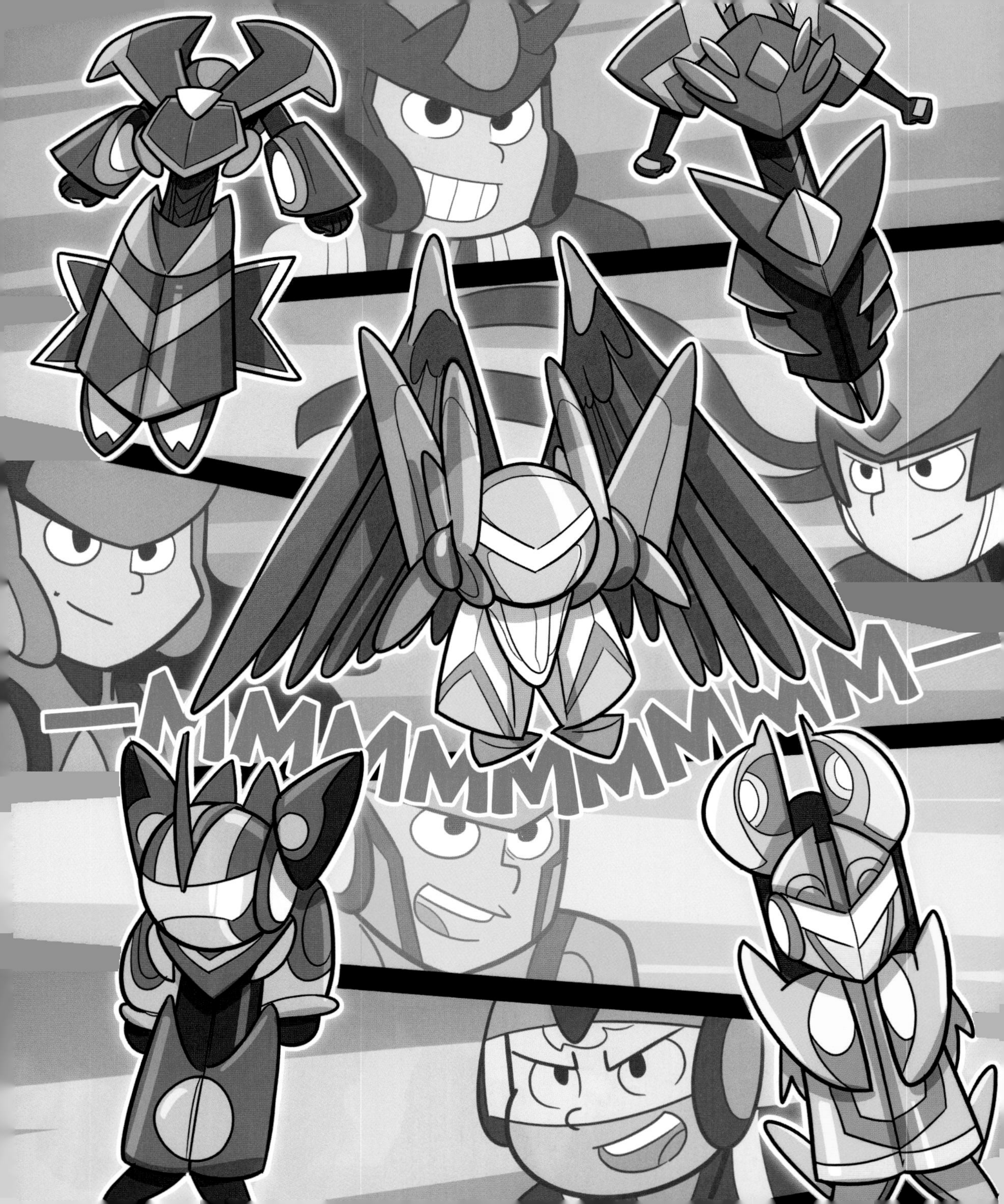
—MMMMMMMMMMMMMM—

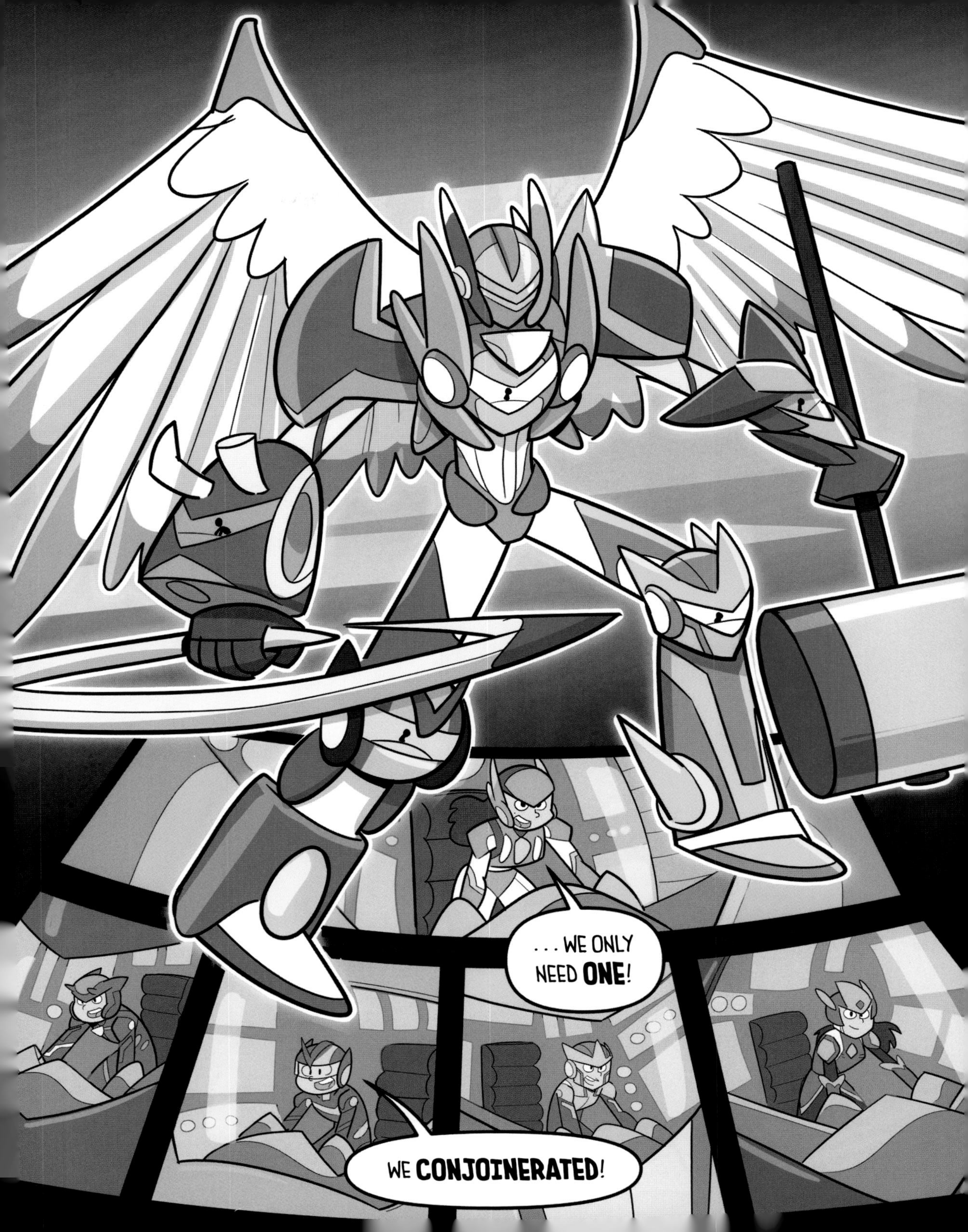

. . . WE ONLY NEED **ONE**!
WE **CONJOINERATED**!

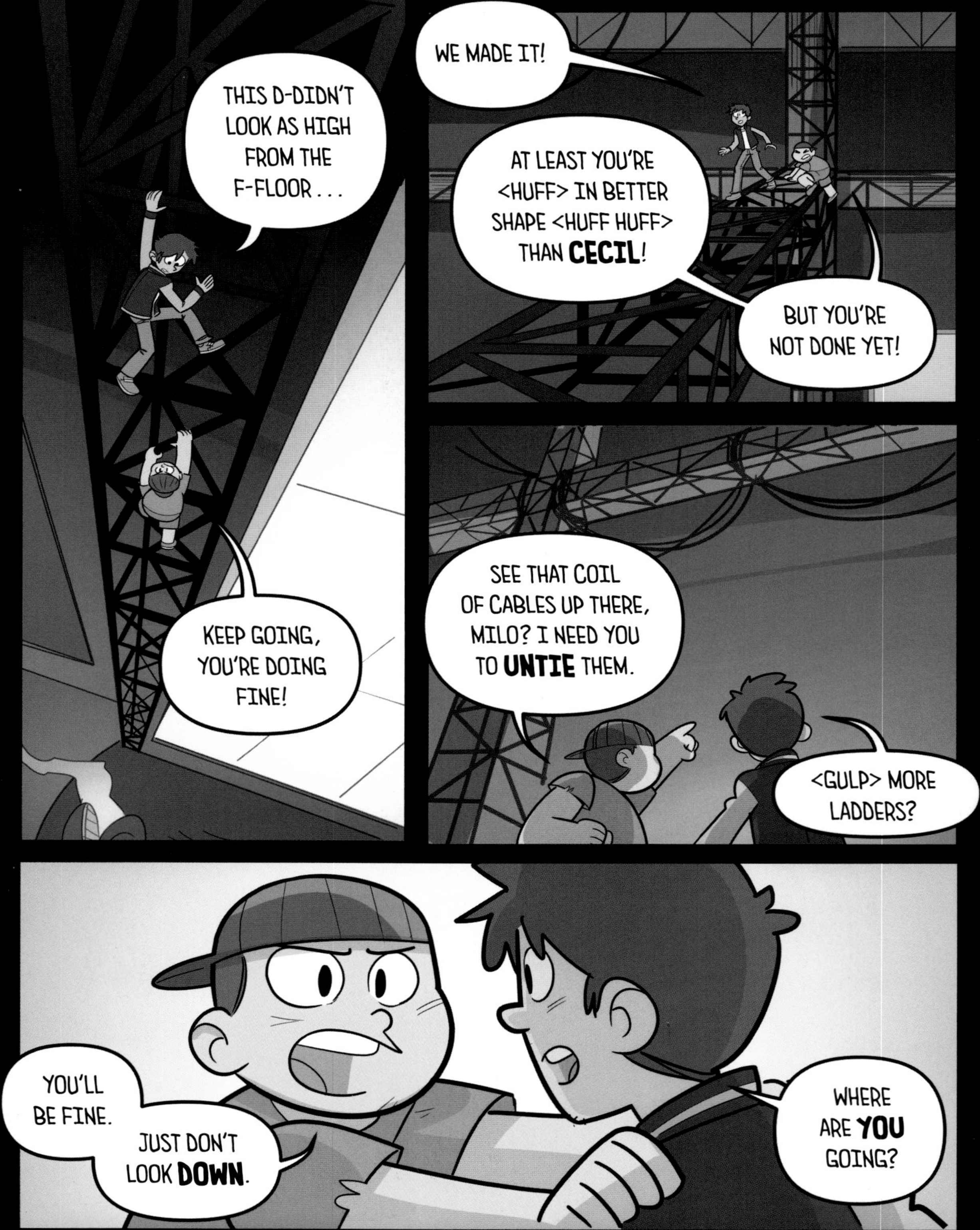
THIS D-DIDN'T LOOK AS HIGH FROM THE F-FLOOR . . .
KEEP GOING, YOU'RE DOING FINE!
WE MADE IT!
AT LEAST YOU'RE <HUFF> IN BETTER SHAPE <HUFF HUFF> THAN **CECIL**!
BUT YOU'RE NOT DONE YET!
SEE THAT COIL OF CABLES UP THERE, MILO? I NEED YOU TO **UNTIE** THEM.
<GULP> MORE LADDERS?
YOU'LL BE FINE.
JUST DON'T LOOK **DOWN**.
WHERE ARE **YOU** GOING?

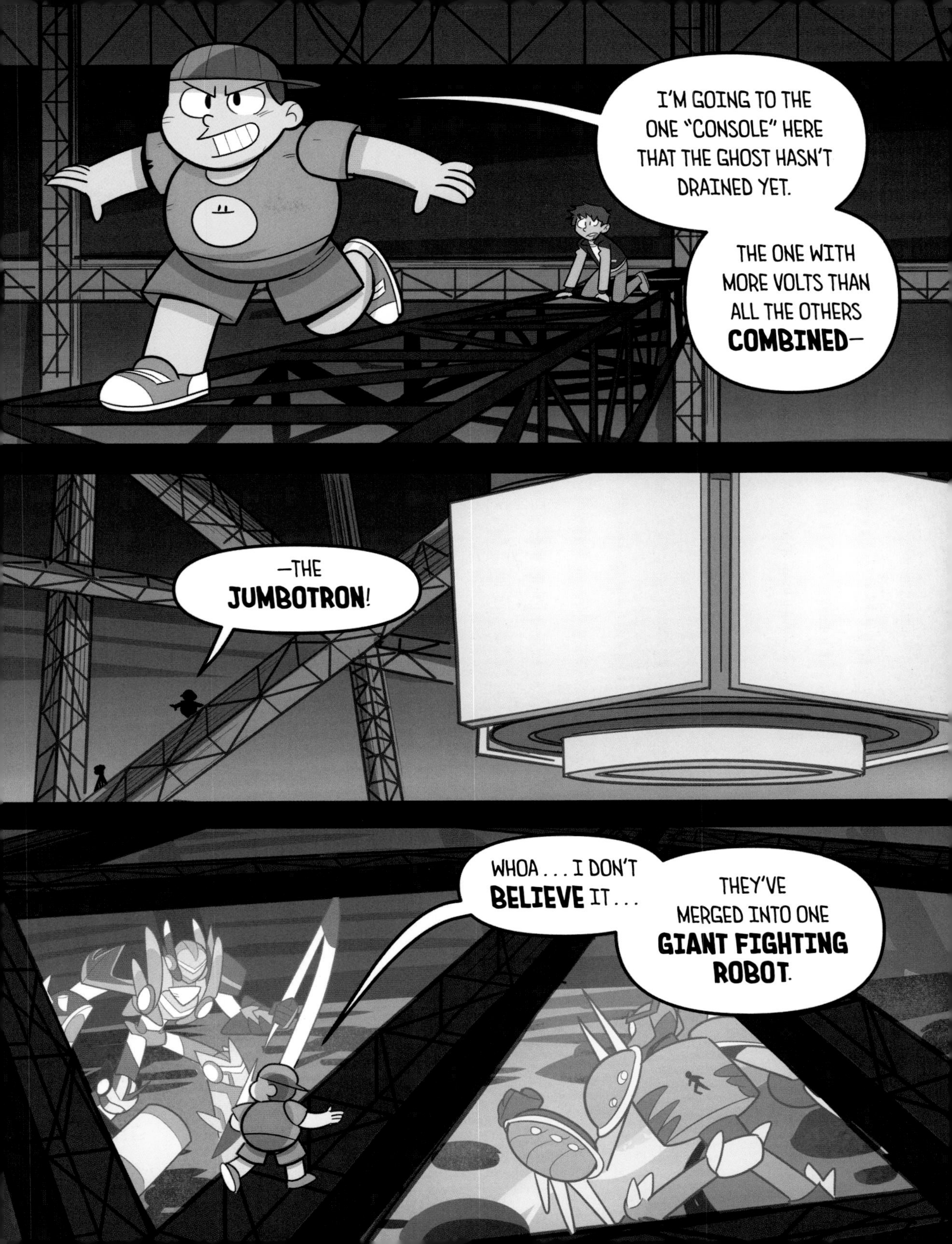
I'M GOING TO THE ONE "CONSOLE" HERE THAT THE GHOST HASN'T DRAINED YET.
THE ONE WITH MORE VOLTS THAN ALL THE OTHERS **COMBINED**—
—THE **JUMBOTRON**!
WHOA . . . I DON'T **BELIEVE** IT . . .
THEY'VE MERGED INTO ONE **GIANT FIGHTING ROBOT**.

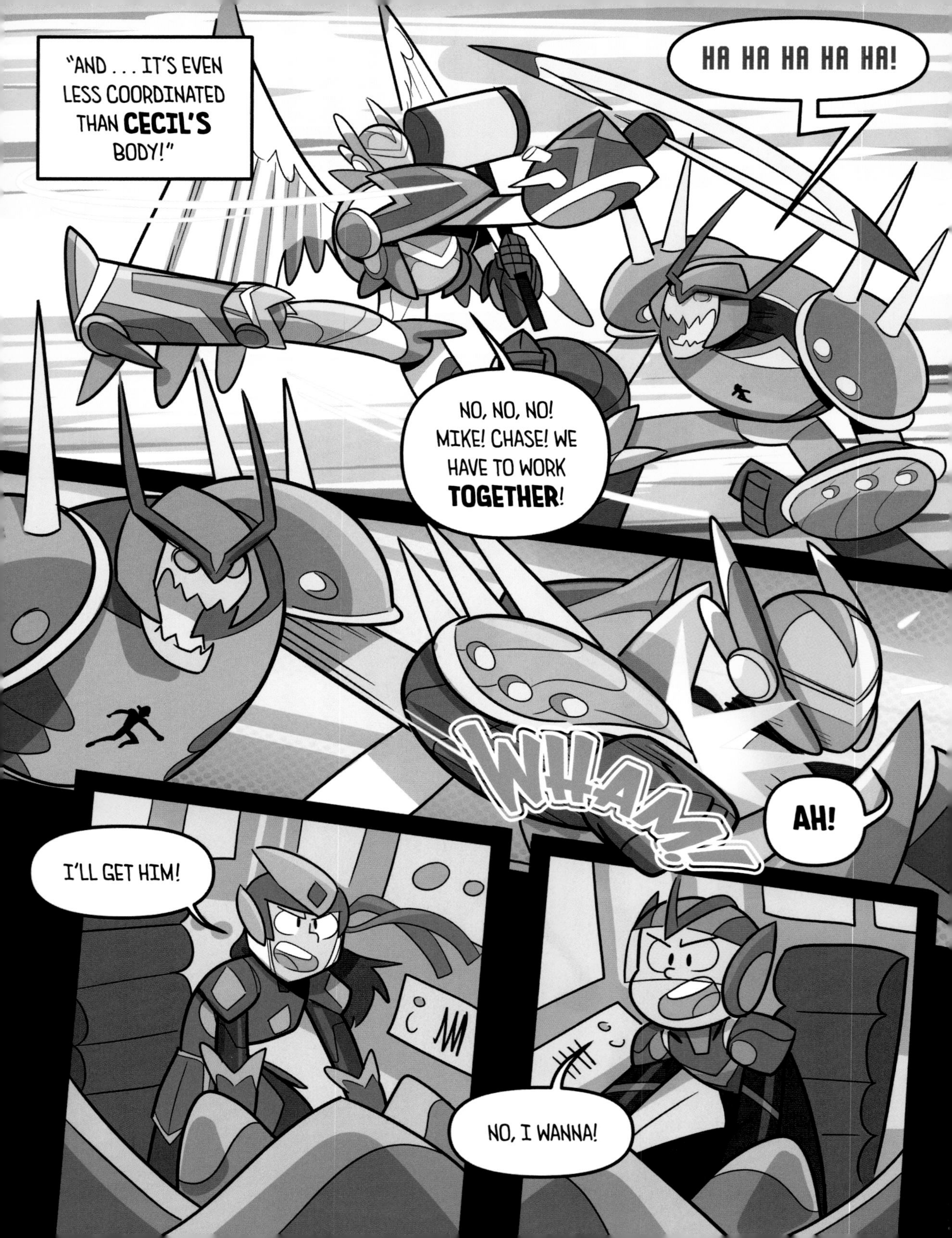
"AND . . . IT'S EVEN LESS COORDINATED THAN **CECIL'S** BODY!"
HA HA HA HA HA!
NO, NO, NO! MIKE! CHASE! WE HAVE TO WORK **TOGETHER**!
WHAM!
AH!
I'LL GET HIM!
NO, I WANNA!

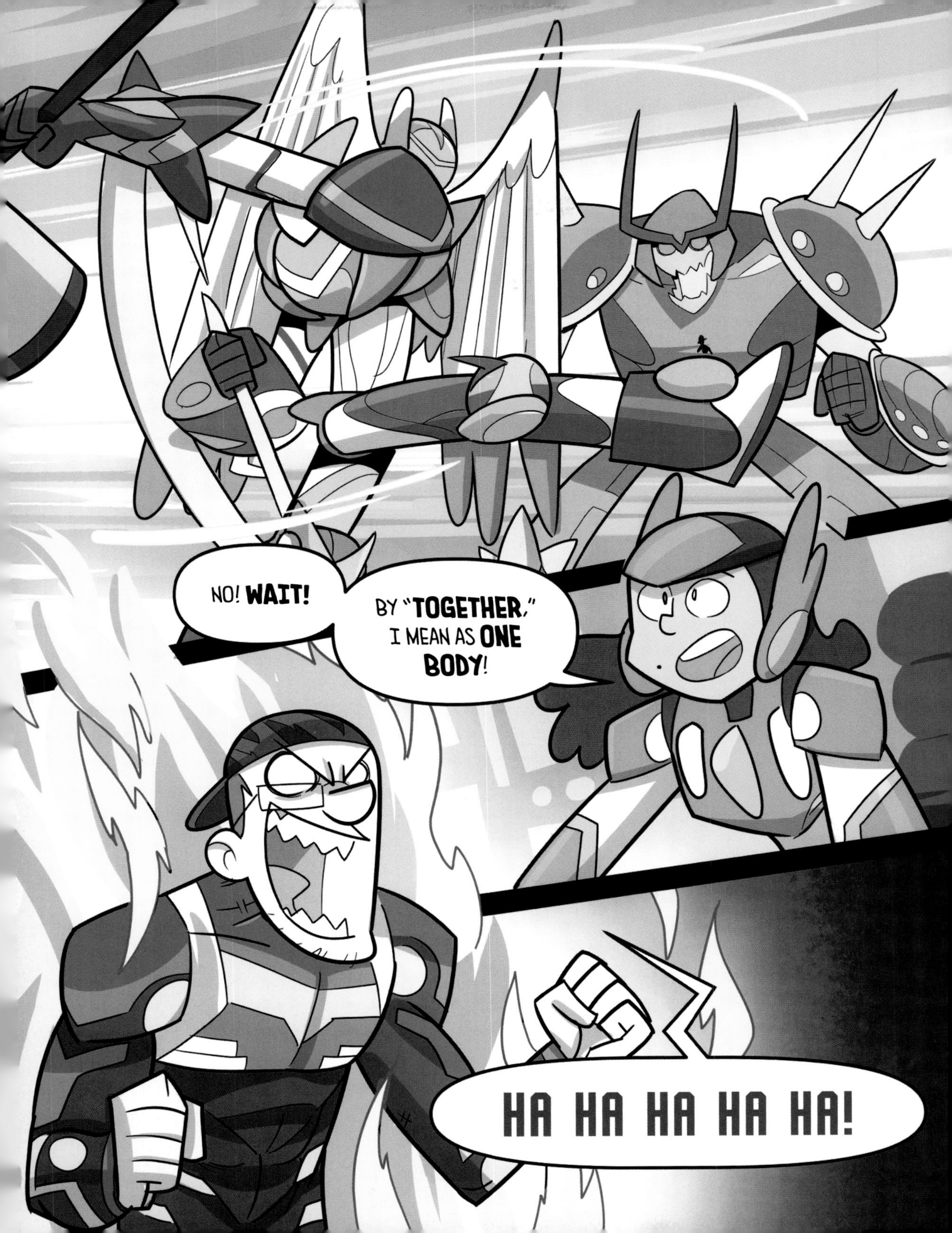
NO! **WAIT!**
BY "**TOGETHER**," I MEAN AS **ONE BODY**!
HA HA HA HA HA!

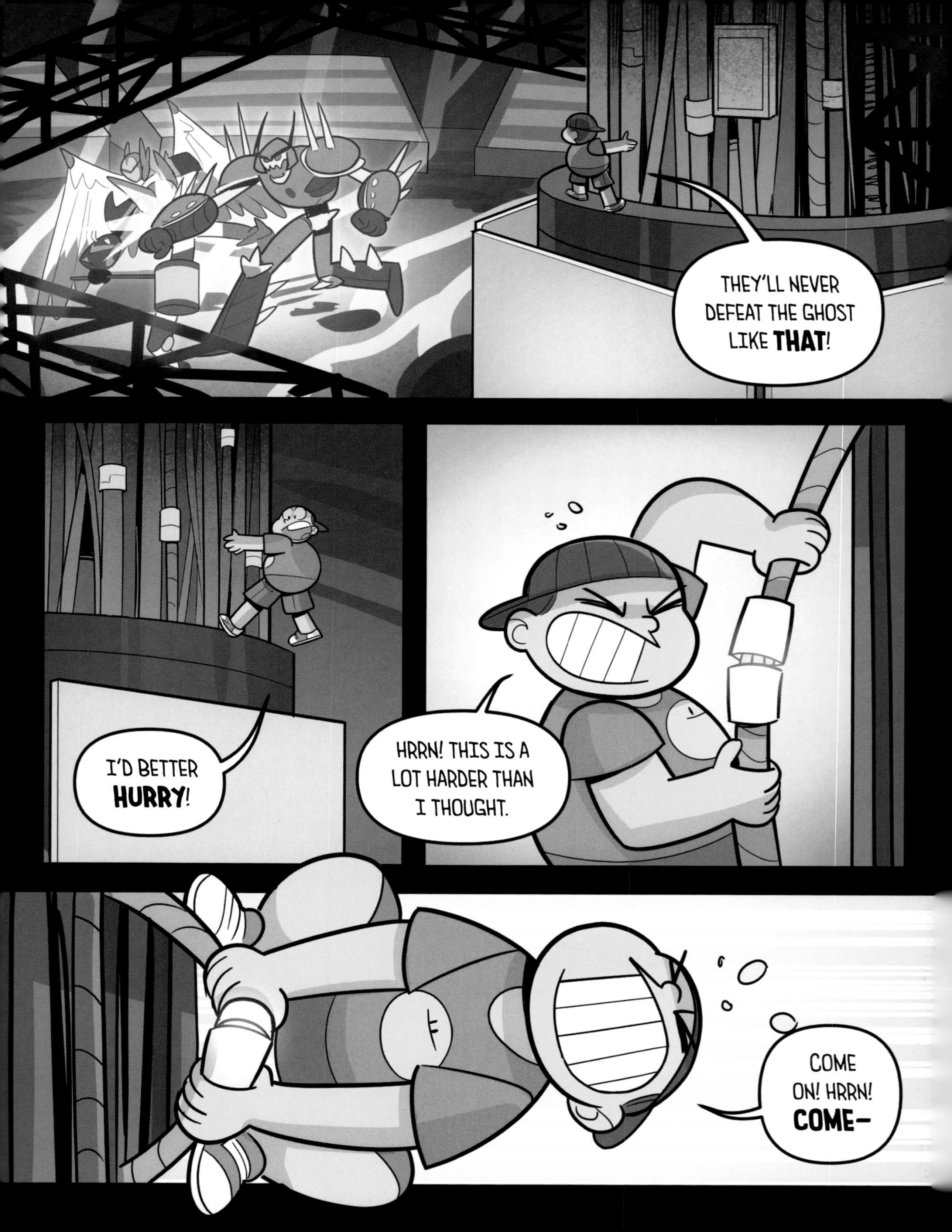
THEY'LL NEVER DEFEAT THE GHOST LIKE **THAT**!
I'D BETTER **HURRY**!
HRRN! THIS IS A LOT HARDER THAN I THOUGHT.
COME ON! HRRN! **COME—**

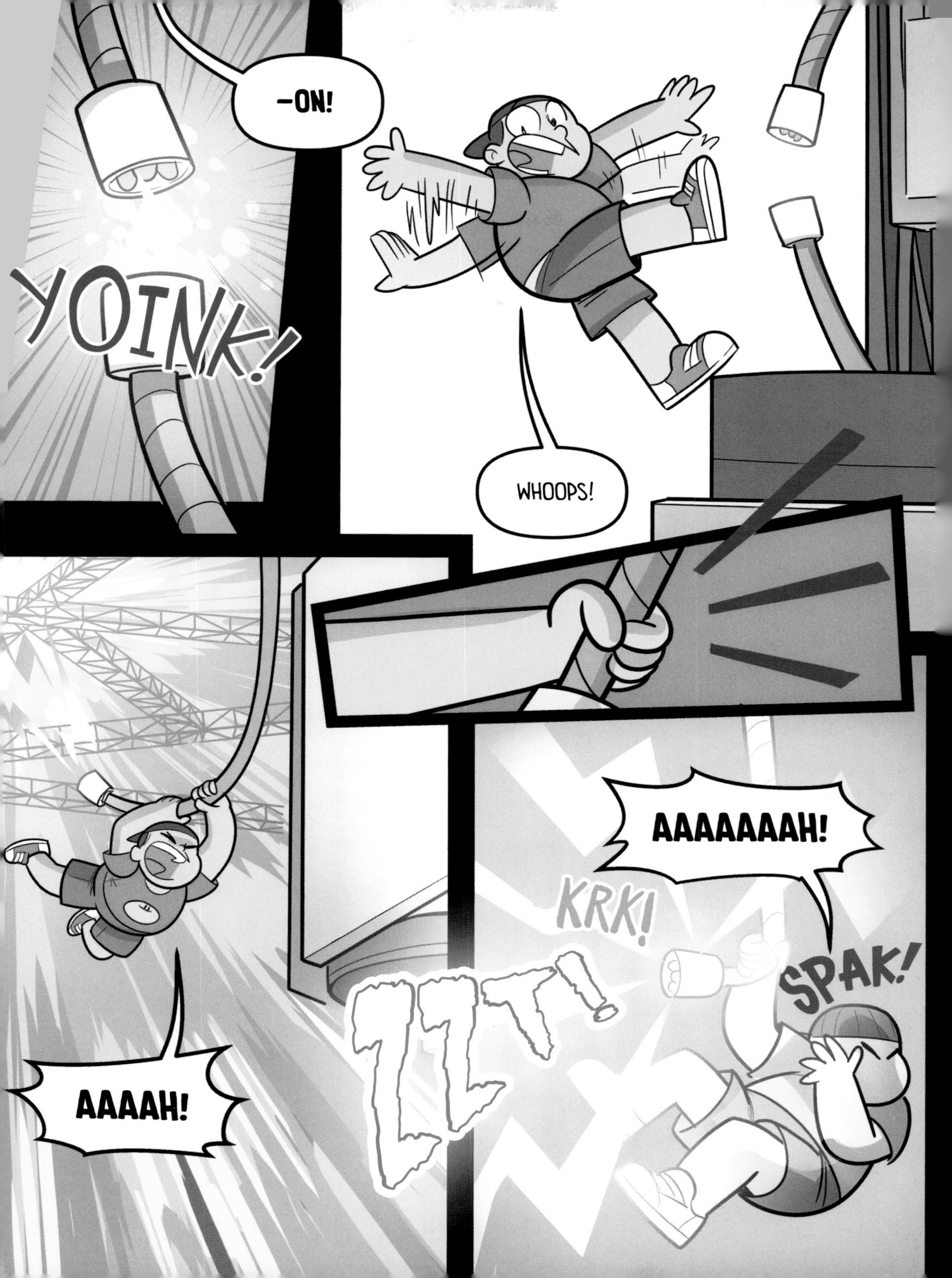
-ON!
YOINK!
WHOOPS!
AAAAH!
AAAAAAAH!
KRK!
ZZT!
SPAK!

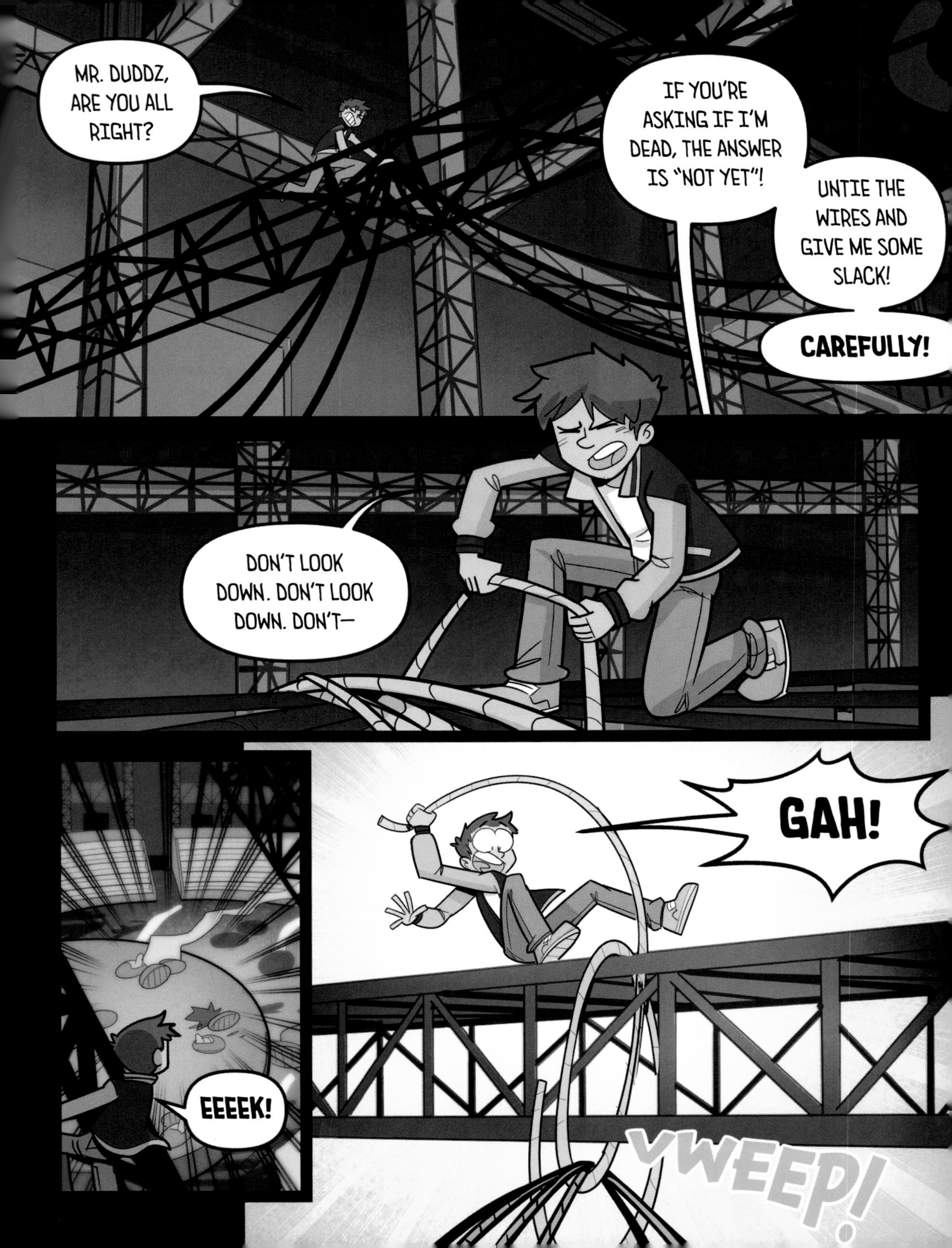
MR. DUDDZ, ARE YOU ALL RIGHT?
IF YOU'RE ASKING IF I'M DEAD, THE ANSWER IS "NOT YET"!
UNTIE THE WIRES AND GIVE ME SOME SLACK!
CAREFULLY!
DON'T LOOK DOWN. DON'T LOOK DOWN. DON'T—
GAH!
EEEEK!
VWEEP!

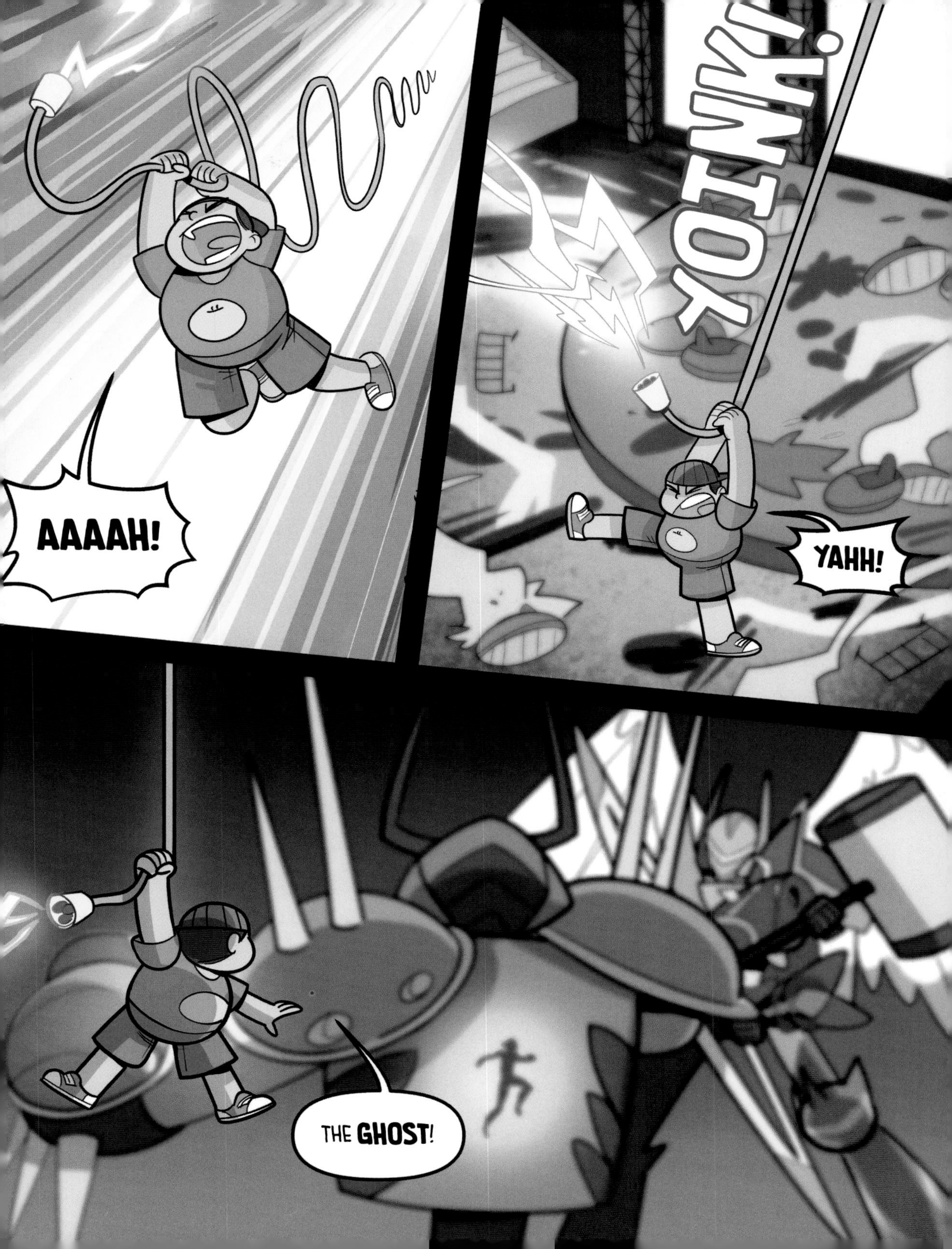
AAAAH!
YOINK!
YAHH!
THE **GHOST**!

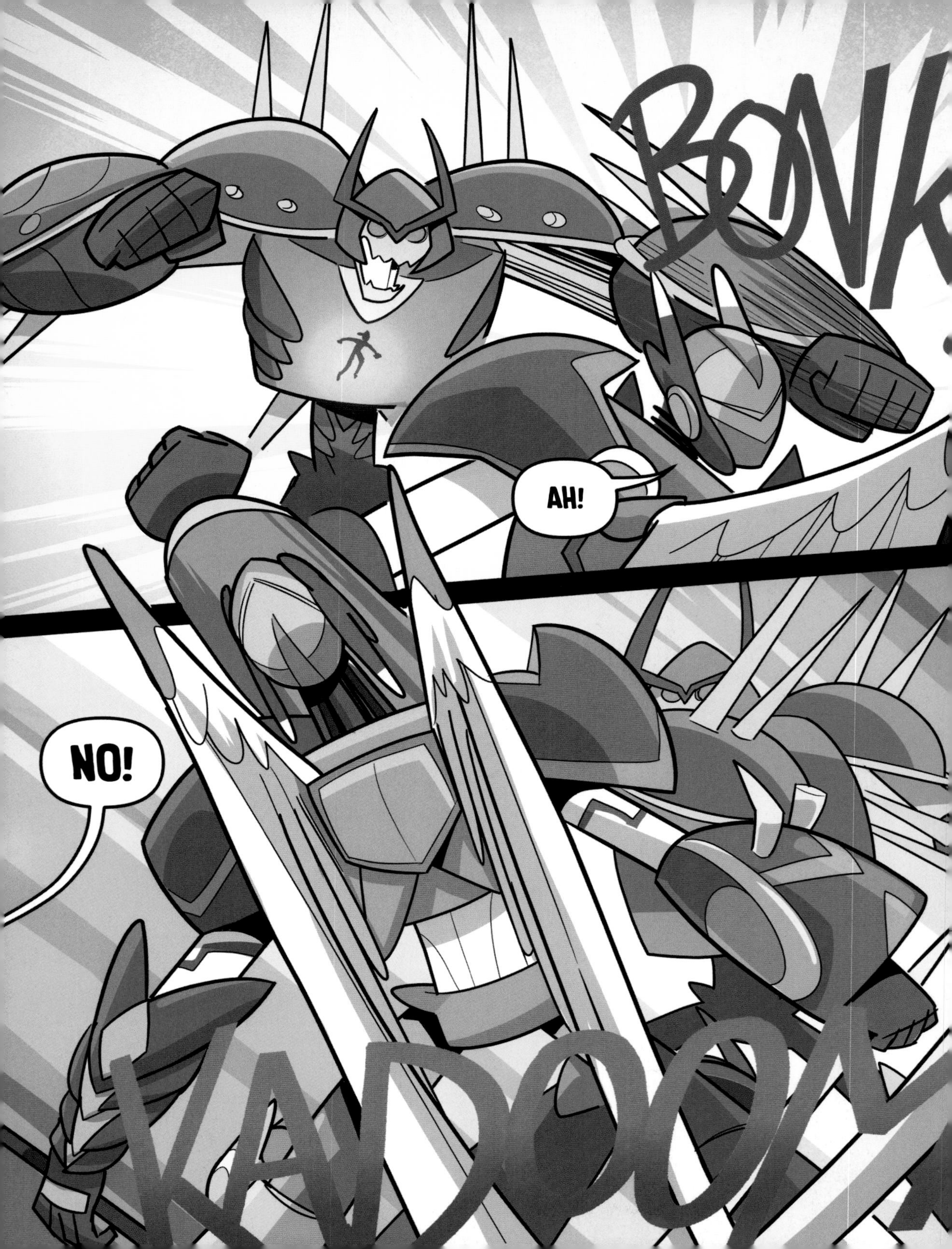
BONK
AH!
NO!
KADOOM

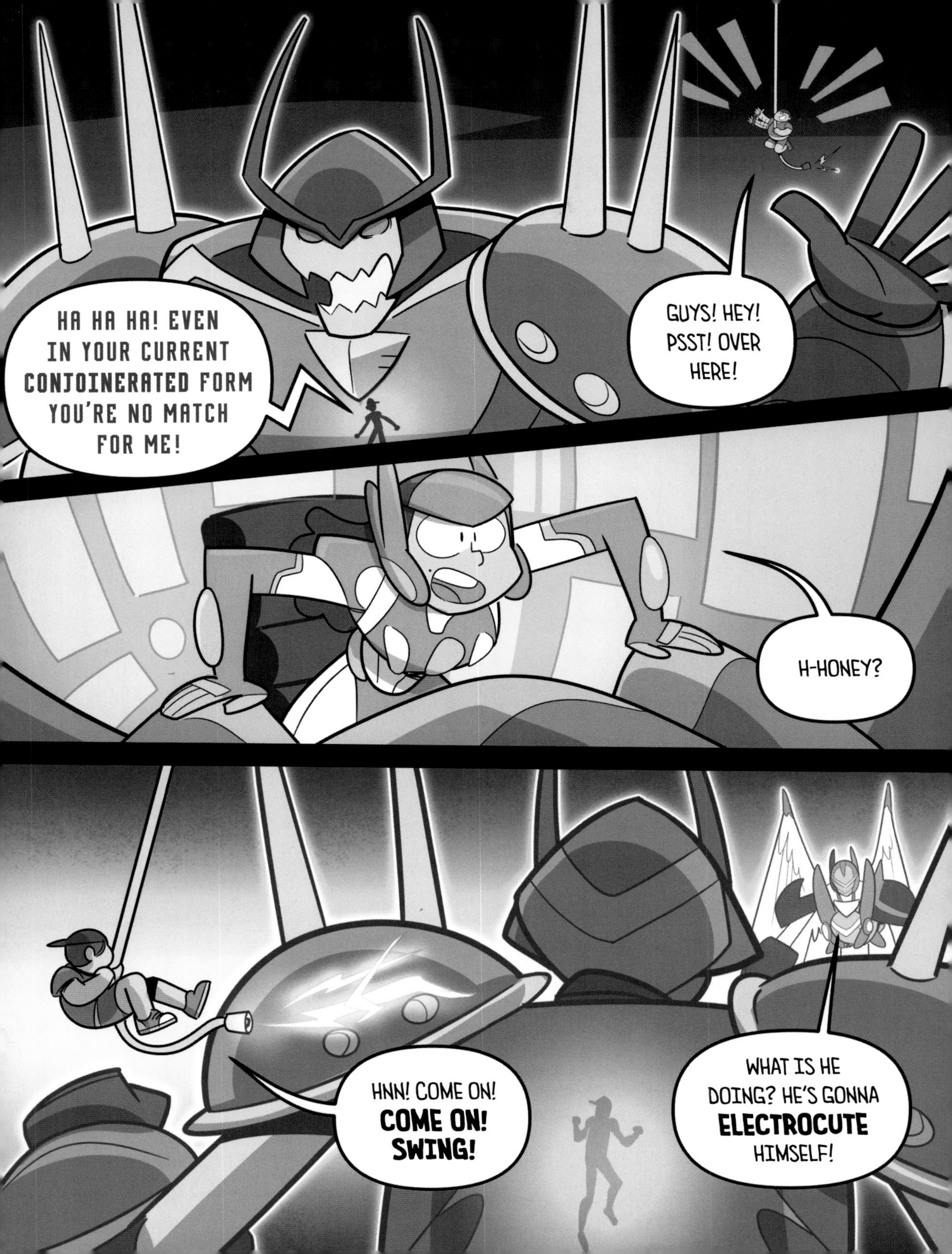
HA HA HA! EVEN IN YOUR CURRENT **CONJOINERATED** FORM YOU'RE NO MATCH FOR ME!
GUYS! HEY! PSST! OVER HERE!
H-HONEY?
HNN! COME ON! **COME ON! SWING!**
WHAT IS HE DOING? HE'S GONNA **ELECTROCUTE** HIMSELF!

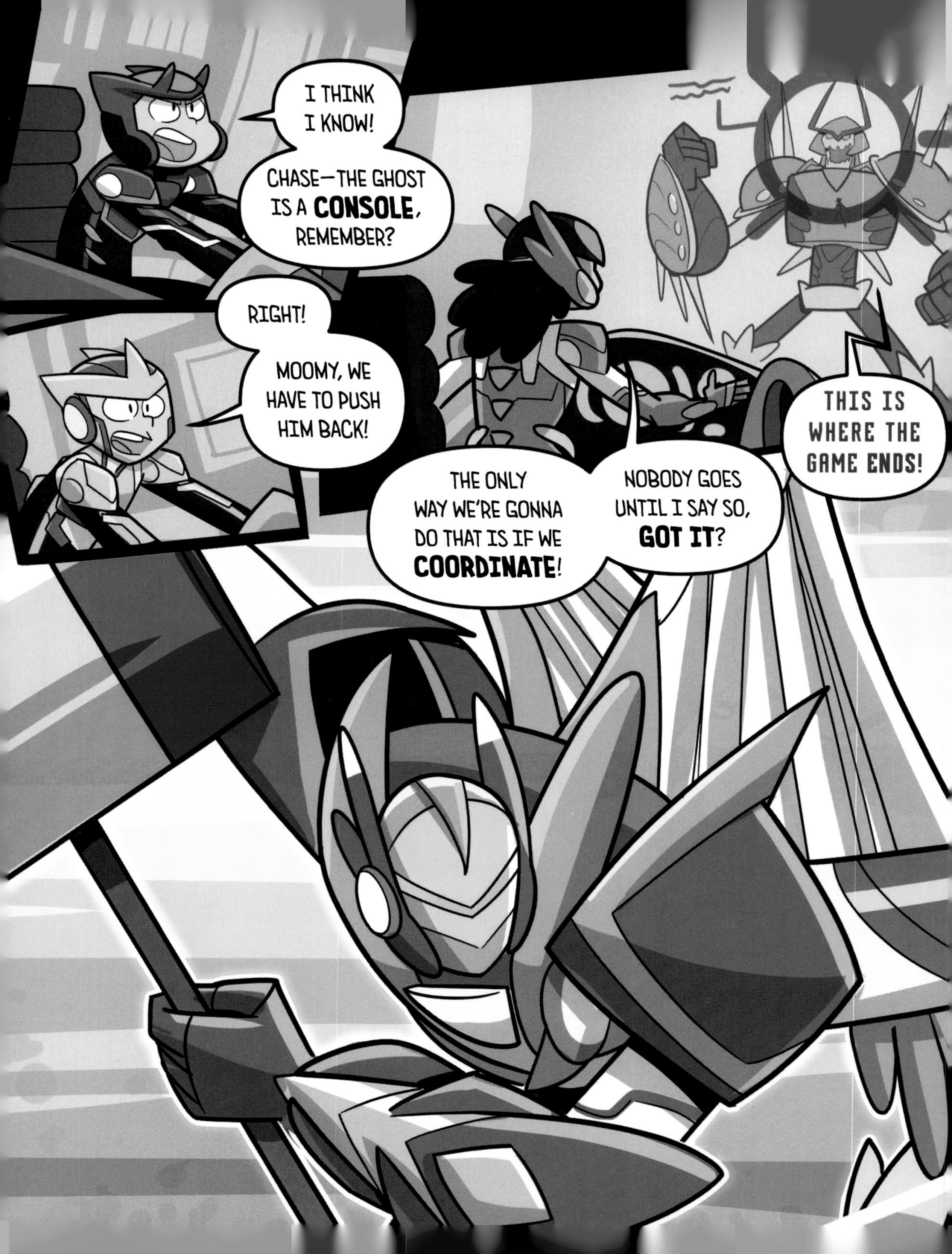
I THINK I KNOW!
CHASE—THE GHOST IS A CONSOLE, REMEMBER?
RIGHT!
MOOMY, WE HAVE TO PUSH HIM BACK!
THE ONLY WAY WE'RE GONNA DO THAT IS IF WE COORDINATE!
NOBODY GOES UNTIL I SAY SO, GOT IT?
THIS IS WHERE THE GAME ENDS!

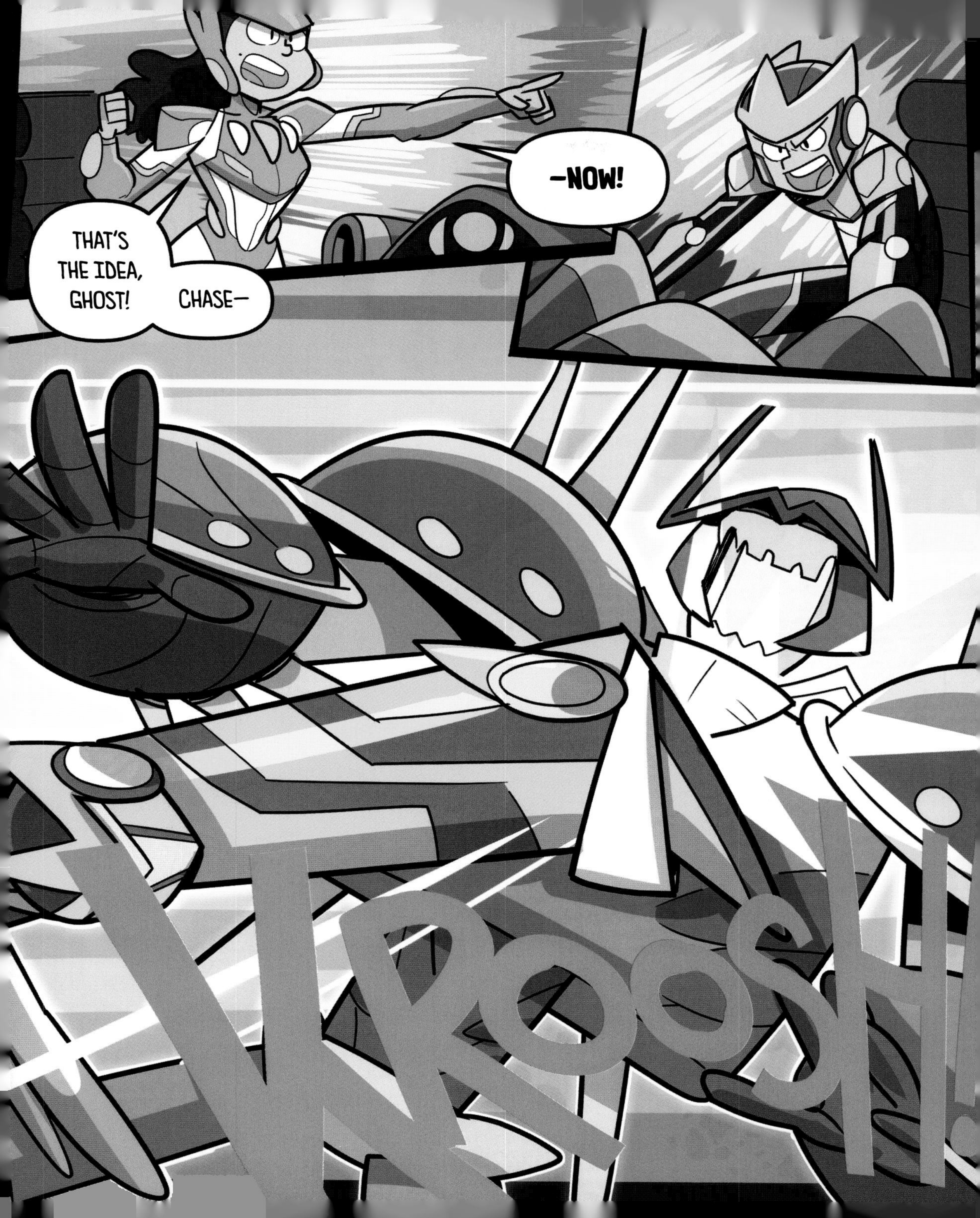
THAT'S THE IDEA, GHOST!
CHASE—
—NOW!
VROOSH!

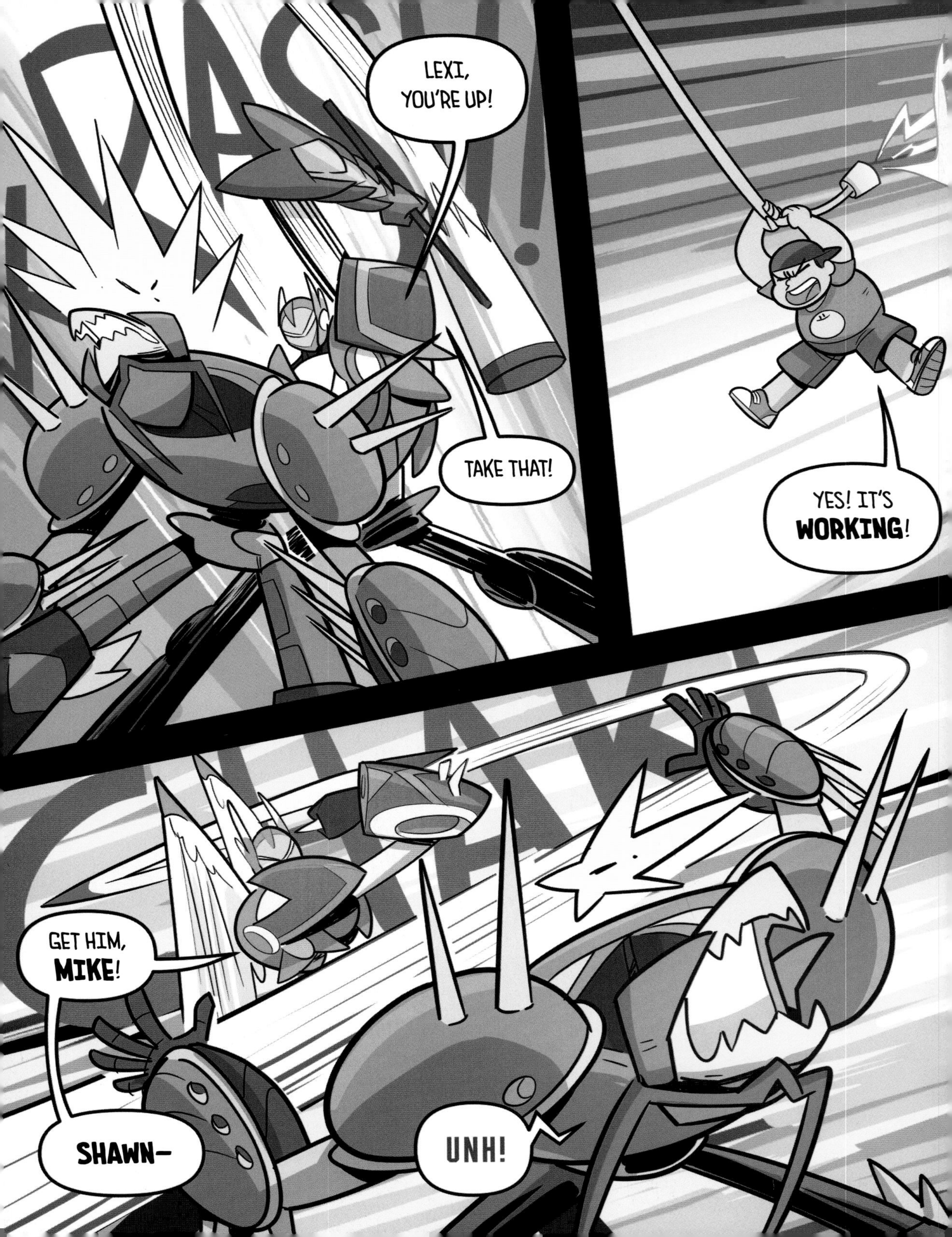
LEXI, YOU'RE UP!
TAKE THAT!
YES! IT'S **WORKING**!
GET HIM, **MIKE**!
SHAWN-
UNH!

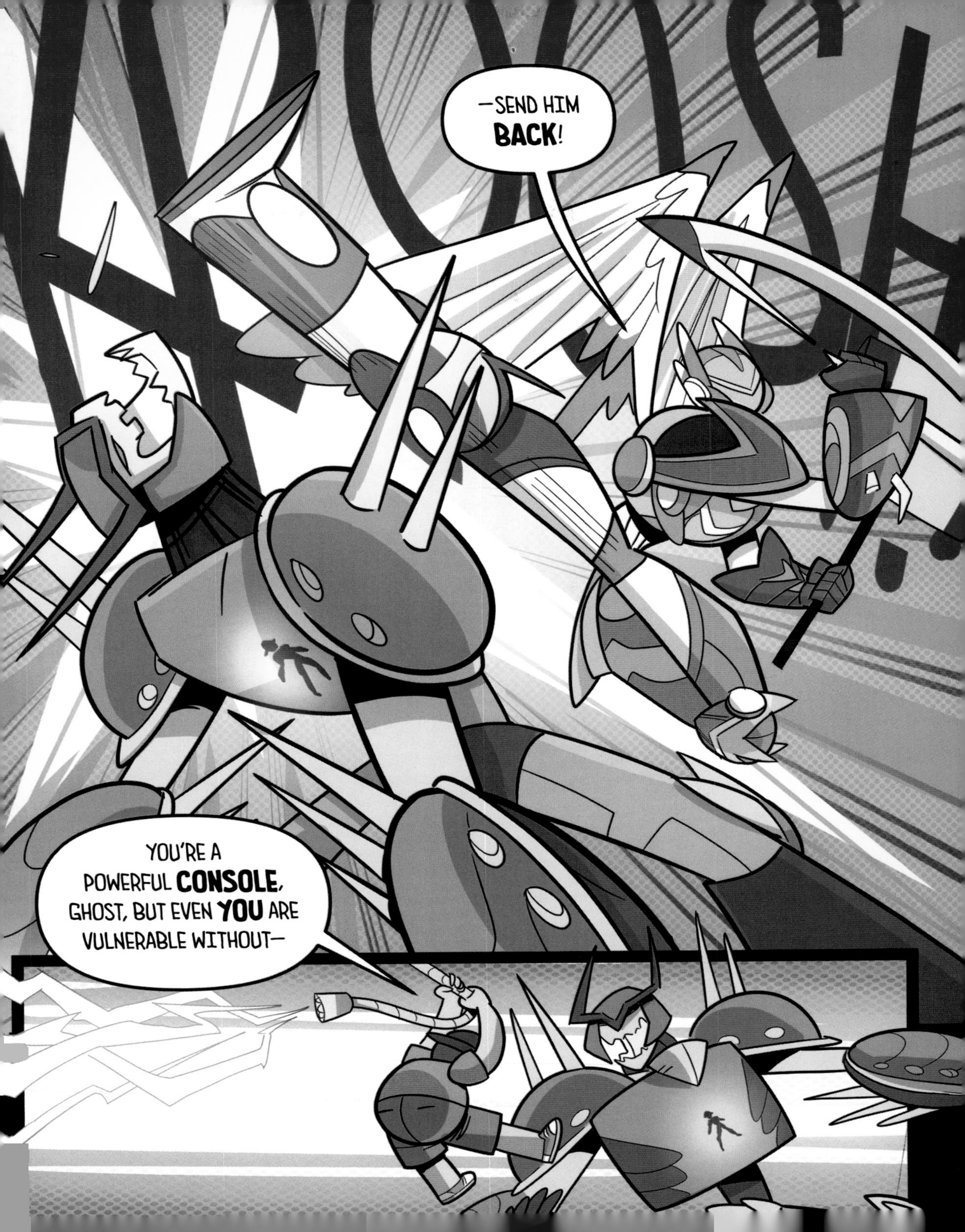
—SEND HIM BACK!
YOU'RE A POWERFUL CONSOLE, GHOST, BUT EVEN YOU ARE VULNERABLE WITHOUT—

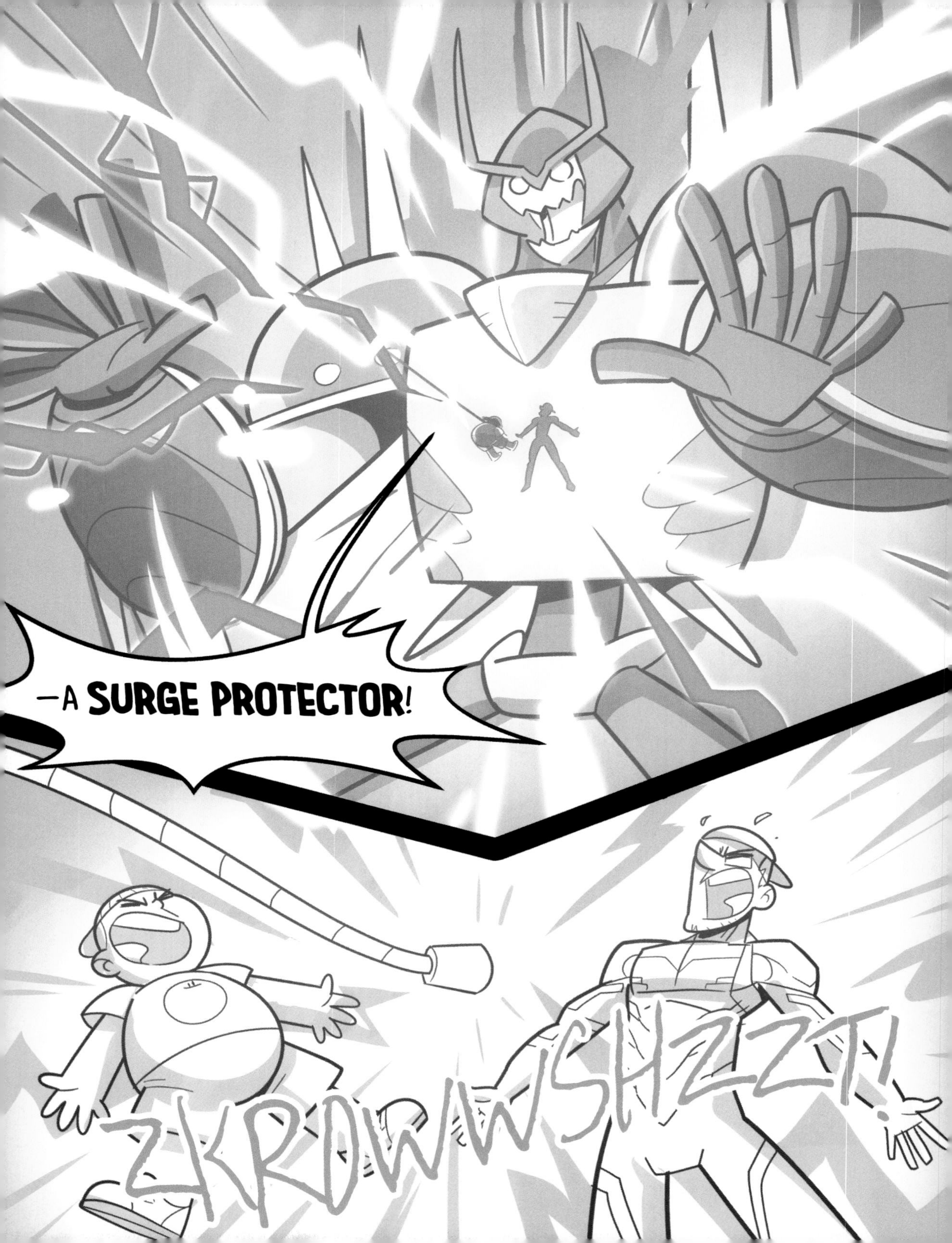
—A SURGE PROTECTOR!
ZKROWWSHZZT!

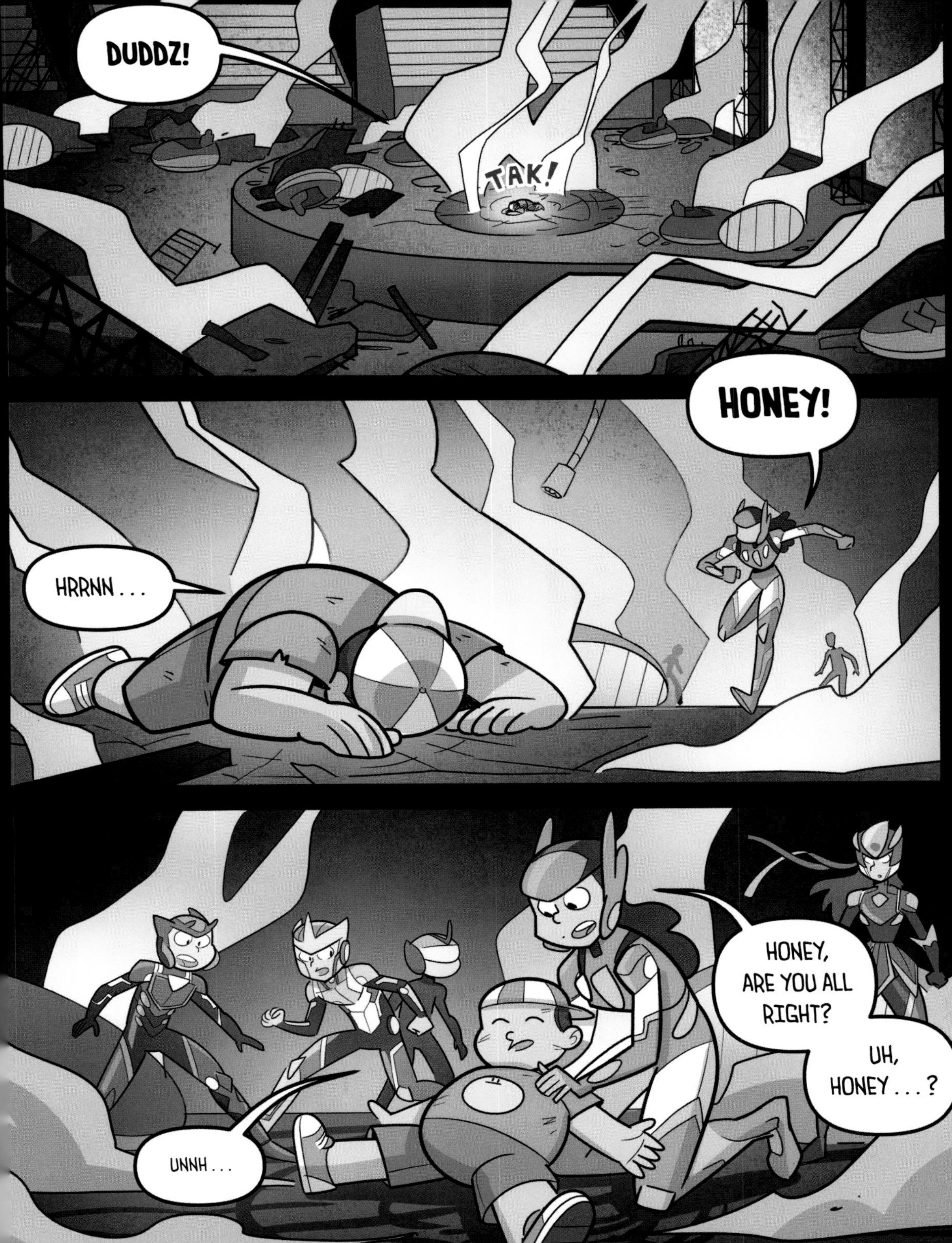
DUDDZ!
TAK!
HONEY!
HRRNN . . .
HONEY, ARE YOU ALL RIGHT?
UH, HONEY . . . ?
UNNH . . .

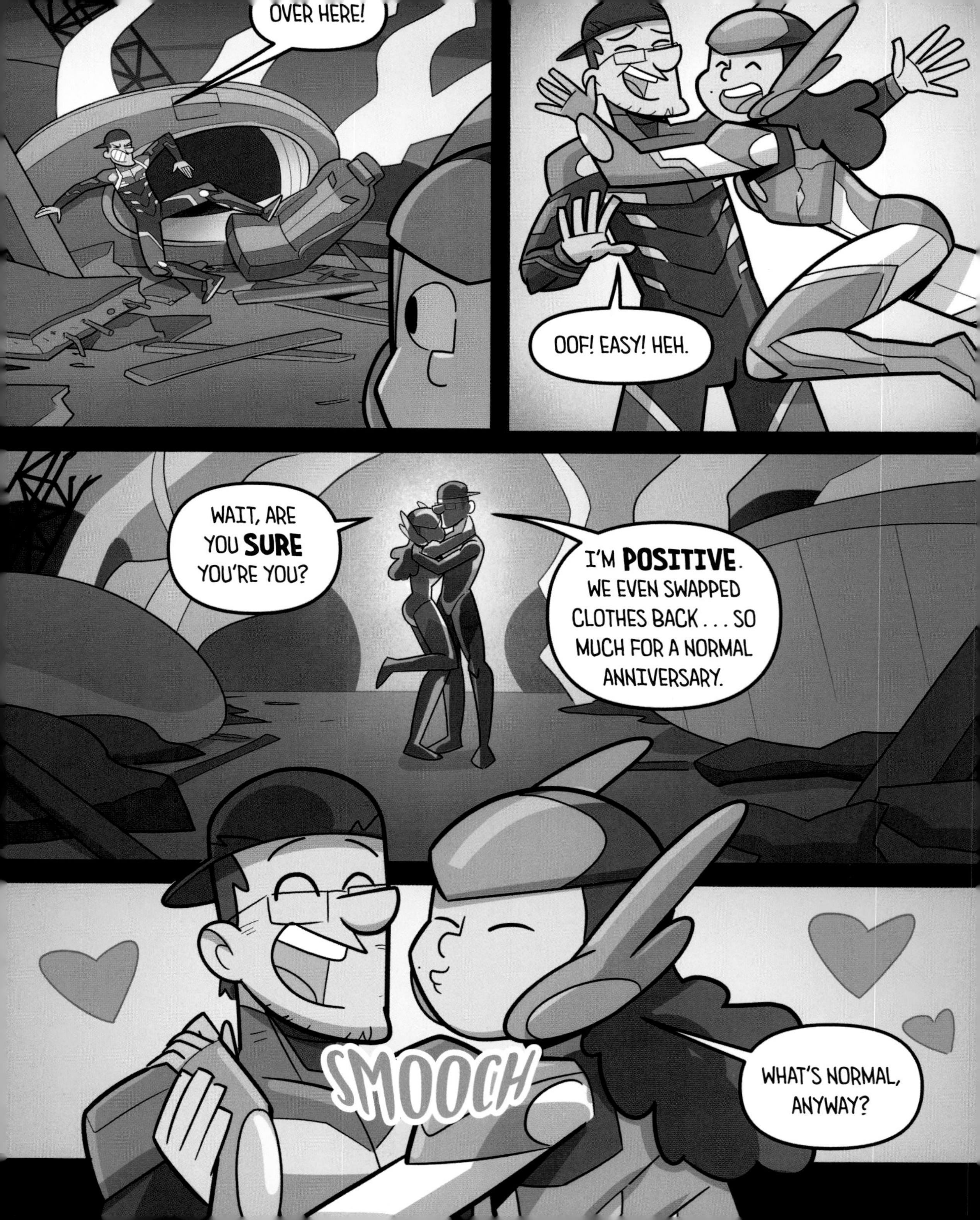
OVER HERE!
OOF! EASY! HEH.
WAIT, ARE YOU **SURE** YOU'RE YOU?
I'M **POSITIVE**. WE EVEN SWAPPED CLOTHES BACK . . . SO MUCH FOR A NORMAL ANNIVERSARY.
SMOOCH
WHAT'S NORMAL, ANYWAY?

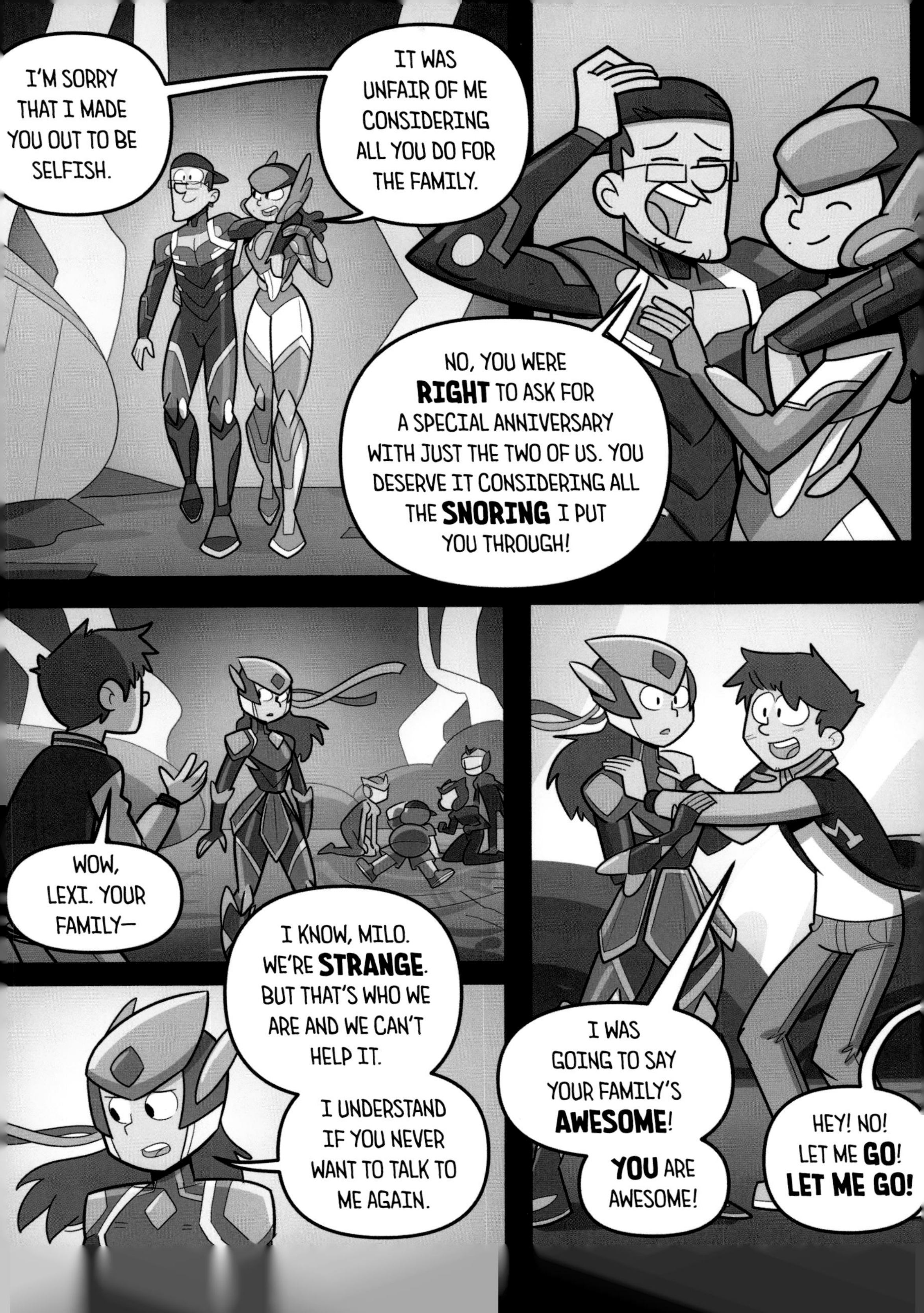
I'M SORRY THAT I MADE YOU OUT TO BE SELFISH.
IT WAS UNFAIR OF ME CONSIDERING ALL YOU DO FOR THE FAMILY.
NO, YOU WERE RIGHT TO ASK FOR A SPECIAL ANNIVERSARY WITH JUST THE TWO OF US. YOU DESERVE IT CONSIDERING ALL THE SNORING I PUT YOU THROUGH!
WOW, LEXI. YOUR FAMILY—
I KNOW, MILO. WE'RE STRANGE. BUT THAT'S WHO WE ARE AND WE CAN'T HELP IT.
I UNDERSTAND IF YOU NEVER WANT TO TALK TO ME AGAIN.
I WAS GOING TO SAY YOUR FAMILY'S AWESOME!
YOU ARE AWESOME!
HEY! NO! LET ME GO! LET ME GO!

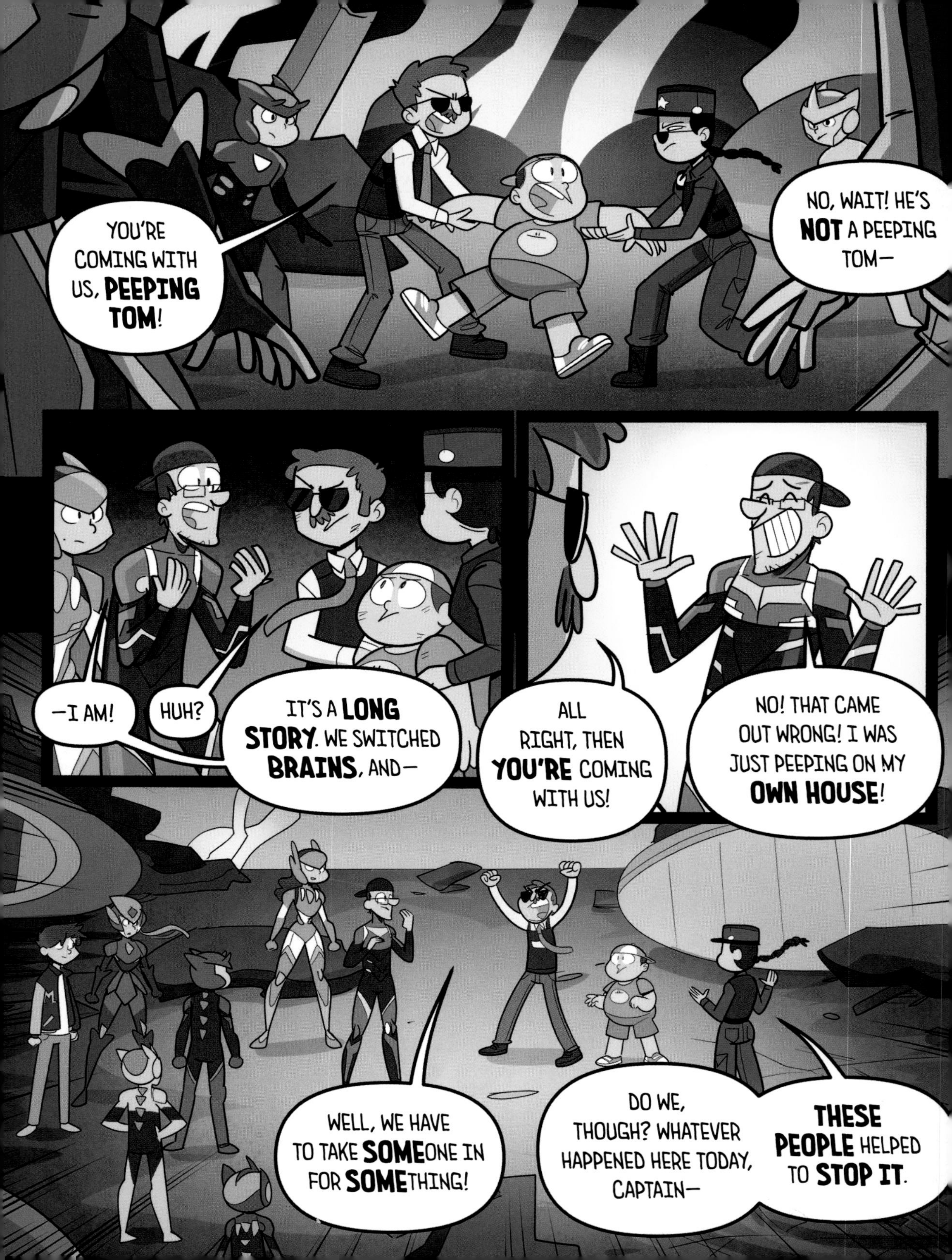
YOU'RE COMING WITH US, PEEPING TOM!
NO, WAIT! HE'S NOT A PEEPING TOM—
—I AM!
HUH?
IT'S A LONG STORY. WE SWITCHED BRAINS, AND—
ALL RIGHT, THEN YOU'RE COMING WITH US!
NO! THAT CAME OUT WRONG! I WAS JUST PEEPING ON MY OWN HOUSE!
WELL, WE HAVE TO TAKE SOMEONE IN FOR SOMETHING!
DO WE, THOUGH? WHATEVER HAPPENED HERE TODAY, CAPTAIN—
THESE PEOPLE HELPED TO STOP IT.

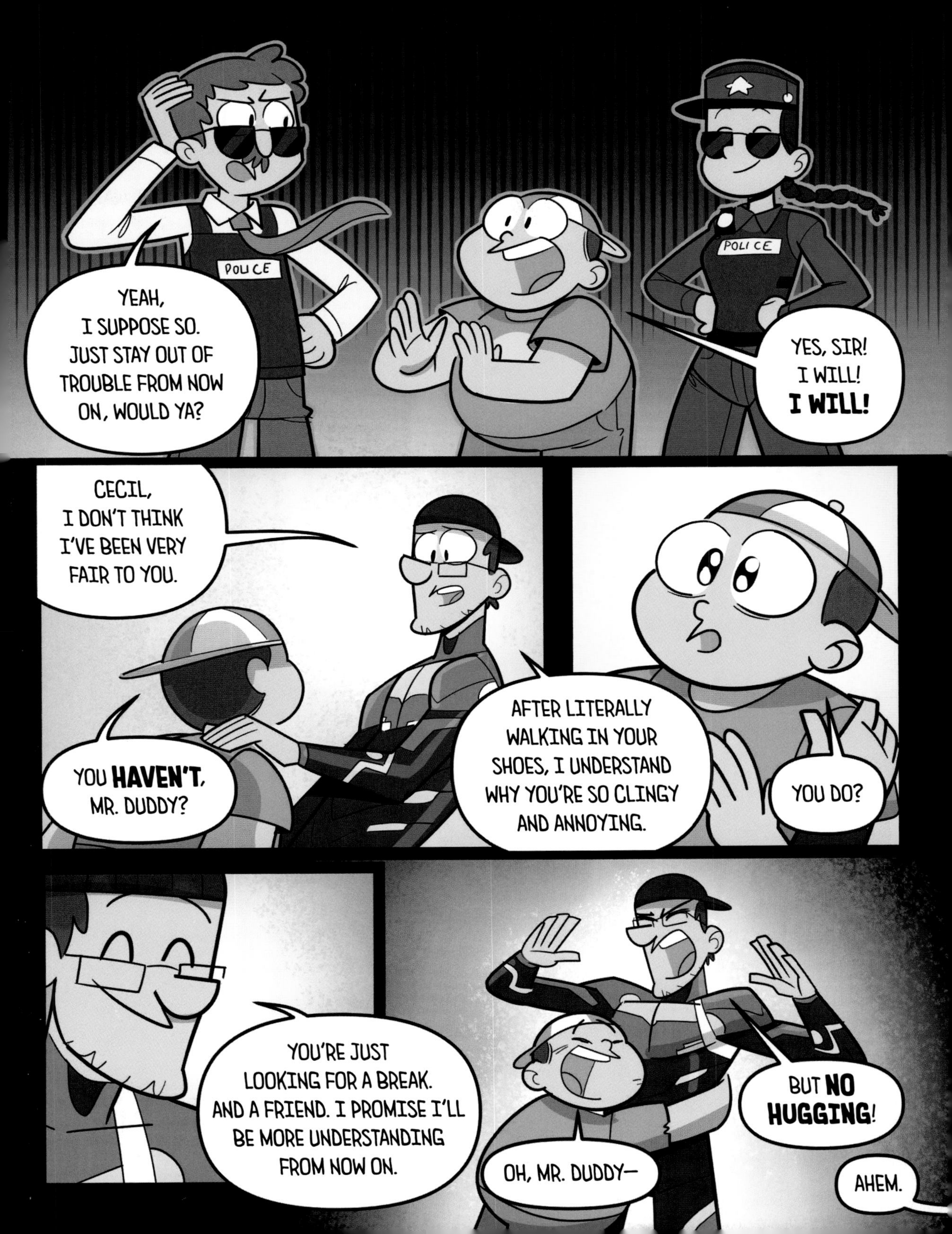
POLICE
POLICE
YEAH, I SUPPOSE SO. JUST STAY OUT OF TROUBLE FROM NOW ON, WOULD YA?
YES, SIR! I WILL! **I WILL!**
CECIL, I DON'T THINK I'VE BEEN VERY FAIR TO YOU.
YOU **HAVEN'T**, MR. DUDDY?
AFTER LITERALLY WALKING IN YOUR SHOES, I UNDERSTAND WHY YOU'RE SO CLINGY AND ANNOYING.
YOU DO?
YOU'RE JUST LOOKING FOR A BREAK. AND A FRIEND. I PROMISE I'LL BE MORE UNDERSTANDING FROM NOW ON.
OH, MR. DUDDY—
BUT **NO HUGGING**!
AHEM.

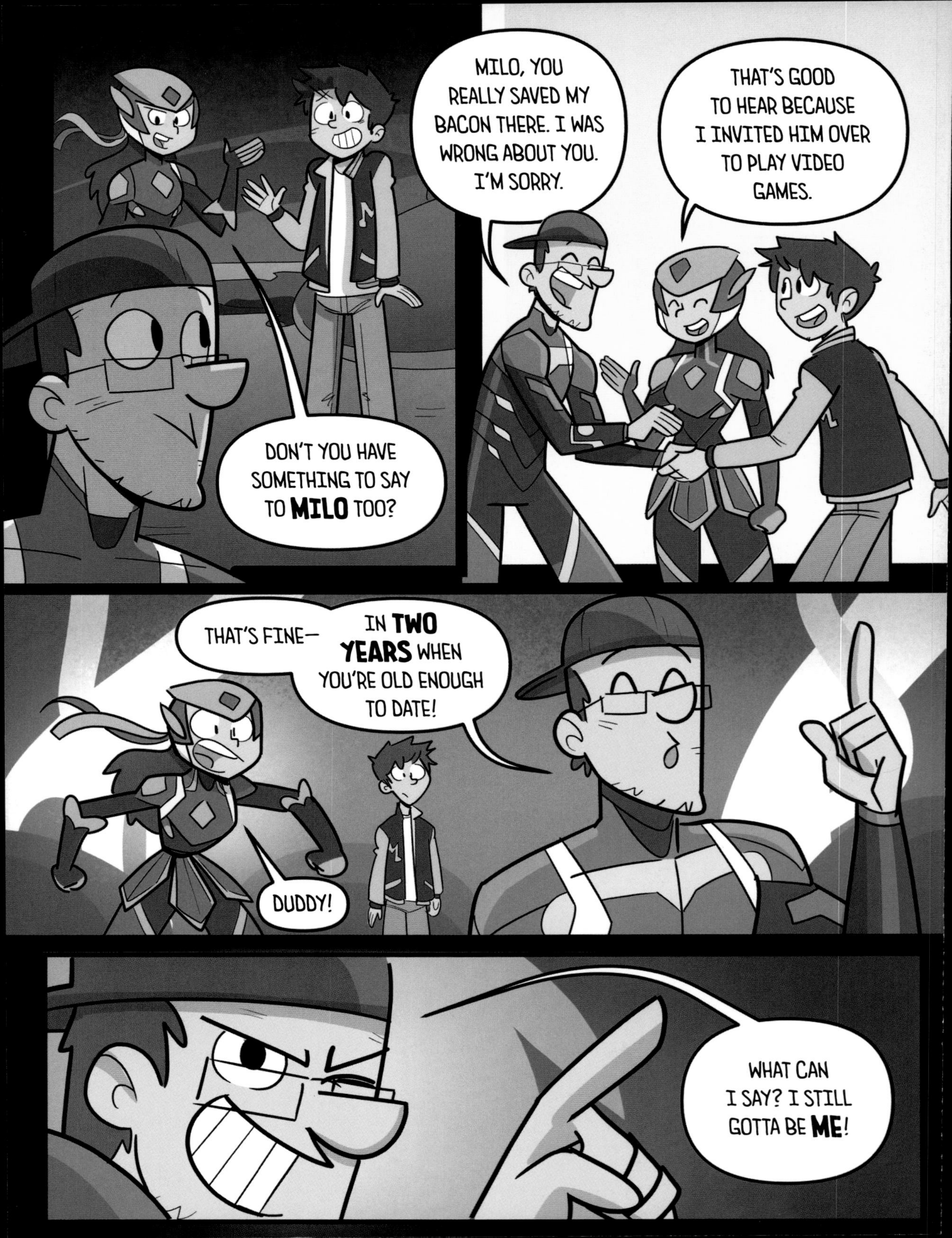
DON'T YOU HAVE SOMETHING TO SAY TO **MILO** TOO?
MILO, YOU REALLY SAVED MY BACON THERE. I WAS WRONG ABOUT YOU. I'M SORRY.
THAT'S GOOD TO HEAR BECAUSE I INVITED HIM OVER TO PLAY VIDEO GAMES.
THAT'S FINE—
IN **TWO YEARS** WHEN YOU'RE OLD ENOUGH TO DATE!
DUDDY!
WHAT CAN I SAY? I STILL GOTTA BE **ME**!

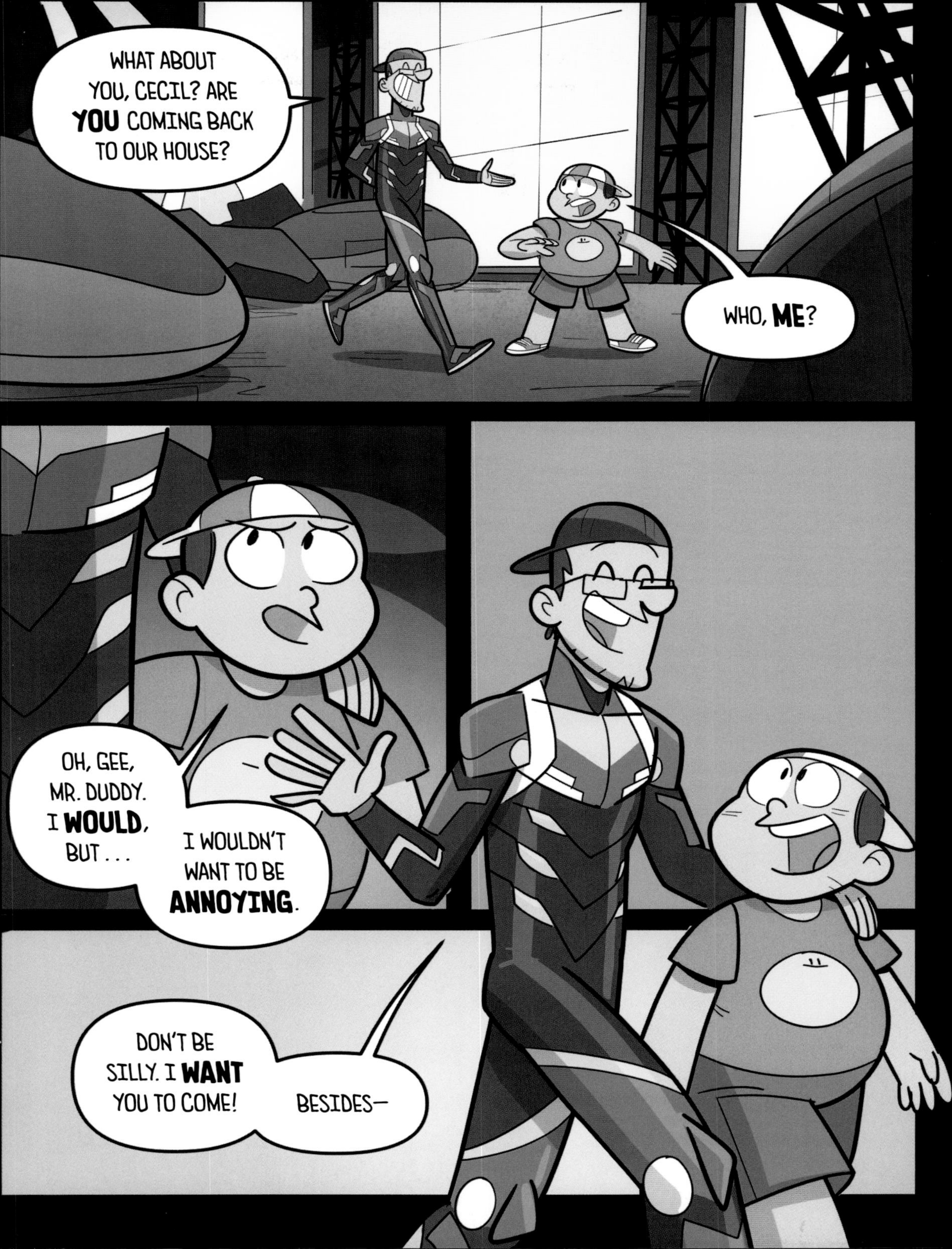
WHAT ABOUT YOU, CECIL? ARE **YOU** COMING BACK TO OUR HOUSE?
WHO, **ME**?
OH, GEE, MR. DUDDY. I **WOULD**, BUT . . .
I WOULDN'T WANT TO BE **ANNOYING**.
DON'T BE SILLY. I **WANT** YOU TO COME!
BESIDES—

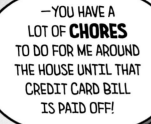

—YOU HAVE A LOT OF **CHORES** TO DO FOR ME AROUND THE HOUSE UNTIL THAT CREDIT CARD BILL IS PAID OFF!

GULP!

DUDDY SHOULD BE ABLE TO GET OUR CONSOLE WORKING AGAIN. WANT TO GO HOME AND FINISH OUR GAME, CHASE?

LET'S GO!

HEY, GUYS—CAN I PLAY TOO?

SHAWN, WE **TOLD** YOU—THE GAME IS RATED TOO **MATURE** FOR YOU.